RECKLESS

RECKLESS

ANNE STUART

THORNDIKE
CHIVERS

This Large Print edition is published by Thorndike Press, Waterville, Maine, USA and by AudioGO Ltd, Bath, England.
Thorndike Press, a part of Gale, Cengage Learning.
The text of this Large Print edition is unabridged.
Other aspects of the book may vary from the original edition.
Set in 16 pt. Plantin.

LIBRARY OF CONGRESS CATALOGING-IN-PUBLICATION DATA

Stuart, Anne (Anne Kristine)
   Reckless : the house of Rohan / by Anne Stuart.
    p. cm.
   ISBN-13: 978-1-4104-3372-5 (hardcover)
   ISBN-10: 1-4104-3372-2 (hardcover)
   1. Seduction—Fiction. 2. Large type books. I. Title.
PS3569.T785R43 2011
813'.54—dc22   2010042443

BRITISH LIBRARY CATALOGUING-IN-PUBLICATION DATA AVAILABLE
Published in 2011 in the U.S. by arrangement with Harlequin Books S.A.
Published in 2011 in the U.K. by arrangement with Harlequin Enterprises II B.V.

U.K. Hardcover: 978 1 445 83628 7 (Chivers Large Print)
U.K. Softcover: 978 1 445 83629 4 (Camden Large Print)

Printed in the United States of America
1 2 3 4 5 6 7 15 14 13 12 11

For my partner in the
circus of publishing —
Adam Wilson,
excellent high-wire artist,
balancing genius,
trapeze artist (a great catcher)
and ringmaster extraordinaire,
all without a whip.
Smooch.

BEGINNING

England, 1804

"Move your bleedin' arse," Miss Charlotte Spenser's maid, Meggie, said to her.

"Isn't that a little too graphic?" Miss Spenser inquired. "I have visions . . ."

"Don't think about it. Just say it."

"Move your bleeding arse," Charlotte said in the polite tones of a well-bred female.

"Bleedin'."

"Bleedin'," she repeated dutifully. "So let me get this straight. Bloody hell, move your bleedin' arse, that's a pile of shit, or shite if I happen to be in Ireland, and," she swallowed, "fuck you. Do I really say that?"

"If you want to. You 'ave to be really mad to say it, and you might get backhanded by your man if you do, but sometimes it's worth it."

"Backhanded?"

"Slapped. With the back of the hand, which hurts more, 'cause of knuckles and rings and such like."

Charlotte looked at her maid curiously. "Did your husband ever do that?"

"Oh, that and far worse. Too bad he took a tumble out that window when he was too drunk to know what he was doing," she said, cheerfully callous. "It'll be a cold day in hell before I ever let a man near me again. They're untrustworthy bastards. Try that one."

"Bastards," Charlotte said, liking the taste of it on her tongue. "Bloody bastard. Bleeding bastard arse."

"No, Miss Charlotte. It has to make sense in English. Arses aren't bastards."

"True. Arses and bastards are nouns, bloody and bleeding are adjectives. Do you say *fucking* as well?"

"Oh, most definitely."

"Splendid," said Miss Charlotte Spenser. "I'll practice." And they continued down the sidewalk, maid and mistress in perfect accord.

They had just attended the weekly meeting of the Richmond Hill Bluestockings and Viragos, a most enlightening afternoon during which Meggie had proceeded to instruct the highborn members how to curse. Charlotte, to her dismay, had been an utter failure, but she was improving with private instruction.

As she climbed the steep marble stairs to Whitmore House, the door was flung open and she was presented with a scarcely controlled chaos. Servants were rushing to and fro, carrying baskets of flowers and gilt chairs and great silver platters. Her cousin Evangelina was throwing a ball, and Charlotte had forgotten about it entirely.

"Drat," she muttered to Meggie. "My cousin is entertaining tonight."

"Try for 'bloody hell,' " Meggie suggested helpfully. "And her's not just entertaining," she added darkly. "Her's got two hundred people coming tonight or I miss my guess."

"She's," Charlotte corrected automatically. "Bloody hell."

Meggie laughed. "Not fierce enough, Miss Charlotte. You need to practice if you want to sound like you mean it." She started toward the side alley that led to the servants' entrance, but Charlotte didn't make any attempt to stop her. She'd learned her democratic ideals were not appreciated by everyone. Charlotte was an egalitarian, and she'd plucked Meggie from the slums, determined to save her. In the beginning Meggie had flatly refused to be saved, but for the last two years she'd become Charlotte's trusted companion. Meggie, fresh from her life as a fallen woman, flat out refused to enter by the front door, even though, as Charlotte's maid, it was perfectly acceptable, and the one time Charlotte tried to join her and the army of servants belowstairs for a cup of tea the atmosphere had been excruciatingly uncomfortable. Charlotte had learned, to her sorrow, that there was no one more snobbish than a British domestic servant, and her lack of welcome was glaringly obvious. She hadn't attempted it again.

She sighed. She would have so much rather have sat and had a cup of tea and a biscuit, her feet up before the fire in the servants' gathering room, than wind her way through the back stairs to the upper floors of Whitmore House, but she had no choice. She nodded as she passed the footmen draping garlands of fresh spring flowers over the massive doorway, handed her hat, pelisse and gloves to the maid who was waiting. Hetty, her name was, and she bobbed a curtsy, eyeing her nervously, as if afraid of an unwelcome gesture of friendship.

But Charlotte had learned her lesson. "Where is Lady Whitmore?" she inquired in a cool, distant voice.

"In her dressing room, Miss Spenser," Hetty said. "She left word that you were to come to her as soon as you returned home."

10

Charlotte didn't bother to hide her grimace. "Any idea why?"

"I'm sure I couldn't say, miss."

"No, of course you couldn't," Charlotte said with a genteel snort, heading for the stairs. She tried to will a wan expression into her face, wrinkling her forehead in a semblance of pain, opening her eyes wide. She was a terrible liar, and Lina would most likely see through her immediately, but it wouldn't hurt to try.

Evangelina, dowager countess of Whitmore, was sitting at her dressing table, regarding her reflection in the mirror as Louise, her French maid, fussed with her hair. Clearly her countenance failed to please her, a fact which Charlotte could only find extraordinary. Evangelina was widely renowned to be one of the most beautiful women in England, from her glossy black curls to her vivid blue eyes with just the tinge of violet, her creamy skin, delicate nose and smiling, sensuous mouth. She'd never seen a freckle in her life, Charlotte thought dangerously. She was tiny, delicate, exquisite and two years younger than Charlotte's thirty. She was staring at her reflection the way Charlotte usually surveyed her own.

"I am looking positively haggard," she

11

greeted Charlotte in a disconsolate voice. "Why is it, whenever I throw a party I end up looking fagged to death?"

"You look gorgeous," Charlotte said briskly, then remembered her plan. "I only wish I felt well enough to join you," she added in a more plaintive voice.

"Oh, no, you don't!" Lina said, turning to glare at her, much to her hairdresser's distress. "You aren't crying off at the last minute on some trumped-up illness. That only works the first three times. I need you with me."

"You aren't going to even notice whether I'm there or not," Charlotte said, sitting down at the end of her cousin's bed, her reflection appearing beside Lina's in the mirror.

She'd long accepted her very ordinary appearance, but seeing it side by side with Lina's beauty couldn't help but be lowering.

Charlotte had no delusions about her shortcomings. She was too tall — at a good six feet she towered over most men. She had awful ginger hair and freckles, she had an over-abundance of bosom, and to top everything off she was shortsighted enough that she needed to wear glasses when she read.

As if these biological indignities weren't

12

enough, she was also poor, unmarried and too smart for her own good, as most gentlemen, including her father, were wont to tell her. Women were supposed to be short and pretty and never dare contradict a man, even if he was spouting utter nonsense. And if they were troubled by shortsightedness, they could damn well get through the season by recognizing people's voices. Who needed to read? Or so her late father had told her.

It was halfway through the miserable year of her coming out that she had put her gold-rimmed glasses firmly on her nose — another point against her, it tending toward the aquiline rather than the more popular snub — refused the milk treatments that were supposed to make her freckles fade, but which only left her smelling faintly of sour milk, and decided to be an old maid. The glasses weren't necessary, but they went well with her acquired scowl, and she wore them everywhere, even when they gave her a headache.

In truth, becoming an old maid had been decided for her during the first disastrous months out, but her stern father had still harbored hope. Until she put on her glasses and trampled on her dance partners, making her an object to be feared.

There had been no second season.

"Of course I'll notice," Lina said. "At least, for the first half hour," she added with her usual honesty, the honesty she kept for Charlotte and few others. "Besides, if you're not there backing me up how can I possibly indulge in a little discreet flirtation with Viscount Rohan?"

Charlotte ignored the iciness in the pit of her stomach. "You could wait for a better time," she suggested. "For instance, next week, at the gathering at Hensley Court."

"Ah, but by then he'll doubtless have discovered some other sweet thing to entrance him. And I'm quite determined to have him. He's gorgeous, he's delightfully wicked and he's rumored to be the very devil in bed," she added with a convincingly lascivious sigh.

"I'm sure he is," Charlotte said, moving away, not even blinking. "However, the amatory prowess of my lord Rohan is of no possible interest to me."

Lina settled back, letting her dresser once more attack the artful array of curls. "You're such a stick-in-the-mud, Charlotte." She sighed. "You really don't know what you're missing. I'm enjoying my widowhood immensely."

Charlotte had her doubts about that, but

14

she wisely said nothing. When her favorite cousin had begged her to come live with her once her horrendous elderly husband died, she'd accepted gratefully. She'd been an only child of distant parents, and their deaths had left her penniless and, if it weren't for Lina, friendless.

Even if the choices open to a poor relation weren't many, sharing a house with Evangelina had been Charlotte's idea of heaven. The only problem had been Lina's feverish gaiety: about as genuine as Charlotte's professed lack of interest in Viscount Rohan. But she wasn't going to think about that.

"I much prefer it that way," Charlotte said, hoping she didn't sound unbearably prim. "Half an hour, standing quietly in the background while you greet your guests, and then I'm off."

"Make it an hour," Lina pleaded. "Rohan might prove difficult. It's always possible I'll need you to help direct him."

Charlotte froze. *Horror* was too mild a word for the emotion that suffused her. "I'm not going anywhere near Viscount Rohan."

Lina batted at Louise's hands and turned to look at her. "Why not?" Her voice was sharp. "I wasn't aware that you were even acquainted with him. Has he done some-

15

thing to offend you?"

"Apart from his appalling lack of moral fortitude?" Charlotte said icily. "No. I've only spoken with Viscount Rohan once in my life, and I've never been alone in his presence, thank heavens." This time she allowed her voice to be as prim as possible, filled with disapproval. Because if Lina guessed the truth it would be unbearable.

"Thank heavens," Lina echoed. "Then why won't you . . . ?"

"I'd rather keep my distance."

Lina shrugged, turning back to face her reflection, and Louise returned to her work, muttering French imprecations beneath her breath. "Suit yourself. If you've taken him in aversion then I'm certain one of my friends will help. I just can't be certain they wouldn't take him for themselves." She made a moue of distress.

"From what I've heard of Viscount Rohan, he's probably had them already."

Lina's laugh was low and earthy. "Most probably. If he hadn't spent the last year on the continent he would have had me. Ah, well, if not tonight, then most definitely at the gathering. I absolutely cannot wait! The Heavenly Host, in all their wicked glory!"

The familiar knot in her stomach tightened. "Nor can I," she said, secure in the knowledge that her cousin's dresser wouldn't understand.

Lina looked up at Charlotte for a long moment. "Are you certain this is the wisest choice, darling?" she said finally. "I'm all for broadening your education, but going from sheltered spinsterhood to a gathering of the Heavenly Host is rather like moving from St. James Palace to the stews of London. I do admire your scientific mind and interest in observing the baser instincts of mankind, but perhaps that might be going a bit too far. You might wish to start a little more slowly."

The fact that Charlotte wanted to agree with her made her even more forceful. She wasn't going to turn craven at this late date. "I understand the basics of animal husbandry and fornication, Lina. I've lived in the country for a great part of my life, and there are no mysteries there. But if I'm intending to spend my life in celibate comfort I wish to observe exactly what it is that you tell me I'm missing. Besides, I have a certain scientific curiosity. The practices I've heard mentioned seem either unsanitary or anatomically impossible, and I'm interested to see just how one manages it." It had all sounded extremely reasonable when she and Lina had first come up with the

17

notion, and she told herself there was nothing untoward about it. To think so would be ridiculously missish.

Lina chuckled. "I can't promise your curiosity will be satisfied if you choose to come merely as an observer."

"You think I should participate?" Charlotte inquired, careful to keep her voice sensible.

"Good God, no! Hardly the proper introduction to the pleasures of the bedroom, my dear cousin," Lina said with an uneasy laugh. "And I suppose there's nothing to be concerned about. If you wish to observe some of the more interesting sexual practices then a gathering of the Heavenly Host is the place to do it. There are always a fair number of guests who derive their primary excitement from watching others, and you'd be dressed in an enveloping monk's robe, with a hood pulled down to obscure your face and hair. No one will know whether you're male or female, and no one would think of accosting you as long as you wear that strip of white around your arm. It's perfectly safe."

"You sound as if you're convincing *yourself*. Perhaps this is a bad idea," Charlotte said evenly.

"And it was mine in the first place, rather

18

than answer your questions. No, I think it will be good for you. If you don't witness anything too bizarre it may even help you overcome your aversion to men."

"I have no aversion to men," Charlotte said. "Only to the institution of marriage, which enslaves women as surely as —"

"Yes, I know," Lina said, having heard it all before. "And in truth, you'll see men at their basest — it could put you off them entirely. Not that I'm in favor of marriage, quite the opposite. I just have different reasons."

"Since no one seems likely to offer for me then that's probably just as well. And you know what a lively intellect I have. This is one area I can't study in books."

"Depends on the book . . . Never mind, love. We should have a great deal of fun once we're back home, discussing what the great men of London look like without their drawers. In most cases it's not a pretty sight."

"Then why —" Charlotte began, honestly curious.

"It's not the looking, dearest. It's the touching. Not that you're to let anyone touch you. If they try I'll cut off their . . . ears. You're my dearest cousin and I intend to protect you." She looked at her for a long

19

moment. "Wear your green sarcenet tonight, and I'll have Louise come and do your hair as well. You may as well give it one last go before all your illusions are shattered."

"I have no illusions, I have no interest in 'giving it one last go' as you so delicately put it, and Meggie can take care of my hair."

"You're impossible!" Lina said with a sigh. "At least wear the green and not that hideous peach thing. It looks dreadful with your hair."

Charlotte rose from the bed and kissed Lina's pale, delicate cheek, resisting the impulse to tell her everything looked dreadful with her hair. Except, perhaps, the sarcenet, which made her eyes green. "I'll meet you downstairs," she said, promising nothing, and took herself off.

Lina watched her cousin disappear, then turned her attention back to her reflection, trying to ignore Louise's ministrations. Surely they were doing the right thing. One glimpse of the goings-on of the Heavenly Host and innocent cousin Charlotte might be so revolted she'd never again countenance the idea of marriage. Keeping her safe from making the same mistake Lina had made.

She knew her cousin much better than

Charlotte realized. She understood perfectly well the look in Charlotte's eyes when Viscount Rohan entered the room. Adrian Rohan was enough to tempt even Charlotte, who persisted in saying she had no interest in men in general or the viscount in particular. And in truth, she was probably safe. Rohan could have anyone he wanted, and usually did. He'd have no appreciation for an over-tall young woman with copper hair who wasn't quite *comme il faut,* one so firmly on the shelf that she may as well start wearing lace caps and sitting with the dowagers. Which Charlotte would, if Lina would let her.

And just in case, once Lina had finished with him he would no longer hold the faintest allure for her cousin.

No, Rohan wouldn't be likely to go near her, and Lina was reasonably certain that Charlotte would be immune to anyone else, no matter how handsome, charming or affluent. As for the kind of man she might be more likely to attract — some plump, elderly widower or, even worse, some pious vicar — once she saw the sort of thing men were capable of she would reject even those unappealing aspirants. In truth, she was taking her into the wilds of Sussex, to Hensley Court and the libertine gathering of the

Heavenly Host, to protect her.

Charlotte knew only a bit of the horrors of Evangelina's marriage to the elderly earl of Whitmore, and Lina had absolutely no intention of telling her any of the unpleasant details, details that were better left in the shadows where they belonged. Those were times she refused to think about, except in the dark of night when she couldn't help it, and she could stuff her pillow over her face to keep from screaming out loud. It was over, it was past. But she wasn't going to chance letting the same thing happen to her darling Charlotte.

Perhaps this wasn't necessary. After all, Charlotte was unfortunately right: no man was likely to make her an offer. She was thirty years old, well past her prime, too tall and too curvy to wear the current fashions well, too strong-minded, too unwilling to flatter the preening males. Observing a few nights of the Revels of the Heavenly Host should be enough to scare her away from ever contemplating changing her stance on love and marriage.

It was a shame, because Charlotte would make a wonderful, loving mother. But motherhood came with husbands, and the price was too dear.

"Voilà, enfin!" Louise cried, stepping back,

clearly well satisfied with what she had wrought.

Lina stared at her reflection. She was exquisite. A work of art. A creation cold and lifeless and beautiful. Good enough to lure the dissolute Viscount Rohan into her bed, further ensuring the necessary demise of Charlotte's hopeless daydreams.

"Eh bien," she said tonelessly. And she rose from her dressing table, ready to finish the job.

2

Charlotte only considered the green sarcenet for a moment before dismissing it in favor of the insipid peach that turned her ivory complexion to ash. She ignored Meggie's objections, waiting until the last minute to head down to the ballroom. Lina would be more than capable of sending her back to change, if it weren't already too late. The first guests had already begun to arrive, and Lina looked resplendent in clinging pink silk that molded her delicate curves. She gave Charlotte a look, then shrugged, as if her poor sartorial choice was no more than she'd expected, and Charlotte took up her place behind her.

Had it been up to Lina she would have been by her side, greeting the guests as an equal, but Charlotte staunchly refused. There were few advantages to being a poor relation, but this was one of them. She didn't have to stand in line and smile and simper at idiotic young men and elderly villains. This was going to be one of the major crushes of the season — Lina had invited everyone, and Charlotte held her place as long as she could. It was only when she could see the black-and-silver mane of Etienne de Giverney overtopping everyone else's as he moved toward them that she panicked. Where the dashing Comte de Giverney went, his younger cousin, Viscount Rohan, was likely to follow, and she wasn't going to take that chance.

She slipped away without a word to blend into the mass of guests, making her way toward the back of the ballroom. The only safe way to escape to her bedroom would be to take the servants' stairs. The main staircase stood just outside the ballroom, and she would be in full view of the arriving and departing guests if she tried to disappear by that route. Not that anyone would notice the movements of a poor relation, but she didn't want to take the chance.

At least she was fortunate enough to have escaped before she had to endure Viscount Rohan's lazy glance, if she even got that much from him. The less she saw of that particular gentleman the better off she was. Adrian Rohan was fully as wild as his father had been, and while most women loved rakes, she did not. She threaded her way through the crowds, invisible as a woman of no wealth, beauty or youth could be, the door to the back stairs almost in sight, when a tall male figure suddenly loomed up in front of her, and she barreled into him, too intent on escape to stop herself in time.

Strong hands caught her arms to steady her, and she found herself looking up into Adrian Alistair de Giverney Rohan's beautiful, exquisite face. He was one of the few men tall enough to make her actually have to crane her neck, and she was too startled to watch her tongue.

Luck was most definitely not on her side. For the first time in her life Meggie's coaching paid off and Charlotte uttered the fateful words *Bloody hell.*

His lordship had already released her, had murmured a polite apology beneath his breath in instant dismissal and was about to move on, her existence barely acknowledged, when her low-voiced but clearly enunciated words stopped him, and his hard blue eyes focused on her for what she was certain was the first time, despite the fact that they'd been introduced at least half a dozen times during the season and danced on one notable, horrible occasion.

He blinked. And then a slow smile curved

his mouth, and it was truly the most wicked, deceitful, appealing mouth, and his gloved hand reached out again to catch her elbow before she could escape. It was just the lightest of touches, perfectly within the bounds of propriety, there was cloth between his flesh and hers, and yet this touch burned.

Bloody hell, she thought again, having finally grown comfortable with the phrase. Of all people, why did it have to be Rohan that she barreled into?

"Miss . . . ?" He clearly racked his brain. "Miss Spenser, isn't it? Have I done something to offend you?"

She dropped a swift curtsy, difficult enough in the swirl of guests, and surreptitiously tried to pull away. How in heavens did he remember her name? She was hardly part of his world. His long fingers tightened. "Of course not, my lord. I do beg your pardon. I have no excuse for such appalling language."

Now that he was actually looking at her, the plague of emotions was even worse, she thought, scowling. It had been bad enough, always watching him from across crowded ballrooms, fighting off the foolish daydreams that went all the way back to the fairy tales of her youth when she knew full well that

27

this was no handsome prince — this was a wicked wizard, an evil faerie out to cast a binding spell on her.

Up close it was far, far worse. The warmth in her belly, the tightness in her chest, the tingling in places she wasn't even going to think about. And the burn where his hand touched her arm.

He was looking down at her. "You're Lady Whitmore's companion, are you not?"

"Cousin," she snapped before she could stop herself. And how in the world did he know that much? She'd counted on her own invisibility.

Again that faint smile. "I stand corrected. Though aren't poor relations often required to serve as *companions?*"

It was a rude question, but nothing compared to the shock of her language. And he still wasn't releasing her. "If you'll excuse me, Lord Rohan," she said firmly, yanking her arm free a bit too roughly.

He released her arm, only to catch her gloved hand in his. Then he smiled at her, a smile faintly tinged with malice. "I think I must insist upon a dance, Miss Spenser. Penance for your shocking breach of manners."

That was all she needed, she thought. She'd danced with him a hundred times, beneath the starry sky, dressed in a gown that suddenly turned her into an irresistible beauty, all in the dreams she'd wickedly allowed herself. Dreams she'd known better than to indulge in, but which she'd allowed herself anyway, and now she was paying the price. She knew from watching him that his grace on the dance floor was something quite extraordinary, his form perfect. And yet there was a certain something in the way he moved that had more than one chaperone shaking her head, looking for some reason to bar him from the innocent young ladies who clamored around him.

She had no chaperone, though at the advanced age of thirty she was too old to be considered innocent, she reminded herself.

"I don't dance," she said. "Please release my hand."

He didn't, not for a long moment. He truly had the most unsettling eyes, she realized. Usually his lids drooped down lazily, hiding his gaze, but she could see their deep blue depths, summing her up quite handily, and she thanked God that years of practice kept her blushes from showing on her pale skin, no matter how she squirmed inwardly.

"Now, why do I get the impression you disapprove of me, Miss Spenser?" he said.

She was feeling curiously light-headed and

she deepened her scowl. Her expression was usually sufficient to scare men away, but clearly Viscount Rohan didn't scare easily. "I don't know you, Lord Rohan. How could I disapprove of you?"

"Perhaps my reputation precedes me. You've got that starched-up look like you tasted something particularly nasty."

People were watching. She'd never held a public conversation with a man for more than a few brief moments, and never with a pink of the ton like Rohan. She was supposed to be invisible, for heaven's sake.

And he certainly had never paid any heed to anyone other than his most recent flirts, all of them stunning beauties. A plain old maid such as Charlotte Spenser would never qualify as the type of woman to interest someone like Adrian Rohan.

He was still holding her hand, she realized with horror. "Where is your dance card?" he persisted.

"I told you, I don't dance," she said through gritted teeth. Lina had long ago ceased insisting she carry a dance card, knowing it was a lost cause. In addition to never being asked, she had two left feet. She tugged at her hand again, but he held fast, stronger than she would have guessed. "Release me. Now."

Her peremptory tone wasn't the wisest choice, she realized as his eyes narrowed. "I think not."

Her slippers were light and soft, made for the dancing she refused to participate in. She gave him a deceptive smile, moving closer, and stomped on his foot with all her weight.

With her light slippers she couldn't have done nearly the damage she would have wished for. Had it been up to her she would have broken his foot — but it was enough of a surprise to have him momentarily loosen his grip, and she pulled free, whirled around and escaped.

She was half-afraid he'd follow her past the green baize door to the servants' passageway, but she'd overestimated her fascination. By the time she dared look back he was gone.

She'd made it up to the servants' narrow staircase when she heard the music start. She was three times a fool, but there was a spot from the second-floor staircase with a perfect view of the ballroom. She'd done just that in her own house with Lina when they were both young girls, fascinated by the workings of society and the behavior of their shallow parents. At that point the two of them had judged it deadly dull.

31

Lina had changed her mind, sailing through a glittering first season, capped with an extravagant wedding to the aging but extremely wealthy and still-handsome earl of Whitmore.

Charlotte, on the other hand, had retreated in abject failure. Her ordinary looks, lack of fortune and unhappy tendency to speak her mind had made her part of a commodity that society had no value for, and she retired back to her family's ramshackle estate, her parents' only child a total failure.

She remembered Viscount Rohan from that disastrous first season, though she'd presumed he'd forgotten entirely. He'd been presented to her as a suitable partner by one of the well-meaning hostesses, and bored though he was, he'd done his duty, standing up with her and displaying barely the trace of a martyred air.

She had never been a good dancer — her family had had no money for a dancing master and she'd had to rely on Lina's lessons. Her nervousness at being in the presence of her secret crush had completely undone her. She'd trampled all over his elegant shoes, missed her cues, throwing the complicated country dance into total disarray.

He'd said nothing, his elegant mouth growing more grim as he tried to rescue the figure, to no avail. When the supreme torture was finally over she'd curtsied to him, and he'd bowed politely.

And then he'd murmured, "I hadn't realized dancing was a blood sport, Miss Samson. You might consider warning prospective partners that they're taking their lives in their hands if they dance with you." His light, casual words were accompanied by a faint glint in his eye that she couldn't read.

She hadn't tried, as her shame overwhelmed her. The fact that he didn't know her name was a relief rather than an added insult, and she'd never danced again. At least never in public, and never with a partner.

There were times, after Lina had chosen to retire to the countryside, that Charlotte would find herself alone in the sprawling manor house. She'd find an empty hallway or a deserted field, and she'd realize she was humming a melody beneath her breath, and it had naturally evolved into a carefree dance, moving with the wind, free and happy.

Still, even Rohan's cruel, casual words hadn't managed to give her a disgust of the man. On the rare occasions when she accompanied Lina to evening parties her eyes would hungrily seek him out, and when he left for the continent her relief had been faintly tinged with disappointment.

She'd come face-to-face with him twice since his return, and his blue eyes had swept over her with the same bored disinterest he evinced toward all and sundry, with the occasional exception of the great beauties. Charlotte Spenser was just a part of the anonymous horde of plain virgins desperately seeking a husband.

Not her, though. Not ever. Her parents were dead, the ramshackle estate had passed on to the nearest male relative, a distant cousin she'd never even met. Evangelina had been widowed, and begged her to move in with her, and Charlotte had done so quite happily. She'd managed to assiduously avoid any social occasion that smacked of the marriage mart, and in truth she'd been happier than she'd ever been in her life. She had her dearest friend and cousin for companionship, the Bluestockings to keep her busy and Adrian Rohan had been abroad.

She knew it couldn't last. Rohan had returned unexpectedly as Europe once again braced for war. Charlotte's peace of mind was destroyed. She had no doubt that Lina would marry again, and despite her inability to give Whitmore an heir, Charlotte was certain a second, happier marriage would provide offspring. Perhaps she could become a helpful honorary aunt, if Lina's new husband would tolerate her.

She looked down at the ballroom for the last time. Adrian Rohan had already moved on, forgetting her, as he leaned over a buxom young beauty. Forgetting her, as he always did. Which was the only consolation her pride could find. She hated the thought of appearing ridiculous or needy. Rohan's attention was elsewhere, and she didn't have to worry about being mocked.

She moved slowly up the back stairs, ignoring the curious looks of the servants as they passed her. She reached the lavish apartments Lina had insisted she use and began to undress herself. There was no telling where Meggie had gotten herself to, but it didn't matter. Charlotte had made certain she had clothes that she could do and undo herself — the advent of a lady's maid had been a recently reacquired luxury. Though whether Meggie's rough ministrations could be called a luxury was something worth debating.

She let down her long, thick hair and brushed it, then fastened it in a braid to keep it from tangling too badly as she slept.

The water in the basin was cool, blessedly cool, against her flushed face.

The sheets were cool as well as she slid beneath them. The spring air had been chilly, and a fire had been laid but not lit. She blew out the candle and burrowed deep under the covers, pulling the blankets up to her nose.

She could still feel his hand on her arm, strong, restraining her. She was a woman who couldn't bear to be forced, bullied, cowed. So why was she tenderly stroking the place where he'd held her?

She was moon-mad. Calf-brained, addle-pated.

But in this one matter her formidable intellect was no match for the dismal, unpalatable truth. She was in love with Adrian Rohan, and had been for years, and nothing, not his rudeness nor tales of his outrageous excess, nor all her own rational self-discourse, could change her.

And once more castigating herself as an idiot, she fell into a deep, troubled sleep.

Adrian Alastair Rohan stared down the dress of the exquisitely beautiful, exquisitely silly Miss Leonard, bored beyond belief even as he said all the right things. Usually an amiable flirtation was as good a way to spend an interminable evening. He would get no more than a kiss from Miss Leonard, and while kissing had long ago lost its charm, he had it on good authority that Miss Leonard had had a great deal of practice at it and was considered something of an expert. It could be entertaining to see if he could manage to teach her something new.

He'd rather be teaching the nervous and thoroughly delicious Charlotte Spenser, though he wasn't quite certain why. Her clothes were atrocious, her manner less than cordial, and whenever he happened to see her she acted as if he'd committed some foul crime. Yes, his reputation was terrible, but in his experience most women found it irresistible.

It was the rest of the time that interested him. Because the honorable Miss Charlotte Spenser couldn't keep her eyes off him, a fact he found amusing. Despite her avowed disapproval of him and everything he stood for, he was fully aware she watched him whenever she thought no one would notice.

As a poor relation and a spinster of no particular beauty she tended to hang back at the edges of the crowds, where she thought she could remain unnoticed while she stared at him. As far as he could tell, she paid no particular attention to anyone else.

He was fully accustomed to having women watch him with appreciation and even longing. He was wealthy, heir to a title and possessed of more than average good looks, all thanks to his parents. His height, his pretty face, his deep blue eyes, so like his father's, had nothing to do with any accomplishment on his part, and he accepted the blessings of fortune with no particular vanity. Those blessings enabled him to indulge his varied appetites and interests, and for that he was casually grateful.

But he wasn't the prettiest young man in society — Montague held that particular office. Nor the wealthiest, and he was a mere viscount, not a duke or even a marquess, though that would come once his father died. And as the honorable Miss Spenser could attest, he was far from the most charming. He had a nasty tongue and was never known to suffer fools gladly.

And yet still she watched him when he danced with the newest beauty, when he laughed with his friends, when he snubbed upstarts and drank too much and occasionally made an ass of himself. And he wondered why.

One possibility, and by far his favorite,

was that she was planning his murder. The poor relation, snubbed once too often, was out for revenge, and he might very well find his next glass of negus poisoned, or a knife between his shoulder blades.

It was nothing more than he deserved, but he doubted she had that in mind. In truth, he knew exactly why she watched him, and it was for the same reason half the women in society, young and old, married and single, plain and beautiful, watched him. She fancied herself in love with him.

If she ever allowed herself to hold a civil conversation with him he would have been more than happy to explain that it was no such thing. Society would have it that women were pure and romantical and men filthy, lusting beasts. To his immense pleasure, he knew otherwise.

Miss Spenser wanted him. Oh, she wanted it wrapped up in posies and flattery and the marriage bed, but she wanted his hands on her starched-up body, stripping those ugly clothes away from her.

And he'd be more than happy to oblige, except that he never touched well-bred virgins. The very thought of finding himself leg-shackled to a scowling, disapproving creature like Miss Spenser was horrifying. And his hypocritical father would see to it that he did the right thing, entirely ignoring his own degenerate past.

Miss Spenser would just have to watch him covertly and sigh. And he'd have to resist the impulse to see if he could make those stern lips soften, and where he could make her place them. He'd be willing to wager that he could have her putting them anywhere he wanted, and he could think of several friends who'd be willing to take up that wager.

But he had a mistress for that sort of thing, or would have, as soon as he found someone to replace the divine Maria, who'd decided she'd rather have a fat old man with an even fatter pocket.

At least there was the gathering of the Heavenly Host. He was looking forward to seeing Montague again, looking forward to indulging his more base appetites. Perhaps he could persuade one of the ladies present to dress in something unflattering and lecture him like Miss Spenser. And then he could proceed to give her exactly what he wasn't allowed to give Charlotte.

The perfect name for her. Charlotte — such a prim, disapproving word. He couldn't imagine why he was interested, apart from the novelty of it all.

He heard Lady Whitmore's trill of laughter

from across the room, and he smiled wickedly. Perhaps he would have to make do with Miss Spenser's exquisite cousin. A noble compromise on his part, one he'd make quite easily. And by the time he returned to London he'd probably forget all about Miss Spenser and her longing eyes.

Because he couldn't just play with the virgin, not if he valued his freedom. But he could have her cousin, and that would more than suffice.

"My dear boy, I have been looking for you everywhere." His cousin's heavily accented voice greeted him as he finished the dance and relinquished Miss Leonard and her impressive bosom to her next partner.

Adrian glanced at Etienne de Giverney. Actually his father's cousin, and closer in age to the old man than to Adrian, Etienne had a kindness for his young cousin, and Adrian found he quite enjoyed the man's company. For one thing, his parents disapproved of him, which was always a boon. For another, Etienne had a taste for things that bordered on the shocking. And while Adrian had sponsored his cousin's entrance into English society, it was Etienne who'd ensured he'd be admitted to the exalted ranks of the Heavenly Host, despite the fact that his father, who had once presided over their revels, now held the group in contempt.

But that was his father. The only man he knew more capable of administering a setdown than he was.

Etienne, being French, had more than a passing acquaintance with some of the darker practices shunned by polite society. He had introduced his second cousin to the pleasures of the opium pipe and ways he could gratify himself alone that were as inventive as they were dangerous.

Unlike his father, who seemed to have forgotten his own disreputable youth, he encouraged Adrian's love of curricle racing, and he played for stakes even higher than Adrian did, with more success.

Adrian never cared if he won or lost. His inheritance, even before his esteemed old man gave up the ghost, was huge, though not quite as impressive as Maria's fat gentleman, the nabob. And at least with Etienne he was never, ever bored.

No, he could look forward to three days of delicious debauchery, as well as a much-needed visit with his dearest friend Montague. He wasn't going to think about Miss Spenser again, he was certain of it.

"There is little sport here, *enfin?*" Etienne said. "Let us see if we can find something to entertain us at Le Rise."

Le Rise was quite the most daring of all the houses of ill repute, the second best thing to the gatherings of the Heavenly Host. The gaming stakes were extremely high and at times quite shocking, the wines were tolerable and the other entertainments were quite irresistible. It was almost impossible to gain entry unless one was of the very highest level. Adrian had been one of the first members, of course, and Etienne was admitted as his guest.

"If we can't then we're pitifully jaded indeed," Adrian said in his perfect French.

Etienne laughed. Leaving Adrian to wonder whether he might not have spoken the ugly truth.

3

Normally the thought of a trip to the countryside would have been Charlotte's idea of perfection. She had never been overly fond of London. It was noisy, smelly and dirty, and while the opportunities for theater and lending libraries and the company of like-minded women were stimulating, the thought of rusticating, at least for a short while, was divine.

But divine had nothing to do with how Charlotte intended to spend her time in Sussex. The Mad Monks were meeting for their debauched revels, and she was to be a part of them.

The trip in Lina's well-sprung barouche had been almost too short. At Lina's suggestion she wore a bonnet that concealed most of her face, and kept her head down. Her height likely gave her away — there were few women quite as long-limbed as she was — but she had every intention of managing a crablike scuttle to appear shorter and more subservient. It was to be hoped that anyone who gave her a second glance would assume she was Lina's maid, because even amid full debauchery a lady still needed her personal attendant. Meggie had been brought along as well, and had anyone asked, the answer would have been that the Countess of Whitmore required her own hair dresser. In fact no one asked. Such concerns over propriety had been absent. By the time they were settled in the distressingly normal rooms at Hensley Court they had seen no one, not even their ailing host, and Charlotte's nervousness began to decline.

"It's very simple, darling," Lina said airily as they drank their afternoon tea, thoughtfully provided by Montague's excellent staff. "The monk's robe will cover you completely, from the top of your head down to the very tips of your toes, and you're so tall everyone will assume you're a man. Just try not to hunch, dearest. Throw your shoulders back but keep your head bowed. You won't need to say a word — your vow of silence is evidenced by the brown color of your robe, and your watcher's status is signaled by the white trim on your sleeves. You may move freely around the grounds, though on no account go near the Portal of Venus. All rules are off there, but I'll point it out to you before I get . . . er . . . distracted. You can go anywhere else, unless a door is locked, but that's usually signaled by a gentleman's neckcloth attached to the outer door. As long as those remain the couple or group inside don't wish to be disturbed."

"Group?" Charlotte said faintly. What had started out as a lark was becoming far too real, and she wondered whether it was too late to change her mind, if she'd wanted to, that is.

"Sweetheart," Lina said patiently, "that's what an orgy is. Two people is simply sex, three or more is an orgy. But don't worry — there are any number of members who much prefer an audience for their activities. I promise you you're more likely to be able to observe an orgy than to be invited to participate in one."

"You relieve my mind," Charlotte said in a hollow voice.

Lina surveyed her. She was dressed in a nun's habit, albeit one made of silk and tailored to her exact dimensions. She hadn't yet taken on the headdress, and with her curly black hair and bright eyes she looked like a very wicked young *religieuse* indeed.

46

"If you've changed your mind, as I'm beginning to think you should, there's no disgrace. I can have John Coachman drive you home, with no one the wiser, or you can stay in these rooms and enjoy Montague's impressive hospitality. He has the finest chefs. And while a few of the guests return here for respite during the revels, the majority of them stay at the abbey, which has been fully remodeled for this purpose, so you'd be unlikely to run into any of them. And one would need a boat to get to and fro, which discourages people from coming back. You could be quite peaceful . . ."

"I'm coming with you," Charlotte said firmly. "Brother Charles, at your service."

Lina shook her head. "Whatever you want, my dear. I am convinced that the only harm you'll suffer is to your innocent sensibilities, but not one will touch you. If they do, all you have to do is scream very loudly."

"Wouldn't that gather too much attention? I'm not supposed to be female, am I? I'm not wearing a nun's habit like you."

"Oh, a great many women enjoy the freedom of a monk's robe. Trust me, if you're not careful the Mad Monks will know the difference from the way you walk."

"I can walk like a man," Charlotte protested.

47

"Indeed, my sweet, you cannot. You have the most delicious sway to your hips, something I've been trying to emulate. To you it comes naturally — I'm very jealous. It's a good thing you refuse to dance. If society saw the way you walk I'm afraid you'd no longer be able to disappear into the wallpaper. Men would be flocking to you." Her voice was wry.

"I don't want men to flock to me," Charlotte protested. "I'm quite happy keeping you company. If you find my presence tiresome I can always . . ."

"*Now* you're being tiresome," Lina said lazily. "You're my cousin and the sister of my heart, the only human being I trust. And you have yet to pass judgment on me, when clearly you're dying to make me realize the error of my profligate ways. I want you with me as long as you can stand it."

"And if you marry again? I doubt your husband would want me along."

"I have no intention of marrying again," Lina said shortly, her voice oddly hollow. She seemed to be looking into the past, at something extremely unpleasant, and Charlotte had a strong suspicion what she found so troubling.

And then Lina shook herself, laughing. "And if I'm fool enough to change my mind you're to beat me soundly until I come to my senses." She rose, reaching for the starched headdress, and a moment later turned for Charlotte to admire.

"I don't know that the lip rouge works," she said dryly.

"It's part of the plan. You need to take off those clothes. They stand out under the monk's robe." She started toward her, and Charlotte slapped her arms around her body, hugging it tight.

"Don't be ridiculous." She was not about to give up anything without a struggle.

"Most of the women wear absolutely nothing beneath their costumes, Charlotte. It's a warm spring night and those clothes can be smothering, particularly since you're covering your head."

"The only time I'm naked is in the bath, and if it were up to me I'd wear clothes there, too," Charlotte said sturdily.

"Tiresome girl," Lina said fondly. "Meggie, bring out the black gown. That will at least cover you without being indecent."

Charlotte looked at the wisp of black silk draped in Meggie's capable hands. "No."

"The only way people will believe you're a man is if you dispense with stays. Trust me, you won't believe how freeing a simple chemise feels. No one's going to be looking beneath your robe. If you want you can keep your garters and stockings on. Many women do, even when they're making love."

"They *do?*" she said, fascinated in spite of herself. Lina's maid began to divest her of her ugly dress, making quick work of the buttons she often struggled with, and the ugly thing tumbled to the floor.

"They do. Men find them exciting. Women do too, both the ones wearing them and the ones . . . er . . . enjoying the women who wear them."

"I still don't understand how that's possible," Charlotte said, not noticing as the maid began to unfasten her stays. "Nor do I understand how men . . ."

"With luck you'll get a thorough demonstration," Lina said, surveying her critically. "My dear, you have quite a lovely bosom. Why do you strap it down like that?"

Charlotte slapped her arms around her chest. "They get in the way," she said, disgruntled.

"Off with the hoops too, dearest. Those will give you away even more than your breasts."

"Could we please stop discussing my *breasts?*" Charlotte begged, her color fiery.

Lina hesitated. "My dear, I really don't think this is a wise idea. You're too innocent . . ."

If there was one thing Charlotte detested it was being told how innocent she was. She'd been half tempted to cry off, but she despised cowardice almost as much as she hated being thought an innocent girl. She was a woman, scientist, and there was nothing she need hide from in her quest for knowledge.

She wanted to know what men and women did. It was a perfectly reasonable curiosity on her part, with no chance for harm to befall her. The Mad Monks were poseurs, playing at vice. Her own biggest risk was a long night of boredom.

She slid off her demi-hoops, standing there in her plain white chemise, knickers, stockings and garters. "This will do," she said firmly.

Lina shook her head. "No, love. Take the rest off. And if I were you I'd remove the stockings — they might impede you if you decided you wished to move swiftly."

Charlotte looked at her, taking in the ominous words. "And why should that be?"

Lina shrugged. "There are undoubtedly some tiresome people here, though they're mostly on their best behavior. I promise I'll be nearby, in case you run into a problem. But humor me. The black chemise and nothing else. You'll adore the sense of freedom it gives you."

Charlotte doubted that, but she did as she was told, divesting herself of every last piece of her own clothing. "Where's the robe?" she demanded nervously.

Meggie produced it, muttering darkly. She'd been against this from the beginning, but Charlotte had been adamant. The monk's robe was made of heavy brown cloth, doubtless far more elegant than traditional monk's garb, and she slipped it over her head, feeling it settle down around her body like a soft caress. She pulled the capacious hood up and breathed a sigh of relief. The sleeves were long enough to cover her delicate hands, her face disappeared into the shadows of the hood. She could do what she wanted with no real fear of discovery.

Lina came up to her with a strip of white cloth, tying it around her sleeve. "Mustn't forget this, darling. It's your safe passage."

Charlotte eyes it doubtfully. "What would happen if I lost it?"

Lina had an odd expression on her face, like a mother sending her child away to school for the first time. "Nothing very terrible. If you lost the riband and someone accosts you simply tell them no. They're honor bound to obey."

"Honor?" Meggie said with an indignant sniff.

"Of a sort," Lina said. She looked at Charlotte. "Are you ready, my dear? It's not too late to change your mind. It's already getting dark, and once the sun sets we're due at the Abbey."

"I'm not changing my mind, Lina."

"Then keep your head and voice down and we'll depart. And Charlotte," she added in a pained voice. "You won't think too harshly of me, will you? I freely participate in these undertakings, and if I thought it would give you a disgust of me I would have refused to bring you here."

"Darling, nothing will give me a disgust of you. You may take your pleasure however you will, just as men do. I promise I will make no judgment."

Lina smiled at her. "No, you really wouldn't, would you . . . ? Nevertheless, I think I'll see if I can arrange for someone else to keep an eye on you. The kind of sport I'm about to indulge in is far from dignified, and I'm not certain I want you picturing *that* in your mind every time you look at me."

Charlotte laughed, ignoring the uneasy pinch of her stomach. "Whatever you think best. As long as no one accosts me or demands anything of me I should be quite fine."

"Trust me, love, no one will. There are few rules among the Heavenly Host, apart from 'Do What Thou Wilt,' but one that remains sacrosanct is that all acts must be agreeable to every partner, and no one is to interfere or criticize a member's choice, be it an unusual act or simply to watch. No one will touch you, darling. I promise."

Charlotte glanced down at the bright white ribbon she'd tied around her arm. "I'll be perfectly fine, Lina. Don't worry. I have complete faith," she said. And wondered if she lied.

Adrian stood off to one side, watching the ceremony. He hadn't bothered with monk's robes or any of the other ridiculous trappings the Heavenly Host liked to indulge in. He preferred his sinning to be flagrant — the idea of hiding behind robes and secret passwords was anathema to him. He liked to think there was nothing he wasn't willing to do, and no one he wasn't willing to let know about it. Including his esteemed, disapproving, hypocritical father, who'd indulged in the same excesses at an even more advanced age than Adrian's twenty-eight.

His mother was a different matter. She worried way too much, but he could rely on gentlemanly restraint to keep most people, including his father, from spreading too many tales.

She wanted him to marry, to give her grandchildren, and he supposed he'd do so, eventually, simply to make her happy. His mother's happiness was one of the few things he cared about, aside from his own determined pursuit of pleasure.

She wouldn't be at all happy to know he was at a gathering of the Heavenly Host. This would have stopped a better man, but, then, he was a very bad man, as Cousin Etienne cheerfully assured him, a rake and a libertine, a seducer of the worst kind. He said it as if conferring a great honor, but Adrian felt no particular pride. In general, he felt nothing at all apart from the pleasure of the senses. The small death of an intense orgasm, the sweetness of the opium pipe, the wild absinthe dreams that could fuel his more intense couplings.

And that was why he was here, despite all the folderol, the Latin which was hardly up to the standards of his classical education. He came for the sex, in all its most un-bridled variations, he came for the total lack of inhibition and restraint. He came for the motto emblazoned across the stone arch that led to this outer garden: Do what thou wilt. He intended to.

Montague was up on the dais, an ironic smile on his lined, elegant face as he exhorted the motley crowd. He looked paler than usual, weaker, and Adrian knew with a sudden, sinking despair that Monty was getting sicker. He lifted a shaking hand to hold aloft the phallus-shaped goblet they were all supposed to drink from, some sort of profane communion. Adrian himself always avoided that part of the festivities — he was much too fastidious to share a cup with some of the worst degenerates in Europe, and he had no great faith in what exactly lay in the concoction of wine and herbs. On one occasion an elixir of ergot rot had sent the entire party into hallucinations of sometimes horrific proportions. Pawlfrey had never recovered; he'd ended locked up in one of his family's country estates, raving mad.

Adrian had more faith in the strength of his own mind, but he preferred to make his own decisions when it came to the ingestion of drugs. He knew how well he tolerated absinthe or opium and regulated his use. The thought of someone else drugging his wine was unacceptable.

He could see Lady Whitmore on the other side of the avid group of nuns and monks, with the occasional bishop's miter thrown in. She was looking fetching, as always, in her habit. She was undoubtedly one of the great beauties, and she'd made it more than clear she was willing to lie with him. All he had to do was nod her way and she'd be on her back, or knees, in minutes.

Something stopped him. For all her flirtatiousness, her languid glances and casual touches, she left him with the feeling that she derived no real pleasure from the actual act. Even the well-paid courtesans he usually cavorted with expressed more enthusiasm.

No, he'd as soon bed her stiff-necked, virginal cousin, Miss Spenser. In fact, that particular fantasy had invaded his dreams recently. Only last night he'd been alone for a change, half asleep, and he felt his body harden at the thought of someone's mouth. The prim, serious mouth of Lina's cousin. He wanted to see if her hair was the same rich copper between her legs. He wanted to see if the freckles covered her breasts, her belly, the insides of her thighs. He wanted to strip the unflattering clothes from her long body, to —

Montague's voice rose to a wavering

crescendo, and he passed the goblet to the next acolyte, disappearing back into the shadows. Lady Whitmore was the third in line, clearly anxious to get started, and Adrian knew he was going to have to make up his mind. Evangelina Whitmore was beautiful, available, he'd never had her. He was a fool to even have second thoughts.

As she moved he noticed the tall monk who'd been shadowing her and frowned. Had she already chosen her partner for the next hour, or for the full three days ahead of them?

And then he saw the white ribbon on the monk's arm. A watcher. He had no particular problem with that — he'd found a number of women enjoyed an audience. It inspired them to new heights. Though he always wondered if their noisy pleasure wasn't then more for the audience and less the result of his own expertise.

Not that that was something that troubled him overmuch. He was quite gifted at the giving and receiving of pleasure. An audience had long since ceased to be a novelty for him — if Lina Whitmore came equipped with a witness then he might look elsewhere.

But to his surprise he saw them part company, and he wondered if he'd been mistaken. He'd been very sure they were together, yet Evangelina was disappearing into the darkness, away from him, and he wondered if she'd gone after Montague. There'd be no joy from that union, for either of them, but that was hardly his problem.

It was the monk who suddenly interested him.

While he considered himself broad-minded when it came to the pursuit of pleasure, he found his own tastes ran to women exclusively. Monty had always chided him for his lack of imagination when it came to choosing partners thusly, but Adrian ignored his old friend. Women were such delightful creatures, so beautifully constructed, as if made for one reason and one alone.

He knew otherwise, but his blood was up and he was focused on that one thing alone. With Lina Whitmore gone, he needed to find someone equally enticing. It shouldn't be that difficult.

"Why the hesitation, my boy?" Etienne had sidled up to him, his monk's habit open to expose a burly chest thick with grizzled hair. Etienne was partial to group efforts, while in general Adrian preferred one woman at a time. There were too many people at an orgy — he tended to lose track of limbs and mouths, and sheer sensation had palled long ago.

Adrian gave him his charming smile. "My intended has gone off with another. I find I must regroup."

"Can you not join them?"

The idea of having sex with his oldest friend was entirely unappealing. He remained close with Montague, whose tastes had made themselves evident later in life, by keeping the question of physical affection at a distance. To put it bluntly, he didn't care who or what Montague fucked, as long as it wasn't him.

"I'll look elsewhere, I think," he said casually, his eyes still on the new monk. He could tell by the way he walked that he was quite young, and he moved farther into the gardens decorated with impressively explicit statues. Adrian could tell by the rigidity in the young monk's shoulders that he had never seen or considered what was going on between the carved participants, and —

A slow smile curved his mouth. "I believe I've found my muse."

Etienne followed his gaze. "You've changed your habits, *mon cousin*. I thought you didn't care for your own sex."

"She's female," Adrian said briefly, watching as she moved away, deeper into the

Garden of Delights. She hadn't screamed or fainted — perhaps he'd underestimated her. She must be far more experienced than he'd guessed.

"Ah, I see. And you've chosen her? Enjoy yourself, then. If she's game, come find us."

Adrian's only response was a faint smile. He started after her, moving silently with the shadows so as not to alarm her, only to find her starting up at the coup de grâce, the undeniably lovely and undeniably pornographic statue of the *Rape of the Sabine*s.

In this case, rape seemed to hold the more common meaning rather than the classical one of simple abduction, as the ever-ready marble Roman was in the midst of mounting his new bride while on horseback.

He'd always found that particular move highly unlikely — even the most reliable animal would have a difficult time not responding to his master's rhythmic movements. He'd tried it once with his most recent mistress during his stay in Italy. After a great deal of tumult, they had retired to a bed, laughing, and he hadn't attempted it again.

The young monk had frozen, and Adrian knew she was staring at the exaggerated member of the Roman soldier, yet another historical inaccuracy that in no way de-tracted from the erotic power of the statue. Adrian could sense dismay in the set of her shoulders, and he chuckled. Poor innocent lamb.

She was walking into the torch-lit gardens, away from the crowds. The Heavenly Host was dividing now, in pairs, in groups, and occasionally voices called to her, inviting her to take off the white ribbon and join them, either to watch or partake, but she shook her cowled head, moving on.

She hadn't taken any of the communal wine as far as he could tell, and there was nothing to ease her fears. How well had Lina advised her? Did she know enough not to pass through the Portal of Venus? Once a celebrant chose to pass through that enchantingly landscaped orifice she would be fair game unless already claimed by another.

What the hell was she doing here anyway? He could think of no earthly reason why a well-bred, disapproving, virginal spinster would come to observe the haute ton at their most libidinous. Nor could he imagine why Evangelina Whitmore would have agreed to bring her.

He strolled after the young adventuress, similarly ignoring the invitations that came his way. She was moving inexorably closer to the Portal, and she probably had no idea what the peculiar gate into the inner gardens signified, not unless she spent time naked with a mirror. Or unless she and Lina were a great deal closer than society suspected.

He chuckled again. As divine as that particular image was, it didn't have the ring of truth. Lina was too devotedly single-minded in her pursuit of men. And he suspected Charlotte Spenser could barely fathom such a pairing.

The ruins of the ancient abbey were growing quieter. Adrian glanced behind him. The Chapel of Perpetual Erection, the newly built gathering place, was ablaze with activity, as most of the celebrants ended up there, at least for the first part of the night. Etienne had disappeared with his partners in that direction. Just as well. Etienne was occasionally a little too interested in his younger cousin's affairs, and no matter how fond Adrian was of him, he still preferred not to have everything he did subject for discussion.

Turning back, Charlotte had stopped beside another statue, this one of a willing young lady using her mouth on what appeared to be a troll. He tried to gauge her reaction, then realized he was getting too close. Close enough to see the distinguishing white tie coming loose. Close enough to sense that she was wishing she were a hundred miles away from here.

What was Lina thinking, bringing her here, he thought again, strangely annoyed. Abandoning her to the doubtful mercy of libertines like him?

Lina knew he had no mercy. He'd done his best to ignore the angry, veiled invitation in the little virgin's eyes, the one she didn't even know she'd issued. But now she'd delivered herself to him, he could hardly resist, now, could he?

"Rohan!" a voice called out. "Come join us." He signaled no, but it was too late.

She whirled around at the sound of his name, and froze. What did she expect? he thought with a touch of irritation. She must have known he'd be there — where else would a young gentleman be when the Mad Monks were congregating?

He could almost hear her gasp from where he stood, thirty paces back. And then in her panic she made her fatal mistake. She pushed through the deliberately overgrown entrance of the Portal of Venus, passing *point non plus.* No turning back for Miss Charlotte Spenser. And the branches caught, pulling at her, so that when she disappeared into the inner sanctum the white tie remained behind, clinging to the overgrown

branches.

By the time he reached the Portal there was no sign of her. He picked up the ribbon, letting the satin length trail against his fingers.

Then he followed her through the gate, smiling.

4

Bloody hell, Charlotte thought with commendable vehemence. When she'd first conceived this mad idea she'd thought there would be enough people that she would be unlikely to see Adrian Rohan — or if she did, he'd be dressed in the same enveloping robe and she wouldn't recognize him.

But not all the gentlemen and ladies wore religious habits. From her brief, nervous glance she'd seen that Rohan was dressed in simple breeches, a loose white shirt and a long, sleeveless coat. For a moment she wondered why he was dressed so informally, and then she realized it was in order to undress easily and quickly, without the aid of a valet.

She didn't even want to think about the beautiful viscount taking off his clothes. The thought of Adrian Rohan naked made her quite breathless, and she was already rattled enough by simply being here. She took

another quick look behind her. He was alone, too close, and looking straight at her.

There was no way he could know who she was — her disguise was too good. And Lina had once casually told her that Rohan had never been part of the peculiar practice of male love, so he couldn't be looking in her direction. Could he?

But still he kept moving toward her, and she panicked, moving deeper into the shadows. The torches were spaced farther apart, the errant moon providing most of the fitful lighting. A temple rose in front of her, a crescent-shaped structure of white limestone, and past the columns she thought she spied a large, shallow pool.

For a moment she breathed a sigh of relief. This was peaceful, safe, lovely in the moonlight, hidden away from the insanity beyond, a haven . . .

"*Demme,* but I knew if I waited long enough I'd find someone young and fresh," a fruity voice said in her ear, and she jumped, panicked, ready to run.

The man was wearing a monk's robe, but his cowl was down and she recognized him. Sir Reginald Cowper, he of the obscenely large fortune, and the seven grandchildren, and the saintly reputation and avuncular charm. There was nothing avuncular about

67

him now.

Before she could move, his heavy hand clamped onto her arm. "Shy, are you?" The old man chuckled. "Well, I like a timid young lad in my bed. You're new here . . ."

A myriad of emotions assailed her. Astonishment that Sir Reginald, he of the numerous descendants, preferred . . . this. Annoyance at the grip on her arm. She shook her head vehemently, trying to pull away, but his thick fingers tightened. Lina had promised her that no one was ever forced, that her strip of white riband was a safe passage. But Sir Reginald didn't seem to remember the rules. She tried to twist in his grasp to show him her badge, but it was gone.

"No need to be so shy, me lad," Sir Reginald said, slurring slightly, and she realized he was very drunk. "I won't hurt you. I'll let you be the one to —"

"No poaching, Reggie." A familiar, mocking voice broke through her struggles, and she froze.

"I saw him first, Rohan," Sir Reginald wheezed. "He came through the Portal of Venus — that makes him fair game. Besides, I know full well you're only interested in *cunt*."

That was a new word for her, but Charlotte had little doubt that it was extremely crude. She glanced up at Rohan's face from beneath her enveloping cowl. He looked the same as always, as if this were a formal ball and he was bored to tears. "Perhaps I'm growing broad-minded," he said in a lazy voice. "I'm in search of novelty and this young monk is perfect. My sainted father has always insisted I treat my elders with exquisite respect, and I would regret having to floor you, but I'm afraid you'll simply have to take no for an answer."

Astonishment was assailing Charlotte from all directions as she listened to this interchange. But Sir Reginald hadn't released her arm, and his lower lip stuck out in a sulky glower. "I'm not giving him up," the old man said mutinously.

Rohan lifted his hand, and there was a strand of white ribbon wrapped around his long, elegant fingers.

Sir Reginald's response was suitably profane, but the grip on her arm loosened, then released her. "Very well. I cede to your earlier interest, and to the sign of favor you hold. Gentlemen must follow the rules of order . . ." he muttered half to himself. "But listen to me, young man," he added, leaning over and breathing alcoholic fumes on her shrouded face. "Next time, don't come through the portal alone, or I might be tempted to ignore those rules."

She wasn't sure what to do. Rohan was watching them, and she knew there was amusement in his eyes. She didn't know whether she ought to nod or shake her head, all she knew was she had to make her way back to Hensley Court, back to the safety of her rooms, before some other gentleman decided he was interested in shy young men.

Sir Reginald wandered off, mumbling to himself, and a moment later he disappeared back through the hedge, back the way she and Rohan had come. She heard a score of ragged cheers on the other side as he emerged, but she had more important things on her mind. Such as getting away from the too-beautiful Viscount Rohan.

She knew of no universal gesture to signal thank-you, so she hoped a gracious nod of her head would be sufficient. His eyes glittered in the moonlight, but there was no sign of confusion or doubt on his face. Just the usual courteous cynicism.

She started to turn, but he caught her hand. "I think not, young friar," he said softly.

She shook her head as she tried to pull her hand free, but he simply followed. "Didn't Lady Whitmore warn you about the Portal of Venus? Yes, I know you were with her. One of her young lovers, I assume. Do you have any idea why she abandoned you to the tender mercies of the Mad Monks?"

She yanked harder, still backing away, but he simply followed her, his grip sure but not as painful as Sir Reginald's had been.

"No answer?" Rohan murmured. "Well, it doesn't matter. We're here now, and my cell is nearby."

She yanked her arm in earnest now, shaking her head, but he simply laughed. A charming, infuriating laugh. "Oh, no, young friar. Not a jail cell. I have no intention of imprisoning you, though I'd be more than happy to teach you other, more pleasurable forms of restraint. No, I'm speaking of my own personal monk's cell. I've paid very good money to ensure that it's a bit more luxurious than the usual, and blessedly private among this circus of sinners. You'll come to like it."

She managed to pull free, and he let her go, laughing, as she ran from him, racing toward the pseudotemple, her sandaled feet clumsy. She kicked off one of the sandals as she ran, then tried to kick off the second, but her foot caught and she went sprawling, flat out on the hard ground.

He was standing over her. She knew he was, even though the cowl had dropped around her head, obliterating everything. And thank God — if it had fallen back on her shoulders he'd know who she was. No one else had curly hair her particular color.

"No need to do penance," he said in that wicked, dancing voice. "You haven't sinned. Yet."

At the ominous, enticing sound of that single word she tried to scramble to her feet, but he caught her, pulling her up against his hard, strong body, one hand around her waist, imprisoning her quite easily. "Are you going to speak, or is this vow of silence permanent? Not that I'm not enjoying this game tremendously, but sooner or later it's going to come down to my bedding you, and you know it. Otherwise you wouldn't be here."

She could push back her hood and declare herself, and he'd release her, horrified at his mistake. He had no interest in plain, virginal Charlotte Spenser — he was here looking for a talented playmate.

But then everyone would know. He'd scarcely keep quiet about it, and doubtless everyone in London society would find it vastly entertaining. She'd never be able to show her face in town again.

Which wouldn't be a terrible fate, but she couldn't abandon Lina. No, her best bet was to go along with him, keep her head down and say nothing and wait for her next chance to run. She'd gotten away from him once, and would have succeeded if it hadn't been for the wretched sandal. Barefoot, she could be fleet and determined — she was used to running through the meadows at home, barefoot. He'd be no match for her.

She calmed her struggles, and his grip loosened. He released her, and she knew a totally mad moment of regret. There had been something undeniably wonderful about being held in Adrian Rohan's arms.

It was hardly the stuff of her fantasies, she tried to remind herself briskly. For one thing, he thought she was a man. For another, this was a place of unbridled licentiousness. He'd probably shag a goat if one wandered by.

"You've decided to be agreeable?" Rohan said. "How mysterious. Either you've taken a vow of silence, young friar, or I know you. That, or perhaps your voice might betray a less than patrician upbringing. Let me assure you I'm wonderfully democratic when it comes to sex. But not to worry — I have far better things for your mouth to be doing."

Charlotte thought of that statue, the one where the female had actually put her mouth on the sculpted male. If he wanted someone so do *that* he was going to have to look elsewhere.

He held out his hand, and she surprised herself by taking it, using it to balance herself as she took off her recalcitrant sandal. She needed every advantage she could get. He took it from her hand before she could drop it on the ground.

"Such a small sandal. You have very delicate feet," he observed. "And lovely hands as well. I think I'm going to enjoy the next three days immensely."

Three days? Good God, what could he possibly find to do with someone for three whole days?

She'd been a fool to attempt this, she thought, sick with misery. She couldn't afford to waste time berating herself now — it would have to wait until she got back to the safety of her room. In the meantime, she had to concentrate on getting away from Rohan and any other degenerates roaming these grounds in search of a victim.

"Are you ready, Brother Silence?" he murmured, his voice mocking, as if he knew very well she wasn't who she pretended to be. Well, of course — he knew she was but someone masquerading as a monk, and he was playing along, barely.

74

But why hadn't he demanded to see her face? He'd made no effort to push the cowl back, thank God, but wasn't that slightly odd? Wouldn't he want to know what the person he planned on bedding looked like? Apparently not, and she could only count her blessings. There was still a chance she might pull this off, escape before he found out her identity.

Adrian was still holding her hand. She simply nodded and let him lead her toward the temple.

Evangelina picked up her heavy skirts and followed the servant out into the darkness lit only by the lantern the footman was carrying. The festivities had already begun — she could hear the sounds of carnal delight fill the evening air, and she suddenly thought of Charlotte. She'd meant to keep a close eye on her innocent cousin, perhaps enlist a few friends to make certain she was safe. One of those friends had been Montague.

She hadn't even noticed his collapse, his sudden disappearance, too intent on her twin purposes of keeping Charlotte safe and getting Adrian Rohan into her bed. Once the servant had found her and whispered in her ear, all Lina's plans had vanished, and she had taken off with the man.

As she climbed back into one of the flat-bottomed boats that were used to carry the revelers to and from the abbey ruins she knew a moment's misgivings. This wasn't beyond the realm of the Mad Monks — one of them could have dressed in Monty's livery to lure her away. Games like this one were simply part of the frivolity.

If that were indeed the case, she wasn't sure whether she'd be pleased or angry. But no, the man holding the torch wasn't anyone she knew, and he carried himself like a servant, not an aristocrat. Monty must truly be ill.

"Hurry," she said in a sharp voice.

"Yes, miss. Mr. Dodson told me I was to get you there as quick as can be. His lordship won't take his medicine and is insisting on returning to the party, and Mr. Dodson's that worried."

"Won't take his medicine?" Lina said grimly. "I'll see to that."

By the time the boat pulled up back at the quay by Hensley Court she was half-frantic, and she didn't wait for the footman to tie up and help her out, she scrambled onto the riverbank and took off across the wide lawn.

Dodson, Monty's devoted manservant,

was waiting for her, wringing his hands and pacing. "Oh, your ladyship," he said, his voice shaken. "Thank goodness you've come. I'm at my wits' end."

"How is he, Dodson?"

He was already leading her into the house. "Not good, my lady, though he could be worse. If I could just convince him to retire for the night, to take his medication and rest, but he insists he must return."

"Insists, does he? I don't think so. He'll have me to reckon with."

Dodson paused outside the salon door. "It's just for tonight, my lady. By tomorrow Mr. Pagett should arrive, and he should be able to help the master . . ."

"What did you say?" came a roar from the room beyond.

Lina pushed the door all the way open. "You always did have devilishly good hearing, Monty." She smiled. "Now stop being a prima donna and let Dodson look after you properly."

In truth, Montague looked awful. His color was gray, and despite the coolness of the night his thin, powdered and patched face was covered in sweat. Nevertheless, he still managed to fix Dodson with a ferocious glare. "What's this about Simon coming early?" he demanded in awful tones.

Dodson had served Montague for too long to be cowed. "I thought it would be for the best, sir. You're getting weaker, you won't listen to your doctor or to me. Perhaps Mr. Pagett will be able to make you see reason."

"The vicar? Pah!" he said in disgust, his voice breathless as he struggled not to cough. "He's a demmed parson! All he'll do is ring a peal over me, preach to me about the error of my ways. I tell you, Lina, there's nothing worse than a reformed hellion. Just because they've found God or some such nonsense doesn't mean everyone else has to."

"You'll pardon my saying so, my lord, but you've given him the living hereabouts. Isn't he supposed to help everyone else find God?" Dodson asked tentatively.

"Demme, but you're a nervy bastard tonight, Dodson."

"Yes, sir," Dodson said serenely.

Lina sank onto the tufted stool near the head of the divan where Montague lay, his body stretched out beneath a silken counterpane. "I imagine he was thinking of me," she said. "You won't listen to the servants and someone must make you behave. Since I'm one of the very few people who can keep you in line, that role falls to me, and he didn't want me to relinquish my entire three days of fun."

Montague surveyed her from beneath his lank blond hair. "Doing it a little too brown, my precious," he murmured. "Dodson has a fondness for you, and he disapproves of all this. I expect he'd like nothing better than to keep you out of it."

"My lord!" Dodson looked genuinely shocked.

"Oh, go away, Dodson. And when the vicar shows up send him straight on to the manse. I'm sure someone has arranged for a housekeeper for him."

"Someone has," Dodson said with real dignity. Since Dodson served as Montague's valet, butler and social secretary, that someone was certainly he. "Milady, would you care for a cup of a tea, or a glass of wine, perhaps?"

Lina smiled pleasantly. If she was to spend the night by Montague's side and not in bed with one of the Heavenly Host, then she had no need to drink. "Tea would be lovely. And a cold supper? Bring enough for his lordship."

"I don't want any demmed food," Monty said fretfully. "Unless you can bring me a sirloin and a pint of ale."

"A good beef broth, I think," Lina said, ignoring him. "With some barley water."

"Barley water? Faugh!" He fixed a glared on both of them. "You may as well kill me now. If Dodson can send for Adrian Rohan instead, you may return to the Revels. Yes, I know you had your eye on him for this occasion, but my needs take precedence. Adrian will understand I can't bear such pig swill."

"Viscount Rohan will be just as strict, my lord," Dodson said. "No one wishes you to die."

A spasm of coughing shook Monty's frail body, and then he lay back against the pillows, exhausted, two bright spots of color on his cheeks. "Do you what you want." His faint voice was querulous. "I don't have the will to fight you. At this rate you'll plague me to death."

"Indeed, I hope not, sir," Dodson said with great dignity before retiring.

There was silence for a moment. The tall windows were open to the cool night air, and in the distance Lina could hear music floating over the water, accompanied by the sound of laughter. And because no one would notice, she breathed a sigh of relief. At least tonight she could be at peace.

"You're terrible to poor Dodson," she said.

Monty sighed. "Yes, I am, aren't I? It never seems to bother him." He paused, his long thin fingers plucking at the quilt covering his frail body. "You'll see to him, won't you, Lina? I've made what arrangements I could, but I worry about the old thing."

"Don't be ridiculous," she chided him. "Dodson's twice your age — you'll outlive him by decades and then you're the one in trouble. You'll never find anyone willing to put up with you the way that brave soul does."

Monty smiled faintly, but didn't bother to argue with her. Instead, he turned his head to looked toward the abbey ruins. The moon was bright overhead, the two spires of the ruined abbey stood stark against the night sky. "It's a beautiful night, Lina," he said. "You know, I hate to admit it, but I'd rather be here with you than romping between the sheets with some lovely young thing. So would you."

She didn't bother denying it — he knew her too well. Though there were times when she wondered how many others saw through her fevered gaiety. Charlotte, for certain. There were doubtless others.

"There will be other nights to romp, Monty," she said, touching his thin hands.

Monty turned his hand over and clasped hers with weak affection. "More's the pity, love," he murmured.

5

The moon had come out. In the distance
Charlotte could hear the strains of music.
There had been a small orchestra set up
near the dais, and the music, simple and
slightly sinuous, snaked its way into her
consciousness. She could see Rohan a bit
too clearly from beneath her enveloping
cowl, and she swallowed nervously, uncon-
sciously flexing her bare toes in the grass as
she walked.

He held her hand. It was unnerving —
she couldn't remember ever having held a
man's hand outside of dancing. When she
was young, her father had certainly never
bothered with her enough to hold her hand,
and all the servants who'd looked after her
were female. Being a short-sighted, overgrown, ginger-haired and befreckled creature, she had obviously never excited the
interest of a gentleman enough for him to
take her hand.

In fact, disposing of Rohan's company would be quite simple. All she had to do was drop the cowl to her shoulders and let him see just who he'd managed to capture. He'd drop her hand as if burned.

That was only as a last resort. His grasp was light, casual. She didn't doubt his fingers could tighten very swiftly, but the longer she allowed her hand to remain in his the more his guard would likely drop.

He wore no gloves. Neither did she. Another shocking circumstance — she'd barely touched anyone without layers of kid leather between them, back when she'd attempted to dance. She'd never been fond of gloves, except for riding or gardening. They made her palms itch.

But she could suddenly see the wisdom of them for social occasions. There was something so . . . intimate about skin on skin, flesh on flesh. His fingers, warm and strong, wrapped around her unresisting ones.

She allowed herself a furtive glance up at him from beneath her enveloping hood. She could see the ruined spires of the abbey behind him, and for a moment they looked oddly like devil's horns. She blinked, then wanted to laugh. She was being ridiculously fanciful. Adrian Rohan was nothing but a man. A spoiled, wicked, far too pretty man, but human. By coming here she hadn't somehow managed to sell her soul to the devil.

Should she dare attempt to speak? If she could manage some kind of low-throated rumble of a voice, it might serve to further convince him she was a man. There was no way he could suspect who she really was — the very proper Miss Spenser would hardly be cavorting with the Mad Monks of the Heavenly Host.

Not that she'd yet cavorted, and she had no intention of doing so. This had all been in the service of a very ill-judged curiosity. Really, couldn't her imagination have sufficed? And who would have thought she'd run into Adrian Rohan?

She had.

The truth came flooding in. She had known perfectly well he would be here, indulging his debauched appetites. She had come here to see him, watch him, if possible, from behind the safety of the disguise. She wanted to see him naked, flushed with desire, so she could capture that in her memory.

She supposed she wouldn't be happy seeing him direct that powerful licentiousness toward some other woman, and if Lina succeeded in bedding him she would walk away, go back to the house and try to forget.

It might even break the powerful hold Rohan had over her mind and her emotions. Because nothing else had managed to have any effect so far. Her longing for him was unbearably painful.

In truth, she looked at the beautiful, spoiled, self-indulgent man and saw a wounded, angry child. One who needed her.

She mocked herself silently. This man didn't need her at all; he needed the next willing body and open bottle and game of hazard. He had no use for someone like her, even though she knew she could be the making of him.

No, if Lina had taken him it would have all been over. Her cousin would have moved on, and Rohan would find other beauties to flirt and dance with, to bed. Nothing would change.

She'd been a fool and a half to come here.

She gave a faint tug on her hand, just to see how alert he was, but his fingers tightened immediately, not to the point of pain, but just short of it. She had the impression that he knew how to judge his strength perfectly, which made her even more uneasy. For him to have such intimate knowledge of pain he must have a fair amount of experience, and that was most definitely one thing she had no intention of witnessing, much less participating in. She should have suspected that would be part of his particular interest.

It was a good thing he hadn't realized the smaller, softer hand in his belonged to a female. In truth, her hands were probably larger than those of many shorter men, and she never used unguents or whitening agents on them, unlike many in the ton. At least that part of her anatomy wouldn't betray her, and that was the only part of her he was going to touch.

They were in a cul-de-sac. The earth had risen around them, leaving them in a landscaped depression, reinforced stone walls all around them, and only one door in the impenetrable fortress.

There was no escape, she realized with sudden panic, only back the way they came. She was certain he must have sensed the immediate tension in her body. His hand tightened on hers, and she knew there was no way to take him unawares.

Kicking him would be useless in bare feet. She could use her elbows, her knees; she could use her fingernails and teeth. She wasn't going to submit to . . .

She took a deep, calming breath. He was under any number of false assumptions.

Once she explained he would let her go. She'd hoped to escape without having to say a word, but escape she would, whatever the price.

She hadn't moved, and he didn't try to rush her, seeming content to take his time in the cool night air. The bright moonlight was unkind — it lit the planes and hollows of his face, only accentuating his dangerous beauty, and for a moment she was back in her dreams where he held her, kissed her, stroked her body until she woke up alone, convulsing, her own hands between her legs.

The memory shamed her, even as it enticed her. But it was her own fantasy, as those hands, embarrassingly enough, had been her own hands fisted beneath her body as she rocked against them. His touch would be anathema.

Fear finally galvanized her. "I'm not what you think I am," she said in a low, gravelly voice in one last attempt to deceive him.

He looked amused, not surprised. "It speaks!" he said in a marveling tone. "And how do you know what I think you are? Believe me, child, I was under no illusion that you were truly a monk under a vow of silence. I'm pleased you've decided to talk — we can't negotiate until you're willing to parley."

"Negotiate?" The word caught her. "What have we to negotiate?"

"Why, the terms of your surrender."

The fear was arcing through her now, threatening to overpower her. "I surrender," she said promptly. "Now let me go."

"I'm afraid you don't understand the concept of surrender, my pet. There is no true surrender until I am thrusting inside you, finding my own completion and yours. There is no surrender until you take me into your mouth. There is no surrender until you beg me for my touch, my kiss, my cock."

Panic washed over her full force, and she tried to yank herself away. But his grip was too strong. Painful now, just a little bit.

"You don't understand," she said, breathless, her voice a notch higher in her panic. "I'm not a man."

"You don't understand," he mimicked. "I never thought you were. I only like to fuck women."

The deliberate crudeness of his language made her flinch. She knew that word, even if some of the others were unfamiliar. That had been the hardest word Meggie had taught her. That he would use it with her was shocking.

Her resolve grew stronger still. "Not this woman," she said firmly. No one gets forced,

Lina had promised her. All she had to do was say no and he'd release her. "We'll go back and find you someone more amenable. As for me, the answer is no."

If she'd hoped he'd look abashed she was disappointed. "It's a bit too late for that, my precious. The moment you stepped through the Portal of Venus you signified your willingness to take on the first man who claimed you. Just be thankful I wrested you from Reggie. He's not particularly nice in his notions, and he would have hurt you."

"And you won't?"

A faint smile curved his elegant mouth. "Only briefly, and I'll endeavor to make it as painless as possible. Losing your virginity always hurts a bit, or so I'm told, but I expect I can soon make you forget all about it."

Oh, God. "What in the world makes you think I'm a virgin?" she protested in her falsely deep voice. "This is hardly the place for innocence."

"Which is why you're so delectable," he said. "And I can tell by the way you walk, the way you flinch when I touch you, when I tell you what we're going to do together. Only a virgin would be so plainly terrified. As to why you're here, I have absolutely no idea. I've been trying to figure it out for

89

some time now."

"Momentary insanity," she said. "I'm recovered now." She pulled at her hand, knowing it was useless, fighting anyway.

"Sorry," he said, not sounding the slightest bit regretful. "We've already come too far."

She could push back her cowl, shock him into releasing her. But she still held off, hoping there was some way to escape this terrible mess she'd gotten herself into without betraying her identity. And the dismal truth of it was that she wasn't so much afraid of the social aftermath of him knowing she'd been there. She was afraid to see that light in his eyes flicker and fade with disappointment once he saw who he really had in his net.

She reached up her free hand to tug the cowl lower over her face. "As for this Portal of Venus you keep going on about, it was a mistake. My . . . my dear friend who brought me here was going to point it out but she got . . . distracted. How was I to know what the Portal of Venus was?"

"I regret Lady Whitmore didn't have a chance to show you," he drawled, shocking her. He knew she'd come with Lina. Well, there was nothing remarkable about that — they'd been standing together during that

90

ridiculous ceremony with its terrible Latin. "But that's hardly an excuse. All you had to do was look. The Portal of Venus," he said patiently, "is the round entrance to the first garden, surrounded by boxwood and maidenhair ferns. It resembles . . ."

"Oh, how *revolting!*" Charlotte cried, with no need for him to continue.

"On the contrary, I tend to find it quite . . . hmm . . . stimulating. But I believe I did mention that I reserve my attentions for women, did I not?"

There was no other way out, she thought desperately. Where the hell was Lina when she needed her? Off enjoying the attentions of who knew how many, her idiot of a cousin forgotten.

"Yes, you did," she said calmly, dropping all effort to disguise her voice. He wouldn't recognize it anyway, not from one short conversation in a noisy ballroom. "But Viscount Rohan is known for his excellent taste. His mistresses are some of the most beautiful women in the world."

"Now, how would you know of my mistresses?" he murmured, amused.

She ignored the question. "You would hardly lower your standards to . . . to . . . bed an unwilling antidote, a plain old maid."

He surveyed her figure in silence for a mo-

91

ment, and she had the odd notion that he could not only see beneath the enveloping hood, but also see through to her flaws and imperfections. "The word is *fuck*," he said deliberately. "And you wouldn't be unwilling." There was a calm certainty in his voice, as if he'd been privy to her awful dreams. "You greatly underestimate your charms." His hand tightened, and he pulled her toward him, slowly, inexorably. She tried to put her hands between them, but it was already too late to fight him, and he simply clamped her against him, against his strong, hard body. She could feel him, as she had in her dreams, and she wanted to cry. So close, so tantalizingly close, and all she had to do was pull back her cowl and he'd release her, shocked, horrified, perhaps disgusted at the thought of the mistake he'd almost made.

But she couldn't get her hands free — they were trapped between their bodies. He'd managed to restrain her with just one arm, and his hand reached up toward her hidden face.

"You don't want to do this," she said desperately.

"Of course I do. I've wanted to for a long time, Miss Spenser." And he pushed the hood from her head, caught her stubborn chin in one strong hand and kissed her.

Lina heard the sound first. A grating noise, like some strange bird, she thought. A jackdaw or perhaps a crow. She opened her eyes and realized she'd fallen asleep beside Monty's chaise. She was sitting on the floor, fully dressed, her head cradled in her arms, and Monty slept on, oblivious to the most irritating bird that was . . .

"Ahem."

No, that wasn't a bird. That was someone clearing his throat, and she lifted her head and turned, not bothering to rise, assuming it was simply Dodson with some tea and toast.

It wasn't. It was a man she'd never seen before, soberly dressed in black with white linen. No lace, no jewels, no ornament of any kind, and he was looking down on her with a shadowed expression that doubtless signaled deep disapproval. She felt herself flush. She, who prided herself on being shameless.

She started to rise, and he held out one hand to assist her. She'd planned to ignore it, but her legs were cramped and gave way beneath her, forcing her to reach to him for support. His was a strong hand, and not soft like those of the aristocrats who touched her.

"Has Montague converted to Catholicism without telling me or are you some part of his depraved activities?"

She was still wearing the wimple, though by now it was on crooked. She snatched it from her head, shaking her long black hair loose around her shoulders, and surveyed him for a moment. "I'm a part of his depraved activities," she said in a cool voice meant to deflate pretension. After all, he was only a vicar, not someone who had any right to judge her.

The man was unmoved. He wasn't a young man — perhaps close to forty if she were to guess by the deeply etched lines on his face. A handsome face, with deep brown eyes, a straight nose, high cheekbones and a stubborn mouth that on a less disapproving man might almost be called sensuous.

Not on this man.

"You must be the new vicar."

"You are very perceptive. I'm the Reverend Simon Pagett, here to take up the living." He glanced down at the sleeping Montague. "Is he dead?" he asked in a voice as cool as hers.

"Of course not!" she hissed. "How could you ask such a thing?"

"Simon's never been one to avoid the truth, no matter how ugly it is." Monty's voice came from the chaise, sepulchral and amused. "I'm afraid I'm not ready to stick my fork into the wall, dear boy. Sorry to disappoint you."

"Good," the man said. "That means there's still time to save your soul." He glanced toward Lina. "And your strumpet's soul as well."

Lina drew a deep, shocked breath, but Monty chuckled. "You know as well as I do that I haven't changed that much, Simon, even if you have. My strumpets are a different gender. Lina's a dear friend and I'll thank you not to insult her."

"From the local convent, no doubt," Simon said politely.

Montague snorted. "You'd best have a care, Simon. This is Lady Whitmore. I have no doubt there are at least half a dozen of her admirers who would gladly defend her honor from your prudish, judging ways. Of course . . . the term *honor . . .*" His smile at Lina took the sting out of his words.

"And where are those half-dozen men, Montague?" Simon said. "When I arrived I saw the carriages, and yet the house seems empty. Where are your licentious playmates?"

"They're at the abbey ruins. I've had it renovated, landscaped. It's really quite delightful, though I doubt you'd appreciate its all-too-human beauty. You'd be shocked."

"You lost the ability to shock me years ago, though you continue to try. How long have you been ill?" he demanded abruptly.

"It takes a number of years for consumption to kill a man. I don't pay any attention to it."

"I know you don't," Simon said severely. "And that's why you're in this current difficulty. You can no longer afford to burn the candle at both ends."

"It's the only way I know how to live. And I didn't invite you here — you weren't supposed to arrive until my guests were long gone. Unfortunately, thanks to Dodson's interference, you've come at a most inopportune moment."

"I am desolate," Simon said dryly.

"Still, I suppose it's just as well. Dodson's infernal meddling has forced Lady Whitmore to miss the first night of the Revels out of kindness for me. Lina, my pet, why don't you run along and play. You can still catch up with the party — it's not far past midnight. Simon will look after me. He's done it enough times before. I have no doubt you'll be able to find some amiable distraction, even at this ungodly hour. The Heavenly Host never sleep."

"I'll be lucky if I can find anyone stirring," Lina said wryly. "They'll all be unconscious from a surfeit of lust and drink."

Simon Pagett was looking at her. When she turned to meet his gaze his eyes were fixed on Monty, but she could have sworn he'd been watching her . . .

It was an easy decision to make, and she didn't bother to consider why she made it. "I'm not going anywhere, Monty," she said, taking the seat she'd abandoned a few hours ago for the dubious comfort of the floor. "There will be plenty of other times of unbridled depravity for me to enjoy. For now I'm not leaving your side." She cast a sly glance at Simon. "Mr. Pig-ett should feel free to partake of the myriad pleasures the Heavenly Host offers. Perhaps he might understand the nature of the sins he's so roundly condemning."

"Pagett." He was calm. And this time when he looked at Lina he didn't try to hide it. "And I assure you, Lady Whitmore, that I have already experienced everything the Heavenly Host has to offer. I'm not interested." He looked down at Monty. "Despite your friend's deplorable taste in both costume and companions I think it probably wise for her to remain here. You've never been an easy patient."

"And you've always been a pain in my arse. Why don't you do as Lina says, and go out to the ruins. Perhaps the decadent souls out there might wish to be saved. I know for a fact they're very fond of succor." He drew out the last word, long and lasciviously.

"You need to be in bed," Pagett said, ignoring him. "I'd have Dodson call the doctor but he'd probably wish to bleed you and you're weak enough as it is." He glanced at Lina. "Would you prefer to go back to your friends, Lady Whitmore? I can make arrangements."

She wasn't quite sure what she preferred. She certainly wasn't pleased with this soberly dressed, high-handed man "making arrangements" for her. She ought to get back and make certain Charlotte was all right. Of course, if there had been any question about her cousin's safety she would never have agreed to bring her, but it wouldn't hurt to set her mind at ease.

"Oh, God, don't leave me to Simon's tender mercies!" Montague begged, his eyes sparkling. "He'll have me in a hair shirt before the day is out. Spare me from reformed rakes — they're the very devil. And yes, Simon, I use that term advisedly."

"I'll stay." Lina pressed his thin, weak hand with hers.

"I knew I could count on you," he murmured, casting a speaking look at the vicar.

Lina glanced over her shoulder but Mr. Pagett was expressionless, offering no protest.

She couldn't imagine a man like him succumbing to the lures of the flesh. His lined face seemed preternaturally grave — as if he were born that way — and she couldn't imagine a time when he had laughed, cried, charmed, kissed. He really did have a lovely mouth when it wasn't drawn into a thin line of what was either worry or disapproval, disapproval seeming more likely. It was a shame it wasn't used for more pleasurable purposes than denouncing the sinful.

Dodson had made a reappearance, accompanied by two of Montague's typically handsome footmen.

"Assist Lord Montague to his rooms and make him comfortable," Simon said in a calm tone that was nonetheless a trifle highhanded. "And Lady Whitmore, may I suggest you change into something more appropriate for the circumstances?"

Prudish little toad, Lina thought rebelliously, ignoring the fact that Simon was neither little nor toad-like. "I thought the habit was eminently suitable, Mr. Pagett, given the spiritual aspect of the occasion and my nursing skills."

In another man she might have recognized humor in his eyes. But this one was surely devoid of humor, and that light in his dark eyes must be impatience. "I wasn't objecting to the nun's habit, Lady Whitmore. I merely thought the décolletage was a bit extreme for a sickroom, and I assumed you preferred to be fashionable. You may wear whatever you please."

"Thank you for your kind permission," she said with only the faintest bite beneath her soft tone. In fact, she'd forgotten that beneath the rounded white collar of the habit the plain black dress was cut very low, ostensibly to allow men to survey her bounty before she actually divested herself of her clothes. She resisted the impulse to yank her dress up higher. Her breasts were firm and well shaped; let the dour clergyman look his fill.

"You have a point, Mr. Pagett," she murmured. "Though it's a shame when you and I are so particularly matched. In costume, at least."

For a brief moment the words hung in the air, seeming to take on a different meaning.

And then Pagett scowled at her, ignoring her breasts as few men had managed in the past ten years. "I doubt we would find we have anything else in common," he said, sounding irritable. "Perhaps it would be better if you were to join your fellow sybarites . . ."

"I will stay." In fact, she'd considered slipping away, but most likely Charlotte was in the room they were sharing, sound asleep.

The footmen were already carrying Montague from the candlelit salon amidst his weak curses and languid protests. The look Simon Pagett cast her was far from promising. "He's in safe hands with me, Lady Whitmore, no matter what he says. It would probably make things a great deal simpler if you went and joined the others."

She looked at him for a long moment. "And it would doubtless make things a great deal simpler if you returned from whence you came and waited until you were supposed to show up. Sometime next week, I collect?"

At first he didn't answer her, and she had the odd, uncomfortable sensation that he saw her too clearly. "Why would you suppose any such thing?"

"Because Montague would scarcely invite a stick-in-the-mud, disapproving parson to a house party composed of notorious libertines, would he?"

Now she could see for certain — he was amused. It barely touched the corners of his fine eyes, and his mouth kept its grim, uncompromising line. Nevertheless, he was amused.

"You think not, Lady Whitmore? In fact, he was expecting me tomorrow, and the Revels usually last a good four days, do they not?"

"Only three this time." She didn't stop to wonder why he'd know that much.

His lips curved in a cool smile. "Perhaps Montague is beginning to accept the fact that he is mortal after all. I expect he hoped to be strong enough to enjoy at least a part of the Revels, and to rub my nose in it." He stared down at her for a long moment, as if he'd forgotten what he was going to say.

She was feeling oddly breathless. If he wasn't going to speak, then she should, rather than stand there in that awkward silence. Of course, the way to break it would be to excuse herself, and that was exactly what she should do. Except she didn't want to.

There was an arrested expression in his eyes, and the silence held. Until something made him come to his senses, and he turned away with a short, dismissive laugh. "Montague will be resting for the next few hours, once the doctor leaves. You may as well get some rest yourself.

"We've got an arduous battle ahead and you'll need your strength."

"Battle?" she echoed, confused. "Battle for what?"

"Montague's immortal soul." He turned, then looked back for a moment. "And likely yours as well."

And without another word he was gone.

6

For a first kiss it was not bad, Adrian thought coolly. Charlotte Spenser froze as his mouth touched hers, too shocked to do anything more, and Adrian pressed his advantage, pulling her closer against his body, wrapping his arms around her so she couldn't escape easily, and proceeded to work on seducing her mouth first. He slid one hand up to her gold-rimmed glasses, slipped them off and deliberately dropped them on the ground before she even knew what he'd done.

She could probably feel his iron-hard erection beneath her silly monk's habit, even if she didn't know what it was. Quite impressive — he hadn't been this excited so early in the game for a long time. He usually needed his partner to be completely naked and under him before he reached this dangerous point, further proof that he'd been far too interested in Charlotte Spenser to begin with.

She was struggling, just slightly, making a distressed sound, and he silently cursed. She was going to have to be handled very carefully or she might bolt, and he'd be honor bound to let her go. Assuming he still possessed a degree of honor.

Except that he knew she wanted this, or would if well-bred, virginal young women had any honesty. If he could just manage to convince her to let go of it all, this could be quite revelatory for both of them.

He lifted his mouth from hers, just barely, and looked down into her shocked, wide-open eyes, now without the annoying barrier of glass. She didn't even seem to notice he'd taken them. "It's easier if you close your eyes," he said in a practical voice. To his astonishment she did, and he kissed her again.

She was no longer struggling, a mixed blessing; her squirming had provided a lovely friction for his erect penis. Then again, it wouldn't help matters if he climaxed in his breeches. Her lips had been tight, frightened, but now they had softened, and he brushed his own lips against hers, once, twice, wanting to hum with anticipatory delight.

If she accepted his kiss he'd have her, he

told himself. Accepted a real kiss, his tongue in her mouth, taking her, not this innocent stuff reserved for young ladies behind the punch bowl, innocent creatures who didn't know what they wanted.

He lifted his head again. "Open your mouth for me."

Her eyes flew open again. "Why?"

It was the first word she'd spoken in quite a while, but her voice was husky and raw as if she'd been screaming.

"Because I want to kiss you that way."

"I don't know what you're talking about. You need to let me —"

He covered her mouth again before she could say the fateful words, and he pushed his tongue into her mouth so he could taste her fully. She froze again, but he knew how to kiss, how to use his tongue and teeth to get the response he wanted. Her body softened first, then her jaw, then her mouth, accepting him.

He took his time then. He wanted her tongue in his mouth, he wanted her to draw his in and suck on it. He demonstrated, hoping she might get the idea, letting his tongue slide against hers, teasing, dancing, sucking, but she still didn't do anything more than let him.

And he wanted more. He'd told himself

that acceptance was enough, but he'd been wrong. He wanted, needed participation.

"Kiss me back," he whispered, his own voice hoarse.

She started to shake her head, but he caught her chin in one strong hand, holding her still. "Kiss me back," he repeated in a rough voice.

Her eyes were huge. In the darkness her rich red hair looked black, and she looked up at him beseechingly. Don't ask me to let you go, he thought.

"I don't . . . know how."

A slow smile curved his mouth as relief flooded him. "I'll show you," he said, claiming her mouth again, trying to control the sheer ferocity of his desire for her. He kissed her slowly, much more slowly than he wanted to, but after a moment he got into the feel of it, the slow, languorous sweep of his tongue in her mouth, the soft little bites, the lift and repositioning of his mouth over hers.

The final, tentative touch of her tongue against his.

He wanted to throw back his head and laugh with triumph, but he didn't want to stop kissing her. He could feel the changes in her body, as it softened, flowed against his, and he wanted to push her against a wall, shove her robe up and take her right there.

He couldn't. He wasn't prone to kindly gestures, but her first time should be in a bed. Hell, her first time should be in her new husband's bed, but he wasn't going to give her that.

He also wasn't going to give her a baby. He would pull out, and her cousin would be able to provide the remedies most of their set used to prevent unwanted conception just in case. She would emerge from his little cave minus her innocence but not much more the worse for wear. She'd still be the same prissy old maid, and she'd conveniently forget her night of love in the bed of London's most notorious rake.

If he ended up letting her stay that long. Virgins were tedious — they cried and then professed themselves to be in love with their heartless seducers, because God forbid they should find any sexual pleasure that didn't come with a lifelong guarantee. Charlotte already thought herself in love with him, whether she admitted it or not. And she would most certainly cry.

Twice should be enough. Once to deflower her and take the edge off his suddenly overpowering need. A second time to go slowly and explore alternatives.

He could make her come, quite easily, but that might be a mistake. She was probably better off not knowing what she was missing, since her future wasn't likely to offer many opportunities. Most men wouldn't be able to see past the glasses and the scowl, they wouldn't appreciate her creamy, gold-flecked skin and rich mouth. If she ever married it would doubtless be to some widower or elderly bachelor who knew nothing about pleasing a woman and cared less, so she'd be happier without too many fond memories. Besides, it would take a lot of work bringing a newly deflowered virgin to completion. He'd be better off moving on to the next partner, sending this one back to the city.

The others wouldn't like it. They'd want to share. Innocence was a highly prized commodity — there was nothing the Mad Monks liked better than to open the eyes of some starry-eyed virgin. They would expect him to pass her along, to be sampled in turn by lechers and degenerates and sodomites . . .

No, he wasn't going to let that happen. She would be his, and his alone, and once he tired of her he'd make certain she was out of reach of his more twisted compatriots.

He thought all this as he kissed her, as his erection pulsed at the front of his breeches, as her hands, trapped between their bodies, slowly began to move, sliding up his chest to finally clutch his shoulders. He thought all this, and then he stopped thinking at all, lost in the taste of her, the feel of her, the sounds of her breath catching in her throat.

And he wanted, needed to hear the sound she made when she climaxed.

He moved her, slowly, carefully, against the door to his hidden room. He turned, leaning against it so that it opened, and he pulled her inside with him as the heavy door swung to a close with a satisfying thud.

Charlotte's senses were flooding her, a delicious cascade of taste and touch, of sounds and scent in the shadowy darkness. She knew she shouldn't let him, but for just this brief moment she couldn't bring herself to resist. This was Rohan, the man in her shameless dreams, the unconscionable rake who'd haunted her waking hours as well. She'd heard the salacious stories — she knew just how depraved he was. She'd read the carefully shielded reports in the newspapers about the Villainous Viscount. His father had been just as bad — it was no wonder he was totally without conscience or decency.

He was also a master at kissing. Even with her total lack of experience she could tell that much. Adrian, Viscount Rohan, was kissing her, tall, gawky Charlotte Spenser, when there were easily a dozen beautiful women who'd doubtless warm his bed quite happily. But he had followed her, somehow divining who she was. Knowing she was plain, spinsterish Charlotte, and he'd come after *her,* and now he was kissing her with such single-minded attention that he must like it, at least a little bit.

As far as she knew, Viscount Rohan never did anything he didn't find enjoyable.

His arms were around her, holding her against him, and her knees felt weak. She wanted to sink against him, just let go and have him gather her body against his. What harm could it do?

Very real harm, she thought dazedly as he kissed the side of her mouth, slow, lingering kisses. In another moment she'd shove him away, in another moment she'd run away, she'd find Lina, she'd . . . oh, God, if he'd only stop she could be strong. But as long as he held her like this she couldn't resist. She'd had so little, and her future was so bleak. Couldn't she have this much?

She felt him shift, turning her around, felt

them both move away from the moonlit sky and the cool night air. She felt dizzy, and she tentatively lifted her hands to hold on to him, afraid she might fall, as darkness closed about them and she could hear the sound of a heavy door closing, and then an odd, clicking sound penetrating the haze of longing that suffused her. Almost like the sound of a lock being set.

Alarm spread through her, and she tore her mouth away, shoving him. He released her this time, moving away in the pitch darkness, and she knew a sudden panic. She hated dark, enclosed spaces, and for the moment she felt trapped, smothered.

And then a light flared in the darkness as he lit one taper, another and another, a candelabrum bringing blessed, welcome light to the darkness, slowly illuminating every corner. Until he started in on the next branch of candles, and she could see all too clearly, and her panic was back, this time rooted in real, not imagined, danger.

It was a small room, cut into the wall of white rock that was so prevalent in the area. A fireplace at one end, with what looked like a fire laid, ready to be lit. Logs to one side, enough for a day or two, but someone like Adrian Rohan would never load his own fire.

There was a sturdy table which held the candelabrum, a bottle of wine and two glasses. A thick rug covered the floors, newer tapestries hung on the wall. Somewhere along the way she'd lost her glasses, probably when she'd fallen, but she could tell, even in the shadowy light, that they portrayed no innocent wolf hunt or Norman Conquest.

They were sexual scenes, woven into the fine threads. Someone had spent years on this blatantly erotic tapestry that now adorned the walls of Rohan's cavelike retreat.

And there was a bed. How could she have doubted otherwise? It was set up against the wall, covered with velvet bedding and a rich fur throw. A bed for indecent activities, not a bed for sleep.

He was watching her from across the small room, still and silent, yet she couldn't rid herself of the sense that he was a predator, waiting.

She turned around, looking for the door. Why hadn't she run when she had the opportunity? She'd stood a good chance of taking him by surprise when he was kissing her, and instead she'd melted like the love-addled idiot that she was, and now it was too late.

Or maybe it wasn't. She was much closer to the carved wooden door than he was, and she leaped for it, afraid he might reach it first and stop her.

He didn't move, and she told herself it was relief that flooded her when her hand found the doorknob. He was letting her go. Until she tried to turn the knob, and it held fast. She yanked, but it was immovable.

She was locked in. With the man of her dreams, the worst libertine in all of England.

"Bloody hell," she said weakly. And she slid to the floor, her back up against the wall, feeling like cornered prey.

When Lina awoke, the early-morning sun was peeping in the window. She sat up quickly, her thin silk nightgown, made for lovers rather than for a comfortable night's sleep, falling down around her shoulders. For a moment her mind was a blank, yet she was conscious of a sense of happy anticipation. It came back to her in pieces — the aborted evening at the Revels, Monty's collapse. And yet her anticipation held. She yawned, then cursed. She'd only meant to rest for an hour or so, but she must have fallen into a deep sleep, leaving Monty in the hands of his unsympathetic vicar. It was the challenge, she realized. Monty's odious friend, the vicar, had arrived and laid down the gauntlet.

And she had snatched it up quite eagerly. Monty needed coddling, not scolding. He needed love and entertainment and distraction from his ills, not some prosy minister reading the riot act over him. She couldn't imagine why in the world Montague would invite him to stay at Hensley Court in the first place. If he'd provided his old friend with a living, why hadn't he simply gone to the manse?

"You're awake, then," Charlotte's maid said in a caustic tone, setting down the tea tray. "What are you doing up so early, and you not in bed till half past three?" Meggie was not looking pleased at starting her duties so early.

Lina pushed the pillows up behind her in preparation for her breakfast. "Did anyone mention that a proper lady's maid does not chastise her mistress for her sleeping habits? You're just lucky I'm alone. My bed in Grosvenor Square might be sacrosanct, but I've come to Hensley Court with the express intention of sin, and it wouldn't do for a gentleman to hear you being so pert."

"I doubt I'd consider your sort of friends to be gentlemen," Meggie said, unchastened. "And there's no one around here to romp with — you know you're safe as houses with Lord M. And your parson isn't going to give you a tumble. Mark my words, he's got a wife and seven children coming after him on the stage."

"If he does it's no wonder he looks so grim," Lina said, breaking apart a light croissant and slathering it with totally unnecessary butter. She was hungry, actually ravenous, yet she'd done nothing to work up an appetite. She finished the croissant in three greedy bites and went to work on the fresh strawberries. She would have happily done with a full breakfast, with eggs and fat sausages and fried toast and mushrooms, when usually such heavy stuff made her faintly nauseous.

"You've never been one for a roll in the mud," Meggie continued critically, "so it's not likely you'll find one of Lord M.'s very handsome footmen in your bed, either. Lord, that man!" She seemed suddenly forgetful of her lecturing mood. "Every single man in this place is bloody gorgeous. From the gardener's boy and the underchef up through the majordomo himself. He certainly liked to surround himself with pretty men. It quite gives a girl pause."

"Likes," Lina corrected quickly. "Likes. Present tense. At least I assume . . ."

"I'm not up with your fancy literary terms, my lady, but if you mean is he still alive, then yes. Mr. Pagett is with him now."

"Oh, Lord," Lina said. "That's all he needs when he's feeling wretched. Get my clothes. Quickly."

"And what clothes might those be?" Meggie said. "The nun's habit again? Or something more transparent?"

"It's never good to educate the lower classes," Lina grumbled. "You shouldn't even know that word."

Meggie grinned, unrepentant. "I listen well, my lady. You were the one to use that word in the first place. I asked Miss Charlotte what that meant, and I was some disappointed to find that it didn't mean something obscene. Just see-through."

"Well, see-through can be quite obscene, depending on what is on the other side." She slid out of bed, spilling her tea on the tray. "The green dress will do."

Meggie's shock was overplayed but nonetheless genuine. "The green dress that you were going to give to Miss Charlotte?"

"Well, I can't very well give it to her now, can I? She's half a foot taller than I am — the hem would be above her ankles."

"It's no dress for an orgy," Meggie pointed out sagely. "The neckline's too high, the cut

117

too refined. What about your red dress?"

"Do you see any orgies around me, Meggie?" she inquired. "I'll be spending the next few days, perhaps longer, looking after Lord Montague. As you sagely pointed out, seductive clothes would be wasted on him, and that prude of a vicar as well. The green dress proves even I can be demure."

"The green dress proves even you can have a sense of humor."

In fact, Lina had ordered the dress from her modiste on a whim. The cut and line of the garment was simple, charming, but most definitely unalluring. It had reminded her of a gown she had worn before she was married, when everything was new and fresh and she still believed in happy endings.

Henry had cured her of that particular notion. He'd been a full forty years older than she was — fifty-eight to her eighteen — but so enormously wealthy her father had been *aux anges.* Henry had already buried three wives and two stillborn heirs, but he hadn't given up hope. A young, nubile beauty should have been just the thing to stoke his fires, he used to tell her, filled with disgust at her ineptitude. His efforts had been desultory, more often spilling his seed outside her in his inability to get hard

118

enough for penetration.

It was a great deal too bad that he accidentally discovered the cure for his affliction. His frustration and contempt for his young wife grew until one night he'd slapped her, so hard she'd fallen against the bed, temporarily seeing stars.

His excitement was immediate and powerful, and the next thing she knew, he was on her like a wild dog, puffing and sweating, hurting her so that she cried out in pain. When she did, his excitement reached a fever pitch, and he spilled his seed deep inside her.

He'd been so rough she'd bled the next day, and he'd been furious, thinking her menses had started early. It had been a blessing. Henry had been a fastidious man and never liked to come near her during her courses.

But a week later he was on her anew. It had taken more and more pain to inspire him. In the beginning he avoided marring her face, but as time passed he enjoyed that most particularly. Seeing the evidence of his brutality seemed to make him feel more virile. Eventually he took his dazed young wife to one of his remote country estates, so no one could witness his increasingly dangerous pleasures.

The only thing that would have stopped him would have been a pregnancy. He wanted an heir with a ferocity stronger than his twisted needs.

In the end it had been her fault, Lina thought. She'd begun to stretch out the time of her menses for as long as possible to avoid the increasingly nightmarish couplings Henry forced on her. She knew full well there was no one she could turn to — a wife's duty was to submit. The only one who would have come to the rescue was Charlotte, and while she would have moved heaven and earth to help her, there would have been nothing she could do.

So Lina had told no one. And one summer her courses were late. Days passed, when her body had been as regular as clockwork no matter what indignities Henry had subjected her to, no matter how brutal his assaults. She lied, of course, to keep Henry from her, anything to have an extra day or two of reprieve.

A week passed, with Henry growing more and more impatient. By the time two weeks had gone by, her breasts were full and tender, her stomach was queasy, and she knew, she simply knew, the old man's foul ruttings had finally taken root.

She'd thought she'd be disgusted, hating

what had begun in her belly. She was wrong. The thought of a baby changed everything. He would leave her alone now, and she would grow large and placid, and by the time she gave birth to his son he would have turned elsewhere for pleasure. He would leave her and her son alone, and sooner or later he would die. He was old and fat, and when he hit her his face would grow purple with rage and excitement, and exhaustion.

She waited too long. Her fault, her fault. She'd wanted to cherish her secret for just a little while longer before she had to bring him into it.

She remembered that day far too well. He'd appeared in her dressing room, sending the servants away.

"Your maid tells me you've been lying about your monthly courses," he said, his voice deceptively quiet. "Haven't you?"

She flushed. "Yes," she admitted. "In fact, I —" That was as far as she'd gotten. His fist had connected with her face, splitting her lip, and after that there had been no chance of speech.

She made the mistake of crying out, enraging him further. The small blessing was that this time he didn't rape her. He simply beat her, with his fists, kicking her with his booted feet when she fell to the floor.

She curled in on herself, trying to shield her body from his blows, but she'd already felt the fierce tearing in her belly, the wetness of blood gushing between her legs. He'd destroyed the one thing he'd wanted most in the world.

He finally stopped. She moaned, and clutched her belly. She could hear him gasping for breath, and she struggled to sit up, knowing the danger any sign of life might bring.

It took her three tries. She could barely see out of her swollen eyes, and the pain in her belly was a ripping, vicious one, but she managed to see Henry half lying on her bed, his legs twitching as he made hoarse, gasping noises. For one moment she thought his sexual excitement had been unbearable and he was using his fist to bring on his own climax — she'd heard those gasping, grunting noises far too many times.

She managed to pull herself to her feet, using a nearby chair for support. She would need a doctor, she thought, dizzy. Would he allow her one?

She could see Henry on the bed, gasping for air like a landed fish. His handsome, florid face was a deep purple, and she realized with almost detached interest that he'd finally gone too far. He was having a fit of apoplexy.

She struggled toward the bed, using various pieces of furniture to support herself, until she reached his side. He managed to focus on her for a moment.

"Get . . . a doctor," he wheezed.

She could feel blood dripping down her legs, into her slippers. She looked down at him. "You sent the servants away, Henry," she said with deceptive gentleness. "They won't hear me if I call for help. You're dying. No one could help you anyway. But I want you to know one thing before you go to the hell you so richly deserve." She moved closer. "I was finally pregnant, and you kicked me in the stomach, Henry. You killed your unborn child. Your heir."

His eyes bulged out, and she could see he understood her. She was unable to walk, so she pulled herself onto the large bed, far enough away that he couldn't touch her with his desperate flailing. She lay there and watched him die, a deep, cold satisfaction filling her. And she didn't allow herself to pass out until he was gone.

There was no scandal, of course. No one mentioned the widow's bruised face and broken arm, and her pale, bloodless complexion they attributed to grief, not blood loss and fever. By the time she called Charlotte to her side, her body, at least, had healed.

Lina looked out the window of Hensley Court, toward the just-visible spires of the ruined abbey, where the Revels went on without her. No orgy for her this time. No chance to once more show herself that men were crude and worthless. No chance to laugh and lie and play the part.

She didn't know what drove her, and she didn't care to find out. The adoration of men distracted her, and if their intense pleasure never migrated to her, she was too good an actress to let on.

Occasionally she would feel a twinge of desire, and she would hope that she would finally feel the pleasure so many talked of.

It never happened.

The green dress was just right for someone who most definitely wasn't attending an orgy. And it would amuse Monty, who knew her better than anyone, even Charlotte.

At the last minute she took an outrageous beauty patch and placed it near the corners of her lush mouth. It would draw the good vicar's attention to her lips, and most probably fill him with outraged disapproval and contempt. He thought she was a whore, knew she was a whore. Even in demure clothes she needed to remind him that his belief was correct.

It was just past dawn when she moved down the deserted hallway of Hensley Court. No one was in sight but an early-morning housemaid, lugging a bucket of coal. She turned in to the center wing of the large, Elizabethan house, built in the shape of the letter *E* to honor the reigning sovereign. It hadn't done much good, Monty had told her, since said ancestor had been deprived of his head anyway, but the house had remained in the family. At least as long as Montague lived. Since he had no issue, God only knew what would happen to the place and the title. He must have an heir somewhere, a distant cousin or the like.

Someone was standing outside Montague's door, and in the unlit, shadowy hallway she thought it was Dodson, her friend and coconspirator. But Dodson was a skinny man, with slightly bowed shoulders. A footman, perhaps, she hoped with a dismal faith that she was right. The shape of the man showed him to be tall, well built, and Monty liked his footmen pretty. But it wasn't a servant.

The man moved away from the door out

of the shadows, and she readied herself for battle.

"He needs sleep," Simon Pagett said.

"I have no intention of keeping him awake. I want to bear him company while he sleeps." She kept her voice calm and reasonable. If it came to a battle of wills she had no idea who Dodson and the servants would choose. On the one hand, they liked and trusted her. On the other, Pagett was a male, and a vicar, to boot, and none of them would fancy the idea of hell.

Someone had heard the sound of voices, and before Pagett could reply, a footman appeared, bearing a candelabrum. She reached out for it, but Pagett had longer arms, and he overreached her, taking it in one capable hand. "We shouldn't argue outside his door, Lady Whitmore," he said, his eyes taking in her somber garb, then rising to see the provocative beauty mark on her cheek. There was an arrested expression in his eyes, most likely disgust, though she couldn't be quite certain.

"I have no intention of arguing with you," she began, only to find her arm taken in his firm grasp as he propelled her away from the door, down the hall. She didn't struggle — it was too undignified. Besides, this proper vicar wasn't going to hurt her.

He took her all the way to the end of the wing, where a small salon waited. There were tall doors onto the terrace that ran the width of the house, and without asking her to leave, he pushed one open, ushering her out into the cool morning air and closing the door behind them. "I don't think we need anyone eavesdropping on our conversation, do you?" he said in a pleasant voice.

"I wasn't aware that we had anything to discuss that the servants would find all that fascinating," she replied.

"We have . . ." He paused, staring at her mouth. Which was exactly what she'd wanted him to do. "Why do you muck up your face with all that paint?" he said.

She laughed, the sound brittle. "Next you're going to tell me I'm too pretty a girl to have to resort to artifice."

"No," he said, his voice measured. "I'm not about to tell you how pretty you are at all. You don't need my empty compliments."

"Empty?" she echoed, mocking.

"And you're hardly a girl."

It only silenced her a moment. "Oh, touché," she said with a laugh. "But hardly Christian of you, sir."

"Why is it unchristian to speak the truth? You must be nearing thirty —"

"I'm twenty-eight," she snapped, unable

to help herself.

She didn't like the faint glint in his eyes. He'd managed to pique her vanity after all.

"I beg pardon," he murmured. "Still, twenty-eight is hardly a girl . . ."

"Point taken," she said irritably. "I'm not a girl. What are we going to argue about?"

"Apart from your age? Most likely everything under the sun," he said, his voice calm. "But I think we're agreed on at least one thing, and that is our concern for Montague."

"Agreed," she said after a moment, controlling her irritation.

"I want the best for him."

"As one of his closest friends I want the same. Why do ministers take so blasted long to get to the point? Say what you want to say so I can go sit with him."

"That's the point. I don't think you should sit with him, or be anywhere near him. I believe the best thing you could do for Thomas is to go out to that wretched playground he built, get your fellow debauchees together and leave this place. Leave him to die in peace."

She laughed without humor. "You think that's what he wants? It was his idea to hold the Revels here. Monty takes joy and pride in his spectacular abilities as a host, even in absentia. He's hired extra chefs, extra servants to handle the party, and it's taking place well out of sight. If the festivities were to be cut short then the guests would descend on Hensley Court to change clothes, retrieve their carriages, all with a great deal of grumbling, which would distress Monty no end. Two more days and their departure will be normal. Everyone will leave, sated and cheerful, and Monty's final social occasion will be deemed a triumph."

"Three days of whoring and degeneracy is a social triumph?"

"It's too late to change him, Mr. Pagett. You aren't going to save his soul, induce him to renounce his . . . his preferences at this late date. And why bother — he's so ill he has no choice but to be celibate."

"You underestimate Montague's stamina," he said dryly. "I've known him all my life — even on his deathbed he'll be pinching the footmen. As for changing him — I don't really care who he wants to fornicate with. It's his soul that concerns me. And it's never too late for that."

Lina eyed him curiously. "Wouldn't you say his desire for other men makes him irredeemable?"

"That's between Thomas and his lord."

"Isn't his soul between Monty and his God as well?"

He stared down at her for a long moment. A breeze had come up, and one by one the candles went out, leaving them in the pinky-blue light of early dawn as the sun rose over the spires of the ruined abbey. "Talking with you is like arguing with the devil."

She found she could laugh. "Oh, I don't think so. Doesn't conversation with Satan involve temptation?" She moved closer, looking up at him. She'd discovered that men liked it when she moved close and looked up from beneath her long lashes. It made them feel powerful, protective, and because she was manipulating the situation it made her feel even stronger. At least, most of the time.

It wasn't that she was feeling weak now, she told herself, uneasy. She just hadn't taken into account how very solid he would feel, standing over her. How he'd feel oddly protective. The soft spring breeze caught her skirts, brushing them against his legs, and she took a quick step back.

"You think you don't tempt me, Lady Whitmore?" he said, his voice dry. "How little you know of ministers. We are men, after all."

She said nothing. There were a number of

provocative replies that came to mind, but that odd, breezy touch of her skirts against his legs had unsettled her. It felt far more intimate to her than lying beneath a naked, grunting man ever had. Strange, she thought. "Exactly what is it you want me to do, Mr. Pagett?" Her voice was deceptively calm. "Apart from making the Heavenly Host decamp early. Do you want me to rejoin the Revels? Stay out of your way. . . ."

"No!" The word was practically an explosion of sound. "The best thing for you would be to go back to London if you won't cancel this ridiculous obscenity of a party. The rest of your friends can follow when they're done."

"Even if I wanted to oblige you, I can't. My cousin is at the abbey. She's an innocent, come simply to observe —"

"An innocent?" he interrupted her again, and there was no mistaking the cold anger in his gaze. "You brought an innocent to that kind of debauchery? What sort of monster are you?"

"She's fine," Lina said stiffly. "No one will lay a hand on her. No one would dare."

"And you're so sure of that? Knowing the kind of men who call themselves the Mad Monks?"

For the first time that niggling uneasiness

131

that had festered in the back of her mind broke loose, and she could have cursed the man. Rohan was over there as well. And between Rohan and Charlotte lay quiet danger.

Indeed, one of her reasons for choosing Rohan as her next lover had been to help sever the connection between her innocent cousin and one of society's worst rakes. She knew Charlotte far too well not to have guessed her secret fantasy, and the easiest way to crush it would be to take the man herself.

Because it needed to be crushed. Falling in love with a rake only led to heartbreak. Falling in love with anyone only led to despair.

But they were both out there, and she hadn't been around to watch over them. "She's fine," Lina said again, ignoring her fears. "Perfectly safe."

And she wondered if she lied.

7

"There's nothing I can do about the door," Rohan said in a lazy voice. "It locks automatically. A servant comes every morning and evening with food, and at that point one can always exchange partners, or request others to join in. But until tomorrow I'm afraid you're quite trapped."

She scowled at him, which pleased him. He'd been afraid he'd have to deal with tears, which always bored him, or worse, too-enthusiastic agreement. He liked to work a bit for his pleasures.

No chance of enthusiastic agreement from her. She was looking deliciously angry.

"Did you take my glasses?" she demanded. "I can't see clearly."

"Glasses? Of course not," he said, all innocence as he remembered deliberately crushing them beneath his boot. If she really needed them then he would be astonished. She used them as a weapon, and he needed her defenseless. "There's not much here you need to see. Except me."

She wasn't charmed. "You can't keep me here," she said in the pinched, disapproving tone she seemed to reserve only for him.

"Don't be tiresome. Of course I can. I just explained. The door won't be opened until tomorrow morning."

"And you think I'll believe you don't have a spare key hidden about the place? I don't believe that the great Viscount Rohan would ever put himself at the mercy of . . . of restraints that he couldn't control."

He smiled at that, letting his eyelids droop lazily. "Ah, child, you have no idea the delight certain forms of restraint can provide. I'll be more than happy to demonstrate — this room comes equipped with all sorts of toys. However, I think you're a little too new at this game to enjoy it, and if I gave you the option of tying me up I tremble to think what sort of revenge you might be tempted to enact."

She just stared at him, momentarily speechless. And then she tried to regroup.

She straightened her shoulders and crossed the room, away from the locked door. She had her choice of one cushionless chair and the bed — of course, she took the chair. She was thinking hard — he should have known she wouldn't be defeated that easily.

"Let's discuss this like civilized adults," she said in her prim voice, reminding him of an old governess he'd once had. That is, if Miss Trilby had ever had a bewitching mouth, gold-flecked skin, an exceptional body and enjoyed dressing in monk's robes. "First, it's absurd to call me child when I'm two years older than you are."

He sauntered over to the bed, stretching out on it and tucking his arms behind his head, prepared to enjoy this. There was no hurry to get her on her back. He could get what she had between her legs from anyone — it was her character that made her different. Interesting. Delightful. "How did you happen to discover how old I am?" he asked mildly enough. "What made you inquire?"

He knew the answer to that, of course. She'd been silly enough to have a crush on him. He could have told her he wasn't worth the bother, but she'd kept herself at a distance, only her eyes touching him. He could tell her now, but he expected she'd already come to that conclusion by herself. He was a useless, vain, ornamental sybarite with nothing to offer the world.

She started to blush, then controlled it. He watched with fascination. He would have thought a woman incapable of controlling her physical responses like that. It made him more curious than ever to see what other kinds of involuntary responses he could bring from her and how she would struggle to contain them.

"Someone must have mentioned it in passing," she said, lying admirably.

"And you happened to remember?"

"I was shocked that someone as old as twenty-eight would still be lost to propriety, a slave to decadence and lascivious riot."

Lascivious riot? He liked the sound of that. "My cousin Etienne is thirty years older than I am and just as debauched. Possibly more so, though I do hope to attain his level someday."

She refused to be baited. "Nevertheless, I'm two years older than you are, and to call me child is patently absurd."

"Sweet Charlotte," he said softly, watching her flinch as he used her name, "you *are* a mere infant when it comes to the darker side of the world."

"I prefer it that way."

He shrugged. "*Tant pis.* You're here now, by your own volition, stepping into the darkness. No one forced you to come to the Revels, to dress in a monk's robe. You took the chance, and now you're going to have to pay the price. But there's no need to look so distraught. I have no doubt you'll emerge from this place a sadder but wiser woman, with no troubling illusions left."

"I had no illusions about you, sir," she said fiercely.

"Didn't you?" He was wearing soft boots, easily removed, and he kicked them off. "I rejoice to hear it. Was there anything else you wished to address like a civilized adult before you come to bed?"

She looked more annoyed than frightened. Good for her. "Be reasonable. I have no idea why you've suddenly decided I'm fair game, but we both know I'm not the kind of woman you bother with. I'm too tall, my hair is too red, I have freckles and . . . and . . ."

"Yes?" he said encouragingly.

She took a deep breath, diving in. "And I'm not . . . pretty. Some of the most beautiful women in the world are here and available tonight, and I'm quite . . . ordinary. You don't want to waste your time with a plain, elderly spinster."

It cost her to say that. He wanted to get up, cross the room and pull her into his arms. To touch that gold-flecked skin, that beautiful mouth, and tell her how pretty she was.

But she wouldn't believe it, not from anyone, but least of all from him. So he stayed where he was, and shrugged. "Perhaps I was looking for something a little different."

"I'm not worth the trouble, I assure you."

And she would be a great deal of trouble, he had absolutely no doubt of it. Making the reward all the sweeter. One thing particularly fascinated him. She was more interested in convincing him that he didn't want her, not that she wasn't drawn to him. He wasn't particularly vain, but he knew women. He knew her. "I'm afraid I like a challenge," he said.

She bit her lip, frustrated. "What can I do to convince you to let me go?"

He looked at her as all sorts of erotic thoughts danced in his head. "Why, I'll let you go, my pet. Once I've had you."

How many women had he brought to this place? Charlotte wondered. There was no doubt they'd all been willing — she couldn't imagine a woman resisting that long, elegant body, those beautiful hands, the hypnotic gaze and rich mouth. They would have to be mad to say no.

What would happen if she said yes? He would strip the clothes off her and she'd lie naked with him, skin to skin. He'd climb on top of her and put his penis inside her, and it would hurt, according to her parents' old cook, the only one who'd bothered to explain the facts of men and women to her. Would he kiss her again? Her mouth still felt tender from his first kiss, when he'd tricked her into coming into this . . . this prison. If she lay naked in the bed with him would he kiss her again? Stroke her? Hold her? Would it be worth it?

But she wasn't going to find out, she reminded herself stoutly. Because afterward he would let her go, and that would be the most painful of all.

She didn't believe him about the lock. If she had enough time she could figure out a way to make it open — her mother had had a habit of locking her chronically misbehaving daughter into her room, and Charlotte had never accepted imprisonment. A hairpin, judiciously applied, could spring most locks. She doubted this was any different.

First, however, she'd have to render the viscount unconscious. Maybe he'd simply fall asleep — she suspected he'd had quite a bit to drink, though of course he didn't show it. If she stayed quiet he might even forget she was there.

She looked around her for a weapon, just

in case. There was the unopened bottle of wine — that could produce a respectable lump on his lordship's fine head. In fact, it might crush his skull and kill him, despite that thick, lovely hair.

While the idea of murder was a fond one as payback for this mess, in truth she was far too squeamish. And as angry as she was, she didn't want Adrian Rohan dead. Just living on a separate continent so she could get over him.

Which was ridiculous — she *was* over him. How could she not be, when he'd practically abducted her, all for wicked purposes?

It didn't matter that it smacked of some of the gothic novels Lina had lent her. Or that being abducted by the most beautiful man in England, simply because he wanted her, was desperately romantic. They both knew all he had to do was snap his fingers and he could have someone else. Anyone else. If she were an idiot she'd be flattered.

But she wasn't an idiot.

The candelabrum sat on the table. If she clubbed him with it, it wouldn't kill him; silver was a soft metal. It might simply bend over his hard head, and then what would she do?

She could pick up the sturdy wooden

chair she sat on and clobber him with it. But that wouldn't slow him down much. Maybe her best bet was to get him to drink the bottle of wine — surely that would make him pass out.

"Are you looking at that bottle of wine so lovingly because you want a glass, or were you considering its efficacy as a weapon?"

She could feel color stain her cheeks. He saw far more than she would have liked. *Stay calm, stay focused, Charlotte,* she told herself. Maybe she'd consider bashing him with it after all.

"I decided I didn't want to risk crushing your skull and killing you," she said in an admirably even voice. "Not that I wouldn't *like* to kill you, but the practicalities convince me it's a bad idea. No matter how much you might deserve it, the Crown would look askance at the righteous execution of a peer. And, besides, blood makes me squeamish."

"You, squeamish? I find that hard to believe. And you'd be surprised what wouldn't kill me. I'm possessed of a very hard head."

She picked up the wine bottle then, annoyed. "I'm perfectly willing to see . . ."

"Put it down." His silken voice held a cool note that would have terrorized a more fragile soul.

She turned it in her hand, reading the label, determined not to do as he ordered. And then, when she was good and ready, she set the bottle back on the table, turning to look at him.

His eyes glittered in the semidarkness. "You're determined to fight me on every level, aren't you?" he murmured.

"Yes."

"Then you're right, we'll have to find a way to compromise." He sat up, swinging his legs over the side of the bed. "I'm not going to rape you, you know."

"No, I don't know."

His smile was devastating. "I have many crimes to my soul, but I'm not a rapist. I've never forced a woman in my life and I have no particular interest in starting now."

"That's because no one has ever told you no, before."

His eyes lit up. "You think I'm that irresistible? How flattering, my pet. Occasionally misguided women have been able to resist me, but they've been few and far between. And you're not one of them."

"No," she said. "Force is the only way you'll have me."

His soft laugh was low and impossibly sexual. "No, my pet, it isn't. But I'll indulge you for the time being. If you come and lie down with me I promise not to touch you below the neck."

"I'd prefer you didn't touch me at all."

"Of course you would. And I'd prefer to push your skirts up to your waist and bury my cock in your body, right now, but we're not going to do that either. Not until you tell me to. You see, we're compromising already."

Her skin felt hot and prickly, her stomach ice cold at his words. She rallied. "You must be very drunk indeed if you think that time will ever come."

"It takes a lot to get me drunk, my love," he said. He'd stopped calling her "child," and she realized she would have preferred it to his mock endearments. "Get on the bed with me, and you're safe. For now."

"And if I don't?"

"Then when the servants unlock the door tomorrow morning they'll find you tied up and gagged and you'll stay right here until I decide to let you go."

"Wouldn't you be more likely to have an enjoyable . . . *orgy* if your servants simply brought you another willing female?"

"Another? I hadn't realized you were willing."

"I mean another female who, unlike me,

143

happens to be willing."

It really was unfortunate. He had the most seductive voice, making the wicked things he was saying sound almost irresistible.

He smiled at her. "I suppose they could, and you could watch, as long as you promised not to make too much noise."

"You're disgusting."

He laughed softly. "I'm healthy. You haven't asked what you'll get if you agree to my devil's bargain. You get on the bed with me, let me touch you, and when morning comes you get to leave, dignity and virginity intact."

"Why should I trust you?"

He shrugged. "My word as a gentleman?"

Her snort expressed a certain lack of faith.

"What kind of assurance can I give you?"

"Unlock the door. Then I'll know I can leave any time I want."

"But you can't. In fact, I can't either. So we're equals, of a sort. I'm not asking much, my angel. No trespass against your maidenly flesh. And I can't fathom why you're protesting so staunchly. You're the one who came to the Revels of your own free will. You walked through the Portal of Venus, dressed in monk's robes. You must have been in search of something, and since you stood side by side with Lady Whitmore I know you weren't looking for Lina. So, tell me, why did you come here in the first place? Were you looking for me?"

At that moment she couldn't remember. It seemed so long ago, lost in the realm of her own monumental stupidity. "Don't be ridiculous," she snapped. "I was . . . scientifically curious. As for your stupid Portal of Venus, Lina was going to point it out to me, but she disappeared."

His expression didn't change, and yet she knew his amusement at her expense was increasing. "Allow me to satisfy your curiosity. I'm more than happy to ensure you experience everything you've ever wondered about."

From this short distance the bottle wouldn't kill him, but it might startle him enough to give her time to escape. Though the door would have to be opened. If he was to be believed that time wouldn't come until morning. "You fail to understand," she said stiffly. "I'm an old maid. A spinster. Happily on the shelf. Since I would have no chance or interest in experiencing the . . . the lust that seems to be of such paramount importance in most people's lives, I thought I could simply come and observe. I'm of a scientific bent, and there's nothing wrong with a little intellectual curiosity."

He laughed again. It should have annoyed her. Instead it sent a trickle of warmth into her belly. "A true scientist does more than observe — he experiments."

"I'm not a true scientist. Observation is enough."

"Then would you like to sit and watch while I disport myself with a more willing female?"

"No," she said instantly. Then regretted it.

"And why not?"

When she didn't answer, he laughed again. "Never mind, precious. Your secrets are safe with me."

"I have no secrets," she said sharply.

"Don't you, now?" he said softly. "Then you'd be the only one." He stretched, slowly, luxuriantly, like a sleepy cat. A tall, beautiful, elegant, sleepy cat. "You really have no idea what you're turning down. I'm accounted to be one of the most accomplished lovers in society. No woman has ever left my bed unsatisfied, no woman has ever refused to return for more."

"Then why don't you get one of them in here?"

"Because I want you."

That silenced her. The four simple words were devastating, both to body and soul. Her stomach reacted with an ache of longing, her breath and heart lifted in unconscious response, and she felt . . . hot . . . damp . . . between her legs.

Reflexively she clamped her knees together, and his soft laugh told her he didn't miss her movement. "Come lie on the bed with me, Charlotte. I won't do anything you don't want me to do. And it's the only way you're going to get out of here in any timely manner."

He was Satan himself, she thought, because she was seriously considering his offer. She was tired, bone tired, and this chair was hard and uncomfortable.

And it was Rohan lying on that slightly rumpled bed — beautiful, haunted Adrian Rohan — who'd just said the very words she'd dreamed about for what must be years. *Because I want you.*

What would the harm be? He'd promised he wouldn't touch her body unless she asked, and that would never happen. He'd sworn he would never rape. She could lie next to him on the bed, close enough to hear his heart beat, close enough to feel his body warmth. He might kiss her again. She could allow him to put his arms around her, chastely. To hold her through the night, her one chance of lying in the arms of the man she loved . . .

147

No, she didn't love him. She didn't even know him, and his reputation was disreputable. But for some reason, sane, sensible, practical Charlotte Spenser had dreamed about the lost and beautiful viscount and his elegant hands, his bewitching mouth. And he was offering her all that beauty, and the lost soul that hid behind it.

Even in the darkness she could see his smile widen, the glitter of satisfaction in his bright, brilliant eyes. "Come to bed, Charlotte Spenser," he said softly, his voice a soft, impossible invitation.

And she did.

8

Adrian Rohan said nothing as Charlotte rose from the chair. She'd squared her shoulders, lifted her chin and crossed the few feet to the side of the bed, but he could see the faint nervousness, the slightest hint of trembling that she doubtless thought she'd hidden. Poor angel. If he were a kind man he'd summon the servant he'd sworn wasn't available and let her go free.

He wasn't a kind man.

He rose as she approached. She was not a short woman, but he was taller, and he was careful not to loom over her too badly. It wouldn't take much to spook her, and then he'd have to start the cajoling all over again, when all he wanted to do was lie down with her. Touch her face. Kiss her mouth. Fuck her senseless.

He could just imagine her reaction if he used those words. He'd have to peel her off the ceiling. He'd wait until it was a fait accompli, until she looked up into his eyes and said "yes" and "please" and "now."

The bed was pushed up against the stone wall. "You get to be on the inside," he said.

She looked up at him. "Why?"

"If you want to escape I'll let you," he said in a deliberately bored-sounding voice. "Just say 'let me up' and I will. In the meantime, I prefer to lie on the outside."

For a moment he thought she was going to balk. But a moment later she'd climbed up onto the bed, pulling the monk's robe up to crawl to the far side. She ended up tucked into the corner, trying to sink into the carved limestone, and he kept a straight face as he lay back down beside her.

"You and I are the only two who are going to sleep in this bed, angel," he said. "You really don't need to be so far away."

"I like a fair amount of space."

He turned on his side, facing her. The tall candelabrum cast a decent amount of light onto her face, leaving him in shadows. He could see the fear in her eyes, on her full, pale mouth. It was too dark to see the gold flecks of her skin, but that was a small price to pay for getting her on her back beside him.

Which was patently absurd. He had never in his life gone to so much trouble to bed one woman. "Move closer, Charlotte," he said in a low voice.

She did. In the close quarters of the bed she smelled delicious. Wet grass, and honey, and heated female skin with its own, indescribable scent. Her wild red hair had been doing its best to escape confinement, and tendrils curled around her pale face.

He reached up a hand to push some of it out of her eyes, and she flinched, annoying him. "I'm not about to hurt you," he said dryly. "You do realize that, don't you?"

If she'd said no he might have been irritated enough to let her go. If she didn't know well enough by now that he wouldn't force her, then this was a lost cause.

Fortunately she didn't know how close she came to being released. "Yes," she said in a low voice.

"Yes, what?" he prompted her.

Her eyes met his. The changeable hazel eyes of most redheads — in the dark they looked almost black. Her forehead wrinkled in confusion. "Yes, Lord Rohan?" she ventured.

He laughed. "No. Yes, I know you won't hurt me. Adrian," he added. "We're in bed together — you may as well call me Adrian."

She jerked, startled, as if just realizing that they were, in fact, lying in the same bed. "I

151

think Lord Rohan is more appropriate," she said in that starchy little voice of hers. Which was patently absurd, with her lying beside him in the shadowy room, her eyes wide, her mouth soft.

"Let's not waste time discussing what is or isn't appropriate. Appropriate behavior tends to be boring. I much prefer inappropriate goings-on. Lascivious riots. Isn't that what you called this?"

"Not *this*," she corrected him. "This is coerced proximity and nothing more."

He touched one errant curl, his fingers brushing against her cheek, and this time she didn't flinch as badly. It was like breaking a horse, he thought. Patience, getting her used to his touch, his weight. He was very good with horses — one frightened, virginal spinster should be easy. At least she couldn't kick him in the head and kill him.

Even if part of her might want to. He smiled at the thought, and her eyes narrowed. "What do you find so amusing?"

"You, dear Charlotte." He let his fingers trace the line of her stubborn jaw. Her skin was soft, smooth, creamy smooth, and he closed his eyes for a moment, breathing in the scent of her, the touch of her. He was quite unaccustomed to working so hard for anything but a horse. And even more astonishing, he was enjoying it.

He opened his eyes again, looking into hers, and for a moment their gazes caught and held, like a physical connection. His fingers carefully cupped her chin, and he felt the tension through her entire body as he moved closer.

"You promised you wouldn't touch me," she whispered.

"I won't touch your body," he said. "I'm just going to kiss you. I promise you, it won't hurt. You survived my first kiss — you'll survive another."

In retrospect, that first kiss had been remarkably unsatisfying. She hadn't known what to do, and he'd been too busy maneuvering her into the room to really concentrate. He wanted to take his time now, see how long it took her to respond.

Because respond she would — he had absolutely no doubt of it. And that would be the first step toward where he needed to be.

It would be too dark for her to see his erection — a good thing. He could feel the faint tremors dancing through her body. If she knew what was going to end up between her legs she'd try to bolt.

He leaned over her, his mouth just above hers. She didn't move, but her eyes were dark with apprehension. "What are you so frightened of?" he whispered against her lips. "It's just a kiss . . ."

She made the mistake of wetting her lips in her nervousness. He couldn't resist, closing the short distance between them, putting his mouth on hers before she realized what he intended.

He'd planned on taking his time, starting soft, but her jaw was clamped shut, her lips tight, and it annoyed him. "Open your mouth," he whispered against her tight lips, "or I'll make you."

Her eyes flew open, staring at him in consternation. It was enough of a surprise to make her mouth unclench, and he slanted his own across hers, pushing it open, using his tongue.

She froze in panic, and he was damn lucky she didn't bite him. He caught her rigid shoulders and pushed her back against the pillow, and his kiss softened, turning seductive, beguiling, touching her tongue, sliding his against it, gently. She was holding herself very still, simply letting him, when her own tongue moved, just slightly, reaching for his as he withdrew, and he let out a groan of muffled pleasure.

She'd put her hands on his shoulders, clinging to him, and he suddenly pulled away as he felt her weaken. "Breathe, Charlotte. You're supposed to breathe."

She let out a *whoosh* of suppressed air, bringing more into her lungs. "How?"

He couldn't resist a small laugh. "A combination of ways. You sneak in a breath whenever your mouths change angles. You breathe through your nose. And you take a deep breath if you know you're about to be kissed. Like now."

He settled his mouth against hers, a second after she drew in her breath, a slow, deep kiss, then lifted his mouth. "Breathe," he whispered before he slanted his mouth against her, changing the angle, reveling in the delight of her untrained mouth. He lifted his mouth to bite her lip. "Again," he whispered. And used his tongue.

This time she was ready for him, kissing him back with real enthusiasm that was all the more arousing for the fact that she had absolutely no idea what she was doing. Clearly no one had kissed her before, and it made her capitulation curiously endearing.

Even touching nowhere but her shoulders he could feel her slowly building arousal. He moved his lips to the side of her mouth, then brushed them against her eyelids, her cheekbones, the soft curve of her ear.

"You aren't supposed to touch me below

the neck," she said in a hushed voice.

He lifted his head to look down at her, and he smiled. "Your hands are on me as well, precious."

She'd been clinging to his shoulders. She released him immediately, but he simply caught her hands and placed them back on him. "Nothing without your consent," he promised, kissing her again, silencing her midprotest.

He already knew how to loosen the monk's robes — it wasn't the first time he'd brought a woman dressed in the plain costume back to these dark rooms. It fastened at the shoulder, held together by the rope belt. He slid one arm around her waist, pulling her closer against him, and managed to get his hand on the rope.

She'd double knotted it, of course, and pulled it tight so that it couldn't accidentally become loose. He had a knife nearby — he would have happily cut it, but he needed to sneak up on her. She wouldn't know she'd been compromised until she was climaxing.

In the meantime, he kept her mouth and her mind busy with his kisses while his fingers fiddled with the knot. It took a while, particularly since he didn't want her to feel what he was doing, but he was nothing if not patient, and once the first knot gave, the rest was simple, the belt opening and falling onto the mattress between them.

And then he couldn't resist. His hand was too close, and he slid it up the front of her until he reached her breasts, closing over one.

She jerked, surprised, and if she hadn't been too busy kissing him she probably would have said no. His fingers toyed with her nipple, feeling it harden instantly in his hand, and he wanted to shove the robe away from her and put his mouth on her, sucking in deep.

Slowly, slowly, he reminded himself, trying to control his rampaging body. Maybe he should leave her here, go find someone else to take the edge off so that he could come back to her and take his time. His need for her was advancing at outrageous speed — it usually took him a great deal longer to get so close to exploding. For some reason, Charlotte Spenser's shy, reluctant responses were setting him on fire.

But he wasn't going to leave her. If it hurt, so be it. He would take as long as he needed to get her cooperation. He couldn't risk scaring her — all he needed was her adamant refusal and he'd be fucked. Or not.

He laughed deep inside as he slid his mouth down her throat. "What's funny?"

157

Charlotte murmured, dazed.

"I am. Going to all this trouble."

Wrong thing to say. She tried to skitter away from him, to the far side of the bed, but the effort made her robe pull open to expose the thin black silk beneath it. She let out a shriek, trying to pull it back around her, but he caught her hands, stopping her by moving closer, so close that she couldn't reach between them to restore her modesty. He put one arm around her waist, clamping her against him, and with his other hand he cupped her chin, holding her still for his soft, seductive kisses, lulling her into a mistaken sense of safety.

He rolled her underneath him, pushing her into the soft mattress as he covered her, his erection up against the juncture of her thighs, his mouth teasing hers, her breasts against his chest, rubbing, rubbing, the nipples irresistibly hard. Her hands were on his shoulders again, clinging to him, not pushing him away. It wasn't complete surrender, but it was moving that way, and his arousal intensified, until he knew he had to slow things down or he'd embarrass himself as he hadn't since he was thirteen years old.

What was it about her that made him so impossibly eager? Was it the adolescent dream of fucking his governess finally coming to fruition? His own hadn't been exciting, but he remembered his cousin's very proper Miss Finster. . . .

He slid his hands up her arms, and he rose, pulling his mouth away reluctantly, staring down at her through the milky candlelight. Her lips were swollen from his kisses, and her usually sharp eyes were dazed. The scowl was gone. Who would have thought starchy Miss Charlotte Spenser could look quite so deliciously aroused?

She blinked for a moment. Her gaze came back into focus as she looked at him, and he felt her initial stiffening.

"What am I doing?" she whispered, horrified. Now she was pushing at him, and he let her go, rolling onto his back to keep from shoving himself into her like a randy bull. It took him a moment to control his breathing, and in the meantime she tried to scramble over him in her need to escape.

He caught her, of course, as one of her legs straddled his in her attempt to get away. He felt the resistance in her body, and he knew she'd say no, so he simply stopped her mouth with his so she couldn't demand her freedom.

Not that he would have granted it at this point. To hell with the rules of the Heavenly Host. He didn't give a damn if she was initially unwilling. She wanted him, and he was going to take her, and to hell with the consequences.

He didn't move his mouth away from hers until he felt her entire body soften. Once more he considered leaving and finding a fast tup to get the edge off. He wasn't going to be able to take the time he wanted to, but at that point he didn't care.

"What are you doing?" he echoed her, faintly mocking. "You're lying on top of the most accomplished rake in London." The robe was open around her, and he used his free hand to push it off her shoulders. Lovely shoulders, and he could see the gold flecks now that she was closer to the light. Stardust scattered on her skin, he thought, and leaning forward, he licked the skin on her shoulder, just tasting.

She made a small, worried noise, and he captured it with his mouth. The garment she wore under the monk's robe was thin, black silk, with no corset, no petticoats, and he suspected, hoped and prayed, no drawers. Just the long silk chemise. It would have come from Evangelina Whitmore — it slid against Charlotte's skin like a caress.

He'd gotten her into the locked room by kissing her into submission. He should be able to get inside her by the same process.

160

He slid his hand between them, catching the silk and slowly pulling it up her long legs. She let out a little shriek of protest against his mouth, and he simply rolled her underneath him again, with the chemise halfway up her thighs, trapped between their bodies.

He looked down at her. "This is going to happen, Charlotte," he said in a soft voice. "You and I both know it. No matter how long it takes, I'm going to end up inside you."

"No," she protested weakly.

No, she'd said. There were rules. The Heavenly Host had a rule of consensuality. A gentleman took no for an answer. No, she'd said.

"Yes," he said. And he kissed her again.

Charlotte lay cushioned in the soft bed, with Adrian Rohan on top of her, his weight holding her there, a captive, as he kissed her mouth.

It couldn't be his full weight. He was a tall man, and strong. She'd have a hard time breathing if he was putting all his weight on top of her.

And the damnable thing was, it felt wonderful. It had felt good through the thick weave of the monk's robe. It felt even better with only that shamefully thin chemise between them. His legs were long, longer than hers, and she could feel his breeches against her skin, feel the mysterious yet unmistakable shape of him against that place between her legs. She knew she was wet, which felt indecent, and she knew the last thing she wanted to do was have him climb off her, unlock the door and let her go.

She had to make the effort. This was the culmination of her most secret fantasies, but if she gave in to it she'd be ruined, completely. It was one thing for her cousin to romp in and out of every young man's bed. Lina was a widow, with a handsome settlement and no interest in the very upper echelons of society or in getting married again. Most people really didn't care what she did, what rules she flaunted, so long as she paid her gambling debts on time.

Why should it be different for Charlotte? It wasn't as if she'd ever contract a marriage, not at her advanced age. And if she did, her loss of innocence would be more understandable.

And she wasn't about to rival Lina in her conquests. She expected that she probably wouldn't do this more than once. But she wanted to. Just this once. She wanted to lie in a man's arms and let him kiss her, wanted to be naked with him and . . . and let him do those wicked things that she wasn't supposed to know about.

And she wanted it with him. With the beautiful, elegant, unattainable Adrian Rohan. It was his mouth she wanted, his arms around her, his body pressed up against hers.

If she was ever going to be naked with anyone she wanted to be naked with Adrian, and the thought of going through her expected long life with no knowledge of this mysterious, magic thing was unacceptable. By some strange twist of fate Adrian Rohan desired her. How could she tell him no?

He'd made it clear he wasn't going to listen. Made it clear that he was going to have her, one way or another, though he'd promised it wouldn't be rape.

His mouth was on her neck, and it was delicious, delirious, and his hands held her shoulders in place for his kisses. The monk's robe had slipped partway down, entrapping her arms so that she couldn't move them, couldn't put them around him. He pulled back to look down at her, his eyes hooded, as she lay there on the bed, *his* bed, pinned by the enveloping robe.

A faint smile curved his usually cynical

mouth. "If you only knew how delectable you look, trussed up like that. I don't suppose you'd . . . no, probably not."

Calm, she told herself. *Stay calm, authoritative.* He was nothing more than an obstreperous little boy, and if she just treated him as such he'd quickly lose interest.

"I'd appreciate it if you'd release me," she said in a remarkably even voice.

He laughed, leaning down to feather his lips against her eyelids, making them flutter closed. He was holding on to the robe, effectively imprisoning her, and it gave her a strange feeling inside, a wrenching kind of . . . of want inside her, which was impossible.

"Truly," she said, trying again. "I'm sure this game must have been great fun for you, but it's time to let me go. My cousin will be awaiting me, and I think I've had enough exposure to the more dissipated parts of life to last me —" Her words ended in a shriek as Rohan leaned forward and ripped the black silk chemise from neck to hem.

She struggled, and the gown fell open. She couldn't cover herself with her arms, she could do nothing but lie there, pinned by him, that strange feeling moving higher, into her stomach and chest, and lower, between her legs.

At some point he'd shrugged off the long vest, and he was now wearing only a loose white shirt and a pair of breeches. She knew enough about mating not to look down at the lower half of his body, and her struggles only made the torn silk gown slide off her body, leaving her completely exposed to his dark gaze.

She had never been naked in front of anyone until today, and now she lay here like some virgin sacrifice for Adrian Rohan to stare at, to judge, to mock.

"Did you know," he said in a casual voice, "that you have the most delicious skin? Your freckles look like little flecks of gold against the creamy white." He leaned forward and put his mouth at the base of her throat, and she could feel his tongue flicker across her skin.

Oh, bloody hell, she thought miserably, the strange feeling getting stronger, heating, clenching inside her. "That was Lina's gown," she said, trying for a matter-of-fact tone of voice and failing. "She won't be happy you ripped it."

"Your cousin sent you out amongst the wolves, unprotected. She's just lucky you fell into my hands and not someone else's."

"Considering that I am lying naked on a bed, my arms trapped, I hardly think that constitutes lucky," she said. There, that was better. She sounded cool and matter-of-fact.

He laughed, his eyes glittering in the candelight. "I think I should demonstrate just how fortunate you are, my precious." And before she realized what he was doing, he'd moved down her body, forced her legs apart and put his mouth . . . *there*.

9

Charlotte jerked in panic at the touch of his mouth, but there was nothing she could do. He was holding her hips, his shoulders were between her spread legs and her arms were trapped by the half-discarded monk's robe. She felt the warmth of his breath, and then his tongue, his mouth, licking at her, tasting her, and a frisson of reaction danced across her skin, pushing away her initial embarrassment.

"You shouldn't . . ." she said weakly, looking down at his golden hair.

He glanced up at her, a glint in his eyes. "Don't you like it?"

She was quivering, wanting his tongue again, wanting him to continue what he started. But it was wrong. Indecent. "No," she said weakly.

"Liar." He put his mouth back again, sliding his tongue against her most private places, and she let out a soft moan of pleasure. He was using his hands now, spreading apart the secret folds, and his tongue caught something that sent a bolt through her.

This was nothing she'd ever witnessed in a barnyard. This was new and mysterious and dangerously powerful, and when he slid one long finger inside her she arched off the bed. He withdrew it, and she let out a cry of distress, only to have him push two fingers inside her, stretching her, filling her, and she wanted more, she wanted him. She wanted what she knew was supposed to go there. Why was he playing with her, why didn't he do what men and women do? What was he —

A rush of feeling swept over her, sparks dancing across her skin, and she let out a small shriek. And then another, as a second wave hit her, and she pushed down against his fingers, needing more.

"Good," he murmured against her, the rhythmic thrust of his fingers a counterpoint to the dancing suck of his mouth. "Again, sweet Charlotte. One more time."

She could no more deny him than keep her heart from beating. She felt his teeth, and this time she screamed, throwing her head to one side to try to stifle the sounds.

He was merciless. The moment one wave

faded another followed to take its place, stronger and more powerful until she couldn't stand it any longer. She was begging him, pleading with him. "No more," she sobbed. "It's too much."

It took her a moment to realize he'd lifted his head, and the crushing, overpowering sensations were slowly ebbing. His eyes were dreamy, half closed, and his mouth was wet, and he wiped it on the shirt he wore.

"You could take more," he said. "You quite astonish me — who would have thought such a little prude could be so disarmingly sensuous? So here's the question, my precious. Do we leave you a virgin? Or do we finish this properly?"

It took a moment for his words to penetrate. "I'm still a virgin?" she asked, her voice not much more than a whisper.

He laughed. "It always amazes me just how ignorant Englishwomen are. Yes, you are still a virgin, at least technically. We can leave you that way if you prefer."

Her brain was slowly returning, and she managed to lift her head. "But . . . but there would be nothing . . . that is . . . why should you . . . ?"

"If what you're struggling to ask is how would I achieve the same blissful state I just accorded you, let me assure you there are

169

any number of ways you can take me that would leave your maidenhead intact." His smile was wicked. "Some variations I'm extremely fond of."

A stray shiver danced across her body, and she realized he still had his long fingers inside her, and his thumb was gently rubbing what he'd been licking earlier.

"It's called a clitoris, angel," he said out of the blue.

"What?"

"That part of you that's so exquisitely sensitive to my mouth and my thumb. I gather you've lived too sheltered a life to discover it for yourself, which is a shame. Self-pleasure is a lovely way to spend a solitary afternoon if an agreeable partner is not available." For emphasis he flicked his thumb harder against her, and she jerked, fighting the hot, liquid rush.

She didn't want to make a sound, but she couldn't help it. The low, guttural moan betrayed her, half of pleasure, half of need.

"So tell me, sweet Charlotte," he murmured. "Where do you want me to put my cock?"

She struggled to come up with something suitable. "A mousetrap," she muttered. "A guillotine."

"Ouch," he said, not sounding particularly

170

distressed. "I'm afraid your bloodthirsty suggestions don't have any effect on me."

"It probably —" flick went his thumb "— made you even more —" flick, flick "— excited." The last word dissolved into little more than a moan.

"I'm not *that* perverse, love. Tell me what you want." He'd moved partly up her body, his hand, his fingers, his thumb still riding her to distraction. "Or shall I make the decision for you? The kind thing, the honorable thing would be to take my pleasure and leave your virginity intact." He smiled at her with a peculiar sweetness. "But you and I both know that's not going to happen. I'm going to take you, Miss Charlotte Spenser, any way I want to. I'm going to lose myself in your delicious body, and when it's over you can go on about your life and pretend it never happened. Or you can try. Say yes, Charlotte."

"And if I say no?"

He was wicked and unabashed. "I'll probably ignore you."

"Yes, then," she said, an edge of wildness in her voice. She would have him, her golden fantasy lover, and nothing and no one would ever take it away from her. "Yes," she said again. "Yes, I want you."

His smile was small, almost smug. "Then

let's get rid of that damned virginity, shall we?"

Before she could guess what he had in mind he put another of his long fingers inside her, thrusting hard, and she felt a sudden sharp pain, a tearing inside her, and she let out a muffled shriek.

Her eyes filled with involuntary tears, but before she could blink them away he'd moved up, over her, his narrow hips between her spread legs. He'd unfastened his breeches at some point, she hadn't noticed when, and she was glad of it. She didn't particularly want to see it, touch it. She just wanted him to make love to her. Let her lie there and feel something other than the stinging pain between her legs.

She waited, bracing herself for the final act, the thrust, the coup de grâce. She could feel him now, smooth and hard against the opening of her sex, and she tensed, prepared for more pain.

He didn't move. He held himself above her, staring down at her, and all amusement had fled from his face. His blond hair fell forward, across his forehead, and there was a thoughtful look in his eyes.

"What are you waiting for?" she demanded finally, moving restlessly on the soft bed.

"I'm hoping one last burst of sanity will

stop me."

She held her breath. Part of her still wanted to escape, and if he released her she'd run to safety. Broken, weeping, but she'd run anyway. Self-preservation was bred deep into her bones, and she was on the edge of total disaster. Willingly.

And then a faint, self-deprecating smile flitted across his shadowed face. "But my cousin assures me that sanity is greatly over-rated. Tell me no one more time and maybe I'll listen."

This is what she'd wanted. He would let her go, and even if he'd broken through her virginity she could still retain some semblance of innocence. After all, no one would ever be near that area of her body to find out otherwise, never again.

Her arms were still trapped by the monk's robe. "Release my arms," she said in a low, determined voice.

For a moment he didn't move. And then he sat back, pulling her up and removing the entrapping fabric. Stripping away the torn shell of Lina's beautiful silk chemise.

He was still dressed, of course, his loose white shirt open, exposing his strong, smoothly-muscled chest. His breeches were unfastened as well, and she wondered if he'd lost interest. No. She refused to look

— but sitting up like this she could still feel him hard against the dampness of her sex, and it wouldn't take much for him to finish.

She sank back on the bed. "You'll let me leave?" she asked, looking up at him.

He reached his hand out to touch her face, pushing the hair out of her eyes, and his fingers were gentle, a caress, as his smile deepened.

"Good God, no," he said, and he pushed into her, hard, one deep, fierce thrust that filled her.

She arched, trying to accommodate his powerful invasion, and her involuntary cry was of pain and satisfaction. No turning back — he'd finished it.

He held himself motionless over her, and she could feel the tension rippling through his hard body. She didn't want to open her eyes, she wanted to savor this moment, this feeling, this possession that should have been something she hated. This possession that felt . . . completely wonderful.

Sanity was overrated, his cousin had said. She had to agree, because this was madness, and she wanted it. For a brief moment in time Adrian Rohan belonged to her, and nothing could ever take that away from her.

"Open your eyes, Charlotte." His voice was rough, and she did so, expecting to see smug satisfaction on his face.

Instead he looked dark, tortured, his blue eyes black in the shadows. His invasion of her body no longer hurt — she had grown grudgingly accustomed to it — but she wondered when he was going to remove it.

"Am I hurting you?" he asked, which surprised her. Why would he care about her comfort?

She searched for her most practical tone, but given the circumstances it eluded her. "It's all right," she said a little breathlessly. "You may remove it now."

She could feel his soft laugh inside her body — a most strange sensation. "I may? And why should I want to do that?"

She started up at him, perplexed. "Because you've done what you wanted. You had sex with me. It wasn't rape, I didn't fight you, so you needn't worry that I'll bring charges against you. As you pointed out, this was my own fault for coming here unprotected. But we're finished now, and if I'm not getting out until morning I'd like to sleep." She could be quite proud of her unemotional reaction to the whole confusing business. Later she could wail and cry when no one was around. For now it was done, over with, and she was deceptively calm. Time to move on with life.

"Oh, my precious angel," Adrian said in a silky, amused voice. "My sweet child, and by god you are a child when it comes to matters of carnality. I thought you had a clearer idea of what went on between men and women. Haven't you ever been in the country?"

"Well, I could hardly stand there and stare when the animals were breeding," she managed in a cranky voice. "My parents would have been horrified. And Lina won't explain these things. Aren't you finished yet?"

"My dear Miss Spenser, we have only just begun."

Before she could say a word he started to withdraw, and she let out her pent-up breath, only to have him push into her again, thick and hard. She cried out, but he simply repeated the motion, his narrow hips moving, pulling partway out and thrusting back in again.

"What are you doing?" she gasped as she clutched his shoulders, the white linen loose in her fingers.

"You want the pretty words, or the truth?" he whispered, leaning forward to brush his mouth against hers. "You're being tupped, shagged, screwed — made love to." Each phrase was punctuated with a thrust, and he was as breathless as she was. "In fact,

176

Charlotte, you're being fucked. It's about this —" he thrust hard "— and this." Another thrust and she could feel her nipples harden in the warm night air, feel the strange heat in the pit of her stomach begin to build and burn.

He slid his hands down her bare legs and pulled them up around his hips, and she could feel the soft cloth of his breeches against her thighs. He pulled her legs higher, and he was deeper, bigger than she'd expected, and she found her body reacting, her hips reaching up, wanting that unspeakable invasion, wanting more and not knowing what it was.

"I'm afraid . . ." he said breathlessly. "Can't wait . . ." He slid his hand up her leg until it was between them, and he touched the place he'd used his mouth on. *Clitoris,* he'd called it. How could he know more about her body than she did?

He pushed inside her again, hard, and he seemed to grow even bigger, swelling, and she knew something glorious was about to happen, when he let out a muffled curse and pulled free from her, and she felt a hot wetness cover her belly as he collapsed beside her on the bed.

He was trying to catch his breath, and she was twisting, restless, confused, when he rolled back, trapping her body with one long leg as she tried to pull away.

"Sorry," he said, not sounding particularly repentant. "You seem to have an unexpectedly strong effect on me. I barely made it out in time. The last thing I want to do is saddle you with a brat."

Part of her understood what he was saying. He had spilled his seed outside her body so she wouldn't get pregnant. Leaving her empty, aching, feeling strange and restless and unfinished.

Why would any woman seek this out? It was messy, undignified, and while the things he did with his mouth had had the most astonishing effect on her, the fact remained that for a few minutes of unimaginable pleasure she'd destroyed her future.

She tried to sit up, but he pushed her back down again with lazy strength. He laughed. "I usually manage these things better. The truth is, you excite me beyond measure, for no earthly reason I can think of." He pulled her closer to his body on the soft bed, and she was feeling too weak to fight him. He pulled her into his arms, curling his bigger body around her back, and she felt some of the strange tension begin to leave her. This was what she wanted, what she had always wanted, she thought. Her back pressed against his chest, his arms around her, holding her against his warm, hard body. Her bum was up against his sex, but he was no longer hard, and she had nothing to fear from him anymore. She started to release a sigh when she felt his hand on her stomach, long fingers splayed across the soft, sticky surface.

And then before she realized what he'd intended his fingers dipped lower, into the soft curls between her legs, and she froze.

"No," she said sharply, trying to pull away.

She'd forgotten how strong he was. He had one arm around her, clamping her body against his, as his other hand continued its wicked descent.

"We're still not finished," he murmured in her ear, his voice low and wicked. "*You're* not finished."

She tried to kick out, but he simply trapped her long legs with one of his, as his fingers slid lower, finding that dangerous place he'd found earlier.

She was wet down there, from him as well as her own embarrassing dampness, and his fingers slid easily against her. He did it with insulting ease — one moment she was struggling, fighting, and in the next she'd gone rigid in his arms, every nerve in her body contracting in shameful delight.

He moved his hand, spreading the wetness around her sex, and she caught her breath. He touched her again, harder, longer, with wicked, wicked knowledge of a woman's body, and she cried out as the cruel delight washed over her again, and again.

Finally he moved his hand away, reaching up to cup her chin, pulling her face back so that his mouth could meet hers, and he kissed her as he'd touched her, long, hard and deep. She started to turn toward him when his hand slid down her stomach once more, and she broke the kiss.

"Please," she begged, desperate. "I can't take any more. Please."

"You can," he said, his voice dark and dangerous. "You can take anything I give you." And when he touched her this time she was shot into a darkness so deep that there was no escape. At the apex of her release she screamed, unable to stop herself.

He turned her in his arms then, and she was sobbing against his chest as he held her, his hands stroking her hair, her tear-streaked face, her trembling mouth. When the last shaky sob died away he kissed her with such tenderness that she wanted to start crying anew.

He was whispering to her, soft, gentle

words that made no sense, words of praise, love, pleasure. "Sleep now, angel," he said. "You need your rest."

She could feel him now. Somehow he'd gotten hard again, but he seemed in no hurry to do anything about it. "Sleep," he said, his lips against her brow, brushing her soft skin.

And so she slept.

Adrian looked down at the woman in his arms, sleeping so soundly, so trustingly. He'd been a bastard to do this to her — he could face that in the few brief moments of post-coital regret, when his own defenses were at low ebb. He should have left her strictly alone.

He'd already known how dangerous she was to his self-indulgent peace of mind. He'd been fascinated by her furtive glances, her well-hidden longing. He'd wanted her for a long time now, he realized, wanted her badly, and he'd been too proud and too vain to admit it. Adrian, Viscount Rohan could have anyone, all the great beauties of London and Paris. Why was he wasting his time with an overtall gawky virgin no one else wanted? Older than he was, though only by a trifle, with ivory skin and freckles and long, luscious legs and he must be mad to be so obsessed with her.

He should have escorted her straight back to the house, accompanied by a stern lecture on the dangers of such reckless curiosity. Or even better, found a servant to take her back. She'd been an idiot to come out here in the first place. If he were a better man he could have rescued her from the mess she'd walked into.

But of course, he wasn't made to be the noble hero. And there would have been no one he could hand her off to — in fact he was less dangerous than most of his compatriots in sin. He shuddered to think what Cousin Etienne would have done to her.

A shaky sigh escaped her as she slept, and he told himself what a bastard he was. At least he'd pulled out at the last minute. In time, he hoped. Just to be certain, he'd make sure Lina shared the herbal infusion ladies of the ton swore by to avoid unwanted pregnancies. He could just imagine his father's reaction. The hypocritical bastard would flay him alive.

His mother, though, would be thrilled.

He rose from the bed, crossing the room to a stand that held an ewer of fresh water and a bowl. He washed, then poured clean water and towels and soaked them. He glanced back at the bed. She was sound

182

asleep, and he shouldn't wake her, but she'd probably be feeling sore and sticky and generally uncomfortable. In truth he'd never had a virgin before, though certain members of the Heavenly Host preferred them, but he could imagine she might be feeling slightly abused. And he wanted her again.

He wasn't that fastidious — he would happily take her already covered with his seed, but he imagined she might balk. He slid back into the bed beside her, tucking her against his body, and began to wash her, slowly, lingeringly.

She opened her eyes drowsily. "Hush, love," he murmured, putting the warm damp cloth between her legs. "You'd probably prefer to soak in a bath, and I'll have my servant arrange it when he comes, but in the meantime this might help. Are you hurting?"

She looked at him as if he were speaking a foreign language. "When your servant comes you'll let me go?" she whispered.

He shook his head. "You won't want to."

"I want to now," she said with sleepy defiance.

He leaned over and brushed his mouth against hers, and he moved the wet cloth carefully, the heel of his hand pressing down on her clitoris while he slowly stroked her.

She made a muffled sound against his mouth, one of pleasure, and she lifted her hips towards his hand, his gentle stroking. He moved his lips to her ear, biting the plump lobe for a moment before whispering again, "Are you still in pain?"

He could find other ways to give her pleasure, to take his own, but for some reason he wanted to be inside her again. Maybe he wasn't a total bastard, because he would give her time to . . .

To what? He certainly wasn't going to wait until she healed. He was hard, and he wanted her now, and there was no reason why he shouldn't take her.

He pulled the damp cloth away and dropped it on the floor, then reached for her. She was already half asleep again, and she moved toward him willingly, tucking her head against his shoulder, her hand on his arm, sighing deeply as her body relaxed against his. Trustingly.

He froze, and an ugly sneer twisted his mouth. He'd really managed to shag her brains out, he thought. She should be fighting him, remembering he was the worst thing in the world for her. Instead she was sleeping in his arms like a trusting orphan.

Then again, she was the worst thing in

184

the world for him. Because she was turning him into a dead bore, when he'd much rather be his wicked, selfish self. There was nothing he could do about it. He simply ignored his aching cock, put his arms around her and let himself sleep.

10

Etienne de Giverney, the ci-devant Comte de Giverney, rose from the bed. Ci-devant — he despised that term. From before, it meant. An insult to the Bourbon aristocracy who were now, in the blood-soaked streets of Paris, mere citizens.

His cousin, Francis Rohan, had blithely handed over the title when he'd left France, the title that should have been Etienne's from birth. A lawyer had drafted a letter to the king, and voilà, all was made right for a few short years. He'd left the tiny surgery where he'd grudgingly worked and enjoyed the life he'd deserved, in the huge old house in Paris, in the countryside château.

The château was rubble now — burned and trashed. He liked to think some of his servants had died inside, but more likely they were the ones attacking the place. His servants had always hated him.

The hotel in Paris was now some sort of

government office, he'd heard. Government! It was to laugh. The canaille could no more govern themselves than they could walk on water. It would only be a matter of time before the bloody new regime would be overthrown, and all the ci-devant aristos would be back where they belonged.

In the meantime, he was an exile, basically penniless, though at least the English respected his title. And his cousin Francis had been generous, as always, inspired, no doubt, by a guilty conscience. Except someone like Francis Rohan, Marquess of Haverstoke, didn't possess a conscience.

It was more likely his wife, with her stupid English sense of honor. She'd done her best to make Francis abandon his profligate ways, ensuring him a damnably long life. How Etienne despised her for her softness. No Frenchwoman would be so weak as to attempt to tame her husband.

Ah, but there was Rohan's son, Adrian, Viscount Rohan. As his father had been granted a higher rank by a foolish English king, his son had taken one of his lesser titles, and at least Adrian was well on his way to the early death his father should have enjoyed. Etienne had taken him under his wing, much to the marquess's disapproval, which of course had only made Adrian more determined. He'd introduced him to all sorts of pleasures, any number of which could foreshorten his life. The English were so ridiculously conventional. Adrian liked to think of himself as a true libertine, a man without a soul or conscience, when in fact he still held to a ridiculous set of rules. Morality was for weaklings; it would be Adrian's undoing.

He wondered who he'd disappeared with. Etienne made certain he kept close to his young cousin. Last he'd seen him he'd been following a young monk. It was too much to hope that the coltish figure in the habit was male. He didn't recognize the woman's walk, but he wasn't concerned. One aristocratic English whore was much like the other. If Adrian developed an attachment, which so far he'd shown no signs of doing, then Etienne could handle the situation with his usual cold-blooded efficiency.

But there was no hurry. If Adrian continued on the path he was leading, the marquess of Haverstoke would be without an heir in no time. His first son had died of an ague ten years before, and Adrian looked to be following shortly, if Etienne had his way. And when he died, all that lovely money and the estates would go to Etienne, as well as the new English title and the old ones.

In the meantime, he was content to wait. Adrian would take care of his own early demise quite handily, and in the meantime, Etienne was enjoying his English life very much, thank you.

He moved to the bowl of water and began to wash the blood off his hands. It was a good thing his own servant, Gaston, accompanied him. Gaston could dispose of the well-paid courtesan who'd shared his bed last night, burn the blood-soaked sheets. He'd been in quite a frenzy last night. By today he was calmed, ready to partake in more genteel English customs.

The whore was staring at him, glassy-eyed, unmoving. She'd stopped screaming several hours ago, and her eyes were dull with hatred. *Tant pis.* He would pay her off, and in the dark no one would notice her scars.

There would be a picnic on the grass this morning. He could count on numerous partners beneath the springtime sun, and by the time he returned to his allotted cell there would be no sign of last night's play.

Still, he was curious about Adrian's choice. It wasn't the Countess of Whitmore — he'd seen her rushing off in the opposite direction with a good-looking servant, clearly intent on a little roll in the mud.

Adrian never kept a woman for more than one night — he'd see who she was at breakfast this morning and then he could decide whether he had anything to worry about.

Which was unlikely. In the three years since Etienne had been exiled, Adrian had held no long-term relationships. He would scarcely start one at a gathering of the Mad Monks.

He laughed to himself. The Mad Monks. The English were so ridiculous in their sins, cloaking them in costume and folderol. At least Adrian preferred, like his cousin, to sin openly. It made his job so much easier.

The woman on the bed tried to speak, but no words came out. He cast a last, curious glance at her, and then walked out into the early-morning sunshine, whistling jauntily.

*"There was a young tinker from Barton
Who wanted a use for his . . ."*

"I don't suppose there's any way I can convince you to regale Montague with something other than obscene poetry?" Simon Pagett said in a world-weary voice.

"What would you suggest instead?" Lina said sharply. "An improving sermon? I imagine he's already heard enough of yours."

"Children, children," Montague said

190

faintly. "Don't squabble. Simon, it wouldn't do you any harm to listen to a few naughty poems. I assure you, Lady Whitmore is quite gifted in their composition. And Lina, my precious, Simon's sermons are actually quite interesting. I would never tolerate him as the new curate if they weren't."

"Don't try to convince me that you were actually going to attend church once he took over, Monty," Lina said. "I wasn't born yesterday."

"No, I do think that's going to be quite out of the question, don't you?" Monty said with a breath of a sigh. "Why don't the two of you go off somewhere and browbeat each other until you come up with a solution. I'm perfectly willing to tolerate either the sacred or the profane."

A wave of guilt washed over Lina, and she held his thin hand. "Oh, darling, I'm sorry. Of course you don't want to hear all this brangling going on about you."

"My precious, you're crushing my fingers."

She immediately released his hand, but found herself casting a worried glance at Simon Pagett. She had been putting no pressure at all on her friend's frail hand, and yet even that had hurt. "Sometimes I don't know my own strength," she said with

191

a shaky laugh, turning back. Monty's color was ashen, his lips bloodless, but his eyes were still sharp.

"Indeed, darling, I don't think you do," Monty said in a soft voice.

Lina moved away from the bed, letting Simon take her place. Why, in God's name had she turned to look at him, as if for help? There was no help coming from someone like Simon Pagett. She was anathema to him, and he was nothing more than a prosing annoyance. Monty didn't need to be subjected to someone lecturing him during the last few days or weeks of his life. He'd always sinned on a grand scale — it was disheartening to see him diminished to a repentant sinner.

"As for you, my dear Simon," Monty continued, looking up into the vicar's lined face, "you need to treat my darling Lina with more respect. She has stayed by me when most others were off consorting with Satan or whatever other bauble has caught their eye at these gatherings."

"You don't know?" Simon demanded, appalled. "You host these gatherings and you have no idea what your guests are doing?"

"Oh, I imagine some of them are trying to summon Old Scratch, but since I don't believe in his existence I hardly need to worry about it. They're just children playing games, the ones who aren't busy with rousing fornication." He glanced at Lina. "Hard to believe this straitlaced fellow ever knew a thing about fornication, isn't it, Lina? But he did. He had quite the reputation."

She really hadn't wanted to be dragged into the conversation, but for Monty's sake she turned back. "Very hard to believe. I suppose, then, that there must be redemption for us all," she said lightly. "Even whores like me."

It was an ugly word, and Monty looked distressed. "I think he's having a bad influence on you, my dear. You aren't usually so self-critical. Trust me, compared to some ladies I know, you've been a model of restraint." He glanced at Pagett. "If you're going to make Lina feel bad about herself then you'll have to leave, dear boy. I can't have my darling girl feeling sad."

Simon had remained noticeably silent on the matter. "Everyone has to feel sad at some point in their lives, Thomas. And Lady Whitmore doesn't need my approval for how she chooses to spend her life — she only needs her own."

"Enough with the spiritual doublespeak," Monty said fretfully. "You two will simply have to learn to get along. I can't have you fighting over my deathbed — I prefer to be the center of attention at all times. Either the two of you go off and make peace, or you can set up a schedule of visiting with me where you won't have to see the other. Either way, I need a rest. Go away."

This was the second time Monty had told her to go off with his disapproving friend. She cast a suspicious glance at the pale man before rising. She could assume this was simply Monty having a temper tantrum, with no ulterior motive, but there had never been anything simple about Monty.

He continued to look fretful and exhausted, and she couldn't tell whether she was imagining things or not. And then Simon Pagett was by her side, his hand on her elbow, leading her away. "You always were a rude bastard," he said in a cool voice. "I'll do my best to convince Lady Whitmore to go away and leave you to me — it's no more than you deserve."

"You won't succeed," she said.

He glanced down at her, and for a moment she was caught, staring up into his brown eyes. Odd, she would have thought brown eyes would be warm and comforting. His were dark and almost bleak. "You underestimate my determination, Lady Whitmore."

"You underestimate mine."

She half expected Monty to shoo them off again, but when she glanced back at him he'd slipped into a restless sleep.

She tried to pull away from her unwilling partner, but his hand on her upper arm was almost bruisingly tight, and he whisked her out of the sickroom before she could even open her mouth to protest.

"You don't want to wake him up," Simon said, loosening his hold once the door was closed. "He'll need all the sleep he can get. And you can surely stand my company for a bit while we thrash things out. After all, we do have the same goal in mind. A peaceful passing for someone we both love."

That sounded much too intimate for Lina's peace of mind, but she decided not to argue. "Indeed," she said calmly enough, hoping to disguise the pain it brought her.

"I've told the servants to set lunch out on the terrace. We can talk without being overheard, and we'll be close enough should Montague need us."

This was fraught with a number of annoyances. First off, what right did he have to high-handedly order lunch, assuming she'd eat it? And to call Monty by his seldom-used first name. And why should he assume she wanted to hear anything he had to say?

He was the vicar and Monty's old friend, she gathered, but still — what right did he have coming in and making decisions and issuing orders?

And what was Monty doing? If she didn't know better she'd suspect him of attempting the single most ridiculous matchmaking in the history of the world. Or maybe it just appealed to Monty's sense of the absurd. One of society's most soiled doves and a pillar of the church. He probably thought if he threw them together enough sparks would fly.

They certainly did. Simon Pagett was looking down at her with what had to be contempt. Oh, to be sure he was all that was polite, at least up to a point, but she knew what lurked beneath his passive exterior. Well, so what? She found him similarly distasteful. They would have to be the last two people on earth to ever consider being attracted to each other.

During her nightmare marriage she'd only tried for help once. Bruised, frightened, she'd escaped to their local vicar, begging for help, for advice, for rescue.

The old man had folded his hands across his ample stomach and told her it was the woman's joy and duty to submit. And that he wished to hear no more complaints.

When she'd returned home she discovered that the vicar had preceded her return with a note to her husband, disclosing their conversation. That was the first night he'd beaten her into unconsciousness.

She'd never set foot inside a church again. And now this . . . this *man* dared to look at her with what she was certain was opprobrium, judging her. "I'll eat in my room," she said and whirled away from him.

He caught her arm again, pulling her back around. "You'll eat with me," he said calmly. "You don't want the servants to know we're fighting."

"I don't give a damn what the servants think," she snapped.

She almost thought she saw a smile in the back of those dark eyes. "In fact, neither do I, but Montague would hear of it and then he'd start this ridiculous matchmaking all over again. We're better off pretending to go along with it."

She could feel the color rise to her face. "I hadn't realized you suspected it, too."

"I've known Montague all his life — it would tickle his sense of the ridiculousness."

She'd thought the very same thing, but for some reason hearing the words from his mouth was particularly annoying. "I'm an extremely wealthy widow, sir," she said in an icy tone, "and not unattractive. Most men wouldn't consider me a ridiculous choice."

He escorted her out onto the terrace, where a table was beautifully laid for two. "Surely I haven't offended you?"

She smiled sweetly. "I'm impossible to offend, Mr. Pagett."

"You may as well call me Simon. Every time you say 'vicar' or 'Mr. Pagett,' I hear poison dripping off your tongue." He released her arm to hold the chair for her. There was no way she could leave without making a scene, so she sat, glaring at him.

"You're hearing your own fevered imagination, *vicar.*" She put deliberate emphasis on the word.

"And I suspect it's a great deal easier to offend you than I would have thought," he added, seating himself opposite her. There were no wineglasses on the table, and she was very much in need of something stronger than Monty's clear, cold water.

"Aren't we to have wine?" she asked.

"I don't drink spirits."

Of course he didn't. And she would have given her right arm for some. But she certainly wasn't about to admit it.

For the first time she had a clear look at him in the light of day. He wasn't as old as she'd thought — the lines on his face were ones of hard experience, not age. The one gray streak in his dark hair was all the more startling, and for the first time she realized he looked oddly familiar.

"Have we ever met?" she asked abruptly.

"Have you been frequenting churches recently, Lady Whitmore?"

"Of course not. I just suddenly had the thought that I might have . . . seen you at some point."

He shrugged. "It's possible. I spent some time in London before I joined the church. When was your first season?"

She remembered it all too well — she'd been seventeen, the toast of London, and innocent. "More than ten years ago," she said stiffly. "But I expect you'd remember me. I was quite the toast."

"I hate to disillusion you, my lady, but I don't remember anyone from that time, no matter how heartbreakingly beautiful. I was too drunk."

She looked at him in surprise. "I thought you didn't drink spirits."

"Not any longer. I find they don't agree with me. I sincerely doubt we saw each other back then, my lady. I spent my time in whorehouses and gambling clubs. No decent hostess would have invited me over her threshold, and certainly no one would have introduced me to a shy young virgin. Which I expect you were, way back then."

"You make me sound like an old crone. I'm twenty-eight. Decades younger than you."

"I'm thirty-five," he said flatly. "Close your mouth, Lady Whitmore. If you're going to be astonished it's better just to raise your eyebrows."

She snapped her mouth shut, starting at him. She could see it now, the signs of dissipation. Her judgmental, self-righteous nemesis clearly must have been a libertine par excellence.

"So you see," he continued in a calm voice, reaching for the crystal glass of clear water, "I know whereof I speak. I know just how vicious and deadly are the paths you and Thomas are following. Thomas is about to meet his maker, and while I have no doubt that God will welcome and forgive him, I think his passing will be easier if he made peace with things beforehand. Which is why I'd rather you didn't sit there telling him ribald poems and gossiping about all your acquaintances."

"You think having been a hellion somehow gives you the right to tell other people what to do, *vicar?*"

"Simon," he corrected in an equally frigid voice.

"Simon," she purred. "Your story is quite touching, I must admit. If I were the sentimental sort I would quite be in tears. But let us examine the truth of the matter. You've just admitted to being the worse sort of reprobate, a drunkard, a lecher . . ."

"A liar and a thief," he added. "Those tend to go together."

"A liar and a thief," she added graciously. "Clearly you've been as despicable as every man I've ever met, with the remarkable exception of your old friend Monty, and you think simply because you no longer whore or drink you've somehow become a good man, a man with the right to pass judgment on other people. I'm afraid I must disagree. You have no right to judge Monty and you have no right to judge me. I will live my life exactly as I choose, and I don't give a damn what you or anybody else has to say about it."

He was watching her, and she had the odd feeling he was no longer listening to her. That something had distracted him in the midst of her tirade.

"Every man you've ever met is despicable, Lady Whitmore?" he said softly. "Then why do you spread your legs for all of them?"

She slapped him. She'd never hit anyone in her life, and yet she reached across the small table and slapped him across the face, as hard as she could.

The sound was shocking in the morning air, like the crack of a gunshot. She froze. Her hand was numb, tingling, and she could see the mark of her fingers on his face.

And then, to her horror, he made it even worse. "I'm sorry," he said. "You're right — I deserved that."

It was the last straw. Monty was dying, her own heart was bleeding and God knew what was happening to Charlotte over there on that island of perverts. She rose so quickly the table tipped over, and the china and glassware went crashing to the ground.

"So much for Monty's matchmaking efforts," she said, her lower lip trembling.

And then she ran, before he could see the tears spill over from her eyes, before he could even begin to guess that the wicked Lady Whitmore's excellent exterior had begun to crumble. She couldn't let it crack until she was alone.

And then, if she had to, she'd howl.

11

Charlotte awoke slowly, cocooned in darkness and warmth, a blissful sense of wellbeing shimmering through her body despite the peculiar feeling between her legs, at the heart of her sex. She was alone in the bed, and she realized that light filtered through a heavy curtain that hid the sleeping alcove from the rest of the room.

She stretched, carefully, not certain exactly what was going to hurt and how much. Was this strange feeling between her legs going to continue? If she held very still she could almost feel him inside her again. Not the pain, but the deep, filling part of it, that had felt strange and foreign and yet somehow blessedly right.

However, she wasn't convinced she ever wanted to do it again.

She closed her eyes, snuggling deeper into the covers. She was naked. She'd never slept naked in her life — it added to her odd sense of lassitude. The soft covers caressed her bare skin, the mattress beneath her cradled her body. Everything was strange and different.

She heard the low murmur of voices then. Adrian, speaking softly, to a servant. The light coming through the heavy curtains was daylight. Her ordeal, such as it was, was over.

She looked about her. The torn silk chemise lay tossed in one corner, but there was no sign of the plain brown monk's robe she'd worn when she entered his bed. She could pull the sheet off, wrap it around her nude body like a Roman toga, push the curtains aside and demand her freedom.

She didn't move.

What had happened to Charlotte Spenser, bluestocking, spinster, the practical, no-nonsense, plain and outspoken creature she'd always envisioned herself to be? She'd fallen into the bed of the man she'd secretly, shamefully dreamed about for three years, and suddenly everything had changed.

She no longer felt overtall and gawky. She felt sleek, sensual, her skin exquisitely sensitive to the feel of the sheets, the remembered feel of his hands that went places they should never have gone.

His mouth had gone there as well.

He'd taken her every way he could, he'd said, and she was exhausted, sensitized. And hungry.

Hungry for the smell of food beyond the thick curtain, the unmistakable scent of coffee and toast and bacon. Hungry for the touch of his hands, his long fingers, his body pressing hers down into the mattress.

She was mad. She'd disgraced herself, been ruined into the bargain, and the only way she could possibly redeem herself would be to scramble from the bed, wrapped in whatever she could find to preserve what was left of her modesty, and insist on being released.

She didn't want to be released. She wanted to stay in that bed all day, within the touch and the scent of the sheets. She wanted to make sure she didn't forget any of it — her fear, her anger, her shattering delight. It wasn't going to happen again, he'd already assured her of that. One night was all he'd wanted.

And there was no one else she'd even consider going near. What she'd done in the darkness with Adrian Rohan, what had been done to her, was so private, so darkly wonderful, that the very thought of one of her occasional elderly suitors trying the same thing was horrifying.

No, this would be enough for a lifetime. Even if she was greedy enough to want more, this would do. As long as she could keep things clear in her mind so that she could relive it.

When she returned home she would write it all down in exquisite detail, just so she wouldn't forget anything. She grinned in the darkness. Did women ever write of such things? There were countless French novels on the subject, hidden in rich men's libraries, and she'd always been unaccountably curious, but if Lina's husband had ever possessed such a thing it was long gone.

Besides, reading someone else's experiences would be almost as bad as lying beneath a stranger. She only wanted her own, to relive over and over when the need arose later in life.

She heard footsteps approach the bed, and she swiftly shut her eyes, feigning deep sleep. She could feel him watching her for a long moment, and she would have given anything to see the expression on his face. Whether it was boredom, distaste or impatience.

She was being pathetic — she was determined to open her eyes, but by the time she did, the curtain had closed again, and he'd moved away.

"Will you be attending the picnic this morning, your lordship?" The servant's voice was clearer now that she was paying attention. "Your cousin has requested that you join his party."

Adrian's laughter was without humor. "I imagine he has. I suppose he asked you all about my partner for the night?"

"He did, sir."

"And you told him . . . ?"

"Nothing, sir. A good servant knows when to keep his eyes open and his mouth shut."

"And you're a very good servant, Dormin," Adrian said lazily. "You may tell my cousin that I'm intending to stay incommunicado for the remainder of the Revels. My partner is more than sufficient for my needs."

There was a clear hesitation from the servant. "And if Lady Whitmore should ask? She's already sent two housemaids out to inquire about her friend."

"We've already agreed that you know how to keep your mouth shut, haven't we?" Adrian's voice was silky with menace. "It would distress me to dismiss you after all these years."

"I've served you well and discreetly for many years, my lord. I would be more disturbed to know I had failed you in any

207

way. No one will discover anything from me." His voice was growing fainter, and she guessed he was moving toward the outer door set in the thick stone wall. "Is there anything else you require from me, my lord?"

He was leaving, Charlotte thought. Her chance of escape was leaving, while she lay abed like an eastern houri, awaiting the return of her pasha. *Get up,* she told herself impatiently. *For God's sake, say something.*

She didn't move. She heard the heavy door close, shutting out the outside light, enveloping them in candlelit darkness once more. Heard the ominous click of the lock. Felt the ominous flow of relief.

He said he wasn't going to need another partner for the next few days. It sounded as if he had no intention of dismissing her, but perhaps the clear insanity that had taken over last night was continuing into the day, and he simply meant he didn't want anyone at all. Perhaps the hours in that bed had been so boring he'd decided he'd rather have no . . . disporting at all.

She managed to shut her eyes again just before he pushed the curtains open, trying to keep her breathing still and shallow. She could smell coffee, surely the most delicious smell in the entire world, could practically feel its heat underneath her nose.

"You may as well open your eyes, precious," he said in that thoroughly annoying, enticing drawl of his. "I know you're awake."

She opened one eye to stare at him balefully. "Of course I'm awake. Who wouldn't be with you wafting hot coffee underneath their nose?"

"If you want some you're going to have to sit up," he said, handing her the delicate bone-china cup before moving away. He was dressed, at least partially, in breeches and a loose white shirt, and his long golden hair was tied at the back of his neck. He hadn't been shaved yet — the servant must be coming back. That was when she would leave. *Thank God,* she told herself.

She pulled the sheet up around her breasts and managed to sit up without spilling the coffee. She took a first sip and felt the blissful strength of it dance through her veins. He was across the room, his back to her, which was a relief. What in the world could they discuss, given the situation? Literature?

She let out a convincing yawn. "Did I miss your servant? Is it morning yet?"

He turned back. "What you mean is, am I willing to let you go yet?"

She would hardly be stupid enough to deny it. "Of course."

"He'll be back. In the meantime, I had him bring you a bath. I thought you'd find it soothing before you left."

Before she left. He'd warned her, hadn't he? One night only.

And really, this was a good thing. The sooner she got back to her normal life the sooner she could begin pulling herself back together.

The coffee was suddenly bitter. She swung her legs over the side of the bed, leaned forward and set the half-empty cup on the table. "A bath would be lovely," she said in an even voice, starting to rise.

She'd overestimated her own resiliency. The moment she got to her feet she felt her balance begin to waver, the shadow-lit room turned into pools of black in front of her eyes and she wondered if she was going to do the most embarrassing thing she could possibly imagine and fall face-first in a dead faint, directly at Adrian Rohan's bare feet.

He moved, fast and graceful, his hand catching her arm as she started to waver, as the sheet started to slip. She grabbed for it, almost going over, and he quickly caught it in one hand, yanking it up around her.

Which didn't make things any easier, she thought gloomily. Now he didn't even want to look at her. Not that she could blame him. She was hardly in the same class as most of the women he'd bedded.

The idea startled her. She was now simply another one of the women Adrian Rohan had bedded. Part of a vast number, no doubt, and easily forgotten. By the next time she saw him he'd have moved on to someone else and forgotten all about her. After all, how could he keep track . . . ?

"Are you going to just stand there or would you like a bath?" He sounded surprisingly patient, almost amused.

She glanced over at the tub. It was huge — and steam was rising in wafts over the cloth-draped sides. "I'm waiting for you to leave."

"We're locked in again. I'm not going anywhere."

"I'm not sure I quite believe in these locks of yours."

He gestured toward the door, his grip on her sheet loosening, and she felt it begin to descend. "See for yourself," he offered as she quickly gathered the falling material back around her body.

"I'm not going to take off this sheet in front of you."

"Modesty," he said with a sigh. "Such a wasted value. What if I promise to keep my back turned?"

"Why should I believe you?"

"Why shouldn't you?"

That silenced her. Indeed, why shouldn't she? It wasn't as if he'd made any effort to touch her, to kiss her, to continue the seduction of the night before. Though come to think of it, once you'd been bedded was seduction even an issue anymore?

"Turn your back," she said in a grumpy voice.

"Will you fall at my feet?"

She stared at him, uncomprehending for a moment. She'd already fallen at his feet, handed herself over . . . oh, he was talking literally, not metaphorically.

"No," she said shortly.

His lids were drooping lazily over his blue eyes, and his smile was small and polite before he released her, turning his back to sit at the little table, addressing himself to the tray of food.

She moved to the side of the tub quickly, dropped the sheet on the floor and slid in. The water was blissfully hot, scented with roses, and her moan of delight was out before she realized it.

The sound caught his attention and he turned to look at her, a cup of coffee in his hand.

"You promised not to look," she shrieked

and sank lower in the bath.

"I most certainly did not. I believe my exact words were, 'What if I promise to turn my back?' You said you wouldn't believe me, so I didn't bother making that promise." He hitched the chair around so that it was facing her, and his eyes were alight with amusement. "You should know better than to trust me."

"You're right," she said in a cranky voice. "Just go away, will you? If you can't leave, then go lie down and pull the curtains and let me enjoy my bath in peace."

"You could always turn your back on me."

Good point. Sinking lower, she managed to shift around so that her back was to him, enabling her to rise enough to let her head rest at the edge of the oval-shaped tub. She closed her eyes, and this time she managed to keep the sheer, sensual delight to herself. She heard him moving around behind her, but she ignored him. She'd never seen such a large tub in her life, and it astonished her that she hadn't heard it being filled this morning. But then, she'd been exhausted, sleeping more soundly than she had in months. Sleep had always been an elusive commodity in her life — there were always too many things to think about, too many things to do.

She wasn't going to think about why she slept so well. If it needed *that* to make her sleep then she was doomed to a lifetime of insomnia.

She leaned back in the tub, spreading her legs slightly, letting the warm water soothe her there. She had a strange memory of Adrian washing her, but that clearly was a dream. The only reason he might have done so was that he was too fastidious to have her again, and after the initial event he hadn't attempted a repeat. So much for magnificent experiences. The steam was rising around her face, and she knew her hair would become even curlier, the bane of her existence, but there was nothing she could do about it. She lifted her arm out of the water. It was faintly pink, but she could still see the smattering of freckles across her shoulder. Had he really called them flakes of gold? Or was that another dream?

He was moving around in the room behind her, doing something, but she wasn't going to think about that. She was going to concentrate on the blissful feel of the warm water moving around her, soothing her, delighting her.

"You're humming." His voice came from somewhere behind her, sounding slightly muffled.

She immediately stopped. She didn't try to deny it — it was a source of embarrassment.

"It's an unfortunate habit of mine." Despite the lascivious delight of the water she managed to find some semblance of her stiff little voice. "I tend to hum when I'm enjoying something. When I'm eating something particularly delicious, when I'm taking a bath, when I'm walking in the countryside."

"I'll have to keep that in mind." His voice was no longer muffled. "You hum when you're particularly pleased with life."

He made it sound as if she was pleased with him, she thought crossly. "No. I hum when I'm enjoying particular physical sensations. I could hardly say I'm pleased with life right now."

"You *could* say so," he said. "But you won't. You're not honest enough."

"If you think being abducted and ruined is cause for celebration you greatly overestimate the effect of your charm," she said in a pinched voice.

"No one abducted you. You arrived here on your own, came with me without fighting, and you were just as involved in your ruination as I was."

"Hardly. I didn't know what I was doing."

"I'm aware of that. You don't even know

215

how to kiss."

She wasn't supposed to know how to kiss, she thought miserably. She was supposed to spend her entire life in virtuous ignorance. "I'm sorry I was such a disappointment," she said stiffly. "Next time perhaps you'll have enough sense to choose someone with a little experience. Someone who's actually enthusiastic about the whole undignified process."

"Very undignified," he agreed, and she could hear the laugh in his voice. He was closer than she'd realized, which made her nervous, but she refused to turn around and look at him. Even without her spectacles she'd probably see him too clearly. "But I think you grew reasonably enthusiastic after a little persuasion. And there are times when lack of expertise can be particularly . . . endearing."

She was getting more and more bothered. By his voice, by the warm, scented water, by the memories he was evoking. "When is your servant coming back?"

"Why do you ask?" He was directly behind her now, so close that she could feel him brush against her loose fall of hair.

"I need time to dress before I leave."

"You aren't going anywhere. Not right now."

"You promised . . ."

"I promised nothing. And you were wide awake when Dormin was here — I checked and you were only pretending to be asleep. If you truly wanted to leave all you had to do was ask."

"I want to leave."

"Ah . . . Too late," he said, moving around the side of the tub. And before she realized what was happening he'd climbed in with her, on top of her, naked, beautiful, erect.

She let out a shriek, dunking her head down under the water. A second later he'd hauled her up, into his arms, laughing at her. "You can lie to me, Charlotte, but don't lie to yourself."

And he set his mouth on hers.

12

She was delicious. In every sense of the word, Adrian thought, moving his knees between her legs with no difficulty as he kissed her lovely mouth. She moaned, a small, weak sound that was pleasure and dismay, and he drank it in, reveling in it. He braced his arms on the side of the tub, letting his hips dance against hers, letting his erection float against the sweet juncture of her thighs.

He heard his own moan, an unconscious mate to hers, as her tongue met his. They kissed, like lovers who knew each other well, and he lifted one hand and cradled her neck, loving the feel of her.

She still hadn't mastered breathing too well, and when he dragged his mouth away from hers, down the side of her neck, she drew in a deep, rasping breath, and he waited for another protest, which he would ignore.

Instead, she lifted her hands and stroked the sides of his face, pushing his damp hair back. He raised his head to look at her, his thumb and fingers slowly rubbing the back of her neck, soothing her.

Her eyes were wide, calm, accepting. But he wanted the words. "Yes?" he said.

She held her breath for a moment. "Yes," she said in a soft whisper.

He smiled then, and he told himself this feeling was smug, masculine triumph. It wasn't. It was simple happiness.

He sat back on his knees. Her full, lovely breasts were just floating at the top of the water, the pink nipples soft and sweet. He leaned down and licked one, feeling it instantly bud against his tongue, and with sudden hunger he latched onto it like a hungry babe, sucking it into his mouth, clinging to it, hearing her quiet moan of pleasure. Her hands slid down to his shoulders, kneading, clinging, and her back arched with instinctive need. He covered her other breast with his fingers, teasing the nipple into matching hardness, as he sucked, sucked, and her hips lifted in the water, wanting him.

He reached down, caught his erect penis in his hand and guided it to her, then thrust, a little too hard, a little too fast, but she took it with only a faint cry. She was wet and sleek and welcoming, and he moved his head, dropping it down on her shoulder as he tried to control his breathing, his fierce need. He wanted to slam into her until he spewed, he was famished, greedy, ready to explode. He dropped his hands into the water and cupped her hips, pulling her up tighter against him, and the sound she made was one of unmistakable pleasure, arousing him further when he thought there was no place else to go. He began to move, slowly at first, letting her get used to his invasion. Dormin had used healing herbs in the rose-scented water, and she took him without protest, without restraint, catching the rhythm, moving with it, her eyes closed, her hips lifting to meet each plunging stroke, faster and faster, as the water splashed around them onto the floor, and he knew he was going to have to pull out, soon now, or he wouldn't be able to leave the tight grip of her body. But this time he wasn't going to come without her. He put his hands between them, slid his fingers into her soft, wet curls, just above where they were joined, and touched her.

It was all she needed. She let out a word-less cry as her body tightened around his, milking him, smooth, shuddering contractions as pleasure engulfed her, and as he felt his seed burst forth he pulled free, hating it, using his own hand to try to simulate the feel of her as he emptied himself into the warm water, cursing beneath his breath.

When his heartbeat had sullenly slowed, he rose, lifting her in his arms, sopping wet. He stepped out of the high tub, onto the wet floor, and carried her across to the bed. There were Turkish towels lying there, and he wrapped her in them like a cocoon, her body soft pink from the water and exertion. As he pulled them around her, drying her, she suddenly looked up at him, and he stilled for a moment, staring back.

Her eyes were bright with unshed tears, and for a moment he was confused. Had he forced her without realizing it? Hurt her? He was still half-erect, or maybe growing so again, and he wanted her with a fierce need that her tears strangled.

He'd pulled the toweling up around her neck, holding it there to keep her warm. "Do you want to leave, Charlotte?" he asked in a hoarse voice.

For a long moment she didn't move. And then she shook her head, reaching up for him. And he covered her body with his.

Charlotte lost track of time. The hours

passed in a blur, aided by the artificial light. He lay on the bed beside her and fed her sweetmeats and bits of cheese and ham, delicious tarts and sparkling wine. He made love to her, in the darkness, in the muted light, on the bed, on the floor by the fire, and when she was too sore to take him inside, he had her use her hand on him, bringing him to an exquisite completion that had her own body trembling.

There was no more need for talk. She was past the point of pretending she didn't want this, and he'd lost interest in baiting her. All he seemed to want was her body, wrapped around his, sleeping against him, shattering in ecstasy, on top and beneath and beside him. She was awash in the touch of him, the taste and scent and texture of his skin. She wrapped her long legs around his narrow hips, she shoved her hands through his thick hair, she kissed him, over and over again, never tiring of it, having no idea how much time passed in that dreamy, dazed state, when she awoke and found herself alone in the cavernlike room, the front door open to the bright sunlight.

For a long moment she didn't move, unwilling to face the daylight. She didn't want this to end, couldn't bear for it to be over.

Her monk's robe lay across the foot of the bed, and she pulled it on, fastening it at the shoulder, then searched for the rope that held it closed. Her sandals were long gone, so she slid barefoot onto the thick carpet. "Adrian?" she said in a small voice.

No answer. There was a scrap of paper on the table, but she didn't want to look at it. She wanted to go back to the bed where such powerful, impossible things had happened, pull the curtains and close her eyes. And wait until he came back for her.

But he wasn't coming back. She knew it immediately, and she wasn't the type to cry. She crossed the room and picked up the piece of paper, then dropped it on the table. *Novelty can only entertain for so long,* it said. *Goodbye.*

Her hair was loose, a mass of curls flowing over her shoulders. She reached back and took the length in one hand, working it into a loop to flatten it before she pulled the hood over her head. She tucked her hands inside the large sleeves, ignoring the faint tremor. The interval was over, it was time to return to her normal life. Time to move on, without looking back.

In the light of day the courtyard looked smaller than she had imagined. There was no one in sight — even his servant had disappeared. Odd, though. She had the strange sense someone was watching her as she walked back toward the Portal of Venus. The grass was cold and wet on her bare feet, and she realized by the position of the sun that it was still early. She moved on, slowly, deliberately, refusing to think.

She passed an occasional servant as she went, but they kept their heads down, refusing to look at her. The Revels must still be continuing, she realized. Everyone else was still in the midst of their debauchery.

It was just as well. She no longer had the strip of white cloth that signified she had no interest in participating, and if anyone decided she was fair game she'd have a hard time putting up a fight. She was lost, defeated. Everything ached. Not that he'd been too rough. They'd made love gently, fiercely, with tenderness and with anger. She was bruised from his hard grip, he was raked by her nails, but the only thing he'd been brutal with was her heart.

She skirted the now-silent chapel with its obscene imagery, headed down toward the river, a narrow stream that carried the small flat boats from Hensley Court and back. She could only hope one was waiting there. Even if there was no servant she could probably manage to pilot the boat herself. It moved by way of a long barge pole, and she probably had enough strength to use it. If she didn't, she'd walk, or swim, or fly if she had to. Anything to get away from this sorrowful place.

The path led down beside a steep embankment overlooking the water, and there were rocks lining the path. She glanced down — when they'd arrived it had been dark and she'd had no idea how dangerous it was. It was a good thing she was barefoot — it made her more sure-footed.

The trees were rustling overhead. New leaves were budding, and the wind had picked up, pulling at her hood. She tugged it closer, keeping her head down, unable to see on either side, her hearing muffled as well. It wasn't until the hands touched her that she realized she was not alone.

And she was falling, down the steep embankment, the rough stones tearing at her arms and legs, the branches slapping at her. The hood fell back, and for a brief moment she looked up, up, to see someone standing at the top of the bluff, unmoving. Someone who had pushed her.

She landed against the boulders. The breath was knocked from her lungs, and she lay perfectly still, unable to breathe, unable to move. Her eyes were open, staring up at the figure above her, and she realized to her horror that he was starting down the steep hill toward her. Not to help her. To finish her off.

She tried to scream, but her breath was still gone, and all she could do was gasp and choke, flailing around. She could feel something wet and warm sliding down her face, and she knew it was blood. She was going to die, she thought. Whoever had shoved her down the cliff was going to kill her.

"Madame, are you all right?" The rough Yorkshire accent came from somewhere beyond her, down at her level, and the man above swiftly turned and began climbing upward, away from her.

Her breath came back in a huge, sucking *whoosh.* "I . . . I . . ." For a moment she couldn't find her voice.

Someone was coming toward her now, someone tall, and the rising sun was behind him, throwing him in shadows. For a moment she thought it was Adrian, and her heart leaped. But he came closer, and it was a stranger, one of the servants, kneeling beside her. "Just lie still, miss," he said. "Help is coming."

Help is coming, she thought dizzily. She tried to look up toward the bluff, but there was no one in sight. "You must have slipped, miss," the man was saying. "That hillside is right dangerous — you could have been killed. Can you speak, miss?"

She moved her mouth, trying to get the words out. She wanted someone to go after him, after the man who'd pushed her. Who'd tried to kill her. But that was ridiculous — why would anyone want to hurt her? "The man . . ." she managed to say.

"What man, miss?"

But by then she gave up, slipping into the darkness that swirled around her head.

Adrian sank back against the velvet squabs of his very fast carriage, closing his eyes. The shades were pulled down over the windows, shutting out the day, and his cousin Etienne was busy opening a bottle of wine. "You almost left without me, dear boy," he said in a faintly complaining voice, his accent just slight enough to be considered charming. "I hardly think that hospitable. I might have had to beg a ride with one of those dreadful chits that Montague invites."

"I told you I wanted to leave by dawn," Adrian said with poor grace.

"I don't see what the hurry was. That tiresome creature you trapped yourself with

227

would hardly come chasing after you, would she?"

"I prefer not to talk about it."

"Indeed, I don't blame you. Though there's something to be said for playing with an amateur for a few hours. But two nights! My boy, you must have been a glutton for punishment. You can just be thankful I made Dormin unlock the door, or it could have gone on even longer. Heaven forbid!" he said with an extravagant Gallic shudder.

"Heaven forbid," Adrian echoed, leaning back and closing his eyes.

"I didn't make a mistake, did I?" Etienne's rich voice was suddenly anxious. "Dear boy, I thought I was rescuing you from a horrid fate. That red-haired Amazon — you must have been desperate to get rid of her. If I thought you actually found the tiresome creature interesting I would have left you alone."

"I don't," he said, his voice flat. Annoyed that he wanted to defend her, annoyed that he wanted to slam his fist into Etienne's florid face. It was bad enough that his cousin had gotten Dormin to unlock the door; Dormin would pay for that transgression.

But with Charlotte sleeping the righteous sleep of one beautifully shagged, he hadn't been able to send Etienne on his way, not without answering a lot of questions he didn't want to think about, even on his own.

"I admit, I was curious about that flamered hair. Is she worth the trouble? I might ask Lady Whitmore to bring her next time . . ."

"No!" Adrian said sharply. And then he managed a dry laugh. "Truly, Etienne, you would find her tedious beyond measure. She's like any sentimental young thing, full of tears and protestations of love. I had to tie her down to take her."

"You know I can be quite fond of that kind of sport."

Adrian kept his face impassive. One of the things he enjoyed most about his father's French cousin was his total lack of conscience. He did what he wanted, with whom he wanted. And Adrian had begun to realize that all he had to do was desire something to ensure that Etienne would go after it. And he didn't want Etienne going after Charlotte Spenser.

He wasn't quite certain why. Why he lied. "You certainly aren't interested in protestations of love, are you?"

"Of course not. In particular, not from someone as charmless as Lady Whitmore's friend. What in the world made you take her in the first place? Oh, yes, I remember. She has the most affecting crush on you, does she not? Always watching you covertly from the back of the ballroom. Clearly this was your semiannual act of charity."

He'd forgotten he'd ever said anything at all about Charlotte. Etienne's malicious tongue could flay anyone alive, and the sooner he stopped talking about Charlotte the happier he'd be.

"I think I may be assured that her crush has vanished. Now, either talk about something else or let me have some peace. Two days of Charlotte Spenser is enough — I certainly don't want to keep reliving it all the way back to London."

Etienne leaned back, a faint, amoral smile on his face. "Perhaps you'd rather hear about Lady Alpen and Mrs. Barrymore? You would have been better off joining us, but then I wouldn't have been able to enjoy the pleasure of two such enthusiastic women."

"I thought you went off with one of the girls from Madame Kate's." Adrian frowned.

"Oh, I was done with her quite quickly," Etienne said with an airy wave of one exquisite hand. "She was merely to get me in the proper mood. And one can be a bit more insistent with those who are being properly compensated, as doubtless you're aware. I'm not sure that Maria and Helena would have been quite as docile as the whore." He glanced at his hand, as if seeing an imaginary stain there, and rubbed at it with the edge of his monk's robe.

"And what the hell are you doing dressed up? I thought you despised that sort of thing."

Etienne gave him his sly, almost secretive smile. "I'm always open to new experiences, my boy. I decided if my dear young cousin was going to try something new then I should attempt something as well." He glanced down at the rough weave of his robe in distaste. "Let us agree to avoid wallowing in the mud in the future, however. These two days have been interesting, but I wouldn't think either of us would want to repeat them, do you?"

"No," Adrian said. "Two days of Charlotte Spenser were quite enough." At least, they should have been. He'd taken her, over and over again, trying to drain the need from his body. All he'd had to do was brush up against her skin and he'd be hard again. He'd taken her so often, so thoroughly, she'd probably have a difficult time walking for the next few days.

The thought should have amused him. He

should share it with Etienne, to convince him how detached he was. But in fact the more he'd had Charlotte Spenser the more he wanted her.

He'd been careless, when he was the most careful of men. He'd pulled out each time, but he'd always waited until the last minute, or even beyond. Lina would have enough sense to make sure her cousin drank the tea the Gypsies provided, wouldn't she? He really didn't fancy having that conversation with the countess of Whitmore. She wouldn't like the fact that he'd despoiled her innocent friend. Not when she'd clearly been interested in being on the receiving end of such a despoiling.

When the door had opened a few hours ago, he'd half expected it to be her, demanding Charlotte. But it had been Etienne, amused, mocking, offering him an escape he could hardly refuse.

He closed his eyes, shutting out the sight of Etienne. His parents had disapproved of his friendship with his French cousin, and the stronger his father's disapproval, the more intrigued Adrian had been. It was silly, childish, but inescapable. Francis Rohan, Marquess of Haverstoke, was an imposing figure, and the only man capable of intimidating Adrian. He fought back any way he could.

But Etienne de Giverney was growing tiresome. There were just so many times one could enjoy the controlled madness of drugs, the visions of the forest mushrooms, the variations and combinations of sex. He was growing bored of it all. In fact, the two days alone with an unsentimental virgin had been the most exciting thing in his recent memory.

But he couldn't regret leaving her. The longer he was with her the more attached she was likely to become, and that would be miserable for everyone. A quick tear and it would be soonest mended. He couldn't linger over such things.

Of course he was entirely immune. He'd enjoyed her while he had her, but now he could forget about her.

Couldn't he?

13

It turned out to be surprisingly easy for Lina to avoid Simon Pagett. If he walked into Monty's bedroom while she was reading him salacious novels, she would simply rise, whisk herself away with a light sally, and there was nothing the good vicar could do short of making a scene. Which such a conventional creature would, of course, never do.

It wasn't that she was such a fragile soul Lina reminded herself. So the man had called her a whore — most vicars would do the same. There was no reason that it should bother her. She had set out to prove something to herself, and she'd never given a tinker's damn for anyone's opinion. The people who mattered loved her — Monty and Charlotte, and if that number was about to be cut in half she'd survive. She'd survived worse.

To her relief Pagett decided he needed to

visit the vicarage where he'd be living for the next few years. At least, Lina assumed he would be. She had no idea who Monty's heir was, but whoever came into the title would doubtless consider the position of local vicar to be the least of his worries. And for a few hours she didn't have to worry about running into the man in the long, empty corridors of Hensley Court.

"So what do you think of the good vicar, eh?" Monty was sitting up for dinner, his color improved even if his strength hadn't seemed to appreciate much.

Lina poured herself another glass of claret, admiring the blood-red color in an attempt to give herself time to come up with a polite answer. Then again, Monty had never been insistent on good manners. "He's a dog."

Monty laughed. "No, darling, tell me what you really feel about him."

"You weren't thinking of matchmaking, were you, Monty? Because if you were, then I think your illness has reached your brain and there's no hope for you."

"I do adore you, Lina, but even I know that you're hardly the kind of woman who'd make a decent parson's wife. Besides, I'm very fond of Simon — I wouldn't think of saddling him with a shrew like you. Why do you ask?"

She decided to ignore her own suspicions. "The vicar thought you might be."

"Really? Wishful thinking on his part, I expect." He took a sip of his own watered-down wine. "Faugh, this tastes like piss. Give me a full glass, there's a dear."

"And how often have you tasted piss?"

"You don't really want the answer to that, do you?"

"You're revolting, do you know that?"

"I do. I'm certain that when Simon decides to marry he'll find someone plain and virtuous, whose knees are so tightly clamped together he'll need a bar to pull them apart. For now I believe he's reveling in the world's longest stretch of celibacy, and the only reason I can think of him breaking it would be if I insisted that the vicar should have a wife. Otherwise he'll continue to mortify his flesh and suffer for his sins."

"Mortify his flesh?" Lina said, startled. "He flagellates?"

"That sounds so deliciously sinful when you say it, darling," Monty said wickedly. He drained his glass of wine, accepting the fact that Lina wasn't about to pour him an undiluted glass. "No whips or hair shirts, just sexual abstinence. He's simply atoning for his sins, darling. He loves them and his guilt far more than he could ever love a woman."

"May they live happily ever after," she said firmly.

"What did you two fight about?" Monty asked with a hint of childish curiosity in his voice.

"Your treatment, my morals, the color of the sky. . . . You name it, we fought over it. How long has he been celibate?" The last came out almost as an afterthought — she had no idea what made her think of it.

"Why do you ask?"

"You said it was the world's longest stretch of celibacy, and I find that difficult to believe," she said airily.

"I am prone to exaggeration, I do confess it. However, I do believe that poor Simon, former scourge of the bawdy houses of London, whoremaster, libertine, rake extraordinaire, hasn't dipped his wick in close to a dozen years. I expect if he ever marries he'd insist on an unconsummated one. Such a waste, if you ask me. While he never shared my proclivities, it seems a shame that no one gets to enjoy his years of experience. Not to mention the fact that he's a fine-looking man, if a little weather-beaten."

"Then we'll have to hope his plain, virtuous wife with the locked knees will manage to overcome his scruples."

"What scruples?"

She'd been too involved in her conversation with Monty to realize her nemesis had returned, and she shot to her feet, catching the racy French novel before it tumbled to the floor. She plastered a bright, vivid smile on her deliberately painted lips. "You're back," she said, stating the obvious. "I'll leave the two of you alone to talk, then, while I —"

"Don't leave me," Monty said plaintively, his eyes laughing. "I want the two people I love most in the world by my side when I leave this mortal world."

"As far as I can see, you're looking a great deal healthier than you were earlier," Simon said in a subdued voice.

"All thanks to Lina's gentle ministrations. She really is quite the loveliest nurse I've ever had. Wouldn't you agree, Simon?"

Lina did a quarter turn, just enough to shield Monty from Pagett's gaze, and smacked him with the discarded novel. Monty immediately began a theatrical cough, strong enough that the vicar, who'd been about to leave the sickroom, immediately paused.

Monty raised his head, smiling angelically. "Stay," he said, sounding wistful. "Both of you."

Lina had been about to leave, but Monty had a grip on her full skirt, and besides, God knows what he'd say to Pagett if she weren't around to keep him in line. She sat back down, with relatively little grace, and glowered, refusing to look at Simon Pagett as he took up a position at the foot of Monty's lavish bed. She could get through this. Indeed, she couldn't imagine why she even cared. She'd been snubbed and insulted by half the grandes dames of the ton, she was persona non grata at the best houses and hopeful mothers shooed their daughters out of her way. Having Charlotte come live with her was already dooming her dearest friend to a life under a cloud, which was one reason she hadn't objected to bringing her out to the Revels. So why should this man's contempt bother her?

She flashed her brilliant smile at Monty, keeping her teeth clenched. "Shall I continue with our book, then?"

"I need to speak to Lady Whitmore," the vicar said in a quiet voice.

"Oh, heavens, you don't need to say anything to me, Mr. Pagett." She laughed an airy laugh. "We really have no need of conversation at all."

Monty chuckled. "You can say whatever you need to say in front of me, Simon. Lina

239

and I have no secrets."

The man made a low, annoyed sound, rather like a growl, and she couldn't resist glancing at him briefly. "I need to apologize to Lady Whitmore," he said finally, his rich voice strained. It would be a good voice from the pulpit, she thought. Full and warm and persuasive when he wasn't criticizing.

"For what?" Monty asked innocently.

"For calling me a whore," Lina supplied after Pagett was silent for a moment. She looked at him openly then, her expression under control now, her smile small and calm. "One would assume he'd know that I've been called far worse by far better people, but he seems to feel guilty about it."

"Not 'far better people,' pet," Monty said. "I'm certain the good vicar is better than anyone else. Or at least he clearly thinks so. Don't you, Simon?" There was a silken edge to Monty's weak voice, and Lina felt a flush of gratitude. Apart from Charlotte there was no one she could trust to defend her the way Monty did.

"Every time I think I've made a little spiritual progress my own idiocy shows me how wrong I am," Pagett said with a frankness that would have disarmed a less stony heart than Lina's. "I have no right to judge anyone, and I apologize to you, Lady Whitmore, and to you, Thomas, for insulting a guest under your roof."

"And do you accept his apology, Lina?" Monty purred.

Lina wanted to tell him to stuff it up his bum, but Monty's thin hand left its grip on her skirt and reached for her hand. She had no choice. "Of course I do," she said sweetly. "Though there's no need for him to make such a fuss of it. I'm used to it."

"There now," Monty said, his frail voice full of mischievous satisfaction. "Now that we're all friends again, let's plan my funeral."

It was a long, oddly companionable night. Monty, having recovered his strength, refused to sleep, and Lina told herself she was loath to leave him to Simon's tender mercies. She almost believed it.

They'd played piquet — two against one. Monty and Lina, whispering and giggling, won seventeen thousand pounds from the vicar's nonexistent fortune. In turn, he trounced them both soundly at silver loo, gloating with unchristian zeal. When night passed into morning Lina's hair was down her back, her beauty patch had long since disappeared and she was sitting cross-legged on Monty's huge bed, dealing like a practiced sharp, while Simon's sedate coat and neckcloth had been tossed aside, his hair had come loose and he was viewing his two opponents with amused distrust.

"Are the two of you cheating?" He was stretched out at the foot of the bed, looking remarkably relaxed and almost human, Lina thought.

"If I were a man I would call you out for that," she replied in a non-offended voice. She'd been cheating quite flagrantly.

"So would I," Monty said with a laugh.

"Maybe I'd best give up gaming as well as whoring and drinking," Simon added. "I appear to be remarkably bad at it."

"In truth, I thought you had," Monty said lazily.

"I'd given up play with real stakes. Since real money wasn't being wagered . . ."

"I beg your pardon," Lina said. "Does that mean you aren't going to pay me the twenty-seven hundred pounds you owe me?"

He laughed. "I believe the final number was in my favor, Lady Whitmore. You owe me three hundred and forty pounds."

"I think he's right there, love." Monty had dropped out of the game an hour ago to simply watch, a wicked smile on his face the whole while. "Best pay up."

She was feeling a little wild and reckless, but in a surprisingly good way. She leaned back against the pillows beside Monty, looking into Pagett's face. Now that he was no longer so grim he was actually quite handsome, and the premature lines only seemed to add to his appeal. He was going to make some pretty little mouse of a girl a most excellent husband. Unless he planned to spend his married life celibate as well.

"La, sir, I came out without my purse," she said archly. "Will you take my marker?"

"Don't trust her, Simon. She's got wicked wiles, and she'll run off without paying."

"You can always take it in trade," she said.

The words hung there for a moment, and the impenetrable, stony expression was back on Simon's face, the one she couldn't read. Contempt and disapproval, no doubt. With a tinge of guilt?

"Don't look like that," she said gaily. "I heard something in church, once, when I wasn't daydreaming. 'The truth shall set you free.' Isn't that right? You think I'm a whore and you said so. I'm not arguing, I'm simply offering you my wares in exchange for the gambling debt."

"Don't." The word was short and sharp.

She'd gotten a rise out of him. Not the right sort, of course. She suspected that particular part of his anatomy no longer worked, not if Simon Pagett told it not to.

Her smile widened. "Oh, yes, that's right, you don't partake of pleasures of the flesh. Well, then, I'll simply have to owe you."

He'd moved down off the bed, reaching for his black coat, and Lina slid off beside him, her wide skirts rustling. She put a hand on his arm. "Oh, don't sulk. Admit it, we've had a pleasant night of it. Quite the best night I've had in years," she said with a yawn she couldn't quite control. "We haven't fought, and clearly I've forgiven you your earlier gaucherie."

"Clearly," he said with a grim twist to his mouth. "It's late. I should go to bed."

"It's early. In the morning," she amended. She suddenly realized she was standing too close to him. Normally that wouldn't be a problem, but for some reason his accidental nearness brought up strange feelings inside her. He was tall, yet he didn't make her feel weak, something that always brought out the worst in her. He gave the impression of quiet strength, when she was lured by noise and brightness. He was waging a battle for Monty's soul, and she fought with the devil on the other side. And yet . . .

She dismissed the odd, vulnerable feeling brutally. "You can always come to my room and I'll give you my voucher," she said in a silken voice. "For the debt I owe you," she added, giving him her most seductive smile. "Don't."

"There's that word again. It must be one of your favorites. *Don't. No.* Shall we add *never* to the list?"

Monty was sound asleep, and they both knew it. "*Never* is a dangerous word, Lady Whitmore," he said in an even voice. "And you know as well as I do that our stakes were artificial."

For a moment she didn't move. She wanted to be closer to him, to press up against him and have him put his arms around her, holding her. He was strong, in ways she couldn't even begin to comprehend, and that strength drew her to a dangerous degree. She wanted to bury her face against the somber black cloth of his coat, she wanted to stop smiling, stop laughing, stop dancing.

She wanted to run as far and as fast as she could.

She took a swaying step toward him, her most seductive smile on her lips. The carmine red had worn off hours ago, but she knew her mouth was one of her best features, full and inviting. Men loved her mouth, and Simon Pagett, beneath everything, was simply a man. "Our stakes were artificial," she murmured, "but my offer is

245

entirely genuine." She reached out and gently stroked his chest, her fingers dancing on the thick wool. He caught her hand, stopping her. But he didn't release her fingers.

"Lady Whitmore," he said, and his voice sounded weary, "there is very little about you that is genuine. You aren't the strumpet you wish you were. In fact, you are a kind woman who loves Montague very much, and for that I'm grateful."

"You have no cause nor right to be grateful," she said, her languor vanishing. "My affection for Monty has nothing to do with you." She tried to pull her hand free, but his grip tightened, and she was right. He was quite strong.

"True. But my feelings are my own. I reserve the right to feel anything I wish. Gratitude, disapproval, desire."

Her laugh was supposed to be light and airy. Instead it sounded bitter even to her own ears. "You don't feel desire, remember, Vicar?"

"I don't give in to desire. It doesn't mean I don't feel it quite profoundly. Unlike you."

She froze. "Don't be ridiculous. As you put it so elegantly, I spread my legs for anyone. I like to sleep with men. Is that so hard to believe? You think only men feel sexual desire?"

"I think women feel sexual desire quite strongly. I just don't think you do. You're a fake, a poseur, Lady Whitmore. You may open your legs, for whatever twisted reason you have, but you never open your heart."

Since he wasn't releasing her hand, she moved closer still, pressing her body up against his, her anger overcoming every other feeling that might have tempered it. "Spare me your homilies, Vicar, they make me ill." She rubbed up against him, like a cat in heat, mocking him, but as he released her hand he caught her arms, putting her away from him. But not before she felt the unmistakable outline of his erection.

"My, my . . . It seems the legendary holy man vow of celibacy might be ready to take a tumble. Unless you walk around with a spyglass tucked in your breeches. It seems you want me to spread my legs for *you*." Her smile was mocking as she waited for him to push her away.

He wouldn't pull her back, she knew she was safe. She didn't want someone like Simon Pagett in her bed — he saw her with uncomfortable clarity. She preferred drunken lordlings and —

"I gave up meaningless couplings outside of marriage for reasons you couldn't pos-

247

sibly understand."

"Try me. And I do mean that."

"No," he said flatly.

"There it is again. *No. Don't. Never.* You really should find new words. Like *Yes. Do. Always.*"

His fingers tightened, and he was going to kiss her. His grip was almost painful, and he lifted her off her feet, pulling her closer, and she wanted this kiss more than she'd ever wanted anything in her life. His hands hurt her, though she doubted he realized what he was doing, and she closed her eyes, waiting for his mouth to meet hers.

And then she found herself plopped down on the floor, unceremoniously. "I refuse to play your games, Lady Whitmore."

She should have left well enough alone. He was far more of a danger to her equilibrium than the men she slept with — he had the capability of destroying all her hard-won defenses. But she couldn't stop herself.

"Coward," she said.

Monty let out a soft snore. Before she realized what was happening, Simon had grabbed her arms again and pushed her outside the tall French doors, out onto the stone terrace in the early-morning light. He pushed her up against the stone facing, holding her there, and put his mouth on hers.

It was astonishing. It was full-mouthed, seething with lust and abandon, and for a moment she froze. She'd been kissed like that before, and she knew all the tricks of a measured response. But those clever tricks evaporated, and she closed her eyes, sinking, sinking. He kissed her with a fierce hunger that shook her to her bones, a deep, carnal kiss that was more sexual than anything she'd done in her entire life.

He lifted his head, glaring down at her. "You think I don't feel desire, Lady Whitmore? That's not a trout inside my breeches. You think I don't want you? You're the only woman to make me this crazy in ten years. You think I couldn't betray my conscience and take you standing up against the wall, right here, right now? Damn you."

He gave her a little shake, and she let out a small, a very small murmur of distress.

"But you don't fool me. You don't like men, you don't like sex, which is far worse than simply being a loose woman. You don't even get pleasure out of the act."

"I get —" Her denial was immediate, but he cut her off.

"No, you don't. Which is why I'm not going to betray everything I believe in, in

249

service to whatever sick game you like to play. I won't do it. Damn you." He pulled her back into his arms, and she looked up at him, torn, confused, longing. "Damn you," he said again, just a whisper, and his mouth found hers.

The kiss was gentle this time, but there was nothing innocent about it. It was sweet and sexual, a kiss of such unbridled longing that it frightened her, and she reached up, meaning to push him away, but instead her arms went around his neck and pulled him closer, down to her, losing herself in the wonder of his mouth.

It was amazing that anything could penetrate the sudden, unexpected, sweet haze of longing that swept over her as he wrapped his arms around her. Just her name, in a hoarse whisper, and she yanked herself away, expecting that Monty had woken up.

Instead she saw three figures at the end of the wide terrace. Two liveried figures, and a limp, berobed woman in between.

Charlotte.

14

Adrian Rohan lounged in the chair, surveying the busy club with a jaundiced eye.
There was a great deal of noise coming from
the faro table, where someone had clearly
just won or lost a fortune. Normally Adrian
would have risen and strolled over to see
who had changed their life, at least for the
day, but he was bored, restless, annoyed.
Gaming had lost its charm for him, wine its
taste, sex its delight. For the past three
weeks Etienne had tried to interest him in
his old pursuits, but nothing managed to
entertain him. He'd made an effort, letting
his father's cousin drag him off to the clubs,
the bordellos, but nothing was able to
capture his interest.

Not even the remarkable prowess of Madame Kate's best fellatrix could do more
than produce a desultory release, when
normally he would have enjoyed the act immensely. He moved through his life with a

stunning apathy. He was tired of everything, including Etienne de Giverney, who was growing ever more tedious in his attempts to distract him. Drink bored him, high-stakes gaming was tepid, he'd had every woman that caught his fancy, everything was flat and tasteless.

"That fool Lindenham," Etienne wheezed as he sank into the chair opposite him. "Wagered the family estate on a roll of the dice. Always a bad idea, no matter how lucky he seemed to have been earlier in the evening. He'll probably blow his brains out in a fortnight."

"Or win it back next week," Adrian said absently. "Etienne, I'm thinking I might rusticate. Town has grown dreadfully stale lately, and I'm thinking a bit of fresh air and exercise might improve my spirits."

"You had plenty of fresh air and exercise at Montague's place. Then again, your little piece of fluff didn't let you out of your cave at all — no wonder you're feeling the need of blue sky. Assuming you'll find it in this dreadful country."

"If you don't like our weather you could always return to France, cousin," Adrian suggested in a sweet voice, unaccountably annoyed.

"And lose my head? I think not! I'm more

than happy to wait out the revolution right here. It won't be long before the canaille give up. As long as they keep executing each other there soon won't be anyone left to rule, and they'll have no choice but to invite us back."

"As you say," Adrian murmured, having heard all this before.

"Anyway, your estate adjoins that of your impressive *père,* my boy. I have a difficult time feeling comfortable in the wilds of Dorset."

"I wasn't aware that I had asked for your company," Adrian murmured, his light tone taking the sting from the insult.

Etienne smiled with just a trace of malice. "Ah, but I know I am welcome wherever you go. Otherwise you risk the chance of becoming sadly bored, and I couldn't allow that to happen to my young protégé."

The word startled Adrian. Did Etienne really see him as a protégé? In what? Etienne's expertise was reserved for depravity and excess, and Adrian considered he did well enough on his own in that area.

Then again, what was the Viscount Rohan known for? The same kind of libertine behavior as Etienne, though in truth his bad behavior tended to be overlooked, due to the fact that he was both titled and unmarried.

Etienne didn't live on quite such an exalted level, and if it hadn't been for Adrian's sponsorship he would have been persona non grata at any number of places. He wasn't well liked. The English distrust of the French, even those exiled by their current bloodthirsty mess, was enough to keep Etienne from joining the uppermost tiers of society, the ones Adrian took for granted. Etienne would be welcome at gatherings of the Heavenly Host, or galas thrown by women of dubious reputation, such as the notorious Lady Whitmore. But he was barely tolerated in his parents' household, and he'd been given the cut direct more than once since he'd been in England.

"I wouldn't think of dragging you away from London during the season," Adrian said with a touch more grace. "I simply find myself in need of a bit of solitude. I expect I'll go mad with boredom and be back within the week."

Etienne surveyed him for a long moment. "Why would you be in need of solitude? I've known you all your life, and I don't remember a time when you weren't ready for a lark."

"I was fairly subdued when my brother died." The words came out before he could stop them.

"Ah, yes," said Etienne in a suitably somber voice. "The poor boy. I wish I could have done more for him. So young, so strong, and then just . . . gone. The fever swept through him so quickly. I think your father blames me for his death."

"Don't be absurd," Adrian said in a sharp voice. "It was scarcely your fault."

"Of course it wasn't. But I expect your father believes that English doctors might have been able to save him. That if he'd taken that fall when he'd been at home, the fever might not have been so virulent."

He hated this conversation. He hated talking about Charles Edward. His death at age nineteen had been devastating for all of them, but for a thirteen-year-old with a severe case of hero worship it had been unbearable.

He surveyed his cousin coolly. "You don't know my father very well. He's not the kind of man who spends time with words like *if only.* He took my brother's death hard, but the only one he blames is himself, for letting Charles Edward ride that horse in the first place."

"The horse belonged to me," Etienne

255

pointed out.

"So he did. And you warned Charles Edward many times. Unfortunately the more you warned him the more determined he became. Being willful and headstrong seems to run in our family."

"Indeed," Etienne said. "You realize that that was when I stopped practicing medicine for good. If I couldn't save my beloved cousin's oldest son then what good was any of it?"

Adrian turned to look at him, biting back his instinctive retort. Charles Edward would have hated the fuss — he'd been young, carefree, determined to live his life to the fullest, and he would have mocked any excessive mourning on their part. And like Adrian, he despised hypocrisy.

Francis Rohan, the Marquess of Haverstoke, was no more beloved than Adrian was a monk. The two cousins, Etienne and Francis, had genially despised each other. Etienne had always been convinced that Francis had stolen his birthright, simply by being born on the right side of the blanket. Bastard or not, Etienne de Giverney was French, and believed that he and he alone should be the comte de Giverney and hold in possession the family estates and the vast house in Paris.

Francis had given them to him. And the Reign of Terror had taken them away, a few short years later.

"I doubt my father appreciates your sacrifice," Adrian said wryly. Etienne's abandonment of his medical career had coincided with his claiming the disputed title — the comte de Giverney would hardly have kept his surgery open, the surgery Rohan money had paid for.

"No, your father has always questioned my affection for him," Etienne said sadly. And then he brightened. "Lady Kate is bringing in new girls, including an African one. Why don't I see if we can take them with us when we rusticate. It would certainly make the time go more quickly. And I can have them ship several cases of the cognac I've just taken possession of. The time will pass in a trice."

"Etienne, I have no desire for the time to pass quickly. No desire for African whores, cognac, or, I'm afraid, your company."

Etienne looked taken aback. "Well," he said. "I see. I had no idea my friendship had become burdensome. I'll relieve you of it . . ."

"Don't be tiresome, Etienne," Adrian said. "You know I love you, and there's no one I'd rather spend time with." A month ago, a week ago, that would have been true. Now, for all his polite protests, he wanted nothing more than to get away from him. "It's simply that I want some time alone. Is that so difficult to comprehend?"

Etienne was clearly undecided as to whether he should continue to be offended or let Adrian charm him out of it. "It's not like you," he said grumpily. "And I don't believe it's good for you. The season has barely begun. If you still feel the need to rusticate in another month then I won't argue."

This was getting as tedious as everything else, and Adrian gave in. "A month," he agreed. He looked around him. "Where's that boy with the wine? My glass is empty." He managed to summon up a smile. "I'll wager a hundred pounds he doesn't come before I have to go fetch him."

"Done," said Etienne, grinning at him. "Though I might have to borrow the hundred pounds. I'm running a bit short nowadays."

"Just get the boy here sooner and you'll win the money."

"But if you lend me the hundred pounds for the wager then when I win I'll have two hundred," Etienne said, practical as always.

Adrian laughed. "So you will. Consider it

done. We'll settle up tomorrow."

He didn't really want to go to the country, he thought, tossing back the glass that Etienne had seen promptly filled. He didn't want to be alone, with nothing to distract him. He didn't want to be thinking about the look on Charlotte Spenser's face when he was inside her. He didn't want to be thinking about any woman. He wanted to get roaring drunk, visit Lady Kate's bawdy house and work out his frustrations.

Charlotte had never taken him in her mouth. There hadn't been time to talk her into that particular delight. Perhaps he could enjoy Lady Kate's specialist again. Or he could simply see if the madam had a girl with coppery hair in her exotic stable.

Faith, one wench was as good as another. He hadn't truly enjoyed those two days in his little cave, had he? It must have been the novelty of it that made it stick in his mind. If he'd had an experienced woman the time would have passed in a much more pleasant fashion.

Then again, if he'd an experienced woman he would have never activated the locked door, and he would have gotten rid of her as soon as he politely could. So perhaps his current edginess was simple boredom, the need for novelty.

He could seek out other virgins, like some of the Heavenly Host were wont to do. Or he could broaden his horizons and consider men.

No, he couldn't see the appeal.

Which brought him around to the question of Montague. After taking off in pursuit of Charlotte, he hadn't seen his old friend again. He'd looked more frail than usual, and it was difficult to tell whether the bright spots of color on his pale face were signs of fever or a lavish hand with the rouge pot. If he retired to the country for a bit he could go by way of Sussex, check on Monty to make sure he was feeling well. He hadn't been in town this season, and Adrian had the lowering feeling that Monty's London days were at an end.

As long as he didn't die. No one had died in Adrian's life, no one he truly cared about, since Charles Edward, in France, fifteen years ago. Of course, he refused to allow himself to care about anyone outside his family, and his mother and four sisters all tended to give birth easily, without the dangers usually inherent. He already had seven nieces and nephews, and while he'd been intemperate enough to adore them, he was cheered by the fact that they were incredibly healthy little monsters. Even so, he did his best to keep his distance from his sisters and their families.

He could just say to hell with Etienne, take off, and by the time he found out it would be too late to talk him out of it. But that smacked of cowardice, and Adrian had never shied away from a challenge in his life.

Besides, the nervy bastard would probably just follow him out to the country. Why Etienne seemed so intent on his company was an absolute mystery. When he'd first appeared on the London scene and attached himself to Adrian he'd been flattered by the older man's attention, not to mention completely in favor of the dangerous excesses he exposed him to.

But the delight had definitely begun to wane.

He rose, sauntering over to the faro table where Etienne seemed to have grown roots. "I find I'm unaccountably tired," he murmured. "I'm heading for an early night. Shall I see you at the ridotto tomorrow night?"

Etienne's small frown turned approving. "It will be my pleasure. Though I would think we'd find more . . . specialized entertainment elsewhere than Ranelagh Gardens. Things tend to be so English there."

Once again the irritation rose. "You're *in* England, Etienne. What do you expect?"

Another night of boredom, Adrian thought as he strolled the few blocks from the gambling club to the small house on Curzon Street he'd bought for a mistress several years ago and then moved into once she'd moved on to greener pastures. The night was cool and clear, the recent rain having washed the stink from the streets, and he was reminded of the night air in Sussex. The chapel that Monty had had constructed, the Portal of Venus.

He slashed his ebony walking stick in the air, annoyed with himself. And continued determinedly onward.

Miss Charlotte Spenser sat in a large, comfortable chair in the solarium in Evangelina, the Countess of Whitmore's mansion. The greenery was abundant, the air moist and warm, and the scent of fresh spring flowers filled the air. She was drinking a cup of tea. Not the wretched stuff that Lina had been forcing down her throat by the gallons, but nice strong, black, English tea, with a little milk and a great deal of sugar. So far it was easier on the stomach than that evil brew.

It had been three weeks since the Revels

of the Heavenly Host. Her twisted ankle had healed nicely, the scrapes and bruises from her tumble down the embankment were almost gone. It should have been hard to believe any of it had ever happened. It was only when her mind started to drift that the feel of his hands, his mouth his . . . *cock,* he'd called it. She could almost feel everything again, and she wanted to weep.

Charlotte Spenser wasn't a weakling. This was hardly that traumatic — no one had to know anything about it.

But she found herself looking at hands. Lina had any number of callers, but for some reason she'd stayed home recently, and no one had spent the night with her. The gentlemen came, and she looked for hands as beautiful as Rohan's. With long, artist's fingers, deft and elegant, and narrow palms. Clever, beautiful hands.

She'd known she'd never find a man with a face that pleased her as much as Rohan's. And no one had that lithe, agile body, that almost feline grace.

But she'd hoped she'd find comparable hands.

There weren't any. The men of the ton had hands that were pale, well kept. But either their fingers were too short or their palms too squat, their fingers stubby.

263

She sighed. It was impossible, and she knew it.

The more time passed, the easier things would be, she promised herself. For the first week she did nothing but weep, something that alarmed poor Lina, who'd seldom seen her stalwart best friend shed a tear, much less become a total watering pot. It hadn't taken Meggie long to ferret out the truth of how she'd spent the time in Sussex — Charlotte was unused to lying, unused to secrets and feeling too miserable to resist Meggie's efforts, and from then on Lina knew everything. It had taken all Charlotte's limited energy and threats to keep Lina from her declared revenge, with only common sense finally tempering Lina's desire to defend Charlotte. "If you make a fuss then everyone will know," Charlotte had said. "It was my choice — I wasn't forced. And the last thing I want to do is end up married to a libertine. I think he was an excellent choice to deflower me, once I decided that was an interesting idea, but anything more than that would be disastrous."

Lina had been distracted. "Just how excellent was he?"

"I'm not about to tell you. Besides, I have nothing to compare him with," Charlotte had said primly, trying not to gag on the herbal tisane Lina insisted upon her drinking.

"But you enjoyed it? He made it pleasurable? You achieved . . . rapture?"

Charlotte had felt her face flush. "Yes."

"Damn," said Lina.

"I beg your pardon?"

"Well, I'm certainly not going anywhere near him now. I consider him your property, and I would never trespass."

"He's hardly my property. Have at him," she'd said with an airy wave of her hand, almost managing to convince herself she meant it. "After all, you wanted him first."

"Now, I know that isn't true. You've been pining for him these last three years, God knows why. Admittedly he's gorgeous, but you're hardly the type to be overset by simple beauty. Why?"

Because he has sad eyes, she could have said. Because he tries so very hard to be bad, to be mean, to be cruel, and all you have to do is look past the studied ennui to see a hurt little boy trying to emerge. And, yes, because he's bloody gorgeous.

But she said none of this. To say it out loud would burn it into her heart.

"I have no idea. But I'm done with him. Feel free to try your luck."

"No," Lina had said firmly. "Drink your tea."

Which she'd done, quite dutifully. And been rewarded, a week ago, with a few betraying drops of blood signaling the onset of her menses. Nothing had happened since then, but it was enough to ensure nothing had come of the two illicit days with him. After all, he'd . . . he'd pulled out of her, hadn't he? To ensure that nothing untoward had happened.

She'd tried to explain that to Lina but gotten hopelessly tongue-tied. "Never mind, darling," Lina had said. "I know what you mean, and I thank God he had at least that much sense. You'll still drink the tea. Accidents can happen, and nothing is ever foolproof."

And so it went. The doctor had declared her right as rain from the aftermath of her fall, and Charlotte refused to let him examine her more intimately. Nothing had happened to her that hadn't happened to most women in the world — it was hardly worthy of medical interest.

In the end it had been an all-around disastrous idea on her part, dressing up to play with the Mad Monks. She knew why she did it. Not for scientific inquiry, it had been for Rohan — she'd been drawn to him

266

in all his self-destructive glory. Seeing him in flagrante delicto was supposed to cure her, wasn't it?

Instead she was even more tethered. If she'd stayed a virgin she would never have known what she was missing, and this was a rare case where ignorance was bliss. Not as much bliss as carnal knowledge . . . but a different sort of bliss. A nice, solid, serene sort of bliss that was much lacking in Charlotte's life for the last few weeks.

The one thing that both Meggie and Lina didn't know was that she hadn't just fallen down that embankment, she'd been pushed. By one of the Mad Monks.

And she had the unbearable suspicion that it might have been Adrian himself.

Lina swept into the solarium, her full skirts dancing on their hoops. "Darling, you're not wearing that hideous old dress, are you? This is your first night out since Sussex. Surely you can look a little more lively."

Charlotte set down her tea. "I was thinking we might wait another few days. I'm not sure that my ankle is completely healed, and I don't seem to have regained my usual energy. We can start with a walk in the park, perhaps tomorrow, instead of a ridotto at Ranelagh Gardens."

"A *walk?*" Lina demanded, horrified. "Sweetings, I don't walk. Besides, Ranelagh will be just the thing. Apart from the masquerade, there will be music in the rotunda, dancing and all sorts of amusement."

"I hate masquerades. Besides, if I'm to have a domino to cover me from head to foot then why does it matter what I wear?"

"In case you wish to wander down one of the private paths with a gentleman and unmask."

"I may have lost my virtue, but I haven't become a trollop," Charlotte said sharply, and then clapped her hand over her mouth. Wandering alone down private pathways was the main reason Lina went to Ranelagh.

"Don't worry, Charlotte," Lina said, totally unperturbed. "It will take a great deal more than that for you to reach my exalted realms. Besides, I've given it up."

"Given what up?"

"Dalliance. You see before you a new woman, above such tawdry stuff as assignations and lovers. I intend to be sober and devote myself to good works."

Charlotte looked at her in amazement. "You're joking."

Lina smiled. "A bit. But I've grown weary of bed sport. It won't harm me to give it up for the time being. So, don't worry, I won't leave your side tonight. We'll have darling old Sir Percy Wainbridge as our escort, and no importunate gentlemen will be allowed to steal either of us away."

"I still don't —"

"And I assure you that Viscount Rohan has never been seen inside the confines of Ranelagh Gardens. He much prefers the tawdrier pleasures of Vauxhall, and even that's too tame for him. He prefers gaming hells and brothels. You don't need to worry about running into him. Does that set your mind at ease?"

"I wasn't worried about that in the slightest," Charlotte lied.

"Of course you weren't. And you'll wear that pretty green dress that you always leave hanging in your closet, and just to make you feel entirely secure we'll both powder our hair. It's out of style except for old ladies, and the tax on hair powder is ruinous, but it's just the thing for a masquerade. Do it for me, love. We need to celebrate! Your recovery and my celibacy! Cheers!"

"Cheers," Charlotte said with a singular lack of enthusiasm. And went upstairs to change.

15

It was a beautiful spring night. After a week of rain the skies had finally cleared, the moon was bright overhead and the air was soft and warm. It was a night made for lovers, Charlotte thought grimly, glad of the mask and domino. Her scowl should scare anyone away, and if Lina forgot her vow of celibacy and decided to seduce their elderly escort she could always manage an early escape.

Unfortunately, Lina showed no sign of abjuring her recent commitment. Her thick black hair was powdered but arranged neatly, with only the most demure of sapphire and diamond-studded hairpins scattered here and there. While she hadn't avoided the rouge pot completely, she'd used a far less lavish hand, and she'd abandoned beauty patches altogether. If her intent was to play down her spectacular beauty it was a failed effort. Amazingly, without the artifice she was practically incandescent.

Her gown beneath the somber black domino was even more demure than Charlotte's. For some reason, Lina had ordered a whole raft of dresses with more sedate décolletage, in softer shades than her usual bright crimson and royal blue. Instead the new dresses were a soft rose, a moss green, a pale blue that perfectly matched her eyes. She was more exquisite than ever.

Fortunately or unfortunately, depending on how Charlotte wanted to look at it, all that beauty was hidden by the mask and domino. With the powdered hair, she could have been mistaken for anyone, even Charlotte.

"It's a bad night," Charlotte said darkly, looking around her.

"Don't be ridiculous," Lina said. "It's glorious out — it would be a crime to spend such a night indoors."

"It's a full moon. Meggie warned me before I left. She said there's trouble afoot. Men behave badly when the moon is full."

"You need to tell that wretched girl to keep her tongue in her mouth. Besides, men behave badly no matter what."

"Maybe we ought to go home," Charlotte said stubbornly. "There's no need to court trouble."

"You're being absurd," Lina said firmly. "We're here and we're going to enjoy ourselves. Sir Percy's going to bespeak us an excellent supper, there's a concert in the rotunda and dancing in the pavilions. We needn't dance if you mislike it, Charlotte, but remember that no one can tell who we are. This way you can enjoy yourself without any fear of being recognized. You can flirt madly, with no consequences, and who knows, you might find you enjoy it."

Charlotte didn't even bother answering such absurdity. She was tired, her appetite was off and the last thing she wanted to do was make a fool of herself on the dance floor. All she wanted to do was go home and go to bed. And clearly Lina wasn't about to take pity on her and release her.

Sir Percy, seventy if he was a day, bowed, his own bewigged head bobbing a little low. Of all Lina's safe escorts, Sir Percy was her favorite, a consummate gentleman of the old school who found all women delightful and flirted so well that even Charlotte lost her reserve and flirted back a bit.

They moved down the well-lit paths, nodding at others in fancy dress. Some were quite recognizable, wearing outfits meant to look like those from ancient Greece or exotic China, but mainly constructed to show off the feminine figure. Most of the men made do with a simple loo mask that they could raise or lower as they willed, and the few who were in fancy dress contented themselves with an enveloping domino.

The gardens were in full regalia, with lights everywhere except the paths meant for flirtations and the lovers' maze behind them. The artificial canal was afloat with small boats meant to resemble Venetian gondolas, there were strolling minstrels in the Italian style, acrobats and jugglers and all manner of entertainment. Charlotte just wished they'd all go away.

Dinner was relatively vile, for all that the meals were famous. The best she could manage was a little bread and the blanc-mange, and even that didn't seem to be sitting too well. Meggie's predictions of disaster had affected her, she decided. In truth, Lina was right. It *was* a beautiful night, and after such a rainy spring it would be foolish not to enjoy it.

Charlotte sat alone at a table in the grass, toying with her glass of lemonade. The thought of wine made her ill as well, but then, she'd never been overly fond of it. Lina had gone off with Sir Percy for a stately minuet, as befitted Sir Percy's age and Lina's attire, and Charlotte glanced around her.

It should have been an interesting sensation, being invisible among all these people, but then, she didn't need a mask, domino and powdered hair for that experience. In truth, she'd always been invisible to most of them.

A lively country dance had started up, and Charlotte began tapping her foot beneath her heavy skirts. Her ankle was almost as good as new, and if she were alone somewhere, out in the countryside, she would have danced.

Sir Percy returned to the table, his florid face flushed with delight. "Lady Whitmore's dancing with young Marchmont, and she sent me to collect you and to take no excuses."

"Oh, I don't dance," she said firmly.

"She told me you'd say that, and not to pay any attention."

She tried her best smile. "Truly, I can't. I hurt my ankle a few weeks back."

"She told me you'd say that as well. You haven't been favoring it. Be a good girl, now. I'm an old man and most young women won't dance with me. I tend to forget some of the figures, and people get impatient. And I do so love to dance."

He was doing his best to look pitiful, and there was nothing Charlotte could do. She could give any importunate young man a thorough set-down, but Sir Percy was the sweetest man in the world, and had always been a good friend to her.

She rose reluctantly, taking his proffered arm. "Wouldn't you rather go for a walk?" she asked somewhat desperately.

"Miss Spenser!" he said in shocked tones. "Are you suggesting we set up a flirtation? I'm deeply flattered, but I'm afraid I'm past such things."

She was about to explain herself, when she stopped. He was looking so pleased with himself at the thought of a flirtation that she didn't have the heart to disillusion him. "I'll dance."

She followed him into the pavilion. No one would ever recognize her, she reminded herself. Her distinctive red hair was now a lavender-white, the half mask covered enough of her face and the domino took care of the rest. She could trip anyone, send them sprawling, and no one would ever be able to attribute it to her.

Indeed, she could use it as an excuse to kick several people she'd long considered deserving of a swift kick.

The melody was an old favorite, "Tom

Scarlett," and Sir Percy drew her into it before she could hesitate, and for a moment she froze as the other dancers made their prescribed moves around her.

And then the music caught her again. One foot started tapping, then she moved the other foot forward, and suddenly the dance took over, and she was moving, dancing, her body alive with delight, her feet sure as she followed the intricate figures.

She would have left the floor once it was done, but the next was a slower, statelier dance, and she couldn't resist, twirling around Sir Percy, around her contrary, around her neighbor, never missing a step. The music sped up, growing livelier, and she moved faster, throwing back her head and laughing with the joy of it. As they performed a figure of eight she passed by Lina, and she didn't need to see her face behind the full mask to know she was mouthing "I told you so" as they went.

She was breathless, laughing when the song finished, and clearly Sir Percy, who was sadly stout, had grown winded, but young Marchmont, a stripling no more than seventeen, all arms and legs and wild enthusiasm, grabbed her, and she was dancing again, a more complicated set, and one she followed with amazing aplomb. It was the first time she'd been able to smile in three weeks — her body felt strong, glorious, as she swirled through the wonderful music.

Lina's new partner was an elderly military gentleman, and they'd joined a different set. Charlotte glanced toward her as she stepped into a poussette, changing partners as she moved toward the outward wall. Lina's face was still covered, but she was gesturing strangely, her hands moving in a panicked figure that had nothing to do with the dance. Charlotte mouthed "what" back at her, but the dance made another turn, and she switched partners to dance with a spotty young man in his twenties, who was almost as clumsy as she once had been.

Her heart melted for the poor boy, who seemed so earnest, and she whispered instructions in his ear every time they did a pass, and eventually he gave her a broad smile as he caught on to the complicated figure.

And then another poussette, and she took the hand of her new partner as she twirled around him. It was God's mercy that the touch called for in the dance was only momentary, because she'd crossed to the other side, curtsying, before she realized she was facing Adrian Rohan.

She almost stumbled in shock, but something kept her moving. She saw Lina in the background, having taken off her mask, and her beautiful face was creased in dismay. Clearly she'd been trying to warn her.

Bloody hell, Charlotte thought a little wildly. He couldn't recognize her, and she was having a wonderful time. She wasn't going to let his unexpected appearance stop her. There were only three more figures with her current partner, and then they'd move on to the next one, and the moment the dance was ended, Lina was waiting to whisk her away. But oh, merciful heavens, it was a Mad Robin, which called for the current partners to maintain eye contact while they slid in front and behind their neighbors.

Her glasses had never reappeared, and in the best of worlds it would leave her unable to see him very well. But in truth, she had only needed them to read, and she could see into his gorgeous blue eyes quite clearly. They were watching her, no discernible expression in them, and she breathed a sigh of relief. She was just a stranger on a dance floor, someone to pass by as the figures called for it. Even if she was taller than most women she was hardly singular. He wouldn't notice. He had no particular interest in her, and he most certainly didn't recognize her.

She moved back into place, dropping her eyes. One more step, and it was the Gipsy. The two of them would meet in the center, circling each other, and it put her uncomfortably in mind of predator and prey.

He didn't know her, she reminded herself, moving carefully as he seemed to stalk her. He danced beautifully, she remembered now, which was probably the reason she'd made such a botch of it the one other time she'd danced with him. She'd already been enamored of him and feeling undignified and silly about it, and his grace on the dance floor had paralyzed her.

This time she was prepared. She knew he was irresistible, moving with catlike grace on the dance floor and off. She glanced at his mouth, unable to stop herself, remembering the feel of it against hers, remembering the feel of his entire body pressed up against hers, skin to skin, warm and moist, muscles taut and straining, hearts pounding . . .

Her face was flushed, her breath coming fast, and she knew it wasn't because of the dance. She held out her hands, crossed, for the final hand-off, and even through two pairs of gloves she could feel his skin, his strength — feel *him* — and suddenly she wanted to cry.

And then he was gone, and she was going through the same movements with a plump, middle-aged gentleman, and she'd survived. She hadn't tripped, hadn't betrayed herself in any way, and Adrian Rohan hadn't even looked back.

She was almost back with Marchmont, and she breathed a sigh of relief. Once she regained her original partner the dance would be over, and she could escape. She wanted to laugh out loud in triumph, she wanted to burst into tears. Her emotions were way too close to the surface, not like her at all. There was one more right to left, as they circled the dance floor, exchanging hands. It would bring her back to Rohan one more time, but he was looking bored, and his partner, a sweet young beauty, was going to lose him once the dance was over, and she told herself she shouldn't be glad of it.

She slid, turned and began the right to left, acutely aware of his approach. His gloved hand touched hers for a brief moment, strong hands, warm hands, and then he moved on, never even looking at her, and Marchmont was back, smiling.

Before he could draw her into another dance, Lina had caught up with her. She'd put her mask back on, but her distress was more than clear. "I'm so sorry, dearest," she said in a muffled voice. "Of all the miserable chances! I couldn't believe it when I saw him here. And to end up in your set! Do you think he recognized you?"

"Absolutely not," she said in a calm, sure voice. "But just in case, don't you think we should leave now?"

"I do indeed. We'll have to find out where Sir Percy went. He's probably in one of the card rooms. He loves to dance, but there's only so long he can keep it up."

Charlotte pulled her hand free. She cast a nervous glance over her shoulder, but there was no sign of the viscount. His erstwhile partner was now flirting with someone new, surviving his abandonment better than she herself had, Charlotte thought. "Lina, I think it best if I go ahead. It's a short walk to the edge of the park, and there are plenty of chairs and hackneys to convey me back to Grosvenor Square. You find Sir Percy and I'll meet you at home."

"I can't leave you alone in a place like this," Lina protested.

"Of course you can. No one's going to mistake me for a trollop, and I can promise you, no one would dare accost me."

"No one might dare accost Charlotte Spenser with her glower," Lina said, "but

281

the mystery woman in the deep red domino who danced so happily is a different matter."

"Don't worry — I can still glower with the best of them. Truly, Lina, the sooner I leave here the better, and you can't very well abandon Sir Percy, now, can you?"

"I suppose not. If you wait a moment I could find Marchmont and have him escort you. . . ."

She glanced back at the dancers, but Marchmont was already in another set and she didn't dare hesitate. "I'll be fine. There are going to be any number of times when I won't have a gentleman to escort me places, and I refuse to allow that to keep me a prisoner. I'll see you back at the house," she said firmly.

"At least humor me by heading toward the south entrance. That way if I can find Sir Percy in time we could meet up with you."

One entrance was as good as another. "Of course," she said, having absolutely no intention of doing so. The west entrance was closer, albeit past the maze and a tangle of lovers' walks. Her earlier elation had vanished, and in its place was a desperate need to cry again. Tears were a weakness she despised, but the catch in her throat seemed to have a mind of its own. The least she could do was find the safety of a carriage and give way to tears there.

She started toward the south entrance with her domino pulled tight about her, her long legs eating up the distance. The west entrance was just past a row of private dining rooms, and she knew a moment's nervousness when she veered to the right, into the dimly lit walkways. If worse came to worst, she could run faster than any of these mincing creatures in their jeweled heels. Not that Adrian had been wearing heels — he was tall enough as it was. Not that he'd be chasing after her.

The catch in her throat had now spread to a burning in her eyes. She was too hot in the domino and mask, but she wasn't about to relinquish them until she was away from this suddenly awful place. No one would know, she reminded herself, pulling the cloak more tightly around her.

The intricate paths looked deserted. Most people preferred to do their courting by the canal that ran through the east side of the park, and the rest were either dancing or eating dinner. There would be no one around to bother her. She headed down one dimly lit path, trying to hold in the tears until she could finally find some privacy.

She'd forgotten the entrance to the maze was disguised. It was part of the game — people out for a casual walk would suddenly find themselves lost. Charlotte had heard about it, but she'd seldom ventured into the pleasure gardens, and she had no idea that she had walked where she shouldn't have until suddenly she was at a dead end, the thick branches blocking her.

Simple enough. She turned around and headed back the way she came. She had an excellent memory, and she'd only made a couple of turns. One more, and she'd be back out on the pathway.

One more, and she came to another dead end. She took a deep, steadying breath. She held still, trying to orient herself, when she heard the breathing.

Someone was there. It shouldn't unnerve her — she was in a public place. Of course people would be around. Perhaps whoever it was could help her get out of the maze.

"Hello?" she said in a hopeful voice.

There was no answer. And yet she could still hear the breathing — whoever it was made no attempt at covering it up. There was a faint wheeze to the breathing, as if whoever was there had raced to catch up with her. Someone older, playing a game with her.

"Sir Percy?" she called out, wondering if this was his mistaken notion of flirtation. There was still no answer, and she realized with sudden discomfort that someone was watching her. Presumably the same someone who was breathing so heavily. The interior of the maze was shadowed and dark, with only the light outside on the path to illuminate it. The walls of the maze weren't as thick as boxwood, and someone could doubtless see through them. She tried to peer through them herself, but there were four sides to try to look through, and she could see no one.

She felt the skin prickle at the back of her neck. She had the sudden, eerie feeling that whoever, whatever, was watching her was malevolence personified.

"I'm not in the mood for games," she said bravely. "Either show yourself or go away."

Her watcher did neither. He did something far, far worse. He laughed, a low, rasping, ugly laugh that caused her heart to slam into a full-blown panic.

"Be damned to you, then," she cried, trying to sound fearless and failing. Whoever was in the maze with her was far from harmless. He was evil.

Wasn't there a trick about mazes, that if you kept a hand on one wall the entire time you'd soon find your way out? Whoever was watching her was somewhere near the center of the maze, and if she kept going that way, she'd run into him. The very last thing she wanted to do. She had two choices, either the right way or the wrong way. She could only pray that she chose the right way.

Putting her hand out, she started moving, quickly, her feet stumbling a little bit over the ground as she moved.

And then she heard him behind her, the noise growing louder as he moved with her. Which meant she was heading in the right direction, she thought, almost sobbing with relief. If she'd been heading toward him he simply would have waited for her, like a spider.

She sped up, ignoring scratches from the greenery, ignoring the lingering pain in her ankle from her recent fall.

Faster, faster, her own breath catching in her throat, the stays digging into her, the branches catching on her flying domino. She was going to be murdered, someone would toss her body in the Thames — no one would ever find her, if she didn't move faster —

The entrance to the maze appeared before she realized where she was. She stumbled out onto the pathway, her breath sobbing in her throat, straight into the arms of a well-dressed gentleman, almost knocking him over.

He put out strong, gloved hands to right her. The night had grown darker, and thank God she still wore her mask.

Because the man who held her arms was none other than Adrian, Viscount Rohan.

16

"Dear lady," Rohan said in that well-remembered voice, "may I be of assistance?"

She pulled herself away from him, stumbling a little on her weak ankle, as a wash of feelings tumbled over her. Relief. He couldn't have been the one chasing her through the maze. Someone else had been the threat, real or imagined.

Relief that he didn't recognize her. She had only a moment to think — should she try a French accent, or the cockney one Meggie had been coaching her on? She could manage a Yorkshire accent from living up north with her family, but it all seemed a bit too complicated. Chances were he wouldn't recognize her voice, but a bit of hoarseness would ensure it.

"Someone was in the maze, following me," she said in a breathless, throaty voice.

He moved past her to the entrance of the maze, pausing to listen. The silence was deafening. He turned and smiled at her, that charming smile that seldom reached into his fine eyes. For some reason it seemed to on this occasion, his hard blue eyes bright. Doubtless a trick of the lamplight.

"Whoever it was is gone now," he said. "But you should scarcely be out alone. Where is your escort?"

"My friend has gone in search of him," she said with all honesty. The problem with keeping her voice soft and husky is that it gave an unwanted intimacy to the conversation. "I decided rather than wait I would hire a hackney or a sedan chair to convey me home."

"Then allow me to accompany you until you procure one. It would be terribly remiss of me to allow a beautiful lady to wander alone on these dark paths."

She had only a moment to consider the wonder of being called a "beautiful lady" before she shook her head. "I thank you, sir, but I am more than capable of seeing to my own welfare."

"To wit, you wandered into a maze alone and were nearly assaulted. A gentleman couldn't possibly abandon a lady under such circumstances." His smile was so charming, so seemingly innocent, that she was both seduced and outraged. Outraged that his charm could be spread so easily to all and sundry, that he could fail to recognize her. Seduced because all the man had to do was look at her and her bones melted.

Had she learned nothing from her sojourn in the country, in his bed? It didn't matter how delicious he could make her feel. She was nothing more than a vessel for his lust, interchangeable, and the glorious, transcendent response he was able to coax from her wasn't worth the shame of his contemptuous treatment and dismissal.

And yet . . .

"No," she said firmly. "No, thank you, my lord. You're very kind, but I cannot be convinced that your company would be any safer than that of the man in the maze."

He laughed then. "You have every right to be careful. I'm capable of very bad behavior indeed. But I do stop short of pressing my attentions on women I don't know. I'm offering you safe escort, nothing more."

She was more than ready to keep arguing, when in the distance she heard Lina's voice, hectoring Sir Percy. "I saw her come this way . . ."

"Is that your companion?" he questioned politely.

"No!" If he recognized Lina it would only be a moment before he recognized her. She had to think fast. "Indeed, I would appreciate your assistance. Let's go."

Was there a trace of triumph on his mouth? She couldn't waste time deciphering his reaction, she simply put her gloved hand on his arm and proceeded to move.

His hand covered hers. "Wrong direction."

Bloody hell, she thought, certain he was about to turn her in the direction of Lina's voice, but instead he simply pulled her onto one of the side paths, into the darkness, moments before Lina and Sir Percy arrived on the scene.

She was moving so quickly she didn't stop to consider that he was making no effort to slow her rapid pace. His long legs kept up with her, and within moments they were out of earshot as well as out of sight, and she breathed a sigh of relief as he led her farther along the darkened path, slowing her headlong pace.

"Was there someone you wished to avoid? I mean, aside from your assailant," he said lazily.

"Of course not. Why would you say so?"

"Because you practically sprinted away from the maze when you heard people coming. Or is it simply that you don't wish to be seen with me?" There was that damnable undercurrent of amusement in his voice, the one she remembered. Did he find all women amusing?

"Why should I worry about being seen with you?"

"Because you clearly know who I am. You called me 'my lord,' and that was no accident. And if you know who I am then you doubtless know my reputation, which is far from stellar. Merely to be seen alone with me is enough to get you compromised."

She considered denying it. He was leading her farther away from the light, and she knew a sudden nervous anticipation. Was he going to make an advance under cover of darkness? She already knew he would never force her. Was there a chance she could enjoy one last, anonymous kiss before he placed her into a coach?

If he tried, she would let him, she decided. Her ankle was throbbing — she'd twisted it in the maze, reaggravating the injury, and she tried not to favor it more than necessary, not to lean on his strong arm.

"Viscount Rohan is fairly notorious, even for those of us who don't travel in his circles." She may as well be bold — pretended ignorance wasn't getting her anywhere. "We shared the same dance set earlier, and someone pointed you out to me."

"Did we?" he said, and her irritation increased. Were all women invisible to him, or only she?

She looked around her. It was quite dark, though she could see the occasional light up ahead. "Where are you taking me?" she demanded.

"Where do you think?" he countered.

She wasn't going to be forced into voicing her secret fears that were just as much desires. "I would hope you were taking me to the hackney stand on the west entrance of the park. Anything else would be unacceptable."

"And I would never think of doing anything unacceptable, fair lady," he said with exaggerated courtesy.

She wanted to kick him. He was flirting with a stranger, his charm given to anyone who took his fancy. This was a good thing, she told herself as the lights grew brighter. It was a salutary lesson as to how interchangeable she was. She'd meant nothing to him, the jaded son of a bitch. And if she hadn't been entirely over him before, she was now, she assured herself. The swiving, self-centered peacock, vain, selfish, offal-munching . . .

"Is something distressing you, oh mysterious one?" he murmured.

"Why would you say so?"

"Because you suddenly dug your fingers into my arm as if you wanted to rip my skin," he observed affably.

She pulled her hand away. "I beg your pardon," she said in her muffled voice. "I was thinking of someone."

"Were you indeed? Perhaps a former lover?"

"Why would you say that?"

"I've found most liaisons don't end well. At least one side is left feeling abandoned and hurting."

He'd pegged her well. She straightened her shoulders, continuing her forward stride. "If that is the case, sir, then why indulge in them? Wouldn't it be easier not to bother in the first place?"

He laughed softly. "The bother, as you sadly put it, is so delightful while it lasts," he murmured too close to her ear. "And I would never resist the call of delight."

She jumped away from him, unnerved, only to realize they'd somehow managed to reach the west end of the park, despite his circuitous route. And she didn't know whether to be relieved or disappointed.

There were hackneys lined up, as well as sedan chairs, a couple of open phaetons and a closed town coach. She breathed a sigh of relief. She was safer in the bright light — by sight she was totally unrecognizable. Granted, she was a tall woman, but she wore flat slippers when most women wore jeweled heels on their shoes, and she was trying to keep her head down. In the dark she was probably just as interchangeable as any of his other light o' loves, but she'd spent most of her time in the shadows with him. There might be other ways to tell him who she was, assuming he even remembered her existence.

She took her hand from his arm and gave him a small curtsy. "You've been very kind, Lord Rohan," she said. "I will bid you good-night . . ."

"Allow me to hand you into the carriage," he said politely, taking her arm and leading her toward one of them. In days to come she would berate herself for being so unobservant, but at the time she was so relieved to have made it through the evening without being recognized that she probably would have climbed into the royal coach without looking.

The door was opened, the steps came down, and he put his wide hands around her slim waist and lifted her into a closed carriage that was far too elegant to be a hired hackney, and then the coach dipped beneath his weight as he followed her in, closing the door behind them, shutting them into the darkness.

She opened her mouth to scream, but he simply stopped her with his mouth, kissing her, holding her still as the carriage moved forward with an almost imperceptible jerk.

She fought him, furious. She had thought he was above such shoddy tricks, absconding with unprotected females. She tried to use her knee, but he simply put one of his long, heavy ones over hers, trapping her in place. She tried her elbows, but his arm snaked around her, imprisoning her against him.

Oh, God, she wanted to kiss him back, she wailed inwardly, keeping her jaw clamped shut. She wanted to taste him, fall back against the squabs and let his mouth wander everywhere. His hand was cradling the back of her neck, slowly massaging it, and she could feel herself begin to melt anyway, soften against the steady pressure of his strong body.

He lifted his mouth for a brief moment, and in the darkness of the unlit carriage she could see the glitter of his eyes. "Open your mouth for me, Charlotte," he whispered. "I've been waiting hours to kiss you and I'm running out of patience."

Her shock was enough that she did as he told her, and his kiss was full and deep, a possessive hunger she felt vibrating through her body. She stopped struggling, when she knew full well she should have fought even harder. She let him kiss her, closing her eyes and savoring the taste of him in her mouth, and he pulled her unresisting body onto his lap.

"You can do better than that, sweet Charlotte. By the time I left you, you were growing quite adept. Give me your tongue."

"Give me yours," she murmured, "and I'll bite you."

She could feel the laugh rumble through his body as it pressed against hers. "No, you won't." And he proved it, tilting her head back, cradling it with one of his hands, and kissing her so thoroughly she felt as if she were melting against him. She made a small, whimpering noise, and she knew what it was. The sound of surrender.

He'd removed her loo mask and tossed it to one side, and he was busy unfastening the ribbons that held the domino close about her. "How could you think I wouldn't know you?" he chided softly. "I know the way you move, the way you bite your lip when you're nervous, the sound of your laughter, your eyes. I know your hands and your skin, your scent, the way you try to pretend that something doesn't bother you when you're very bothered indeed." He slid one hand down between them, between her thighs, and she tried to squirm away from him. "Though I must admit I'd like to hear your laugh more often. Perhaps see you scowl less and smile more."

"Leave me the hell alone," she said breathlessly, hoping the curse added the peremptory note that her aching voice lacked.

He caught her chin, pulling it up to meet his face, and she looked into his devastating smile. "I can't do that, love. That's been my problem for the last three weeks. I can't stop thinking about you, and I'm afraid no one else has managed to distract me."

So she wasn't alone in this, she thought miserably. That was something, at least. He lusted after her. She could feel his erection beneath her hips, and she moved, just enough, a subtle caress that made his arms tighten around her.

"Holy Christ," he muttered in her ear. "Don't do that."

"Why?"

"Because I'd like to wait until we get back to my house."

Her heart leaped into her throat. "I'm not going to your house."

"I'm afraid you are, love. You're in my carriage, and that's where we're heading. Don't worry — I'll send a note to Lady Whitmore, telling her you're safe. No one else will have any idea you've gone off for a libidinous interlude."

"I'm not going anywhere at all with you. Leave this carriage."

"It's *my* carriage," he said apologetically. "I made arrangements after I saw you dancing. You told me you didn't dance. Come to think of it, I remember an occasion when you trampled on my feet hard enough to cripple me for days. Do you save your wicked clumsiness for me alone?"

She could feel the color flood her face. Suddenly it was three years before and she was gawky, clumsy, so in awe of the man that her feet didn't move. New strength swept through her, and she yanked herself out of his arms. He let her go, and she ended up on the opposite side of the coach, glaring at him.

"I don't dance."

"Don't be ridiculous. You danced with me, and with several other fortunate gentlemen. I was quite annoyed with them."

He was lying. It was all part of his mockery, and she couldn't understand what pleasure he derived out of being so cruel.

"Have you ever seen me dance in public, my lord? Normally I would assume you wouldn't have paid attention one way or the other, but I assure you tonight is the first time I've danced since that unfortunate time you were forced to partner with me at Lady Harrison's." Her voice was flat, emotionless. If he wanted to embarrass her, cause her pain, she wasn't going to let him see it.

"Do you expect me to be shamed by that? How foolish of you, to let a dandy's stray comments affect you. If I listened to all the malicious things people have to say about me, I'd be curled up in a ball somewhere." He paused, looking at her. "Is that what you did? After I effectively demolished you?"

"You don't even remember," she muttered, not wanting to look at him.

"Lady Harrison's. You were wearing some abominable pink creation that clashed with your glorious copper hair. We danced a country dance, a complicated one, I believe. I think it was 'Prince William.' "

To this day Charlotte couldn't hear the strains of "Prince William" without feeling ill. She stared at him in disbelief.

"And you remember all this because . . . ?" she said severely.

His half smile was barely visible in the coach. "Because I'm seldom such a total bastard, and I try not to pick on the defenseless. You looked so crushed that I never forgot it."

"And this is the way you apologize? By abducting me?"

"No, my precious. My apology was that delicious fuck we had three weeks ago. Abducting you now, as you insist on calling it, is my way of repeating that most excellent activity."

She stared at him, openmouthed in astonishment at his gall. *How dare you* was too mild a response — she simply stared at him in disbelief. And then she moved, lunging for the door.

The carriage was going at a fast clip, and she was halfway out the door when he caught her, dragging her back in before she could tumble to the hard, filthy streets. She landed on the floor, and he held her there as he locked the carriage door.

"You idiot," he said, all humor and sly seduction vanishing. "You could have been killed. I don't travel at a leisurely pace — you could have broken your neck."

"Good," she snapped.

"Death before dishonor? Too late, my precious. I've already dishonored you quite completely, and I have every intention of doing so again."

She lunged for the door again, but he caught her easily enough, pulling her up onto the seat. And then he let go of her.

"You're so gullible, precious," he said in a weary voice. "How many times must I tell you I won't force you. Did I make you do anything you didn't want to do?"

"You tricked me," she said darkly. "You seduced me into it."

"Of course. That was my intention. I'm very good at what I do. Isn't that the reason you gave in? If you were going to have sex, it might as well be with a master."

"So humble, too," she murmured.

He moved his mouth close, so close. "Accept it, sweet Charlotte. I can take you home with me and make you come just by kissing your breasts, and you know it. Don't you, love? And you want me inside you."

She was having trouble breathing. She could almost feel his mouth on her as the words hit her ears. Her nipples hardened against her corset, and she felt wet between her legs.

At this rate he could make her come just by talking to her.

Adrian Rohan was a dangerous man. Too dangerous for her.

"No," she said, her voice wobbling slightly

when she wanted it firm. "I'm telling you no."

"All right," he said amiably, not at all shattered by her rejection. "There are endless women who'd happily lift their skirts for me. I don't need to force anyone. I thought you might enjoy another taste of the forbidden, but since you so clearly regret our time together I'll find someone else."

Her head was going to explode. She needed her mask, but in their wrestling match it had been crushed. She reached behind her for the hood of the domino and tried to pull it over her head, but his hands caught hers. "No, you don't. Not that I don't despise the hair powder — that must have been Lady Whitmore's asinine idea. It's a crime to cover hair as glorious as yours."

"Stop it," she said. Good. Her unshed tears were making her voice hoarse, and it came out sounding calm and angry. "Why did you . . . did you . . . ?"

"Why did I fuck the sweet hell out of you a few weeks ago at the gathering of the Heavenly Host? Because you were there, and I must admit I enjoyed myself tremendously. I'm afraid I don't need a great deal of motivation for these things. In your case I imagine it was the novelty of it all. I'd forgotten all about you, and then there you were, right in front of me. Just like tonight. I have to say it seems like Providence, since I hadn't made any other arrangements for female companionship tonight. But if you'd rather not, then so be it. Perhaps Lady Whitmore might be interested in providing me with entertainment."

His calm, cruel words were like knives, and yet she didn't flinch. Later, when she was alone, the words would sink in, but for right now she was too angry, too proud to let him see how he'd wounded her.

"I doubt Lina would be interested," she said in a cool voice. "She doesn't usually want my leftovers."

"Brava," he said softly. "Fight back."

Which was exactly what she planned to do. "As for novelty, you'd be a fool to try to repeat it. You can only deflower someone once, and as you've pointed out, I'm hardly the kind of woman you usually dally with. You prefer beauties, women who are adept at pleasing a man, who know all sorts of tricks and games to please you. You wouldn't want to bother with a clumsy spinster again."

"True . . . But she was so delightfully besotted with me."

She wanted to kill him. If she'd had a

knife she probably would have stabbed him. As it was, she had nothing but words to hit back with.

"You took care of that, my lord," she said, not bothering to deny it. "One night with you is a most effective cure."

It was supposed to infuriate him. Instead he laughed softly. "Of course it is. And it was two nights. You don't want me to kiss you, do you?"

"The thought disgusts me."

He moved closer, and she could feel his body heat in the cool night air. "And you don't want my mouth on your breasts, sucking your nipples into hard little berries."

It didn't need his mouth — his words had had the same effect as she felt her nipples tighten. Fortunately he couldn't see beneath the layer of clothes she wore. "Absolutely not."

"And you don't want my mouth between your legs, my tongue teasing you into such peaks of pleasure that you cry out?"

She was wet now. He probably knew it, but it didn't matter. "I'm not fond of perversion."

"I suppose that means I can't talk you into taking my cock into your mouth then."

She was so shocked she couldn't find the words to refute it. Finally she said, "You sick bastard."

"Oh, my love, not sick at all. It's quite lovely, and some women, the very best of women, enjoy it as well. So I gather this means you don't want me inside you, riding you, pumping you, making you cry and scream with pleasure?"

"You're a pig," she snapped.

"It's a pig's world. So the answer is no, my precious?"

The smug, cruel bastard. The beautiful, wicked, hurtful man with the hands of a devil and the mouth of an angel. He would take her back to Grosvenor Square, and she would slink into the house, go up to her room and curl up into the ball he talked about.

"The answer is yes," she said. And had the pleasure to see his face freeze in shock.

17

Never would Adrian Rohan have thought that a woman's acquiescence would send a cold chill down his back. It had no effect on his cock, which had been painfully hard since he'd put his hands on her, which had been at least at half-mast since he'd spotted her on the dance floor and moved heaven and hell to join her set. This was supposed to be a salutary lesson, a way to get over her. Instead he was seducing himself as he was seducing her.

She was supposed to slap his face, demand that the carriage take her to Grosvenor Square, and he would cheerfully accept her dismissal, proving to her, and to him, how little she mattered.

Instead it was all he could do to keep from throwing her down on the seat, yanking up her skirts and taking her.

And she'd said yes. He didn't bother to hide his astonishment. Though he could . . .

ahem . . . rise to the occasion. "I beg your pardon? Was that agreement I hear? How delightfully refreshing. I thought you decided to regrow your hymen and be the same prissy, starched-up female you were before I put my wicked hands on you."

Now he was sorry he hadn't lit the carriage lights. He couldn't see her expression very well, and she seemed to have turned the tables on him.

In fact, that was probably why she'd done it. She was calling his bluff. Or was it the other way around? He was the cardplayer — he was usually much better at sizing up his opponents.

He could imagine that she had her hands in her lap, clasped tightly, but her voice was calm and smooth. "Like you, my lord, I had no other plans for this evening short of returning home with my cousin. If you're that desperate to have me I could hardly argue. It's quite flattering."

"Well played," he said softly. "And now it's my turn to tell you that I'm not the slightest bit desperate. That I chose you simply to torment you — that picking on lovelorn virgins . . . I beg your pardon, I forgot that you are no longer a virgin. Picking on lovelorn *spinsters* is better entertainment than sampling the pussy at Madame

Kate's." He wondered if she knew that word. From the slight flinch he decided that she probably did.

"Are you trying to hurt my feelings, Lord Rohan? If you receive such pleasure from inflicting pain I'm surprised you didn't suggest you whip me."

"What do you know of whips, child?" he said with a laugh.

"I live with Lina, in case you've forgotten. She's quite . . . broad-minded when it comes to her search for pleasure. Though from my experience men usually prefer to be the ones who are whipped, not the ones delivering the pain."

"I'm not like other men — haven't you realized that yet? And I doubt I'd trust you enough to give you the upper hand. I could end up with the very skin flayed from my body."

"We could see," she said sweetly.

Damn, he was enjoying himself, he realized. After his initial shock at her seeming agreement, he was finding this sparring the best thing in weeks. "You're quite surprisingly resilient, Miss Spenser. I would have expected you to go into a languishing decline after my rough treatment of you."

"Was that rough?" she asked innocently. "It perhaps lacked a bit of finesse, but you managed well enough."

He wanted to laugh, he wanted to kiss her. "I didn't really consider you deserved my best effort, since you had absolutely no idea what you were doing."

"Indeed. I would hope that wasn't your best effort. I would be sadly disappointed if society considered *that* to be masterful."

"Society does not have an opinion of my expertise in the bedroom."

"Of course it does. Where do you think you get your nicknames? Skirtchaser. Whoremaster. Libertine. Gamester. Drunkard —"

"Bitch," he returned pleasantly.

"Oh, dear," she murmured. "Does that mean you've changed your mind? Perhaps you only like sweet, inexperienced women."

"Are you going to tell me you've suddenly gained experience other than the quite effective swiving I gave you?" His voice was silken.

"It's been three weeks, my lord."

"Has it? I haven't been paying any attention." *Point to me,* he thought.

"Ah, but I've been enjoying myself immensely. I suppose I should thank you for introducing me to the sport of lovemaking. And I don't mean to criticize — you did your best, and for a halfhearted effort it was

310

a good beginning. And truly, I don't mind bedding you again. I'm certain you improve with practice."

He was quite in awe of her. She was carrying this off beautifully. She was expecting she could infuriate him enough to let her go. Unfortunately the more inventive her insults the more enchanted he was with her imagination. It was, of course, possible that she'd spent the last three weeks imitating her dear friend and shagging everyone in sight. But he sincerely doubted it. She still moved like an innocent.

A woman changed. Not through the magic of sex — the women in his family, in society, still walked demurely, at least for the most part. But women who spent the majority of their lives in their lovers' beds walked differently. With an erotic sway to their hips. A knowing way of carrying themselves certain to draw the attention of any randy young buck.

Charlotte walked like a virgin, kissed like a virgin, reacted to his ridiculous attempt at abducting her like a virgin.

But she fought him like a woman, an angry one. A hurt, abandoned one. And part of him wanted to stop playing this ridiculous game and hold her. The rest of him was having too much fun.

"I'm honored that you're giving me a chance to improve on such a shoddy performance," he said. And grinned in the darkness when he heard her distressed intake of breath. If she'd ever played cards with him she would have known this wouldn't work. "What else?"

"What else what?" Her voice quieter in the darkness. They were nearing Grosvenor Square — the best way to reach his home was to go directly past Whitmore House. He wondered if she knew that.

"What other insults are you planning to lob at my head?" he said. "They're quite entertaining."

"I'm so glad I've amused you," she said, some of her bravado fading. "But in truth, I think we can both agree that what happened three weeks ago is something not worth repeating. You can certainly find much better company for that sort of thing."

"But Miss Spenser, now that you have all this expertise, don't you want to form a more experienced opinion on my technical prowess? Size, stamina, imagination . . ."

She said nothing.

"Admit it, Charlotte," he said lazily. "You've spent the last three weeks mooning over me. Crying your eyes out over my rude departure. I think you'd give anything to have me again."

"Do you, indeed? When I've had so much better?"

He laughed softly. "Prove it."

He heard her swift intake of breath. "I beg your pardon?"

"If you've spent the last three weeks on your back with various men, show me what you learned."

The coach had pulled to a stop, but no one came to open the door. His servants knew not to disturb him until he rapped on the roof of the carriage.

She sat there frozen, holding her breath. And he was holding his, hoping against hope that she was going to try to continue this charade to its natural conclusion. In his bed.

And then she let it out in a whoosh. "Take me home," she said in a small voice.

"So you lied."

"Yes. Take me home. Take me home or I'll scream."

"I'm shocked," he said cheerfully. "I would never have thought you'd succumb to such a weak defense. I'll tell you what. We'll wager for your release."

There was more light coming in the carriage now, and he could see her clearly. Unfortunate, because his wanting her became stronger than ever.

"So you can get away with saying you never rape," she said bitterly. "I suppose you want to play cards so that you can easily cheat."

"Nothing so crass. Just come over here and let me kiss you. And then it's up to you whether you go or stay."

She stared at him in disbelief. "You've already kissed me tonight," she said flatly. "Half a dozen times, if anyone's counting. And I still want you to let me go."

"Well, then you shouldn't worry about the wager. You'll win. All you have to do is let me kiss you for, let's say, three minutes, and then if you want to leave I'll have my coach take you straight back to Grosvenor Square."

He could see her swallow, and he wanted to put his mouth against her throat. He stayed very still.

"I don't think it's a good idea."

"Why not? I'm perfectly willing to live with the consequences. In fact, it's more than clear that I happen to want you. I don't know why — you're clumsy and red-haired and too smart for your own good. I'd be much better off with a whore, or at least someone like your friend Lady Whitmore. Someone marginally familiar with the delights of bed sport. But for some inconceivable reason I happen to want you."

"I'm so flattered," she said in acid tones.

He knew her weakness. She wanted to be pretty, and thought she wasn't. When in fact he thought she was quite the prettiest thing in his memory. With her sun-flecked skin, her round, gorgeous breasts, her long, exquisite legs. Everything about her was pretty.

But he wasn't going to tell her that. He was going to tell her everything that was wrong with her, in hopes of keeping her away.

"I may want you, but if you say no it won't trouble me. We had unfinished business when I left Sussex. Tonight it will be finished, one way or another. Are you game?"

"And if I refuse?"

He hadn't considered that one. "I suppose I can let you down here and you could walk back to Grosvenor Square. I wouldn't recommend it — a woman alone on London streets might be mistaken for a woman of easy virtue. Which, unfortunately, you are not. Come, my sweet darling, take the wager. We can't sit here all night."

She looked at him for another long, contemplative moment. "All right."

He kept his smile hidden. "Come over here and climb on my lap again."

315

"We were talking about a kiss and nothing more."

"No, we were talking about three minutes of kissing and whatever that entails. Surely you don't think I could get into that much trouble in three minutes, do you?"

The blessed girl looked torn. Clearly she had no idea just what he could manage in that period of time. "All right," she said again, and moved across the seat toward him.

It would have been entertaining to make her climb into his lap, but he had a real fear as to what her knee might hit, so he picked her up and placed her there, crossing his legs to provide a cradle for her. "When do the three minutes start?" she asked, some of her nerves finally showing.

"Now," he said, one hand pulling her head down to his. The other reaching beneath her skirts.

He was ruthless, Charlotte thought dazedly as his mouth covered hers, hot and wet, breathing in her breath, using his tongue with such thoroughness that she started to think it was her favorite part of his body. He leaned back against the seat, pulling her with him so she half sat, half reclined, the ever-present reminder of his own arousal beneath her bum. His kiss was a reminder of everything she had felt in that small room in Sussex — the emotions, the sheer, blazing passion, even the shame.

And she was lost in it. Lost in him. Just for a moment, just for now, she could have it back, that which she thought was gone for good, and she was done fighting. She felt him slide his hands under her voluminous skirts and she didn't try to stop him. When his fingers slid between her legs she didn't clamp them shut in maidenly modesty, she let him push them apart, touching her in her most private place where she knew she was shamefully wet from his words and his promises, wet and she didn't care. His fingers slid easily amid the moisture, touching the place he'd told her about, the place that held such power over her body, and she whimpered in response.

He moved his mouth across her cheek, to the soft edge of her hairline, and his tongue was at her ear. "That's right, my precious Charlotte. Don't fight me. You'll like this, I promise you." And he slid one finger inside her, deep.

She arched off his lap, struggling for a moment, but he simply pulled her back against his body, clamping her there, while he replaced one finger with two, as his thumb brushed above.

The feeling was electric, powerful, disturbing. It was one thing when they were both naked in bed, but here in his coach, fully dressed, the driver above and people walking by on the streets, he was touching her so intimately that she wanted to die of shame. And pleasure.

Her hands had been trapped between them, but when he'd shifted her they were free, and she knew she ought to push his hand away, push his body away. He'd lied, he said he was only going to kiss her, and instead he was doing this unspeakable thing to her.

But instead, she put her arms around his neck and brought his mouth down to hers, kissing him back as he rubbed her, slowly, deliciously, his fingers pushing in deep as he brought her to the very edge of rapture, so that she was barely able to breathe, her fingers clutching him, her hips pushing at him, wanting more, needing more.

It was too much, it wasn't enough. She needed him inside her, she needed him to unfasten his breeches and push her down on the seat and take her, take her now . . .

And then he stopped. Just as she was about to explode in delight, he pulled his hand away, pulled her skirt back down,

318

caught her arms and set her down beside him on the seat. "Three minutes are up."

She was shaking, dizzy, unable to think straight, unable to speak. She was having trouble catching her breath, and she clamped her legs together tightly, trying to re-create the feelings he'd been bringing forth. She was so close, so close . . .

"Are you coming in with me?"

It took her a moment, but eventually she released her pent-up breath, forcing herself to relax. Slowly, carefully, so as not to jar her body onto that desperate ride once more.

"You don't fight fair," she said in a small voice.

"No, I don't. Not when I want something."

She looked at him in the filtered lamplight. He was beautiful, she thought, from his tawny mane of hair to his long, wicked fingers, to that hard, thrusting piece between his legs. Everything about him was beautiful, and she wanted to lie next to him, kiss him, roll in his arms.

She was still wearing her thin kid gloves. She peeled one off, very slowly, looked up at him with a sweet smile and slapped him as hard as she could.

She had a lot of strength. It whipped his

head back, and she knew the blow had to have hurt, because her hand was numb. And she didn't have an ounce of regret.

"Now, if you're tired of playing games," she said coolly, "I'd like to go back to my house."

He didn't move for a moment, didn't touch his face. The mark of her hand was beginning to show, the outline of her fingers against his pale, cold skin. And then he smiled.

Leaning forward, he knocked against the small window that connected to the front of the carriage, and gave the driver the address in Grosvenor Square. Then he sat back patiently as the carriage moved forward.

The drive was a short one — less than five minutes, and during that time he said absolutely nothing. She could feel his eyes on hers, as tangible as a touch, but he made no effort to move closer, no effort to change her mind. He seemed almost pleased with the outcome of their battle, which surprised Charlotte. Did he want her or didn't he? Was this all some elaborate game? Were there wagers at his club as to whether he could once more entice the red-headed virago into his bed? If so, he must have bet against himself to be so cheerful.

She wouldn't ask him. She was being foolishly fearful. If he had planned this then word would get to Lina, and her cousin would tell her. So he hadn't lied. He'd simply run across her when he had no other, more pressing plans. Doubtless he was telling the truth, that he'd forgotten about her entirely after their brief liaison in the country. Which was a good thing, was it not? Everyone needed to forget about it. Most importantly, she did.

She could see her crumpled loo mask on the floor of the carriage, and she leaned down to pick it up, ignoring the little shiver of reaction that tightening her muscles had given her. She felt exquisitely sensitive, ready to explode, like a mirror shattering into a thousand pieces. He took the mask from her and tied it on her face methodically. Just in time; those ridiculous tears were starting again. She'd be delighted when she finally moved past this absurdly weepy stage in her life. She had barely cried when her parents had died. These tears made no sense — they were totally unlike her.

With a great effort she summoned an impressive scowl, willing herself to be still. When the carriage came to a stop, Adrian hopped down, reaching up a hand to her. She would have liked to ignore it, but the narrow steps were unwieldy, and falling into the mud would be the coup de grâce of the night. She took his hand, stepped down and tried to pull away, but his fingers had closed over hers.

He smiled down at her, but she could see that odd, haunted expression in the back of his hard blue eyes. "I expect this has given you a complete disgust of me."

"Is that what you wish?"

"It would certainly be for the best. For both of us."

She looked up at him in the lamplight. She could see the imprint of her hand quite clearly, and it shocked her. And pleased her.

The street was solid beneath her feet, and she locked her knees so they wouldn't betray the lingering weakness. "Goodbye, Lord Rohan," she said. The door to Lina's house stood open, the footman waiting patiently. "I don't expect we'll see each other again."

His smile was slow, mocking, irresistibly devilish. "Would you care to wager on that, my love?"

18

To Charlotte's relief Lina hadn't returned home yet. She wouldn't have to make excuses as to where she'd been, and by the time Meggie appeared from belowstairs, looking both rumpled and pleased with herself, Charlotte had managed to get her tears in check and regain some measure of composure. Her body still felt on the very edge of exploding, but by taking calm, deep breaths she seemed to be able to maintain her calm. To fight the crazed, irrational urge to run out the front door and down the streets back to Adrian's house.

"You've been tupped," Meggie said flatly, taking one hard look at her. "Miss Charlotte, I thought you knew better —"

"I certainly have not!" she said, managing to sound both innocent and indignant. "Lina and I got separated and I took a hackney home." She took a closer look at her lady's maid. "If anyone's been misbe-

323

having, it's you. I thought you swore off men."

"Have you seen the new undercoachman?" Meggie said with an appreciative smirk. "He could tempt a saint to lift her skirts, and Lord knows, I'm no saint. But don't try to change the subject. You've got that look about you."

"That look comes from being tired. I just want to go to bed."

"As long as you promise you haven't already been to bed," Meggie said smartly.

"Or what? You'll refuse to serve me?"

"Don't be daft, Miss Charlotte," Meggie said, her voice softening. "You need a nice cup of tea, don't you? I can have Cook —"

The knock on the door stopped her in the midsentence, and Charlotte's heart flew into her throat. It was Rohan, come back for her. It didn't matter why or how, she'd do anything he wanted. No one would make a social call at this hour — there was no one else it could possibly be.

She jumped to her feet, moving toward the door, when Meggie moved in front of her, a troubled expression on her face. "Mr. Jenkins will answer the door, Miss Charlotte," she said.

She felt herself flush. At this rate she'd never be able to fool anyone. She sat back

324

down, determined to be calm. Why had he come back? He must have been feeling as bereft as she was. Was there any way she could throw herself into his arms and beg him to carry her off and finish ravishing her?

Of course there was. All she had to do was ask. Tell him. Proving to everyone she'd finally lost her mind.

Jenkins appeared at the salon door, his long face showing no reaction to the unexpected visitor. "The Reverend Simon Pagett to see Lady Whitmore. I explained she wasn't at home, but he's asked to wait, and I wondered if you might be willing to receive him in her place, Miss Spenser."

Not by a blink of an eye did she show her reaction. And yet Meggie moved close enough to put a comforting hand on her shoulder. "Sorry, love," she whispered.

Meggie had always known more than she should, and been far too quick to guess the rest. Charlotte straightened her back, cursing herself for a fool. "Of course we'll receive him, Jenkins. Lady Whitmore should return at any time now."

A moment later the vicar was ushered in, and Charlotte had her first chance to get a good look at him. She'd seen him at a distance when she'd arrived back at Hensley Court, bruised and battered and badly shaken from her fall, but she hadn't been able to form an opinion. Now she needed a distraction quite badly, so as she rose and curtsied she took covert stock of him.

Interesting. Lina had told her he was old, and sour, and mean-spirited and quite the most miserable human being she had ever met, and if she never saw him again she would be very glad.

She'd lied. Simon Pagett was probably somewhere short of forty, with a lean, wiry body and the kind of face that had seen too much. It was a serious face, but he had really fine eyes, and some women might find his mouth to be sensual. Which of course was wrong in a cleric, but the vicar didn't appear to be someone who'd lived a sheltered life of abstinence.

"I'm sorry to disturb you, ma'am, but I'm looking for Lady Whitmore."

"Do sit down, Mr. Pagett. Is Lord Montague . . . has he worsened?"

He didn't sit. "I'm afraid so. He's asked for Lady Whitmore, and I'm hoping she'll return to Sussex with me. If she can tear herself away from her pressing social obligations."

There was a note of censure in his voice. "You disapprove of social obligations, Mr. Pagett?" Charlotte asked, wondering if this was how Lina had formed her negative opinion.

He smiled then, ruefully, and Charlotte was momentarily charmed. He must not have smiled at Lina, or her opinion would have risen considerably. "Of course not, Miss Spenser. I must confess it's been a long ride from the country and I'm worried about Montague. It's made me a bit short-tempered." He glanced around him. "If I might ask, where *is* Lady Whitmore?"

"At Ranelagh with Sir Percy Wainbridge," she said.

"Do you expect her to return tonight?"

"Yes, she expects me to return tonight," Lina's sharp voice came from the doorway. "I'm not in the habit of traipsing off to spend the night with my lovers."

Mr. Pagett turned abruptly, and there was an immediate tension in the air. "I have no idea what you're in the habit of doing, Lady Whitmore. I was given to understand that you do exactly what you want to."

But Lina had already moved past the insult. "Is Monty dead?" she asked in an anxious voice, tension vibrating through her body.

"Not yet," he said, and Lina's shoulders relaxed slightly. "But I'm afraid it won't be long. Thomas has asked if you would like to come say goodbye."

"No, I would not," Lina said flatly, shocking Charlotte as well as Pagett.

Pagett nodded grimly. "In that case I'll take my leave . . ."

"I won't say goodbye to him," Lina said. "I refuse to let him die, and that's exactly what I shall tell him. Do we leave tonight or is the morning soon enough?"

Was there a look of approval in Pagett's eyes? If so, Lina didn't notice it. "Traveling at night is more difficult."

"So it is. I gather by your answer that tonight would be better. Meggie, go upstairs and pack for me. Charlotte, I presume you want to stay here?"

Alone, in London, with Adrian Rohan a few streets down? "I want to come with you," she said, rising. "I'll go help."

"Is there anything you need to do before we leave, Mr. Pagett? I keep a coach in London — there's room for you if you'd like to leave your horse here." Lina's voice was cool again. Odd, when she was usually so warm and flirtatious, even with those who disapproved of her.

"I prefer to ride," he said.

"Then I'll simply have to send Sir Percy on his way, change my clothes and we'll be ready." She disappeared out the door, and they could hear her voice just beyond the door. "Percy, my love, I'm afraid I've been called out of town, but Jenkins will see that you're properly looked after."

"I wouldn't think of interrupting your lovers' tryst," Pagett said.

Sir Percy hobbled in, aided by one of the sturdy footmen. "Demme, afraid I twisted me ankle," he wheezed. "Just call me a carriage, love, and I'll be fine."

"Percy, your house is more than an hour out of town. You'll stay here. It's horribly rude to leave you like this, but I know my servants will take most excellent care of you."

Amid much protestation and fuss Sir Percy was aided up to one of the second-floor bedrooms by three footmen and the austere Jenkins, and then Lina turned to the vicar, who was watching her out of half-closed eyes. "I'll be ready in less than an hour."

"Isn't he a little old for you?" Pagett drawled, deliberately provocative.

Lina turned to Charlotte. "You see why I told you he's an odious human being?" she said brightly. She looked back over her shoulder. "Indeed, you need to ride your horse, Mr. Pagett. There's only room for three in the carriage and we'll need to take

Meggie. I can only hope the weather will change and there'll be a nice, icy rainstorm to accompany our journey."

"We're not likely to have ice in April, and I doubt you'd enjoy traveling by coach in that kind of weather anyway. I have one more call to make, and then I'll be ready to accompany you."

"Another social call? At this time of night?" Lina said archly. "There are other people you treat as rudely as you do me?"

"Would you have preferred I wait until morning, Lady Whitmore?" he asked in his steady voice.

She glared at him. "Point taken. We'll be ready within the hour. If you're not here we'll go ahead without you." She swept from the room without another word, not even looking at Charlotte.

Simon Pagett met her curious gaze with a wry smile. "She doesn't like me, I'm afraid."

"Perhaps you might get along better if you didn't criticize her."

"I'm not sure if that's a good idea," he said, half to himself. "By your leave, Miss Spenser."

After he left, Charlotte found Lina rushing around her rooms, flinging clothes around as Meggie and one of the upstairs maids tried to keep up with her. "Do you need help, dearest?" she called out to Charlotte as she paused in the doorway.

"It won't take me that long," she said. "You didn't tell me that Mr. Pagett was so young."

"Didn't I? Well, I suppose he is. Younger than he looks, apparently. But he's got the soul of a crabby, mean old man."

Charlotte remembered his wry, charming smile and the odd expression in his eyes when they rested on Lina. "If you say so," she said doubtfully.

Lina already had a trunk mostly filled, with enough on her bed to fill another.

"How long are we planning to stay?" Charlotte asked. "You're packing enough for the entire season."

"Well, one never knows what might come up. I need to bring my new dresses, but I wouldn't want to be without some of my other clothes. I wouldn't want Mr. Pagett to think my new colors and necklines have anything to do with him."

"Why should they?" Charlotte asked, momentarily mystified.

Lina's laugh was brittle. "Indeed, why should they? Are you packed, dearest?"

"It won't take but a moment. No, Meggie, you stay and help Lina. You know it won't take me more than a minute or two to get what we'll need, and Sussex is not at the end of the world. We can always send back to London if we've left too much behind."

"Of course we can," Lina declared feverishly. She came over and gave Charlotte an exuberant hug. "I'm glad we're leaving, aren't you? You don't want to risk running into Adrian again, and I'm dreadfully, dreadfully tired of town right now. The countryside will be perfect."

Charlotte looked at her askance. "But Lord Montague . . ." she said doubtfully.

"He's not going to die, Charlotte. I refuse to let such a dreadful thing happen. He's got years left, I've been assured of that."

"Who assured you?" she asked, remembering Lord Montague's pale, frail appearance. "A doctor?"

"Well, in fact I believe it was Adrian Rohan," Lina admitted. "But his cousin, that awful Frenchman, used to be a doctor, so I imagine that's the next best thing. Adrian says that in another month or so Monty will be out doing something absurd like rowing on the Thames or dancing half clad and well to the boughs in Hyde Park after midnight."

Charlotte said nothing. Clearly Lina had no desire to believe anything else. If Lord Montague lasted another month Charlotte would be much surprised. There would be no reason for Pagett to summon them if the end wasn't near. But they would take things as they came. At least she was getting far enough away that she wouldn't be tempted by Adrian Rohan ever again.

Adrian was in a thoroughly foul mood. His insouciance had only carried him so far. Once Charlotte Spenser walked into the house, his lazy smile vanished. He dismissed his carriage — the walk back to Curzon Street was short and he needed to work off his bad temper.

He'd certainly handled that well, he thought savagely. He'd thought to make her so mad at him that she wouldn't ever countenance touching him again. Then, when he'd decided to have her after all, he'd worked her into such a state of excitement that his own arousal had been painful. And then she hadn't given in.

He cursed at the thought. What kind of games was he playing? He wasn't sure if he wanted to win or to lose. And what the hell was wrong with him? Charlotte Spenser? She was older than he was, for God's sake. She was an antidote — no one wanted her. She'd had at least one season, he supposed, since he remembered dancing with her, but

333

clearly no one had offered for her, and by now she was a complete spinster, thirty if she was a day, with no possibilities, no future except as a companion to Evangelina Whitmore. Why in God's name had she rejected him? Shouldn't she take her pleasure where it was offered? It wasn't as if she could lose her virginity twice.

Her lie about turning into a whore like Lina was totally unbelievable. But that didn't mean it wouldn't always be the case. He'd shown her, quite effectively, the kind of pleasure that could be had between a man and a woman. With Lina's habits there'd be scores of randy men, and Charlotte would be there. With her glower, to scare them away. With her deliciously long legs and copper-colored hair and luminous eyes, with her creamy skin and delectable mouth. Once someone got her in bed they wouldn't let her go, and the thought infuriated him.

If she was going to have an illicit affair it was going to be with him. The little idiot didn't realize that partners weren't interchangeable. That what went on between them had been, for want of a better word, *special.* There'd been something rare and dangerous between them during those two dark days, some kind of connection that he'd never felt before. And the damned feeling had lasted, disturbing with his sleep, leaving him bored with the beautiful, experienced women he could easily have.

In truth, he wanted Charlotte and no one but Charlotte, and his efforts to get over her were only making things worse. He could have had her in the carriage. His release might have been enough to finally let go. There was no way that the sex had been as good as he remembered. Impossible. All he had to do was tup her again and he'd know that for a fact.

He was almost home. The full moon had set, and the night was dark. Perhaps that was his problem — folklore had it that everyone got a little crazy during a full moon. Certainly the watchmen were busier with miscreants and Mohocks. By tomorrow he might feel entirely differently.

But tomorrow was too far away. He could see his cozy little house up ahead, but he stopped, looking back the way he'd come. Not quite ready to admit defeat.

But what could he say? If he had any idea which was Charlotte's bedroom he'd damn well scale the walls of Evangelina's house to get to her. Perhaps he could just charge in like some bloody pirate and demand her, throw her over his shoulder and carry her off. Who could stop him?

He laughed at the thought. Charlotte would probably break his head for trying it. And he suspected Evangelina wouldn't be any help — she was damnably protective of the woman. Girl. Woman.

If he had any sense he would spend the night blessedly alone with a bottle or two or three.

He had no sense. He turned, moving back the way he'd come, when something rushed out of the darkness, straight at him. More than something — three men, brandishing clubs, and the first blow took him off guard, hitting him in the head, momentarily stunning him.

The next caught his knees, and he fell to the ground, reaching for the pistol he carried beneath his coat.

"Watch out, 'e's got a popper," one of them called, and his arm went numb from another blow.

"Finish 'im off, Jem," one man said. "We wants to get paid before the cove takes off. Besides, we gots other work to do tonight besides this one."

Presumably it was Jem who moved closer. Adrian looked up at him dazedly, his head still ringing. The next blow would most likely crush his skull. And for some reason all he could think of was Charlotte's re-action to his untimely demise.

"You there!" someone shouted, and just like that the men scattered into the shadows like the rats they were, Adrian thought dazedly.

He tried to sit up, and someone came up to him, putting his hand under his arm to haul him to his feet. The arm they'd hit, and he let out a string of blasphemous curses as he struggled to his feet, only to see that his savior was wearing the collar of a vicar.

"Bloody Christ," he muttered weakly.

The man laughed. "You're in one piece, Rohan. You can thank God for that, not curse him."

"Fat lot you know," he said. He narrowed his eyes. He was still seeing a shadow around everything, but he was fairly certain he'd never met this man before. "Who are you?" he demanded, suspicious. "How do you know who I am? Did you set those men on me?"

"I'm the one who saved you, remember? I know who you are because I've come to see you. I'm Simon Pagett. I've come from Lord Montague."

He was already dizzy, and the man's words weren't helping. "He's not dead, is he?" he

337

said in a dangerous voice.

"No. But he doesn't have long. He wants his closest friends to come and say good-bye."

For a long moment Adrian didn't say anything. And then he nodded toward his house. "I live just over there. Come in with me and you can tell me about it."

"I don't have much time —— I'm to meet with some people and escort them to Sussex."

"I don't have much time either. My head is killing me and I damned well want to get drunk and go to bed."

"It might not be a good idea to get drunk after someone slammed you in the head," the vicar said mildly.

"Are you a doctor?"

"No."

"Then I'll take my chances. Come along, Vicar. There's drinking to be done."

19

Charlotte, normally the best of travelers, was totally miserable on the seemingly endless drive to Sussex. It took all her willpower not to throw up as the traveling coach lumbered along the bumpy roads, and when they stopped to change horses she couldn't manage more than a few sips of weak tea.

It was late morning by the time the coach pulled up at Hensley Court and discharged its bedraggled passengers. Mr. Pagett had gone ahead of them for the last hour, in order to make certain all was in readiness for their arrival.

Indeed, the interaction between Lina and Mr. Pagett provided Charlotte with much-needed distraction from her current woes. She couldn't very well think about Adrian Rohan without fury churning her poor beleaguered stomach. How dare he? How dare he tempt and taunt her like that, as if she were some idle plaything. She could console herself with the knowledge that she hadn't given in, no matter how much her body had cried out for it. She'd won the battle.

It just happened to feel like she'd lost the war.

At least thinking about Lina and the vicar kept her mind off her stomach. Listening to Lina's fuming diatribe had been wonderfully distracting.

"Isn't he the most odious man, Charlotte?" Lina had demanded early in the trip. Mr. Pagett was riding outside, having to keep his horse's pace slow to match the heavy coach. "You were spared much of his company, or you'd realize how abominably high-handed he is. The Lord preserve me from small-minded vicars and their prosy ways!"

"He didn't seem particularly prosy," Charlotte said, a hand clasped to her roiling stomach beneath her loose pelisse. "He mainly seemed concerned about Montague. A concern you share."

"That's the only thing we do share," Lina said with an angry sniff. "And he has no right to cast judgment on anybody — his own early life was fully as sordid as the most depraved libertine's."

"How do you know that?"

"He told me," Lina said artlessly. "You just need to take a good look at him to realize the truth. He looks a good ten years older than his real age, all due to excesses of brandy, of whoring, of ruinous behavior. How dare he tell me what I should be doing?" She fumed as Charlotte had rarely seen her.

"What were his suggestions?"

Lina was too busy muttering imprecations beneath her breath to immediately notice her cousin's question. She was dressed most becomingly in a demure gown of soft rose, and for the first time Charlotte didn't have to worry that her cousin would succumb to inflammation of the lungs from having vast amounts of her beautiful chest exposed. Even her hat was a subdued affair, instead of the usual outrageous confection, awash with feathers and silk flowers and the occasional representation of a woodland creature.

No, something or someone had inspired the notoriously unrepentant Evangelina, Lady Whitmore, to abandon her wild ways, and Charlotte couldn't help but wonder if the vicar had anything to do with it.

"It's a waste that he's so attractive," Lina went on, half to herself. "All that lovely, diffident grace, that world-weary air, that handsomely debauched face. He'll marry some whey-faced miss who'll keep his house and present him with whey-faced children, and all the whey-faced women in his whey-faced parish will adore him, of course. He'll pretend not to notice, the righteous Mr. Pagett, but underneath he knows full well the effect he has on vulnerable women."

"Then it's a good thing that neither of us are vulnerable women," Charlotte said, more out of a wish to see Lina's response than a belief in the truth. Not that she planned to say anything about it, but it seemed to Charlotte that Lina was completely vulnerable from the top of her neatly coiffed and braided black hair to the hem of her demure dress.

And how typical. The unfairness of life was quite extraordinary. If one of them was to fall in love with a sober parson and the other with a libertine, surely their roles should have been reversed.

She made a sudden, choking sound.

"What's wrong?" Lina demanded, her concern momentarily distracting her from her anger with the vicar.

"Nothing," Charlotte muttered, secretly horrified. *In love with?* Where had that thought come from? It was ridiculous, absurd, sheer madness. How could anyone

342

fall in love with a self-indulgent sensualist like Adrian Rohan? It was as absurd as thinking Lina had fallen in love with the parson.

Except that Lina had changed her clothes, her behavior, and couldn't seem to keep her mind off Mr. Pagett. And Charlotte felt her recalcitrant stomach lurch.

But she was nothing if not resilient, and she smiled brightly at Lina, not revealing her inner turmoil. "Mr. Pagett sounds most unpleasant. Which is a shame. He seemed like a most pleasant-spoken gentleman."

"Don't be misled by his handsome face," Lina said darkly. "He's a snake."

The more Lina protested the more Charlotte was intrigued. Lina was much too interested in Montague's friend, no matter how much she denied it, and Charlotte was tempted to point it out to her, then thought better of it. She was too weary to argue.

She slept, and dreamed of Adrian, his hands caressing her body, his smiling, handsome mouth brushing hers. She hoped he was suffering. Men were less able to hide their arousal, and she'd had no doubt at all that he'd wanted her, quite badly.

Was he lying alone in his bed, hard, aching, regretting his stupid, callous treatment? Probably not. He could take care of the problem himself, couldn't he? Lina had explained it to her one time — that men, that Adrian, would use those deft, beautiful hands on himself, bringing his own release.

And presumably she could do the same. She remembered waking occasionally, lying on her stomach, rocking against her fists, feeling flushed and feverish. She certainly wasn't going to do that again. She had no particular interest in getting better acquainted with the mysteries between her legs. She was for more curious about his parts. She wanted to look at him, touch him. During those long hours she'd never had a chance.

Adrian probably didn't plan to endure a night of frustration or the substitute ministrations of his own strong, beautiful hand. There would be scores of women who'd shared his bed. All it would require would be a note, or a surprise visit, and they'd lift their skirts for him as easily as she did. If he wanted to avoid entanglements he could always do what his friends had suggested and visit the notorious Madame Kate's.

He had countless ways to deal with their unfinished business, and she had nothing. Heartless bastard, she thought, feeling her bile rise again.

She made it to Hensley Court but not

much farther. The carriage pulled to a stop and she took a dive out the door, not even waiting for the footman to lower the steps. She landed on her knees in the gravel and proceeded to become embarrassingly, miserably sick.

"Travel sickness," she said wanly when Lina and Meggie rushed to her side. "Too much jostling in the coach. I feel fine now."

Lina eyed her, unable to disguise her worry. "Have you been ill before today, dearest?"

"No, thank heavens. That is, my stomach has felt a bit off for days now, but this is the first time I've cast up my accounts."

Out of the corner of her eye she saw Lina and Meggie exchange glances. "I'm fine," she said again, nettled. "Just happy to be out of that wretched coach." Unbidden, the memory of the last coach she'd been in returned, Rohan's mouth on hers, his hand between her legs, his hot, solid body beneath hers in the velvety darkness. She groaned.

Simon Pagett met them in the massive front hall, and Charlotte had just enough energy to notice that his eyes went straight to Lina. So whatever lay between them wasn't one-sided. "Thomas is sleeping," he said. "Your rooms are ready — you may as well use the time to rest. The doctor's just been here. He's mystified — just when he thinks it's the end, Thomas rallies. He says there's no telling how much longer."

"Are you suggesting *I look tired?*" Lina demanded, looking to take offense.

"No, Lady Whitmore. I'm suggesting that you rode all night over rough roads and unless you're superhuman you'd doubtless like an opportunity to relax. If you'd rather go for a brisk hike in the woods and then organize a house party, I wouldn't think of arguing."

Charlotte could practically hear Lina growling beneath her breath. It was fascinating to observe. She didn't ever remember a gentleman speaking to Lina with such a deliberately aggravating tone. Most men fell all over themselves in an effort to ingratiate themselves with her. And she couldn't remember Lina reacting so strongly to provocation.

"My cousin is feeling unwell after the trip," Lina said in her stiffest voice. "She's suffering from travel sickness, and I want to make certain she's comfortable. And then I will come downstairs and sit with Monty until he wakes up, since *you* had a long, difficult ride. I imagine you need your beauty rest. Unless you have any objections."

Mr. Pagett stiffened, but Charlotte finally

decided that even the interesting contretemps between the vicar and her cousin wasn't enough to distract her from her current state of misery. She allowed herself a small whimper, feeling truly pathetic, and Lina rushed to her side, studiously ignoring her newfound nemesis.

When they got to her rooms Meggie stripped her and wrapped her up in a fine lawn nightdress, tucking her up in bed with a warm brick at her feet and a cool damp cloth for her head. She lay back, trying to keep from sniffling miserably. She was just so bloody pitiful. She felt queasy, she had no energy, all she wanted to do was sleep. And if that weren't enough, she had the lowering feeling that her heart was broken.

It wasn't fair.

She had no reason to fancy herself in love with a selfish sybarite who cared for nothing and no one but his own pleasure. But once the idea had managed to creep into her thoughts there was no way she could banish it. If she had any kind of sense at all, that last meeting with him, in the closed confines of his town carriage, should have given her a complete disgust of him.

It only made her long for him more.

She moaned, softly enough that Meggie and Lina couldn't hear her. If she just man-

aged to keep her distance she could probably manage to get over him. After all, she'd
been recovering, albeit at a ridiculously slow
rate. If only she hadn't seen him at
Ranelagh, danced with him, let him lead
her to the supposed safety of a hackney.

Duplicitous bastard. She liked heaping
epithets on his head, the more the merrier.
He was sneaky, dishonest, amoral, selfish,
mean . . . there weren't enough bad words
to describe him. The more she saw of him
the more she disliked him. Or if that wasn't
precisely true, at least she was more and
more determined to keep her distance from
him. If she simply stayed in the country she
would never have to see him again. Viscount
Rohan was notoriously unmoved by the
countryside, avoiding it at all costs. If she
could just convince Lina to remove to her
Dorset estate then sooner or later Rohan
would go abroad, and maybe he'd fall off a
mountain or marry a Chinese princess or
be eaten by a tiger. She didn't care which
fate befell him, as long as it happened *soon.*

Lina and Meggie were whispering about
her. Their voices were low, and clearly they
were self-assured enough to think she'd
never hear them. They'd forgotten her child-
hood. She'd spent many of her formative
years growing up alone in the old house in

Yorkshire, her parents paying no attention to her, the servants whispering their shock over the poor, abandoned child. She knew the concerned tone of the whispers, even if she couldn't make out the actual words.

It didn't matter. All she needed was sleep, and she'd feel wonderful. All she needed . . .

Lina found Simon Pagett on the terrace overlooking the winding canal that led to the ruins of the old abbey. It was a beautiful late-spring morning, the scent of damp earth in the air, the promise of new life . . .

She didn't want to be thinking about new life. She and Meggie were probably jumping to conclusions. After all, Charlotte had assured her that the blasted viscount had been careful, and from what she knew of Adrian Rohan, she could well believe it. Society would know if he had bastards littering the countryside, and from what she'd seen of the old marquess, she could well believe Adrian wouldn't dare risk impregnating a girl of decent breeding. Not that the marquess wasn't utterly charming. If he wasn't clearly so besotted with his wife she might have been tempted to see whether an older man might be the answer to her problem. Not that it was a problem, per se. Nothing like the mess Charlotte would find herself in if the tisanes didn't work and Rohan hadn't been careful enough.

There were more drastic ways to deal with things if they'd progressed to that point, but Charlotte wouldn't want it and Lina wouldn't let her. They could go abroad together, providing the bloody French didn't decide to start another war. Or simply retire to the country.

"You're looking perturbed, Lady Whitmore," Pagett said. "Is there something troubling you?"

She looked at him. With the sunlight shining full on his face she could see his ruined glory quite clearly. He must have been devastating when he'd been a hellion, she thought. Even now, with the lines of weariness and an abandoned dissipation writ on his lean face he was still quite . . . appealing to someone with no sense.

She had a great deal of sense. "My dearest friend is dying. Of course I'm perturbed."

If she'd hoped to put the vicar in his place she failed. "You've had a while to come to terms with that," he said, though his voice gentled. "I had the impression that there was something new and disturbing."

"If there is I would hardly be likely to share my concerns with you, now, would I, Mr. Pagett?"

"I don't know why you wouldn't. I'm a vicar — it's part of my job to hear people's concerns. I'm accounted to be a very good listener."

"I'm not part of your parish, and my concerns are my own." He was standing too close to her, and she ought to move away, but for some reason she was more tempted to move closer. As a result, she stood her ground.

He looked down at her. He was somewhat above middle height, though not nearly as tall as Adrian Rohan, but she was small and he seemed to tower over her. "I could tell you that a trouble shared is a trouble halved, but I doubt you'd believe me."

"I don't believe you'd even quote such a hoary old line at me. Next you'll be telling me that confessing my sins to you would get me into heaven sooner."

"No," he said, looking oddly troubled. "I don't think I want to hear your sins."

"That's right, you're getting quite elderly. I doubt you have enough time left to hear everything I've done," she said brightly.

For a moment he frowned, and she knew she'd pricked his vanity. And then he laughed. "You're very good at being annoying, Lady Whitmore. I've already told you I'm thirty-five — I expect to live many

351

decades longer, and I doubt your sins can encompass that much."

"You'd be surprised." She tried to sound merry, carefree. Instead her voice came out with a hollow note.

He said nothing, watching her with a contemplative expression on his handsome face. And it was a handsome face, she thought ruefully. His premature lines only made him more interesting looking — he was probably far too pretty when he was younger. It was a good thing they hadn't met then . . .

A sudden horrifying thought hit her. To her knowledge she had never entered the bed of anyone without having a considerable amount to drink, enough to shut out the clamor of fear and darkness, and it was possible she didn't always remember them. And he must have been very pretty.

"I didn't meet you before, did I?" she asked in a sharp voice. "When was your blinding encounter on the road to Damascus?"

He laughed, having read her mind. "No, Lady Whitmore, I can safely assure you that I never bedded you in my wild years. You would have been far too young. And if I'd run into you later I promise you, you wouldn't have forgotten."

She flushed, at a disadvantage, but she rallied. "I've forgotten any number of them," she said airily. In fact, a lie. She'd only forgotten one, and been aghast that she had, until the shame-faced young man admitted that he hadn't been able to consummate the evening. "In fact, if I tried to count them all I should fail sadly." Another lie. While she would have loved to have a lengthy list of her amatory triumphs, she still had a strong regard for her own health, and finding men who were both careful and game was difficult.

"Of course you should," he said in a soothing voice, clearly doubting her. Which would have made her determined to find the next man she could and bed him, but for some reason she'd lost interest in it. She was having a great deal more fun arguing with Simon Pagett.

"I must compliment you on your new taste in clothing, Lady Whitmore. The subdued colors bring out your beauty far more than the garish ones you chose before."

"I have no interest in your sartorial advice, Vicar," she said, ignoring the rush of pleasure. "You gave me no warning — my maid packed whatever was clean."

"Of course," he said in an infuriatingly

calm voice, and she was determined to go upstairs and see if ham-handed Meggie was capable of immediately cutting down the necklines of her demure dresses. She glared up at him.

And then she found she had to laugh. "You really are the most annoying man in the world, aren't you?"

He smiled at her then, and the world seemed to shatter and split. "So I've been told."

She stared at him for a moment, unable to come up with a single word, as something inside her began to melt.

She panicked, though she wasn't quite sure why. "I wonder, though . . ." she said in the drawling voice she used to such good effect.

He looked at her warily. "Wonder what?"

"Are all men the same? Even those who've found God?" she mused.

He was very still. Like a fox, she thought, afraid a bitch had caught his scent. She laughed at the thought, mirthlessly.

"How do you mean? I can assure you I sleep better at nights. I'm happier."

"You don't strike me as particularly happy. As for nighttime sleeping situations, my thoughts were running more along those lines."

"Of course they were," he said, and there was no sting in his wry voice. "If this is your tactful way of asking me about pleasures of the flesh, I can assure you that becoming a vicar didn't castrate me."

"I'm *soooo* glad to hear it," she cooed. "Monty told me you'd taken a vow of celibacy, and I didn't know if that was out of necessity or inclination."

"Montague has been way too free with his tongue," Simon said, clearly annoyed. "If you're so interested, Lady Whitmore, I can tell you that I haven't taken a vow of celibacy. I've simply decided that I've fornicated enough outside of the marriage vows."

"You have plans to marry then?" she asked brightly, ignoring her inner pang.

"Not at this point." He looked at her for a long, hard moment. "I may change my mind."

She breathed an unobtrusive sigh of relief, emboldened. "Be certain to invite me to the wedding. I give wonderful presents."

"If I marry, Lady Whitmore, you'll definitely be there." There was an odd note in his voice, one she couldn't decipher.

She was feeling restless, edgy, and it was a shame Charlotte wasn't there to stop her. "So, has your vow of celibacy . . . I beg your pardon, I mean your informed decision . . . affected other things?" She moved closer, so close that her hooped skirts swayed against his dark-clad legs.

He stood his ground. "What other things?"

She wasn't actually touching him, but she was acutely aware of him. His lean, wiry body, his narrowed eyes, his mouth. He really had the loveliest mouth she'd ever seen on a man.

"Like kissing," she said. And she slid her arms around his neck and pressed her mouth against his.

20

She expected him to freeze. To stand there awkwardly while she kissed him, to shy back in horror as she teased him with her tongue, to lecture her on her impropriety while she laughed at him.

He was just inches away from her body, and his lips were motionless against hers. He reached up behind his neck and caught her wrists, pulling them down, and she knew a moment's melancholy triumph.

And then a moment later he pulled them around his waist, yanking her up against him, and he was the one who used his tongue, deepening the kiss, pushing her mouth open.

She was so astonished she could do nothing but cling to him, reveling in the feel of his hard, warm body up against hers. And hard it was. Most of the men in society were soft, pampered. He wasn't. He was strong, and determined, and she closed her eyes, her head falling back against his deliberate onslaught.

There was nothing hurried, nothing rough about his kiss. Once he took charge he took his time, slow and steady, kissing her with a thoroughness that left her weak in the knees. She never thought she particularly liked tongues, but she liked his. No, she loved his. Any doubt as to his checkered past was now thoroughly dispelled. No one could kiss like this without a very great deal of practice.

She moaned, swaying against him. Who would have thought a kiss could be like this? It was heavenly, distracting, almost . . . arousing. She could feel a strange flutter in her belly, an odd sort of ache in her heart, and she let her hands slide up his strong back, pressing herself closer against him as the kiss went on. And on.

"Mr. Pag—" Dodson's voice broke off in embarrassment as the butler realized what he'd walked in on.

He was in the midst of trying a hasty retreat, but it was already too late. Simon had released her, setting her away from him with calm deliberation before turning to the butler. "Yes, Dodson?" His voice was completely calm. One might have thought he was totally unmoved by the deep kiss he'd just shared with her, but Lina wasn't fooled.

His breathing was almost imperceptibly quickened, and she thought she'd felt a burgeoning arousal against her stomach.

Yes, most definitely, since he turned his back to both her and Dodson and seemed suddenly fascinated with the wide expanse of well-manicured lawn. She should feel smug, triumphant. Instead she wanted to curse Dodson.

"I beg pardon, sir. I didn't meant to interrupt. Lord Rohan has arrived."

"What?" Lina shrieked as Simon was dismissing the butler.

Simon turned his head to look at her. "Viscount Rohan," he said. "Thomas's dear friend. I went to see him after I visited with you, to request his presence at Montague's bedside. Thomas had asked for him as well as you."

"And when were you going to tell me?" she demanded, her discomfort over the truncated kiss making her testy.

Except in fact it hadn't been truncated. He'd had time to kiss her quite thoroughly, and his hands had just slid down to her narrow waist. If they'd covered her breasts she had no idea how she'd react. No truncation, it was a promise, rather.

"I didn't realize I needed to present a list of Thomas's guests for your approval."

"I don't give a bloody hell who comes and goes here. It's *Rohan* who's the problem. He . . ." Her voice trailed off as Rohan came out onto the terrace. He wasn't his usual graceful self. He had a decided limp, a black eye and bruising on his face.

"Good morning, Lord Rohan," Simon said. "I'm happy you were able to come so quickly. You're feeling quite recovered from your ordeal?"

Adrian made a bow. "It was trifling," he murmured. "Lady Whitmore, you are looking as beautiful as ever. I'm delighted to see you."

"Your servant, my lord," she said, giving him a brief curtsy. She couldn't tell whether he was surprised to see her or not. It seemed highly unlikely that he would have come here if he'd known Charlotte would be in residence, but Adrian Rohan had always been an enigma.

"Are you here alone this time?" he asked.

She was saved from having to answer by Dodson's reappearance. "My lord Montague is awake."

"You've timed your arrival perfectly," Simon said in an easy voice, annoying Lina even more. Personally she thought his timing was execrable, but there was nothing she could do about it. They all filed into

Monty's bedroom, and Lina took a moment to appreciate its outrageousness.

Monty had always had a flair for the dramatic, and his bedroom was a fitting backdrop. The bed was huge, a rival to the Great Bed of Ware, though the rich brocade hangings seemed better suited to a sultan's palace. There were cupids and seraphim and sea monsters carved into the bedposts, and enough pillows tucked behind Monty to outfit half of London. The French doors were open to the wide terrace and the spring air, but a fire was blazing in the huge stone fireplace as well.

Monty was sitting up, and if his thin body was even more wasted, his eyes were alight with mischief. He didn't look quite at death's door, thank God, though Lina couldn't help but wonder what games he was up to now. "How delightful to see you all!" he said in a strong voice. "I'm so sorry I was asleep when you arrived — that damned doctor keeps giving me laudanum and it makes me sleep too much. Lina, you're looking exquisite as usual. I'd say the same for you, Adrian, except you look as if an angry husband caught up with you. Whose wife did you make the mistake of seducing?"

Adrian laughed, leaning against the bedpost as Lina took the seat beside Monty and held his thin hand. "No wives recently. They all wanted to leave their husbands for me, and you know how boring that is."

"Dear boy, send their husbands to me and we'd *all* be happy," Monty said, the immediate strength of his voice fading somewhat. "But we're missing someone, are we not? Where is your so-charming cousin, Lina?"

Lina kept her face averted from Rohan's. She didn't want to see his expression. Pleasure or discomfort would be equally bad. Charlotte needed to keep her distance from Rohan, at least until they knew . . .

She refused to consider the possibility. "She's taking a nap, Monty," she replied. "We drove all night to get to you, darling. Some people aren't as resilient as I am." She did her best to keep her shoulder between Monty and Pagett. She was going to have to escape, to get upstairs and warn Charlotte before she blundered in on Adrian's presence. With ample warning she could spend the time in bed until Adrian left. The stomach grippe was a totally reasonable complaint. In fact, she ought to start embellishing, to set things up for Charlotte's sake so that her disappearance didn't seem odd.

Too late. The opposite door to Monty's

ceremonial bedchamber opened, and Charlotte popped her head in, looking human again.

"Come in, dear girl!" Monty said in a fair approximation of his most florid voice. "So kind of you to visit this poor invalid."

Charlotte had known Monty for years, and she moved into the room with the smile on her face masking the concern in her eyes. "You're looking well, my lord."

"I look like death and you know it," Monty said charmingly. "Have a seat and tell me all about what you've been doing. Rohan, get the girl a seat."

It would have been comical if Lina weren't so worried. Adrian Rohan had been hidden by the lavish bed hangings. Charlotte took one look and blanched, and for a moment Lina wondered if her stalwart Charlotte was going to faint for the first time in her life.

But Charlotte was made of sterner stuff. A moment later she had dropped a curtsy, murmured a polite greeting and taken the chair that Simon, in the first act she approved of, had been quick to provide.

"So here we all are," Monty said cheerfully, his voice weak, his eyes alight with a curious mischief. One might almost think he knew what had gone on between Charlotte and Adrian, but that was impossible.

One might almost think he'd been privy to that absurdly ill-advised kiss she'd given his straitlaced vicar. Or he'd given her, in fact, when he'd turned things upside down.

But he couldn't know any of these things. Lina wanted to reach out with her other hand, clasp Charlotte's in support, but Monty was clinging tightly, and Charlotte was doing a magnificent job of looking impervious.

"Here we all are," Rohan said in his lazy voice. "So what have you got planned for our entertainment, Monty? Surely you're not going to wither away in front of us? We need a full recovery."

"Wish I could oblige you, dear boy," Monty said faintly. "I used to lead you all a merry dance, did I not? But I'm afraid my dancing days are over."

"You don't need to dance, Monty," Lina said soothingly. "You just need to stay with us."

"For as long as I can. In the meantime, Lina, I'm delighted you brought your cousin. And Rohan, I'm delighted you *didn't* bring yours. Etienne is far from my favorite person in this world."

Rohan looked startled. "I hadn't realized that. Is there a reason?"

"I knew him in Paris years ago. You were

just a child then, but I never trusted him."

"You never said anything about it before," Rohan pointed out.

"I'm dying," Monty said flatly. "I can say what I want and no one can object. People have to do my bidding."

"Hardly," Lina said with a laugh.

"You're all here, aren't you? I have things I want to say to all of you, and I'll need privacy to do it. I'm certain you can manage to amuse yourselves while I meet with each one of you."

"Of course we can, Monty," Lina said. "Charlotte and I could use a walk after being cramped up in a carriage for so long."

"Ah, but I wish to talk to you first, precious," Monty said.

Lina opened her mouth to object, but Charlotte had already risen briskly. The color was good in her pale face, and she seemed perfectly recovered from her early-morning bout of illness. Clearly she'd been worried for naught, and the Charlotte she knew was perfectly capable of making short work of Adrian Rohan should he offer any kind of insult. Besides, he was far more likely to run in the opposite direction. The viscount went through women like water and a repeat engagement would be unheard of.

"And Simon, dear fellow," Monty added. "I gather there's a leak in the church roof and your sexton is somewhat fond of the bottle. In fact, he's a total inebriate."

"He is, indeed." Simon had a wry look on his face. "However, he's been an inebriate for the past ten years, and the roof has had a hole in it for at least three. Is there any particular reason you wish me to deal with it today?"

"No time like the present," Monty said innocently.

Rohan pushed away from the bedpost and moved to Charlotte's side. "I believe we have our orders, Miss Spenser." He held out his arm, and Lina wondered if Charlotte would refuse. But in another minute they were gone, out onto the terrace, with Simon Pagett disappearing in the opposite direction.

"You're a very bad man, Monty," she said evenly. "I never would have thought you capable of matchmaking. You always had too much respect for human individuality."

"I always had too much respect for the trouble I could cause. Nowadays it doesn't matter —— I won't be around to worry about it. So tell me the truth, my precious. Do you like him?"

Lina considered it for a long moment. "I

don't actively dislike him," she said carefully. "But I don't think he has any intention of offering for Charlotte, or for anyone, and it would take more than subtle threats to bring him up to scratch."

He stared at her for a long moment, seemingly mystified. "My dear, there are times when you astound me." He hesitated, as if he would say something else, then shook his head. "Never mind, my dear. There's none so blind as will not see."

She stiffened. "What are you talking about?"

Monty's smile was a ghost of his usual insouciance. "I'll tell you later, precious. When you're ready to hear it."

The moment they stepped outside onto the wide terrace Charlotte yanked her hand away from Adrian's arm. "What in God's name are you doing here?" she demanded.

His slow, lazy smile was as devastating as it was infuriating. "You left me high and dry, my dear Miss Spenser. We have unfinished business."

"No, we don't." She hid her hands in her skirts so he wouldn't see she was trembling. Her common sense, which had fled the moment she caught sight of him, was slowly returning. She could only hope her equanimity would return as well. "I'm sorry, I'm being absurd. There is no way you could know we'd be here. I'm sure if you did, this would have been the very last place you would have appeared."

"As you say." His voice was enigmatic. "But in truth Montague is my dearest friend. I would have been here no matter what monsters I had to face."

Her smile was brittle. "Only one monster, Lord Rohan," she said. She allowed herself a moment to survey his battered countenance. "What happened to you? Did fate finally deliver you the comeuppance you so richly deserve?"

"Why would I deserve a beating? What great crime have I committed? You willingly put yourself in my hands. I would have released you any time you requested it." His expression was limpid, innocent, but Charlotte was unmoved.

"I didn't willingly get in your carriage yesterday. At least, I didn't know it was yours," she corrected, scrupulously honest. "As for several weeks ago, tell me truthfully. Would you have been able to unlock the door when I first requested you do so? Or several times thereafter?"

"No," he said, and she believed him. For a moment.

"And could you have had someone come to unlock the door if you requested it?" she persisted.

This time his smile was slow and rueful. "Yes."

She stared at him. She should have raged, stormed, she should have stomped away, she should have accused him of every crime imaginable. And yet all she wanted to do was cry in relief. He'd wanted her. He could have had anyone, he wasn't trapped in that room with her. He'd chosen her. He'd kept her.

He was looking at her quizzically. "Aren't you going to slap me?" he said. "I'd appreciate it if you didn't — I'm in a great deal of pain already, though I expect in your case it's not much of a deterrent. So we've established I deserved this beating. Did I deserve to die?"

She made a concerted effort to get past her emotions. "Die? Was someone trying to kill you?"

"I was set upon by street ruffians, who were clearly intent on killing me. If Pagett hadn't shown up we wouldn't be having this conversation."

She ignored the dark pain in her heart at the thought. "Why would someone want to kill you? Of course, that's a ridiculous question — I would like to kill you. I'm sure countless other women would as well. But I think that most of us wouldn't have bothered hiring thugs — we'd rather have the pleasure ourselves. Who have you offended?"

He seemed amused. "Most everyone, though I would presume not to the point of killing me. If someone wanted me dead I would think they'd challenge me to a duel. Of course, I'm a fairly lethal shot, and if someone challenged me I could choose the weapons, so perhaps my enemies are cowards. Right now you're the only one I can think of who'd want me dead, and while I sympathize, I don't think you'd have time to arrange it. I'd just left Curzon Street when they set upon me."

"You live on Curzon Street," Charlotte pointed out. "Why were you leaving there?"

For a moment he looked uncomfortable. And then he laughed. "I may as well be truthful. I was going to see if I could find some way past Lady Whitmore and finish what we'd started."

The day was very quiet. She could hear the sounds of birds in the distance, the quiet hum of bees in the late-spring flowers. A soft breeze had picked up, pulling at his hair so that it fell into his face. She wanted to reach up and brush it away, but she kept her hands still.

"I assumed you would have taken care of the problem yourself," she said, then wished she'd kept her mouth shut as his smile widened.

"My hands are not nearly as much fun as yours. Though I suppose I could have closed my eyes and pretended . . ."

It was awful being so fair-skinned — she could feel hot color stain her cheeks. "I beg your pardon," she said. "That was most improper of me."

"Aren't we past the point of being proper with each other?"

"I think we should do our best to return to that state. We're likely to run into each other on occasion, and we'd be better off pretending we never . . . er . . . never . . ."

"Tupped?" he offered helpfully. "Swived? Shagged? Screwed? Fucked? There are any number of words for it."

"Are they all so ugly?"

He moved closer to her, as if he couldn't help himself. "I don't think they're ugly at all. They're honest. Physical. Arousing. Come to bed with me."

The last followed so suddenly upon the previous words that for a moment she didn't comprehend. "I beg your pardon?"

"You heard me." His voice was low and hungry. "Come to bed with me. It's a huge house — no one will walk in on us. We'll find a place. A nice, private place. I want you, I've been driven mad with wanting you, and nothing I do seems to change it. Take my hand and come with me."

The blood was pounding in her body. In her ears, between her legs, in her heart. Time seemed to stand still. Now was the time to claim her revenge. Now was the time to finish it for good. To say "no, thank you" very politely and walk away. There were hundreds of other women he could have. He was poison for her, beautiful, glittering poison. Walk away, she told herself.

He put his hand out, his long, gorgeous fingers outstretched to her. She stared down at them, and to her astonishment she saw a faint tremor.

"Yes," he said. "I'm shaking, I want you so badly. What do you want me to do, Charlotte? Beg?"

She knew the answer, they both knew the answer, but neither of them spoke it. He'd make a terrible husband — he'd whore and gamble and drink and break her heart.

"What do you want, Charlotte?" he said again, sounding almost angry.

She met his hard blue eyes. "You."

21

He took her hand in his, his grip sure and steady, and led her into the house. She followed him almost in a daze. Was she really doing this? She most certainly was.

He was lying to her, of course. Not for one moment did she believe he was so caught up with longing for her that he'd throw caution to the winds. And yet he seemed to be doing just that. A romp between the sheets at a notorious gathering was one thing. With a pillar of the church and a vengeful Lina around there was a good chance he'd be forced into marrying her.

So why was he taking such a chance?

He said he'd been mad with wanting her. The madness she could believe. The wanting was more of a question. He'd let her go last night, and she still wasn't sure who'd won that particular battle. If she thought she'd proven she could walk away from him, she'd failed. He might be convinced she was invulnerable. She knew she couldn't think, couldn't eat, couldn't sleep. All she could do was long for him.

No, he must be lying about how much he wanted her. Once more he was trapped someplace without a more beautiful, experienced alternative. But he was such a lovely liar that she was willing to believe him.

Just as she'd believed him when he told her they were both trapped in the room near the abbey, and he'd lied about that as well. He could have had anyone else, and he'd chosen her.

In the end, his reasons didn't matter. This was her choice, her decision. She would have him, for an hour, for a day, for as long as he wanted. She was tired of lying to herself.

The servants looked at them curiously as he pulled her through the house. It was a huge old place, with whole wings of it shut down. He seemed to know his way around it — within a few minutes they were climbing higher and higher into a part of the place that clearly hadn't been occupied in decades.

"Where are we going?" Not that it mattered. She would follow him anywhere.

"The children's rooms," he replied. "Unfortunately Montague hasn't been able to fill them." He glanced back at her. "We used to visit Montague's family when we were young. My sisters and I were relegated to the nursery, while my brother got to sleep in the main part of the house. I was very jealous."

"You have an older brother?"

"No," he said. "Not anymore. He died."

Of course he did, she thought, stricken. He wouldn't be Viscount Rohan if there was an older son to take the title. She didn't make the mistake of saying she was sorry — his voice precluded sympathy. Clearly it was a pain that still clung to him.

He pushed open the door to a room shrouded in shadows and Holland covers, and pulled her in, closing the door behind them. He dropped her hand, and they stood there in the darkness, unmoving. "Why did you come with me?"

A trickle of fear danced in her belly, and for a moment she wondered if she was going to be sick again. He'd been toying with her, seeing how far she'd come, and now he was going to laugh at her and tell her he'd never wanted her, that this was revenge for leaving him last night. She panicked, and before he could strike the first blow that would devastate her she managed a cool laugh. "I was bored."

She could see his responding smile, seeing straight through her. "So was I . . . Aren't we glad we have each other to keep us entertained in such a tiresome place?" He took a step forward, and without thinking, she backed away, the uncertainty still moving through her body.

"It's not going to work if you do that," he said softly.

"Maybe that's a better idea."

"Coward," he said. He took another step toward her, and she took another one back, coming up against the closed door. He leaned forward and brushed his mouth across hers, so gently it seemed as if she'd imagined it. "Poor Charlotte," he whispered. "You're as bad as I am."

"What do you mean?" Her voice was only a thread of sound as his mouth traced the line of her jaw, ending up just beneath her ear, against her throbbing pulse.

"It's a waste of time to keep fighting it. We're doomed. We may as well give in." His hands were in her hair now, and she heard the hairpins fall on the floor as her neat braids fell loose around her. "Turn around, Charlotte."

"W-why?"

"Because I want to unlace your dress."

"Is that strictly necessary?"

He laughed against her throat. "Yes, it's strictly necessary. I want to see you naked. I want to lick every inch of your body. Turn around."

She turned. His hands were on her back, and she shivered, leaning her forehead against the solid door as she felt his fingers unlace her, deftly, as he'd unlaced so many other women before. She wasn't going to think about that, she told herself. She wasn't going to think at all.

The dress began to slide, catching on the narrow hoops. And then he set to work on her stays, which was a very good thing since she was having a hard time catching her breath. He freed them, then untied the ribbon that held her hoops and petticoats around her waist.

Everything fell down around her ankles in a *whoosh,* leaving her standing still in her chemise and stockings and drawers. She started to turn, but his hands caught her shoulders, to stop her.

"You're not naked yet."

"I know," she said, reaching for asperity and ending up with nervousness.

"I thought we agreed you were going to get naked."

"You still have your clothes on."

"So I do," he said. "Shall we change places?"

She turned then, and he let her. In the half light, with his bruised face, he still looked beautiful. "No," she said. "You can stay there." And she reached for his neck cloth.

She'd never removed a man's neck cloth before, and it took her a moment to figure out how to untie its intricate knots. The fact that her hands were shaking didn't make things easier. At one point she tugged when the folds weren't free, and he made a faint choking sound. "Perhaps I'd better do this myself if I'm going to survive long enough to pleasure you."

She froze. Suddenly the memory of their first meeting came back to her, when he'd mocked her clumsiness, and she tried to pull back from him.

He wouldn't let her. He caught her hands and placed them against his chest. "You're going to have to figure out how to deal with me, darling Charlotte," he said, brushing a kiss against the corner of her mouth. "I'm a very insensitive fellow half the time, and if you take offense we'll be spending all our time fighting. Or making up. On second thought, perhaps you should keep getting angry with me."

"Why?"

"Because when we make up we'll have sex, and it will be delicious."

"Can't it be delicious without fighting?"

He'd pulled the neck cloth free and handed it to her before dropping his arms. "Why don't we find out," he said in a soft voice. "Do you think you can manage the buttons?"

She could. He shrugged out of his coat. He was still in riding clothes, so he wore no vest, and the tiny pearl buttons on his snowy shirt were difficult but not impossible. At least she didn't run the risk of strangling him in the process. The shirt opened beneath her fingers, exposing his smooth, beautiful chest with just a faint sifting of hair in the center. She was fascinated by that hair. She pulled the shirt free from his breeches and pushed it off his shoulders. And then she leaned forward and pressed her face against his chest, rubbing her cheek against the softly furred part, turning her mouth against him and licking delicately, breathing in the scent of him.

He let out a ragged breath. "Get to my breeches," he begged. "Please."

"But you said we're in no hurry," she murmured against his chest. She rubbed her face against him like a kitten, and found herself making soft purring sounds as she did so. While she was luxuriating in the touch and texture of him, he was growing ever more tense.

He took her hand and slid it down the front of his breeches, holding it there against the solid ridge of flesh. She smiled against his skin, moving her mouth downward to the flat bowl of his navel, rubbing, purring, until she sank onto her knees, pressing her cheek against his erection, letting her nose and mouth and chin brush against it through the fine wool of his breeches.

"Oh, merciful God," he muttered weakly. She put her hands up to his narrow hips, needing to hold on to something, as she caressed him with her face, her mouth, loving the feel, the freedom of it.

He held himself very still, letting her play for long minutes, as he seemed, impossibly, to grow harder and larger beneath the constricting breeches. Finally he spoke, and it sounded as if the words were being forced out. "I hate to bother you," he said politely enough, "but my breeches are becoming positively painful. At this rate I'm going to pop the stitching. The buttons are at the side."

Yes, she could feel them beneath her hands as she held him. She decided not to hesitate. These buttons decided to open easily beneath her fingers, and she caught the fabric of his breeches and underdrawers, and pulled them down, releasing him.

Even in the murky light she could see him quite clearly. His heavy penis jutted out, an invitation, and still, oddly enough, a threat. She didn't care. Grasping his hips again, she leaned forward and gently rubbed her face against him, against the solid thrust of him, against the crinkly hair at its base, rubbing and purring, letting her lips brush against his skin, rubbing her eyelids and forehead and mouth against him.

He was trembling now. And she was wet. "Take me in your mouth, Charlotte," he said with a soft groan. "I beg of you. Suck me."

She could claim her revenge now, she thought dazedly. She could rise and walk away, leaving him as insanely aroused as she had been the night before.

But she knew what she wanted, and she was tired of games. Very delicately she put her mouth on the tip of him, tasting a strange sweetness.

"More," he said in an anguished voice. "Please, Charlotte. Take more."

There was no way she could take all this into her mouth. But she wanted to try. She closed her mouth over the head, circling it, tugging at him. And then she sucked more in, slowly, inch by inch, her tongue touching, tasting, wetting him to make the slide easier. His hands were in her hair, not forcing her, just holding her as she pulled on him, closing tight around her so that her mouth embraced him, held him.

"Can you take more?" he whispered hoarsely.

She released him for a moment to answer, and he let out an anguished cry. "Oh, God, don't stop."

"You're too big," she said. But she sucked him in again, going deeper, taking more of him, so much that he brushed the back of her throat, and she made a little singing noise of pleasure.

She'd never imagined feeling like this, wanting this so badly. It was doubtless perversion, but she loved it, loved the taste of him, the feel of such strength inside her mouth, the way her tongue could sweep against him, the way her mouth could wrap around him. He was prompting her, and she realized he wanted her to move up and down on him, as if he were between her legs and not in her mouth. And as his pleasure grew, and his strong legs began to tremble, so did hers, so that when he suddenly pulled her away she cried out in distress, fingers digging into his hips, trying to pull him back.

Instead he hauled her to her feet. "You're not quite ready for that part, love," he said, and for a moment she was mystified.

She looked up at him. "What part? What happens next?"

"You know what happens next," he said in a hoarse voice. "I spill my seed."

"And then what happens that I'm not ready for?"

"You swallow it."

She started to sink to her knees again, but he laughed a shaky laugh. "You'd be better served if you gave me a moment to regain my self-control and let me remove my boots. It's the least a gentleman can do."

"And you're such a gentleman."

"Not with you, love. But I'm trying."

He leaned against one of the covered beds, pulling first one boot off and then the other with more ease than she would have expected. And then his clothes followed, and he was naked, gorgeous, just a little bit frightening.

"Take off your chemise and your drawers," he said. "You don't want me tearing them again. You'd soon run out of clothes."

She was suddenly shy. Silly way to be,

considering what she'd just done to him, but her hands shook and she wondered how she could reach up under the chemise without exposing herself to his curious eyes —

He moved forward, took the hem of the chemise and whipped it over her head with one smooth movement. And a second later, the drawstring to her drawers was loosened, and they fell to her feet, and she was wearing nothing at all but her stockings.

"Oh, God," he said, a curse, a supplication, a prayer. He pushed her up against the door, just behind her, lifted her by her legs and thrust inside her, hard.

She was shocked by his sudden move, his immediate invasion. That they were standing shocked her, that it felt so good. He slid deep, painlessly, and she knew that was why she was wet. For him. She threw her arms around his neck, holding on tightly, as her body did what her mouth had done, clasping him, holding him, as he thrust up into her, a hard, steady, relentless rhythm that had her gasping for breath, shivering in reaction, unable to move herself as he pinned her against the door, simply receiving his half-frantic thrusts, wanting more and more.

His skin was covered with a thin film of sweat, his face against her neck, his fingers tight on her hips. A climax rocked her, the climax she'd been cheated of the night before, and she could feel herself shatter, losing all sense of anything but the blinding, mindless pleasure he gave her.

He held still, letting her ripple and clench around him, and when the first throes had died he swung her away from the door, never breaking their joining, carrying her across the room to the Holland-covered bed. He tried to set them both down without breaking their connection but she tumbled away from him and he slipped free, and she found she could giggle.

"Heartless wench," he growled, coming down on one knee on the bed. "Turn over."

She stilled, looking up at him questioningly. "Turn over," he said again. "And get on your knees. You know I won't hurt you. Don't you?"

Yes, she knew. She did as she was told, for a moment feeling embarrassed, undignified. But there was no dignity to be sought in sex, and she felt his mouth at the small of her back, heard his sigh of dreamlike appreciation. "You're beautiful, you know," he murmured, his hands sliding over her back, pulling her forward so that she rested on her elbows. "Your skin is like cream. I want you every way I can." His fingers slid over her buttocks, hard, caressing, then moved down between her legs, to the wetness there, and she jumped, her sensitized flesh quivering.

He rubbed her, spreading the dampness, and he slid his long fingers inside her, making her start. And then she pushed back against his hand, wanting more.

A moment later she felt his hard thighs at the back of hers, his cock nudging at her damp sex. And when he pushed in again it was tighter, deeper, rubbing against a different place that suddenly made her climax again, a long, powerful shudder. He held her, one hand palming the front of her to hold her steady.

"Try not to come so hard, love," he said in a shaky laugh. "You're pushing me out again. And I need to be *deep* inside you."

His words made another paroxysm hit her, and she was powerless to do anything about it. "I can't . . . stop it," she said, dropping her head down on the heavy linen cover that smelled of bleach and sunlight and dust. "Just let me . . ." Her momentary breath was enough, and he pushed in, deeper than he'd ever been before, so deep she could taste him again.

His fingers tightened on her hips, and it was as if permission had finally been granted. He thrust into her, fast now, so hard she had to muffle her cries into the covers beneath her, again and again and again, and she knew if he pulled out she'd die, she needed all of him, spilling inside her, she needed him filling her, over and over.

He took one hand from her hip, slid it around in front of her and rubbed his palm against that magic place, just as his cock slid along a spot so powerful inside her that even the mattress couldn't muffle her shriek, and with a final, slamming thrust he climaxed, inside her, and her body pulled him deeper rather than pushing him away as she dissolved.

It seemed to last forever, his rigid outpouring that seemed to scald her very heart, her shivering, clenching, mindless release, and all she could think was more, more, more, and then suddenly it was enough, and they collapsed together onto the narrow, dusty bed.

22

Etienne de Giverney was a very unhappy man. He had spent a lifetime in search of the legacy he deserved, he'd broken the laws of God and man, and just when it looked as if it was in his reach that overgrown, red-headed bitch had thrown all his plans in the sewer.

It was impossible. Three weeks ago, when he saw Adrian head after her instead of sharing drink and decadence with him, he'd assumed he was perfectly safe. The girl was awkward, older than his cousin's son and heir, ordinary looking and too outspoken. He would fuck her once and abandon her.

But he hadn't. He hadn't emerged from that little room he kept, preferring his privacy to the audience most of the Heavenly Host preferred. And Etienne was there under sufferance. Not a member, not even a guest, but a hanger-on to be tolerated. Oh, they laughed with him, gambled with him. But he knew the English and their misguided sense of superiority.

Etienne had finally chosen to interfere. It hadn't been that difficult, to tease Adrian into leaving her behind. And just to make certain she didn't cause any more trouble he'd arranged her tumble down the cliff before he caught up with Adrian.

She hadn't hit her head, or suffered more than a few bruises. More damnable luck. And the men he'd hired to finish Adrian for good had bungled. They'd waited too long. He'd turned away from home instead of coming toward them, and their necessary pursuit had ruined everything.

Etienne had been waiting at Adrian's house, prepared for the tragic news, when that stupid English vicar had helped him into the house. It had taken all Etienne's sangfroid to keep from screaming in rage.

And then the moment Pagett had informed Adrian that Charlotte Spenser would be in Sussex what must he do but go haring off almost immediately, like a love-starved moonling. Who would have thought it?

Etienne had done everything he could to stop him, but for some reason his influence over Adrian was waning. It wouldn't be long before he was dropped, and he'd lose his entrée to anywhere in English society.

He wasn't going to let that happen.

Indeed, it wasn't his fault. The heir, Charles Edward, had been too much like his father, with a neck-or-nothing style in all of life. He rushed into things without thinking them through, and it hadn't taken long to goad him into riding Etienne's favorite horse, Meutrier. With typical English arrogance he hadn't known that the horse's name, and temperament, meant "murderer." The horse was mad, there was no other word for it. He'd been abused, and only Etienne could ride him.

But Charles Edward didn't like being told he couldn't do something. The fall had broken his back. The pneumonia that followed had finished the job, leaving Francis Rohan with only one heir.

It had been child's play to corrupt Adrian. He was already well on his way by the time he was twenty-five, old in the ways of sin and decadence. It wouldn't take much for Adrian to succumb. Opium was a dangerous drug, the interesting concoctions he made from plants could be even worse, and he had watched Adrian use them indiscriminately, with his help, of course.

An overdose would be so easy, but he preferred not to help things along. Adrian had been doing just fine by himself. His wretched father, Francis, was old now, close to seventy. He couldn't live that much longer, though he seemed damnably healthy. If Adrian predeceased him Francis would quickly follow, and there would be no one but Etienne to step into the title, the house, the monies.

He intended to be kind to Francis's wife. He would remove her from his houses, of course, but he would settle a small amount on her, enough to keep her relatively comfortable if her needs were few. And what needs would she have? She'd be in mourning, unable to attend social functions, which made things a great deal simpler. After that time was up he expected her to simply fade away without her husband. They were far too attached to each other — Etienne considered it bad ton to be so besotted, particularly after so many years and six children. No, she would die soon and he wouldn't have to worry about even the tiny stipend.

But none of that would happen, that rosy future would vanish if Adrian lived long enough to reproduce. And Etienne could no longer afford to be patient.

The small village of Huntingdon boasted an indifferent inn, but they were used to the strange comings and goings connected to Hensley Court, and no one paid any notice to the big Frenchman. They weren't even concerned about traitors. Most of the stupid English expected him to sell them out the first chance he got. They didn't realize that the so-called French government would rather have his head on a pike than theirs.

Fortunately he knew Hensley Court and its grounds very well — he'd been most observant on the few occasions when he'd been invited to join their silly games. It would be easy enough to slip in unnoticed, once he'd decided how he was going to handle the situation.

In retrospect, he'd clearly been mistaken in thinking things could resolve at their own speed. Instead of getting weaker, Adrian was growing stronger, and there were times when Etienne caught him looking at him with the same cool contempt he saw in Francis's eyes. It infuriated him.

He could blame all this on Miss Charlotte Spenser, a woman who'd never known her place, who had somehow managed to ensnare Adrian when Etienne had done his best to throw women of his own choosing at the man's head. Women who owed him a favor and would do what he told them to.

He took a deep breath. Indeed, it was

most aggravating, and it would take days to handle this. He would have to kill them both, of course. Adrian because he stood in the way, Miss Spenser because there was always the remote possibility that she carried an heir.

An heir who would be just as much a bastard as he was. And yet, Etienne had no doubt Francis would contrive to allow his grandchild to inherit the title. His English cousin had had things his way for too long. The loss of a second heir would slow him down where age hadn't managed to.

And how it would gall him to know that Etienne would inherit everything. The pleasure in that was almost better than the inheritance itself. The smug bastard who'd always had everything that should have been Etienne's by right, who'd given back his French title and estates just in time to have them confiscated by the canaille. A man who'd done everything he could to make sure Etienne was disliked. It would be revenge most sweet.

There were times when he wondered how he had come to this. He'd been a healer — Francis had paid for his medical training and bought him a surgery in Paris, a poor compensation for the title he'd stolen. But still, he'd spent decades helping people.

Perhaps it would be tallied into the final reckoning, perhaps not. He wasn't sure he believed in anything after this life.

Which made him all the more determined to get what he wanted from it.

"I think she's pregnant," Lina said in a disconsolate voice. "And you know what a disaster that is."

"No," said Monty, "I don't. Babies are lovely, new life is divine. If you're worried about what society will think then that's a new experience for you. To hell with society."

"You're right, of course," Lina said, managing a smile. "I tell you what, why don't we move in here with you? Charlotte can have her baby, and we'll make our own odd little family."

"I get to be the mother," Monty said with a faint grin. "I'm not cut out to be a pater-familias."

"Of course you are. You're very grand and controlling, like all good patriarchs are. You have to get better, though. No lolling about in bed like this. If we're going to have a baby we'll be very busy."

"I'll do my best. Of course, we haven't taken Rohan into account."

"How did you know it was Rohan?" she

asked. "You've been in bed for the last three weeks."

He looked affronted. "Do you think my servants don't report everything to me?"

"Everything?" she said.

"Everything. I do think Rohan might have other plans for Charlotte, my pet. But that doesn't mean I don't want you to move in here. You'll make a perfect mistress of Hensley Court. I've long imagined you here."

"Bless you, sweetness. I'll marry you. I think we should do very well together. Sexual congress is really a great deal less important than people say."

"Sexual congress is really a great deal more important, my pet. You just haven't had anyone do you right."

"Fat lot you know," she said.

"I do. I know very well how men make love, and I can tell you don't. So no, my sweet, I won't marry you. I don't think there'd be time even if I wanted to."

"There'll be all the time in the world," Lina said, leaving the chair and climbing up onto the bed, curling up next to him.

"If you say so." His voice was faint. "But if, by any strange occurrence, I don't, I'll be very happy to think of you here. I think you should have many, many children."

She was already feeling close to tears, and

is they threatened to spill over. "I can't ve children, Monty."

"I think the right man will give you many children."

"Then I'll need to find the right man," she said with a watery chuckle.

"I'll take care of it."

She took his frail hand, and they lay there in companionable silence. "Do you think Rohan and Charlotte could possibly be happy? He's a rake and a libertine."

"His father managed to reform with the love of a good woman. Adrian's the man his father is, despite his current shortcomings. I expect he and Charlotte will end up disgustingly happy, doting on each other into old age." He shook his head. "There's nothing worse than a reformed rake. Just look at Simon. He'll probably end up the same. It quite breaks my heart," he said cheerfully.

Lina laughed. "I promise I'll be wicked till the end of my days, Monty."

He lifted her hand to his and kissed it lightly. "We shall see, my precious."

Charlotte rolled over, stretching. Sunlight was coming in through the shuttered windows of the old nursery, and dust motes danced in the air. Adrian lay beside her, sound asleep, naked and beautiful, and she lay back, cradling her head in her arms, and watched him, her eyes sliding over all the mysterious parts of his body that were so different from hers. She felt wonderful, full of life and energy, as if she could dance and fly and sing.

"Go back to sleep," he muttered, not bothering to open his eyes.

"I can't. I'm too happy."

At that he did open one eye to survey her. "Delighted I could help . . . If you let me sleep I can do it again and you'll be even happier."

"I can't . . ." His arm shot out and caught her around the waist, pulling her back against his body. He was cool, lovely, all that flesh against hers, and she could feel his penis begin to stir at her backside, and instinctively her nipples hardened.

He felt them against his arm, having positioned himself deliberately. "Then again, now's as good a time as any," he said in her ear.

She pulled away, and he let her go, reluctantly. She sat up on the bed, looking down at him for a long moment. "Lina's going to raise a fuss."

"Then we avoid Lina. She doesn't need to know until it's too late."

"Too late for what?" she asked, confused.

e'll get married, of course. It's not the
st possible solution — I certainly had no
ntention of marrying anyone, but there
doesn't seem to be any help for it. I don't
seem to be able to get you out of my system.
It requires long familiarity for that to happen — I was enchanted with my favorite
mistress for more than two years before I
finally tired of her. I fully expect it to take
that long with you."

She stared at him, her face expressionless.
"And what happens then? If we're married
you can't pension me off with a diamond
brooch."

He laughed. "It costs a lot more than a
diamond brooch to dispense with those
kinds of entanglements, my sweet Charlotte.
No, we should do fairly well together once
society recovers from the shock. Even when
desire fades and we move on to other
partners I imagine we'll still be friends."

Her skin was like ice. "I would get to move
on to other partners as well . . . ?"

"Of course. Would you think I would be
so unfair?" He frowned. "Though I must
admit that right now the idea makes me
furious. But I'll change my mind, of course.
I always do."

"You always do," she echoed.

"In fact, that's why it took me so long to

get here. I was able to obtain a special license from my godfather, who happens to be the bishop of London. I imagine we could prevail upon Pagett to marry us."

"I don't think so," she said in her sweetest, softest voice.

He raised an eyebrow. "You don't want him to marry us?"

"No, my lord. I don't wish to marry *you.*"

His expression was almost comical. "Don't be ridiculous. Of course you do."

"No," she said calmly. "I do not. You're a cold-hearted, arrogant son of a bitch, and I deserve better."

He just looked at her in astonishment, as if she'd suddenly grown a second head. "I beg your pardon?"

She rose, ignoring her own nudity, and grabbed the Holland cover off the adjoining bed, wrapping it around her with great dignity. "I'm smart, I'm talented, I'm essentially kindhearted and I'm not a complete antidote. I shouldn't have to settle for the kind of cold-blooded union you're suggesting. It's so kind of you to condescend to offer for me, but you can take your proposal, if that's what it was, and stuff it up your bum. I'm worth more, I deserve better, and I'm not settling for someone like you."

She started toward the door, the heavy

trailing behind her, and he was up off bed, at the door before she made it here. He looked confused, furious, bewildered.

"You're not making sense, Charlotte," he said patiently. "The sex between us isn't like ordinary people's. You won't find this with someone else — it's special. I'm offering you the chance to be a viscountess, to have your own establishment, perhaps even children . . ."

"You're willing to make a great sacrifice on your part in order to scratch a curious itch. Find someone else." She put her hands on his bare chest, resisting the urge to stroke him, and shoved him away.

By now he was angry, affronted, and he fell back. "To hell with you then — do you know how many women would give everything to be in your place?"

"Go find one of them and shag yourself silly. You can't have me." And she yanked open the door and strode out into the hallway, feeling majestic, righteous and furious.

It was probably just as well that she got lost. Her defiant mood could only last so long. By the time she'd taken her third wrong turn, her lower lip was trembling, and when she came to the end of a hallway with no staircase in sight, she simply sank onto the worn carpet, the cover draped around her, and began to cry silently.

The linen was useless for blotting her tears. She lay there in a miserable welter of sorrow, sobbing quietly into her arms, when Lina found her.

She put her arms around her, murmuring soft, comforting things, helping her to her feet, repositioning the cover around her naked body. "Where are your clothes, dearest?"

"I . . . in . . . the . . . nursery," she said between hiccups. "Don't go there. He's in a rage."

"He doesn't know the meaning of the word *rage*," Lina said darkly. "Did he hurt you?"

Charlotte shook her head. "No."

Lina knew the halls as well as Adrian had. Within minutes she'd brought Charlotte back to her rooms, Meggie bustling around her, making clucking noises as she helped her bathe. "He certainly marked you, that one," she said. "I hope you did the same to him."

Charlotte closed her eyes, refusing to think about it. Refusing to think about the bite mark on his shoulder, the scratches on his back.

on't worry, sweeting," Lina said. "He'll arry you, make no doubt about that. If he ninks he can get away with this without offering for you . . ."

"He did offer for me. I told him no."

Lina's astonishment mirrored Adrian's, and Charlotte's ire began to rise again. "Why does everyone assume I should be grateful for the tidbits of attention he's tossing me?" she demanded. "I don't want a cold-blooded marriage of short-term lust and long-term politeness."

"It doesn't have to be that way," Lina protested.

"Yes, it does. That's what he's offering me. He was quite astounded that I would refuse such a magnanimous offer. He probably thought I would be struck dumb with gratitude. Well, I'm not grateful. I'd rather spend my life a fallen woman. I'd rather marry a rag-picker and live in the stews of London than marry that . . . that arrogant pig bladder."

Lina was sitting on the bed beside her, a troubled expression on her face. "Charlotte, you have to marry him. I think you might be increasing."

Charlotte looked at her blankly, the words making no sense. And then the meaning was clear. "No," she said flatly. She thought about it a moment. "Absolutely no." Th strange sense of lassitude and energy, the feeling of fullness and growth. "I can't be."

"Meggie says you haven't had your monthly courses. Just a few drops of blood, and that's often a sign of pregnancy. You've been tired all the time, sick in the morning, the smell of bacon makes you ill when you used to eat it by the pound. We won't know for sure, but you have all the signs. You have to marry him."

"No," she said stubbornly. "That just makes me even more convinced. I'm not going to bring a child into the world and give him a . . . a . . . *jackass* like Adrian for a father."

"You want to bring a bastard into the world?"

"We can raise her together. That is, unless you're sending me away for gross immorality."

Lina's laugh sounded suspiciously close to tears. "No, darling, I'm not. And if you don't want Adrian then you don't have to have him. We'll figure something out. Go away to the continent, or out to the country during your confinement. No one need ever know."

"I'm not giving the child up," she said.

"We'll tell everyone the baby was an

we've taken into our home. Don't ⌐ ⌐, darling, it will be —"

⌐er bedroom door slammed open, and ⌐drian was standing there, fully dressed, vibrating in rage. "You didn't think it worthwhile informing me that you're pregnant?" he roared.

Charlotte stiffened, her own rage flooding back. "Where did you get that idea?"

"From Monty. He wants to know why you won't marry me as well."

"Because I don't love you."

It was the wrong thing to say, but she was goaded. He looked at her in complete astonishment, and then laughed. "Why in the world would you think love has anything to do with what's between us? It's healthy lust that we ought to enjoy as long as it lasts, and then —"

"That's enough," Lina broke in hastily. "I believe you've put your foot in your mouth enough for one day. Why don't you go back down and chew on it for a while. Charlotte needs her rest. If she is increasing, and we're not even sure of that, then we need to take extra-special care of her."

Adrian's eyes narrowed. "You told me you've been entertaining gentlemen nonstop since you arrived back in London. What makes you think the child is mine?"

Meggie had just set the tea tray down in her lap, and Charlotte didn't hesitate. She picked up the pot and flung it at him, scalding tea spewing out over the bedroom.

It hit him on the unmarked side of his face, slamming against his cheekbone and breaking. The tea drenched him, but he didn't flinch, even as blood began to trickle down his cheek from the spot where a shard of china had sliced through the skin.

"Be damned to you then," he said, and slammed the door as he went.

For some reason Lina had a half smile on her face, one she quickly wiped away when Charlotte glared at her. "Let me get this straight, dearest. You won't marry him because he doesn't love you, is that it?"

"You heard him. Love has nothing to do with what's between us," she said angrily.

"But we know differently, don't we? You're in love with him. I'm not sure why, but I accept your choice."

"It's not my choice. He doesn't want me for the right reasons, and I won't take him for the wrong ones." She could feel the tears welling up again, and she dashed them away. "And why am I crying all the time? I never used to be so pathetic."

"Another sign of pregnancy, Miss Charlotte," Meggie said in her practical voice.

ne me mum got knocked up she'd
bawling all over the place. I used to
k it was just because she didn't want
other bastard clinging to her, but she told
me no, it came with the baby. You're pregnant."

Enough was enough. Charlotte stopped fighting it. She burst into tears, flinging herself face down on the bed. And it wasn't until later that she realized that Lina had quietly slipped out.

23

Adrian made it as far as the stables. He spun on his heel and turned back. He was making a habit of this, he thought wryly. She really did have the ability to make him insane.

He was damned if a child of his was going to be born a bastard. She didn't like it — she could damn well make the best of it. The best of a title, a fortune, better sex than she'd ever find in her life. There were worse fates for an overtall spinster with red hair and freckles. He didn't care what she wanted or didn't want.

Except that he loved her rich, coppery hair. He loved her creamy skin and the flecks of gold that danced across it in the most deliciously unexpected places. He hadn't gotten around to discovering all those places, and he was never a man to leave a job only partly done.

And what if she wasn't pregnant? he

strolling back into the house as if her future weren't at stake. Then he'd do his best to ensure she soon would be. He wanted her to be pregnant, he realized with a sense of shock. Wanted her to be carrying his baby. The thought of her, round and waddling, heavy with child, filled him with an odd sense of what might almost be called delight. Not that he would go that far. But his father would probably appreciate an heir if she had a boy, and his mother worried about him incessantly. If he were married she might calm down a little.

Of course his mother wanted him to fall in love. He could lie to her, though she tended to see through his prevarications even more quickly than his father did. But he imagined he could do a pretty good approximation of a man besotted. The kind of man who'd wake his godfather up in the middle of the night, demanding a special license. The kind of man who'd then jump on a horse and ride all night after her, ignoring the fact that he'd just been bashed in the head and leg and couldn't walk without limping. The kind of man who'd drag a woman off and shag her senseless in the middle of the day in an abandoned nursery.

The kind of man who wouldn't admit how much he needed her.

Simon Pagett was coming out the front door just as Adrian was about to enter. He had a troubled expression on his face, and when he spied Adrian he didn't look particularly pleased.

"You really are a vicar?" Adrian demanded abruptly.

"No, I wear the collar because it limits my fashion choices," he replied icily. "What do you want, Rohan?"

Adrian reached in his pocket and pulled out the crumpled license, handing it to him. Pagett frowned, looking it over. "How did you manage this?" he said finally.

"He's my godfather."

"It's dated today."

"I know when it's dated, man," Rohan said irritably. "I went and woke the old man up right after you left me. He wasn't best pleased with me — I'm not expecting much of a wedding present."

Pagett surveyed him for a long moment. "I didn't realize you knew she was pregnant."

"Bloody hell, did everyone know she was pregnant but me?" he exploded.

"If you didn't know she was pregnant why did you get the special license?"

Adrian said nothing.

"If I'm going to marry you I'll need an

409

know, you're a pain in the arse," Ro-
_ot back. "You'd think you'd spent
_ life being a saint."

"You're never too old to change your
ways," he said. "Why?"

"It seemed like a good idea at the time."

"And Miss Spenser agreed?"

"Miss Spenser is refusing to marry me,"
he said in a cranky voice. "I expect you to
show her the error of her ways."

"I'm afraid I can't do that. I want what's
best for her, and I doubt you're it."

"For God's sake!" Adrian shouted, goaded
to distraction. "What the hell do you want
from me?"

"When you figure it out, let me know. In
the meantime I have things to do." He was
about to walk past Rohan, when Lina appeared at the door, her black hair coming
undone, a look of wrath on her perfect face.

"I'm going to kill you," she said.

Pagett paused, looking back. "No, you're
not. Leave him alone, Lady Whitmore. He
needs to figure this out on his own."

"Don't you dare tell me what to do!" Her
fury at Pagett seemed oddly misplaced.
"This is between me and Lord Rohan."

"No, it's between Charlotte and Lord Rohan. It's none of your business," Pagett

returned. "This is your fault, for taking M
Spenser to the Revels in the first place, fo
someone like Lord Rohan to prey upon."

"Excuse me!" Adrian protested, but the
two were facing off against each other, and
he was forgotten.

"I brought her here to show her just how
worthless men are. She was curious, and I
thought she'd be better off knowing that
she wasn't missing anything," Lina said furi-
ously.

"How very altruistic of you, Lady Whitmore. Had I known you were capable of
such charitable gestures I could have come
up with a number of ways you could better
use your misguided energy."

"I can think of any number of ways . . ."

Adrian slipped into the house, going in
search of Charlotte once more. Their angry
voices carried after him, and he stopped,
glancing back at them.

"Why did you kiss me?" Lina was saying,
glaring at him.

The unruffled vicar was looking ruffled
indeed. "I believe you were the one who
kissed me. Inappropriately, I might point
out."

"I started it, you finished it."

"I thought you needed a lesson," he said
stiffly.

n in what? Kissing? I assure you
a great many men."

your reputation, Lady Whitmore.
rtain you've lost count of how many
you've . . . kissed."

"And what business is it of yours?" she
demanded, incensed.

"Absolutely none."

Idiots, Adrian thought, taking the marble
stairs two at a time. When he slammed open
Charlotte's door she was alone in the bed.

He came and stood over the bed. "You're
marrying me. I'm not giving you a choice in
the matter. I won't have my child born a
bastard."

"I won't have my child be the son of a
swiving, mean-spirited, libidinous troll who
—"

"Troll?" he echoed, momentarily distracted. "Surely not a troll, my precious."

"Troll," she said firmly. "I won't have
you."

"You have no choice. He's my child, and
he's not being born on the wrong side of
the blanket. I've spoken to Pagett. Six
o'clock at the parish church. I'm not taking
no for an answer. If you're not there I'll drag
you there by your hair."

She reached for the closest thing she could
find, a heavy book, and she threw it at him,

412

but he ducked. He was already in rou
enough shape — another few days and the
wouldn't be enough left of him to mangle.

He'd calm her down once he got her
naked. If he had to haul her out of bed and
carry her to the church in his arms she was
going to marry him. This was making him
crazy, and the only way he knew to calm
things down was to get her back in bed with
him. Legally. Permanently.

In the meantime he needed to keep as far
away from her as possible, or they'd either
end up back in bed together or she'd kill
him. And he wasn't sure which he preferred.

Charlotte looked at the door, vibrating with
fury. How dare he think he could just come
in and order her about? He thought she was
just going to show up at the church? Ridiculous.

She slid out of bed. Meggie had gone to
fetch her discarded clothes, and she dressed
quickly. It wasn't that she didn't trust Lina
to keep Rohan at bay, but Lina had her own
troubles with Simon Pagett. If Charlotte
simply disappeared for a little while it would
be better all around.

How she was going to accomplish that was
the challenge. She wouldn't be able to leave
the house without one of Monty's countless

eing her, and they would have no
report to Rohan. But perhaps
made it out of the house she could
direction. The village was only a
mile walk across the fields, and there
s a coaching inn directly in the middle of
t. She could safely assume that at least one
of the available coach routes would lead to
London, and once there it would be a fairly
simple matter to come up with an alternative. At least, she hoped so.

The hall was empty when she slipped out
of her room. She did her best to appear
cheerfully casual as she walked down the
stairs, ready to break into a run if Rohan
should put in an appearance. But for once
luck was with her. Even the faithful Dodson
was nowhere around, and Monty's bevy of
handsome footmen were in short supply as
well. She didn't bother trying the heavy
front door; instead she slipped through the
library, coming out on the wide terrace that
led down to the formal gardens.

She moved quietly, keeping to the edge of
the walled gardens. By the time she reached
the end, her heart was pounding in her
chest. Turning the corner, she barreled into
a huge figure, and she let out a frightened
shriek that quickly turned into a cautious
sigh of relief.

"Monsieur de Giverney," she said. Adrian's cousin. What the hell was he doing here?

"Monsieur le Comte," he corrected. "The French government may have outlawed my title but I still account it as worth something."

"Indeed. I beg your pardon, my lord," she said swiftly, mentally cursing him. She didn't have time to deal with the man's vanity, she needed to get away.

"I'm here to offer you my help, Mademoiselle Spenser."

She was just about to come up with a quick excuse and exit when his words penetrated. She glanced up at him.

He was a handsome man in a barrel-chested, florid style, with thick lips and eyebrows, a strong blade of a nose and flat black eyes. She'd never liked him, and she didn't like him now. Unless his idea of helping was to get her away from Adrian.

"Help me with what, my lord?" she asked in an even voice, resisting the impulse to look over her shoulder. For all she knew, Rohan had realized she was missing and at this rate it wouldn't take long to find her.

"You're trying to get away from my young cousin, are you not? A good lad, but importunate. I presume you've fought?"

She said nothing for a moment. She didn't like him and she didn't trust him, but at that point she didn't have much of a choice. If she was to get away before Adrian came searching for her she was going to have to take the help offered. "Yes," she said. "He's trying to force me to marry him and I don't want to."

His thick eyebrows rose. "Indeed? Then you shouldn't have to. I can help you get away, *mademoiselle.* Otherwise you might find yourself . . . how do you clever British say it . . . leg shackled before you know what happened."

She looked at him for a long, cautious moment. Why would this man help her? He was Adrian's cousin — wouldn't he want to help him instead?

It wasn't as if she had any choice. "I would appreciate your help, *monsieur,*" she said politely.

He smiled at her, a warm, avuncular smile that wreathed his thick lips and didn't reach his eyes. But then, he was French, she reminded herself. Perhaps it took a lot more to make him smile. "Then I will take care of things. *En avant!* Come with me and I'll spirit you away where no one will ever find you."

"And where is that, Monsieur le comte?"

she asked in a calm voice.

He took her hand in his heavy hand, bringing it to his mouth, and she wished she dared to pull it away. "You will have to leave it up to me, *mademoiselle*. Trust me, I can be quite ingenious. He may scour the earth to find you, but he will instead find failure."

"And how will you manage that? Sooner or later he's bound to figure out where I am. Where I've gone. Which is . . . ?"

He smiled at her benevolently. She could see tufts of black hair in his ears, his nostrils, creeping over his high neck cloth. It wasn't his fault he was incredibly hairy, but it took all her social graces to keep from retreating in distaste.

He breathed on her, breath laden with odd cooking flavors that clung most unpleasantly. "Where will you be, *mademoiselle,* where no one can find you?" he echoed politely. "Why, I'm afraid you'll be dead."

Adrian couldn't find her anywhere. No one could. At some point, in between the time he went storming into Charlotte's room and gave her an ultimatum and when her maid had brought her a late luncheon, Charlotte had disappeared, taking her clothes, leaving a scribbled note for Lina and vanishing into

...in air.

For a moment he wondered if they were all lying to him — some mass conspiracy to help Charlotte escape from the hideous punishment of marriage to a lenient and engaging husband. But they were just as mystified as he was, and the muted warfare that had existed between them all faded into worry, and in his case, something akin to panic.

He felt as if he were walking on ice, with no sense of when he would find steady ground again. He didn't know what he wanted, what he needed, but he couldn't shake the sense that something was very, very wrong.

No one else seemed to share the measure of his panic. They wanted him gone, he knew it, and indeed, he was ready to — inaction making him crazy — when he was called once more into Montague's bedroom.

Montague's color was ashen, and he seemed to have shrunk inside his skin. His eyes were closed when Adrian walked in, and for a moment he had the sick feeling that Monty had died. But his eyes fluttered open, and there was a ghost of his familiar, faintly malicious smile.

"You need to find her." He spoke so softly Adrian wasn't sure he'd heard him clearly.

"How did you know she ran off . . . ?
Idiotic question. "You knew I'd slept with
her. You knew she was pregnant. Is there
anything you don't know?"

"I don't know where she is," Monty said,
his voice barely more than a whisper. "No
one saw her go. One of my gardeners spotted her several hours ago at the bottom of
the walled gardens, talking with a tall man.
I presume that was you?"

Rohan shook his head, the unease that was
filling him beginning to spill over. "I haven't
seen her outside. She's refused to marry me,
and every time I try to talk to her she throws
something at me."

"My dear friend, you must have bungled
that badly. Which surprises me — you're
always so good at handling angry women.
Of course, this case is very different."

"Because she's pregnant?"

Montague sighed. "I don't understand
how you can be so thickheaded when I've
always considered you an eminently intelligent man. Save for the times you've been
under your cousin's influence. All of you
are complete dunderheads — at this rate I
don't dare die. You have no sense at all."

"I have no idea what you're talking about.
I can manage my life perfectly well," he said
with a trace of hauteur.

"Yes, you've just demonstrated what an excellent job you're doing. I've got Evangelina pining over Simon, I've got the vicar mooning after her like an adolescent girl. At least Simon seems aware of it, unlike Lina, who doesn't seem to realize she's fallen in love."

"Lady Whitmore's in love with the parson?" Adrian said, momentarily distracted, remembering their argument. "That should turn a few heads."

"You're no better. Charlotte's totally besotted with you, heaven only knows why. To be sure, you're pretty enough, but Miss Spenser is far too intelligent a woman to be swayed by simple beauty."

"It's not my beauty," he said dryly. "She thinks I'm not the lecherous profligate I pretend to be."

"I did mention she was intelligent, did I not? You, on the other hand, are a complete idiot. You're not likely to find another woman who's worth even half of what Charlotte could bring you. And you go stomping around, totally oblivious to your own feelings."

"What feelings?"

"Never mind," Montague said wearily. "Do you happen to know where the so-

420

estimable Etienne de Giverney is rig
now?"

Adrian's rebellious streak flared. "Don't,
pray you, become like my parents and tell
me all the reasons Etienne is a danger to
my health. Surely you are more broad-
minded when it comes to indulging one's
appetites. Etienne is inventive and entertaining." Which wasn't strictly true. He was
tired to death of Etienne and his constant
need for distraction. Distractions that led to
a profound weariness of the soul. But he
was damned if he was going to admit it. "In
fact, I told him I didn't want him ac-
companying me here. He tried to insist, saying he had a fondness for you, but acquit
me of being a total idiot. He despises you
and you return that regard."

"I rejoice that you see that much," Montague said.

"In truth, I've felt sorry for the man. He's
lost everything, he's trapped in a foreign
land, forced to exist on the limited kindness
of my father, who's never liked him. If it
weren't for me I doubt he'd be received
anywhere."

"And yet you didn't bring him?"

Adrian paused for a moment, looking at
his friend's tired eyes. "I admit it. I'm sick
to death of him," he finally said. "Why do

u ask?"

"He's a tall man, is he not? He knows where you and Charlotte are. And he hates you."

Adrian laughed, ignoring the uneasiness building inside him. "Don't be absurd, Monty. I've taken him everywhere, brought him into society. He owes me as much as he owes my father."

"And he hates your father. As he hates you. No one likes to be made grateful all the time. Why do you think your lovely girl decided to run off? She didn't appreciate your noble sacrifice."

"I didn't say that," Adrian protested. "I was perfectly logical. And I'll have you know I told her we should marry before I even knew she was increasing."

"You told her *the two of you should marry.* And you still haven't figured out why you failed so miserably?"

"She could hardly have expected a declaration of love and a promise of lifelong fidelity," he said, irritated.

"It sounds as if she did."

Adrian said nothing for a long while. "Right now I simply want to find out where she is. We can argue about the marriage later. If you know where she went then for God's sake tell me."

"I think Etienne has her."

"In heaven's name why?"

"I can think of any number of reasons. He's not your friend — the Etienne de Giverney I've known since my early days in Paris is not a friend to anyone. He gets rid of anything that stands in the way of what he wants. I think he's decided that having lost his French title and lands he now wants the English titles and estates. And he's going to get them."

"Of course he wants them. He always has. I'm not a complete idiot," Adrian said.

"No, only a partial one. Though I admit, I had no idea how far he'd be likely to go or I would have warned you. You're in his way. So is your possible heir. And if I were you I wouldn't be languishing, waiting for Charlotte to return."

The feeling of dread that he'd been fighting returned full force. "You think Etienne has taken her?"

"Haven't I said as much?" Montague spoke with a trace of his old asperity. "I haven't much time or energy left, and I really don't wish to waste it solving the mess my friends have made of their lives. I wish to depart mine knowing that things are well on their way to at least a reasonably happy conclusion. I'll be very annoyed if something appens to Charlotte. It will depress me, and if I have to die young, I at least deserve to die happy."

"Nothing's going to happen to Charlotte. I'll find her and force her to marry me."

Montague closed his eyes wearily. "I can't live forever, dear boy. Stop being so stubborn. You're in love with the girl. Admit it and go tell her."

Adrian narrowed his gaze, but he didn't bother arguing. "Where would Etienne have taken her?"

"How should I know? It depends on how mad he is. He may have strangled her and dumped her body in the canal by now, while you've been sulking."

"No," Rohan said, his heart like ice. "No."

"You think he's not capable of doing such a thing?"

"No," he said, the blind fury threatening to overwhelm him. "I believe he's capable. But I would know if she were dead."

"Would you? And you still deny you love her? What kind of bond could you possibly have that would allow for you to know any such thing?"

"I need to find her. We can argue about whether I love her or not once she's safe," Adrian snapped.

"Well, at least that's a step in the right

direction. You're allowing for the possib·
when any fool can see you're totally bes·
ted with the girl. Which gives me muc·
greater hope for your future. In the meantime, there are any number of places
Etienne might have taken her. He may have
driven her back to London — she'd probably go with him willingly enough in her
need to escape your ham-handed behavior.
Or he could have taken her to the ruins.
There's lots of privacy there. Send Dodson
to me and I'll have him organize a search
party."

"I can't —" Their conversation was interrupted by one of Monty's beautiful footmen.

"Excuse me, my lord, but a gentleman left
a message for you."

The fear suddenly went bone deep, and
when Adrian held out a hand for the folded
scrap of paper he could see it shake slightly.

He recognized Etienne's scrawl immediately: *Your bride awaits you at the Chapel of
Perpetual Erection. I suggest you come at
once, and alone.*

He looked up, meeting Monty's gaze. And
then he walked out without another word.

24

At first Charlotte was aware of nothing but darkness and the smell of what seemed uncomfortably close to fire and brimstone. Her recollection was hazy — she'd been running from something, hadn't she? And why couldn't she seem to move? There was something over her head, blocking out the light, and she tried to shake it off.

She squirmed, and heard a low, evil chuckle, the same sound she'd heard in the maze at Ranelagh Gardens. Memory came flooding back, along with a full-blooded fury. She tried to speak, only to discover something was tied around her mouth, silencing her. She tried to shake it off, furious, when she heard the laugh again.

"You don't like that, do you, my pet? If you'd had the sense to hit your head on a rock when I shoved you down the cliff you wouldn't be going through this now."

Etienne, she thought. Etienne had pushed

her. She allowed herself a brief moment relief. She thought she'd long ago dismisse the idea that Adrian had tried to kill her, but there must have been a lingering doubt, now vanquished.

She was good and trussed, like an angry chicken, she thought. Her legs and arms were tied to a chair, and she struggled, wildly, the chair tipping when a heavy hand clubbed her across the face. The hood over her head muffled the blow, and she struggled, desperate for a way out of the darkness. She didn't like being tied up.

"If you're going to behave yourself I'll let you see where you are." He pulled the hood off, and she blinked, looking around her. She appeared to be in some kind of church, and for a moment she wondered if Etienne was in league with Adrian, if he'd brought her to the village church to force a marriage upon her.

And then she noticed that the cross was inverted, the altar was a bed, and the leaded glass was patently obscene. There was a brazier nearby, a fire burning, taking some of the damp chill off the air. Fire and brimstone. She must be in the blasphemous chapel of the Heavenly Host. The Church of Perpetual Erection, Lina had told her. Wishful thinking on someone's part.

She turned her head back, her eyes setting on Etienne de Giverney's bulky form.
She glared at him, but he merely watched
her, unmoved, one leg swinging negligently
as he perched on the edge of a table. Names
for him swirled inside her head, and her inability to spit them out at him was almost
worse than being tied up.

"Don't worry, *mademoiselle.* You won't be
in this deplorable condition for long. Your
noble knight will be rushing to your rescue
momentarily, and you will have the chance
to die in his arms like a true heroine. Just
be patient, or I'll be forced to hit you again."

She ignored him to look around her, her
vision somewhat encumbered by her restraints. The chapel was a new construc-
tion, made of wood. Ecclesiastical-type
hangings lay across the low-slung altar,
blasphemous ones, and she wondered what
Simon Pagett would say if he saw this place.

There were piles of wood set at intervals
around the sides of the small church, and
she could smell the resin scent of pitch. The
place was set to go up in flames, and there
was a certain poetic justice to it. A chapel
dedicated to the fires of hell succumbing to
a conflagration.

Her eyes met de Giverney's expressionless
ones, but his smile was eerily affable. "Yes,

mademoiselle, there will be a sad accide⁙
You and your lover will die in a fire. It w⁙
be a very great tragedy, do you not think⁙
No? You look as if you were quite desperate
to tell me something, but I think I will leave
the gag in place for the time being. I'm
afraid I have a very hard heart, and your
tears and pleading will leave me completely
unmoved. They will only annoy me."

She'd been frightened and angry, now her
fury overwhelmed any lingering fear. As if
she was so poor-spirited as to beg for mercy!
She glared at him, trying to put all her anger
and contempt into her gaze, but he remained completely unmoved. "It won't be
long, *mademoiselle.* I expect him to come
charging up on a white horse — oh, no, he
won't be able to do that, will he? He'll have
to use the ornamental canal to get here,
which will cut the drama. But I expect him
to make any number of heroic declarations
before I kill him. In fact, I think I hear him
coming now."

Charlotte's fear escalated, and she began
to struggle anew, to warn him, when de Giverney's low, eerie laugh sent chills along her
spine, and he called out, "We're here, dear
boy. Your lady love awaits."

She half expected Adrian to charge in, as
he had into her bedroom earlier in the day,

429

l of rage and demands, and she braced erself, ready for rescue.

Instead he pushed the door open and strolled in, seemingly at ease. "Etienne," he said in a charming voice. "What is all this?"

The *comte* laughed, amused. "Oh, I think you know, dear boy," he replied. "It should come as no surprise to you. If you'd listened to your father's warnings you'd know that I never give up on what I want. But then, what headstrong young man ever listens to their elders? I suggest you put that pistol down on the chair. I have one trained on Mademoiselle Spenser, and she would be dead before you managed to get off a shot."

Adrian's wry smile was all charm as he removed the dueling pistol from inside his riding coat and set it down carefully. "Of course, you knew I would have to try."

"Of course," Etienne said with equal courtesy.

"So how can I convince you to let Miss Spenser go? She has nothing to do with what lies between your family and mine."

"Ah, but she does. You think I don't know that she's carrying a possible heir? The moment you became infatuated with her I knew she was a potential problem, and I tried to dispense with her earlier. If I let her go now, not only would your father contrive

430

to have your child inherit, but it would l
a witness. And they're much more likely
believe a silly English girl than a despise
Frenchman, don't you think?"

Silly English girl, Charlotte thought, fuming. Now she was truly angry.

Adrian must have sensed her rage because he glanced over at her. "You've already tormented her enough. Trust me, being unable to talk is sheer torture for her. I know she's dying to tell you what she thinks of you."

"*Dying* is, I'm afraid, the operative word," Etienne said, trying to sound regretful and failing utterly. "Go over there and untie her, but don't let your body get between her and the gun, please."

"You're letting her go?"

"Don't be stupid, Adrian," Etienne said wearily. "Move slowly. I would prefer not to have to shoot you, but I'm willing to take the chance."

Charlotte looked up at him as he towered over her. His back was to Etienne, and the expression on his face was startling, filled with regret and guilt and longing. "Am I allowed to talk to her?"

"Feel free," Etienne said grandly. "I'm afraid she won't answer. My tolerance for romantic declarations is minimal."

431

e knelt in front of her, his hands on her
kles, and began to untie the ropes that
ound her there. "I'm sorry I got you in
this mess, sweet Charlotte," he murmured.
"If I had any idea there was insanity in the
family I never would have come near you."

Etienne made an angry sound, then managed a laugh. "Unlikely. You are too much
like me, Adrian. You take what you want
and be damned to the consequences."

Her feet were loose, and he reached for
her bound wrists. "I'm nothing like you.
I'm not some pathetic old man whose
empty life needs to be filled with other
people's titles and money." He dropped his
voice to only a breath of sound, and if she
hadn't been staring up at him she wouldn't
have heard it. "When I turn, drop to the
floor and stay there."

At least, that's what she thought he'd said.
His coat hung open, and she could see a
tiny pistol tucked inside, and she let out a
muffled sound of protest. That small gun
would be useless against the firearm Etienne
carried, and Adrian would die in front of
her, and she couldn't bear it. She loved him
— it was too late to deny it any longer.
She'd been an idiot not to take whatever he
offered — it was more than most people got
in this life.

"What's she fussing about?" Etien. demanded sharply. "You wouldn't be plar. ning anything, would you? Move to one side so I can see her clearly."

Adrian did as he was told, keeping his back to Etienne, one hand working on the knots at Charlotte's wrists, the other reaching for the tiny pistol.

She lifted her gaze, turning to look at Etienne, and froze in horror. He'd lifted the gun and was pointing it straight at Adrian's back.

It was shadowed, gloomy, and there was no way she could see him depress the trigger, but she moved anyway, surging to her feet, driving her shoulder into Adrian's belly to knock him out of the way just as the small area exploded in sound, and they both went down, hard. She felt an odd burning in her arm, a strange pressure as she landed on top of Adrian. He shoved her off him, and when he rose he had that tiny, useless gun that was almost swallowed up by his long-fingered hand.

She thought she heard another shot, but her ears were still ringing from the first, and he'd used his other hand to shove her down onto the floor, keeping her there. She felt his body jerk slightly, and she knew he was shot, knew Etienne had killed him, and she

...reamed behind the gag, despair washing ...ver her. She would kill him, she would . . .

She tried to scramble to her feet, but she was feeling oddly weak, and strong hands shoved her down again. Adrian's hands. The small building was filled with smoke from the pistol fire, and she could hear nothing but a loud ringing in her ears. She lay on her back, stunned, staring up to see Adrian rise, limber and graceful as always, and she wanted to scream at him to get down.

She could smell blood. Adrian's? Or Etienne's? Worse than blood, an indescribable stink on the air, one of violent death. But Adrian was still moving. Adrian still moved.

She managed to get her bound wrists under her and push herself up to a sitting position. Etienne de Giverney lay splayed out on the floor, a tiny, thoroughly effective bullet wound in the middle of his forehead, his discarded gun at his foot. Adrian picked up the gun and stood over his cousin's body, kicking him with his booted foot just to make certain, kicking him hard. And then he turned back to Charlotte, and she'd never seen such rage on anyone's face in her life.

"How dare you!" he shouted at her. "That's my child you're carrying — how dare you

put yourself in danger."

She reached up and pulled the gag fre
even with her wrists still bound, and
struggled to her knees.

"Bastard," she said succinctly. "It would
be nice if you cared whether I died, but
instead you just don't want your precious
heir put in danger. Well, to hell with you,
you bloody-minded, pig-swiving, ridiculous
man! I was trying to save your worthless,
damnable life."

Apparently he realized there had been
something missing in his protest. "Why?"

"Why *what?*" She tried to stand up but
instead fell back again. She felt weak, her
shoulder was paining her damnably and she
was tired of fighting him.

"Why were you trying to save my worthless, damnable life?"

She considered passing out, just to avoid
coming up with an answer. After all, she
was pregnant — she no longer had any
doubt about the truth of it — and she
hadn't eaten, and being kidnapped by a
madman and nearly murdered was surely
enough justification for even the most
stalwart of females, which she hoped she
was, to faint. But where was light-
headedness when you really needed it? she
thought.

Because I love you," she shouted back at .m, furious. "You do not deserve it. You're almost as worthless as your murderous cousin, and I still refuse to marry you, but whether I like it or not, I don't want you dead. I'm in love with you, but I imagine it's simply because pregnancy disarranges women's minds, and I plan to do everything I can to get over it as quickly as I can."

He stared at her. It would make life so much simpler if he wasn't so damned beautiful, she thought. She was really pathetically shallow, because looking at him made her heart melt. Her only choice was to close her eyes as she repudiated him, but that made the room swim, and she decided she really didn't want to faint after all. She summoned up a suitably truculent expression, glowering at him.

"You're bleeding. Goddamn it, Charlotte, the bastard shot you."

"Oh," she said faintly. In that case it was perfectly all right to swoon. It would have been nice if she'd known that a little sooner and avoided having to tell him she loved him. But at least she needn't say anything more.

And she happily slipped into darkness.

25

As if things weren't bad enough, Adrian thought, facing the tribunal that sat across from him in Montague's library. Even Monty seemed to have rallied enough to be carried in, though Adrian suspected he'd come more for amusement's sake than anything else.

He'd been carrying Charlotte's bleeding, unconscious body toward the landing when he saw them running toward him: Pagett, Dodson, half a dozen footmen and, to his utter and complete horror, his father. He hadn't wanted to let go of Charlotte's limp body, cradling her tightly in the boat as Pagett ripped away the sleeve of her dress to expose what was, in fact, nothing but a graze. If his father hadn't been watching him out of cool, assessing eyes he might have started crying. Instead he just held her closely, letting her bleed all over him as they made it back to the estate.

hey were waiting for her with a litter, ..d by this point he relinquished her. He .new when she'd regained consciousness — sometime in the boat — but she'd elected not to let anyone know. He couldn't blame her. If he could manage to fake a fainting spell he would, anything to avoid his father's icy rage.

Even now she was tucked up into bed, a hot-water bottle at her feet, his mother sitting in a chair beside her. At least she wasn't here in the library, ready to have his liver served up to the wolves.

He surveyed the grim-faced row of judges. The only one who terrified him more than his father was Lady Whitmore, who would have most definitely gutted him on the spot if she could. She was sitting as far away from the vicar as she possibly could, which didn't fool most of the people there. Monty was right — they wanted to shag each other silly, and he wondered if he could deflect attention from his own transgressions by pointing this out, then thought better of it.

"What do you have to say for yourself, Adrian?" His father was quite a remarkable old man, considering he'd spent a life of debauchery that presumably put Adrian's career in the shade. Adrian could thank his godfather for his parents' unwanted appearance. No sooner had Adrian taken off his special license in hand, when the bish. had sent a message out to Dorset, inform ing his parents of their son and heir's upcoming nuptials. He should never have told his godfather where he was going, but he'd just escaped from Etienne's paid assassins, and he wasn't thinking too clearly.

"If I'm supposed to apologize for blowing Etienne's head off then you'll have to excuse me," he said stiffly. Never in his life had he wanted a drink more, but no one seemed to be offering.

"You didn't blow his head off with that tiny peashooter," his father said with a genteel snort.

"Well, I'm sorry that I didn't have a bigger gun," Adrian retorted.

"I'm sorry you didn't as well. I regret even more that you didn't listen when I warned you about him," the marquess said in icy tones. "If you had kept your distance in the first place this might never have happened."

"If you've brought me in here to say 'I told you so' then I have more important things to do," Adrian said, starting to rise.

His father didn't need to say a word, he simply looked at him, and Adrian sat back, restless. He hadn't seen Charlotte since the doctor had patched up her shoulder and

ounced her fit and pregnant. His
other had taken over from Lady Whitmore, and he'd been shut out, away from
her, with no chance to hold her as he so
desperately needed to do, to assure himself
she was safe.

He needed to tell her the truth, that he
was a worthless idiot, blind and stupid and
shallow, but that despite all that he loved
her.

They wouldn't let him.

It was a conspiracy, he thought grimly. He
was going to have to take his punishment
before they'd let him go to her.

"I want to know what you intend to do
about the situation."

He deliberately chose to misunderstand.
"About your cousin, sir?" He let the deliberate emphasis be his one form of fighting
back. "I'll have to deal with the local
magistrate, I expect."

"I'm the local magistrate," Montague said
with a trace of his old energy. The doctor
hadn't wanted to leave him, but Montague
had sent him away with a querulous wave
of his bony hand. "I declare you innocent of
any wrongdoing. As for de Giverney, I
imagine there's space in the village grave-
yard to dump him."

"Presumably he's Catholic," the vicar said.

"If he's buried in Protestant ground he'll
to hell."

"Oh, let's, then," said Lady Whitmore
"I'll be happy to help dig."

"I mean, what's to be done with the young
woman you ruined?"

With anyone else Adrian might have taken
issue with the term *ruined.* Ruined her for
any other man, perhaps, which was just
what he wanted. "In case the others haven't
told you, I've been trying to get her to agree
to marry me. You know that I have the
special license, and Pagett there could
perform the ceremony. But she won't
agree."

"And who could blame her?" Lady Whitmore said. "With the idiotic way you asked
her. Would you believe, Lord Haverstoke,
that he told Charlotte that he was willing to
marry her, and that he had no intention of
keeping his marriage vows?"

"I said no such thing," Adrian protested.
"I simply told her that once the . . . er . . .
passion faded from our union she would be
free to find other amusement, as would I.
It's what everyone in society does."

"Your mother would take exception to
that. In fact, I believe you just slandered
her." His father rose to his still-impressive
height.

ut Adrian stood his ground. "You could rdly convince me that your marriage is in ny way indicative of what usually goes on. Your devotion to each other is so extreme that it's almost bad ton."

There was a dangerous glint in the marquess's hard blue eyes, so like his son's. "Tread carefully, boy."

"You could hardly expect me to duplicate your good fortune in marriage."

"And why not? While it's true that no woman could ever equal your mother, I trust you have the good taste to come close. And as appalling a reprobate as you are, you're merely a child when compared to my reputation."

"Then I would think you'd appreciate how I got in this situation." Adrian fired back, unwisely.

"No, I do not. I never seduced an innocent of good family."

"Except for my mother."

The marquess's eyes narrowed, but Pagett hastily interceded. "I think we need to look at the situation calmly," he said in his measured voice. "I believe we're all agreed that our most pressing concern is Miss Spenser."

"She's my *only* concern," Lady Whitmore snapped. "I suppose you think she's a

strumpet who should go into a hom...
fallen women."

The vicar looked at her with cool dislı...
but there was fire simmering beneath ı...
"Hardly a strumpet, Lady Whitmore. Even
you don't deserve that term." Before she
had a chance to fire back, he continued. "I
believe the best outcome would be for her
to marry Lord Rohan, which is why I agreed
to perform the ceremony. The church in the
village stands at the ready. But I also believe
that Miss Spenser's wishes should come
first, and being shackled to a man of Lord
Rohan's reprehensible character might be
too unpleasant for her to contemplate."

"I beg your pardon!" Adrian protested.

"Adrian's not reprehensible," Monty said
in his faint voice. "The rest of you have
hardly lived more stellar lives. I do believe
Charlotte will be the making of him."

So, in fact, did he, Adrian thought, wondering how far he'd get if he simply walked
out. He *needed* to see her.

"She doesn't have to waste her life on
him," Lady Whitmore said. "She and I can
live very happily together. I've grown quite
weary of society, and a life in the country
will suit both of us very well."

"I would prefer her to join our family in
Dorset," his father said. "I agree — she

n't need to marry Adrian. We can find
ay to work around it."

She is welcome to stay here for as long
s I live," Montague said. "After that it's up
to my brother."

"She will always have a home here,"
Simon Pagett said.

Everyone turned to look at him in surprise, Lady Whitmore with slowly kindling wrath.

"Good for you," Monty said faintly. "I knew I could count on you after I'm gone."

"Your brother?" Lady Whitmore demanded, incensed.

"Half brother," Montague clarified. "And heir. I wish he wouldn't insist on remaining a damned parson, but there's nothing I can do about him choosing a 'respectable' life. You'll marry her, won't you, Simon?"

The two brothers' eyes met, a look of silent understanding moving between them. And then Simon smiled ruefully. "You know me too well, brother. Of course I will."

Lady Whitmore was on her feet, pale and shaking. For a woman so adept at hiding her feelings she looked quite devastated. At least everyone's attention was off him, Adrian thought, wondering if he could slip out.

"You're not going to marry Charlotte!"

she cried.

The vicar looked back at her, and th might have been the only two in the room "Of course I'm not. That is, I'll perform the ceremony for her, but she's not the woman I'm going to marry."

Lady Whitmore failed to look mollified. "Then who?" she demanded.

"You, darling," Montague said airily. "He's madly, stupidly in love with you. Now sit down and be quiet."

Lady Whitmore sat, too stunned to say anything more.

There was a faint smile at the corner of Haverstoke's mouth, one that vanished when he turned back to look at his son. "We still haven't decided what —"

Adrian rose, finally having had enough. "I'm afraid, sir, that it's not your decision. It's Charlotte's. I think you've kept me from her long enough." And he strode out of the room, without a backward glance. Though he could have sworn he heard his father's approving chuckle as he went.

He took the steps two at a time in his haste to get to her. Charlotte was lying in bed, her red hair a coppery halo around her pale face and he felt the unfamiliar panic fill him. She looked so unlike her usual fierce self.

s mother looked up from her needle-
rk and gave him a warm smile. "Did they
ng a peal over you, dearest boy?"

"Of course." He moved to her side and
kissed her cheek. He adored his mother, but
he needed her out of the room. "Do you
mind if I speak to Charlotte alone?"

"Don't leave!" Charlotte protested, but
Elinor, Marchioness of Haverstoke, had
already risen.

"I'm sorry, my dear, but I believe he's
about to abase himself, and you shouldn't
miss the chance to let him." She drifted out
of the room on the scent of lilacs, and
Adrian turned back to Charlotte.

He did look chastened, Charlotte thought,
staring up at him. Which everyone probably
told him he deserved, but she was more
charitable. He'd saved her life. He'd tried
to do the right thing. And when she'd been
trapped in that hellish church she'd told
herself she should have said yes to him,
taken anything she could get of his love.

Now she knew she had no choice but to
say no.

"I'm sorry I yelled at you," he was saying.
"Back at the chapel. I was afraid he was going to kill you."

"I understand," she said politely. "And I

446

should thank you for saving my life."

"If it hadn't been for me you wou__
have been in danger in the first place."
moved closer.

Her arm ached, her head hurt, and she
wanted to cry. But first she needed to let
him go. "I think you've been blamed too
much for one day," she said. "You shouldn't
be blamed for . . . er . . . compromising me.
I never said no to you."

"Until today. When I asked you to marry
me."

She could do this, she told herself, putting a calm smile on her face. "In fact, you
didn't ask me to marry you. You told me we
would get married."

"I know," he said ruefully. "I botched it
completely. Do you want me down on one
knee? I'll do it."

She shook her head. "No. I won't marry
you, Adrian. You don't need a wife you
don't love. You're only twenty-eight, you
have more than enough time to contract a
respectable marriage and have heirs. This
probably won't be your first by-blow." She
put a protective hand against her stomach.

"*Don't* call it that," he snapped. "In fact, it
would be," he added more calmly. "If the
child were going to be illegitimate. But it's
not going to be. Remember, I came here

wedding license before I knew you
pregnant. I already knew I wanted to
rry you."

She stared at him. "Why?"

"We would deal extremely well together.
You're just being stubborn — you know you
love me, you've admitted it. Why wouldn't
you want to marry the man you love?"

"Because I deserve better. I deserve a
good man who loves me."

He reached out and brushed his long
fingers against her cheek, and they came
away wet with tears, when she hadn't known
she was crying.

"I'm not a good man," he said. "But I do
love you. And I can do better." And without
another word he climbed up onto the bed
with her, pulling her into his arms.

And finally, finally she believed him.

By the time Adrian carried his new bride to
the tiny church in the village it was already
bedecked with flowers. Lina had worked on
the preparations, a whirlwind of energy
keeping her as far away from Simon Pagett
as possible. They hadn't spoken a word
since Monty's unexpected announcement,
which was fine with her. She was never going to get married again, certainly not to a
prosy old preacher who'd lied about his

identity.

She was half tempted to put on her n̶ outrageous ball dress with the shocki. décolletage while she acted as Charlotte' attendant, but something stopped her. The ceremony was short, sweet, with Lady Haverstoke weeping happily and even the marquess looking pleased with the situation. She had suggested they wait a day or two, but Adrian had insisted he wasn't leaving Charlotte's side, and Simon had announced that he couldn't countenance cohabitation, and it suddenly seemed all for the best to just do it before Charlotte could change her mind.

They had left to go back to Hensley Court, where everyone would most likely retire to bed. Everyone but Lina, who'd waited in the shadows until they'd left. The last thing she wanted was a tête-à-tête with Monty's disapproving brother. She'd always known Monty had a malicious sense of humor, but she'd never realized that Simon might share it. Then again, everyone had failed to mention that they were half brothers.

She'd seen him climb into the carriage that held his frail brother, and she'd ducked back into the shadows. There was one small chaise left, and she moved out into the light. She could sneak back into Hen-Court and no one would ever see her.

"I wondered when you were going to emerge." His voice came from out of the shadows, and she whirled around.

"It's been a long day," she said, trying to hide her unaccustomed nervousness. "Don't start with me now."

Simon Pagett looked at her with wise, knowing eyes. "I believe we started weeks ago, whether you realized it or not." He took her hand. She knew she should snatch it back, but he wasn't wearing gloves, and neither was she, and the night was cold and his hand was strong and warm.

"Lady Whitmore," he said in his rich, minister's voice, "would you do me the honor of becoming my wife?"

"A vicar's wife? Me?" she said in a sarcastic voice. "I believe you've taken leave of your senses. The parishioners will rise up in outrage."

"The good thing about being the heir as well as the vicar is that I don't have to listen, and if the parishioners have a problem I'll give sermons about redemption and casting the first stone."

"Even though you're marrying Mary Magdalene?"

His smile was warm. "Am I? I'm so glad

you're being more sensible than cousin. But I'm afraid you've got a long to go before you can equal Mary Magdalene. She ended up a saint, you know."

His thumb was rubbing back and forth against her fingers, a small caress that felt strangely erotic. Arousing. Why *this* man? she thought. Why did this man have to be the only man to move her?

"I don't want to get married again," she said in a small voice, trying to avoid temptation. Something she'd never been very good at.

"And why not?"

"Because I don't enjoy the marriage bed." There, the awful truth was out.

He looked confused. "Then why have you been so, shall we say, experimental?"

"Because I was hoping I was wrong. But I'm not. A man's touch leaves me cold. So unless you're thinking of a celibate marriage, you definitely don't want me."

"My dear Lina, celibate marriages are a dead bore. And if you think you don't like making love then you simply have to trust me. My many years of practice are good for one thing after all. I can make you change your mind."

She looked at him, long and hard. It was foolishness beyond hope. But then, she was

l. "You can try," she said.

Does that mean you'll marry me?"

She took a deep breath, and said the one thing she thought she'd never say again. "Yes. I'll marry you."

Adrian sat in the pew, Charlotte tucked close beside him. It was three weeks later and they were here again, watching Lina marry her vicar, and a glow of contentment, that unlikely condition that now seemed permanent, washed over him. Charlotte was healing well, even though she did have a distressing tendency to cast up her accounts at inopportune moments, but he didn't care. They'd been able to enjoy wickedly vigorous sex despite her injury and pregnancy, and he had to admit that it would take two hundred years for them to tire of each other. She leaned her head against his shoulder, and he put his arm around her, drawing her even closer.

"Do you think they'll be as happy as we are?" she whispered.

"No one will be as happy as we are, not even my parents," he said gravely, glancing over at his mother's cheerful, tear-streaked face. His mother always cried at weddings — she'd been practically sobbing at theirs.

"Still . . . Lina looks really happy, doesn't

she? For the last three weeks she's bee͟
panic and then suddenly this morning s͟
positively glowing. I'm not sure why͟
thought I was going to have to drag her t͟
the altar."

He let his fingers trail along the side of her neck surreptitiously, delighting in the softness of her skin. "Oh, I can explain that. I saw her leaving Pagett's room very early this morning, a ridiculously happy smile on her face. I think she must have convinced him to anticipate the marriage vows by a day. The vicar must not be as strong-minded as he thought he was," he said with a soft laugh, leaning over to placing his lips against her temple.

"Who would be when faced with Lina's charms?"

"Not even tempted, my precious," he whispered, brushing his lips against hers. Why his darling wife needed reassurance was beyond him, but he was happy to give it. She was exquisite, even in the most wretched of circumstances, and he loved her.

There was an ominous throat-clearing. His father was giving him a disapproving look for whispering in church. Adrian simply smiled at him, undaunted, and his mother reached out and caught her hus-

's hand, drawing his attention away.

the first time he really began to under-
nd what lay between his parents.

But for once in his life his formidable
father was wrong.

He and Charlotte were going to be just as
happy, just as besotted with each other, for
the rest of their lives.

And, in fact, they were.

ABOUT THE AUTHOR

Anne Stuart loves Japanese rock and roll, wearable art, Spike, her two kids, Clairefontaine paper, quilting, her delicious husband of thirty-four years, fellow writers, her three cats, telling stories and living in Vermont. She's not too crazy about politics and diets and a winter that never ends, but then, life's always a trade-off.

Visit her at www.Anne-Stuart.com.

We hope you have enjoyed this Large Print book. Other Thorndike, Wheeler, Kennebec, and Chivers Press Large Print books are available at your library or directly from the publishers.

For information about current and upcoming titles, please call or write, without obligation, to:

Publisher
Thorndike Press
295 Kennedy Memorial Drive
Waterville, ME 04901
Tel. (800) 223-1244

or visit our Web site at:

http://gale.cengage.com/thorndike

OR

Chivers Large Print
published by AudioGO Ltd
St James House, The Square
Lower Bristol Road
Bath BA2 3SB
England
Tel. +44(0) 800 136919
www.audiogo.co.uk

All our Large Print titles are designed for easy reading, and all our books are made to last.